THE IRIDUAN'S MATE

BOOK 7: IRIDUAN TEST SUBJECTS

SUSAN TROMBLEY

Disclaimer:
This is a work of fiction. All of the characters, names, incidents, organizations, and dialogue in this novel are either the products of the author's imagination or are used fictitiously. References to ancient civilizations, myths, and mythical characters are not intended to be historically accurate. Alien character biology may not align completely with the terrestrial biological inspiration in function or terms.

 Created with Vellum

ONE

Shulgi stared down at the emaciated body of a deceased Iriduan male, a heavy sigh escaping him. The corpse's wings curled against his bony spine, shriveled from dehydration, though the healers had tried their best to pump fluids into him before he passed. His dulled teal blue skin clung to light and delicate bones, shadowed by deep hollows beneath his high cheekbones. Bright red eyes stared lifelessly from their sockets. Bedraggled green hair tangled around his head, the knots and snarls of the dry and broken strands so matted they concealed most of his long, pointed blue ears.

"Red eyes." Shulgi shook his head. "An ill-favored color in combination with his skin and hair. I'm surprised he made no effort to have them changed."

"Red is an ill-favored color even when it coordinates," Professor Namerian said as he stood on the other side of the exam table. "It's a true shame. His queen tortured him as a parlor pet for years before his creche-kin brought him here. His condition had already advanced too far for us to cure him of the affliction. His body couldn't survive the process."

Shulgi turned his focus to Namerian. The former Iriduan professor and medical researcher now worked on the secret project that kept Shulgi and his team hidden below the suspended streets of an Iriduan male "dreg," an out-caste district beyond imperial space where males hid from—and flouted—the laws of the Iriduan Empire, engaging in various criminal activities that put Shulgi on edge and increased his cynicism about his own people.

"Red *is* a favorable color for war-class." It was an idle comment, more an aside as he studied the teal flesh of the corpse. "Pity he didn't have that choice, given his build."

"Choice?" Namerian laughed bitterly. "He went through meta in a creche. The empire chose for him." He lifted a hand to touch the ports on the back of his neck reflexively. "Still, leisure-class seems a harsh fate for one such as him. The least they could have done was fix his eye color before exposure."

"It's clear he was ill-favored from the moment he crawled out of his egg," Shulgi said in a dour tone. "His creche probably decided re-engineering him wasn't worth the investment."

Shulgi flicked his wings, the fluorescent lighting of the lab streaking over the viridescent veins flush with fluid that kept his wings ready for flight. He shot another glance at the body, shaking his head as a deep sadness gripped him. "This process is frustratingly slow. There are so many others like him, and so few of them know about this clinic."

Namerian met Shulgi's eyes, plucking a scalpel from the cart beside him. "There's another complication. I was hoping to speak to you about it later this evening, during our daily debriefing, but now that you're here...."

The muscles in Shulgi's shoulders and back tightened, his heartrate speeding up at the warning tone in the other male's voice. A trickle of combat stimulants pumped from his glands into his bloodstream. "I take it this is news you would prefer not to give me."

Namerian adjusted the corpse so it lay flat on its back, then made the incision to begin his autopsy. He would study this corpse to find out what level of damage had been sustained that even the nanites couldn't repair in time to save the male. "We had a case of re-imprinting."

Shulgi's wings vibrated with the knotting of his back muscles. "What? That's.... that *can't* be!" He growled, unwilling to accept this news. "The cure is supposed to be permanent."

Namerian continued the motions of his work as he explained, the sounds of him cutting into the corpse warring with the low hum of lighting and equipment in the stark lab. "Our chimeric genome is creating an issue with the persistence of the cure. The imprinting and compulsory exposure genes inherited from the Menops occur in both gene clusters *and* tandem arrays in our genome, and which type and how many are in an individual's DNA varies wildly across all subjects. That's why it was impossible to find a cure before the creation of the nanites that can mutate from within by tracking biochemical responses to their associated genes. If we could reprogram the nanites to allow them to persist inside the subject instead of self-destructing after only the active relevant genes are rewritten, they will find each additional cluster or array when it activates and rework it to cure the new affliction."

"Absolutely not!" Shulgi slashed the air in front of him with one hand. "The risks of allowing the nanites to persist and continue to modify the patient's genome remain too high. We must stick to the current program to avoid the chance of them reactivating latent memory code and reawakening one of the high lords." He clenched his fists as he turned away from the sight of the corpse being autopsied. "The last thing the Iriduans need right now is the return of a creature like Ninhursag."

"This puts our plans for phase two on hold," Namerian said, his tone laden with disapproval.

Not all the healers and researchers in the clinic agreed with Shulgi's insistence that the nanites shut down after rewriting the genes involved in the patient's affliction. Fortunately, none of them had been able to reprogram those nanites, and the only people who could were out of their reach.

Shulgi had no intention of changing the plan he'd agreed to several years ago when Nemon had given him the cure and the override code to keep the nanites from automatically shutting down after executing their primary function. The Lusian captain, Roz, had warned him of the potential dangers if he ever used that override. At the time, he'd wondered why they'd allowed him to have the code considering the potential outcome of using it. Now, he suspected that the Lusian had foreseen this possibility, and—like disseminating the cure itself —Roz was leaving the decision of what to do about this new complication up to Shulgi.

"This complication will only temporarily affect phase two," Shulgi insisted, keeping his tone and expression neutral, despite his roiling thoughts. "We will re-inoculate any patients who present new imprintings, and study the data provided by the nanites to see if we can isolate patterns in the chromosomes that will allow us to target all inactive imprinting genes as well as the active ones before shutdown."

"I *know* you want to implement phase two as badly as the rest of us." Namerian's gaze fixed intently on Shulgi rather than the body on the slab.

Shulgi shifted his eyes to the dead Iriduan male, his chest now spread open to reveal his ravaged internal organs. "I *do*. More than anything, I want to see this affliction ended for all our people, but I won't do whatever it takes to reach that goal. There are some outcomes that will end up worse for us than the affliction itself—worse for this entire galaxy. 'For the greater good' is no longer an excuse I will tolerate."

Namerian regarded him through violet eyes that coordinated well with his medium purple iridescent skin. Silvery hair framed his face, which would have been well-favored by an Iriduan female, but the empire had decided his mind was too useful to waste on the leisure-class.

"Shulgi, you and I are both from the bloodline Amanat. Creche-kin. You trusted me with this mission. Now you must trust me to do what's necessary to complete it!"

Shulgi sighed, running a hand through his hair, his body humming with combat stimulants that seemed to pump into his bloodstream more often now than ever before. "The worst crimes Iriduans ever committed were carried out to complete missions we justified by claiming virtuous intentions. I don't want to see my own kin go down that path, Namerian. If you intended our familial relationship to sway me, you chose the wrong argument."

Namerian straightened from his work, slamming down a bloodstained tool whose purpose Shulgi didn't bother to guess. "Curse the web! Your blighted 'honor' is driven by fear rather than altruism. I know that silkless egg-blighter Ninhursag forced you to do things you'll always regret, but you're allowing her memory to inhibit our efforts to save our Iriduan brothers from suffering a similar fate!"

He pointed at his chest with a bloodstained hand covered in a skin-coat glove. "My focus is on saving our people!" He stabbed his finger towards Shulgi. "What is your focus *really* on? Will you condemn our project to this criminal hole forever, saving just a handful of Iriduans at a time—those *lucky* enough to have heard about the cure through inconsistent channels? Or will you allow us to alter the program, and save the entire male population before our enemies find a way to stop us?"

As Shulgi glared at Namerian, both frustrated and angry at his dismissal of the danger posed by the nanites, Namerian gestured with a hand to the corpse. "*Look* at this poor male. He suffered for *years* before his kin found out about us. Do you really think the high lords are the only creatures capable of destroying us? Our civilization is dying, and the carrion eaters are already circling the empire, just waiting to pick apart the remains. If we can't regain our former glory with a cure for this affliction that eternally weakens us, then the light of the Iriduans will disappear forever from this galaxy."

Shulgi did look down at the fallen male, shaking his head sadly. "You know my final word on this. Even if I wanted to change it, the choice isn't entirely my own. Our benefactors do not want the return of the high lords any more than we do. We will delay deployment of phase two for now to see if we can modify the existing program to seek out and rewrite inactive genes before shutting down. That's all that I can offer."

He turned his back on Namerian as the other male muttered under his breath, returning his focus to the corpse.

Without another word, Shulgi left the lab. His jaw ached from his gritted teeth, a jaw muscle ticking beneath his breather mask as he stalked away from Namerian and yet another failure to save an afflicted male.

That sense of failure followed him up the narrow stairway to the basement of the algae production and packaging plant, Ma'Nah, that served as a front for their clinic. Only his team had the code to the "Management Only" section of the basement, though many of the employees were aware of the existence of the lab since they had come to this world in search of the cure.

At least Shulgi's team had found marked success, and

rarely lost a male to the ravages of deprivation. The tormented, red-eyed male in the lab below was an exception, rather than the rule.

The need for secrecy had driven Shulgi's team deep into the underground of the dreg, which was itself an underground of sorts in column 212 of the city of Za'Kluth. The basaltic behemoth of a city was formed by columnar jointing in the wake of lava flows that still pooled in lakes and moved sluggishly in rivers even on the dark side of Igoth, a planet tidally locked to the red dwarf star Zik.

Zik's system skirted the very outer edge of the CivilRim, though there was nothing civil about the star system or the city of Za'Kluth. In fact, the inhospitable environs beyond the massive black columns of the city still offered more safety than some of the neighborhoods inside those columns.

Many pirates and slavers made their home on this world, along with outcasts from every species capable of space flight. Some of the columns contained special environments created specifically for species unable to live within the "Ubaid Standard Band" of life support parameters that most of the members of the Cosmic Syndicate could endure.

Generally, Iriduans had little need to travel to those parts of the city, but Shulgi had visited some of them on occasion in the process of doing business. Despite being out-castes, the Iriduans of the dreg possessed some of the most advanced environmental suit and combat armor technology in the entire city, not to mention a devastating array of imperial weaponry the out-castes smuggled into the city and sold for high profit.

Even on this world, where brute strength often ruled supreme, the Iriduans had gained a certain degree of dominance among the many other species. Their numbers alone made them a threat to other factions that might be intent on taking over their territory and mechanized and Iriduan security provided heavy guard for the dreg itself.

Nothing got into the dreg without passing through that security. The out-caste neighborhood was as tightly guarded as any male district in the empire, so that even the air filtration systems were extensively regulated to keep potential exposures from afflicting the unmated males that lived there.

Shulgi's passage through the utilitarian factory offices garnered a few greetings and friendly gestures, but most of the males kept their heads down, focusing on their work. The factory did a booming legitimate business throughout Za'Kluth and neighboring CivilRim systems, and Ma'Nah paid its extremely high fees to the city bosses in full every quarter without complaint.

The smell of the algae pools drifting up to the offices from the production floor made Shulgi's stomach turn, and he adjusted his mask's filter to cut out all external odors. The appearance of his mask wasn't out of place in the factory, though many males went without masks inside the dreg, feeling as safe as they would ever be from exposure to female scent signatures that could afflict them. No female of any species was permitted beyond the imposing gates of the dreg and the guards always scanned visitors to keep them from smuggling in a scent bomb.

Outside the factory, pungent steam curled misty fingers around his boots as he strode over granite paved streets flanked by massive, boxy warehouses devoid of any of the architectural beauty usually so ubiquitous in imperial colonies. Neon lights reflected off the wet pavement as he passed through the factory sector and into the entertainment district.

Automated advertisements emanated from every business he passed, promising every manner or form of entertainment or pleasure that an Iriduan could enjoy in the galaxy. In this sector of the dreg, more effort had been made to improve the appearance of the buildings, though most of the architectural elements were simple facades concealing far less visually appealing colonial pop-ups.

The only uniquely beautiful and imposing structure in the entire dreg was the ziggurat at the center that held the temple to the Grand Spinner. No expense had been spared in that building's construction, but not out of any zealotry for religious beliefs mostly abandoned by the hopeless population of the dreg. Though the temple had been built at exorbitant cost, most of those reported funds had been embezzled under the noses of the city bosses who decreased levies on religious constructions.

From this sector, the outline of the ziggurat against the hologram of a false-starred sky projected above and around the entire dreg dome looked distant and insignificant.

His stomach growled in hunger as he stalked past a variety of eateries and food stalls, but his frustration at the latest news about the cure had combat stimulants boiling through his blood. He needed an outlet rather than a meal, though he couldn't recall the last time he'd eaten. Time seemed to flow away from him since he'd come to this world, focused as he was on the cure and getting it out to as many Iriduan males as possible without gaining the attention of the empire or its enemies.

Roz had warned him of many possible futures in the flux for the Iriduans. If he wasn't careful, his mistakes—his poor decisions—could doom his people instead of saving them.

Beyond the stimulant lounges, arcades, theaters, and bars sat the final structure designated for the entertainment sector, built right up against the rough-finished internal wall of the basaltic column itself. Bright exterior lights illuminated the combat arena, turning false columns and the domed roof into gaudy displays of flashing color.

Despite the exterior display, no customers occupied the spacious lobby at this hour, and a sole attendant manned the sign-in counter, his gaze lifting as the entry doors slid closed behind Shulgi, whose wings flicking out of the way reflexively.

When the attendant spotted him, he shook his head with a rueful smile of greeting. "There's no one signed in right now who will fight you, Shulgi Amanat."

Shulgi smirked beneath his mask as he approached the counter while the attendant muted a comedy play he'd been watching on a screen below the countertop. "I never expected a dreg to be filled with so many cowards."

The attendant chuckled. "It wasn't, before you came here. Your undefeated record has many questioning why you waste your time hiding from the empire instead of fighting in the resistance."

Shulgi unhooked his mask and removed it, inhaling deeply. The air smelled of sweat and male pheromones laden with aggression. His already heightened senses sharpened even more as his glands pumped out additional combat stimulants. He felt eagerness for battle—and victory.

He set the mask on the counter and then displayed his wrist implant for the attendant's scan to debit his account. He usually paid a premium to the arena for live battles, but often had to settle for the simulated ones due to a lack of willing opponents.

"I see no point in the resistance," he muttered as the attendant handed him the disposable skin-coats for use in the combat rig. "They have no chance of defeating the empire and changing anything. Not as long as the imprinting affliction remains."

The attendant snorted. "That and the fact that a bunch of males can't continue the species alone." He leaned on the counter, lowering his voice. "I heard some resistance males are eyeing the humans now that more are flooding into Syndicate space. It turns out that Iriduan-human half-breeds are live born and don't need a meta to progress from juvenile to adult. That means no need for Spinners." He straightened, shrugging. "Of course, that also means diluting our bloodline with the ape-bloods, but I suppose it's better than having our offspring trapped forever in juvenile form."

"You forget the affliction," Shulgi growled, collecting the skin-coats and his mask from the counter, "what difference does it make to be mated to an Iriduan female or a human one? Both would still have control over you for the rest of your life."

He pushed away the memory of a particular human female who had proven to him that not all women would take advantage of their mates—and that some females could love their mates as fiercely and loyally as they were loved in return. Sometimes, he wasn't sure if he still admired Paisley as he had after she'd saved his life—or despised her for forcing him to carry on living when she could have put him out of his misery with a quick shot to the head. She had made him understand what true loneliness and a yearning for a mate of his own felt like, and he hated it. He hated the false hope she had given him that had quickly died in the reality of the bleak dreg and the filthy criminal city beyond it.

"I think there are worse fates than being mated and having sex all day, even with a naked-ape female," the attendant said in a defiant tone. "They loaded some holos of the most beautiful ones from Earth in the stimulant lounge, and I have to say, they're not that bad."

Then he gestured to a rig room to the left of the lobby. "You know the drill. Stow your weapons in the locker before going in. The equipment is all in standby. I take it you don't need assistance hooking up." He grinned, looking painfully young, though he had probably gone through meta decades ago. His face lacked the lines of strain that many of the older males in the dreg couldn't hide any longer.

Though if he continued to use stimulants to spur an arousal in defiance of unmated impotency, the signs of addiction would carve deep hollows in his cheeks and darken the skin around his eyes, aging him far more than stress did—and the sexual stimulants could end up killing him.

Shulgi didn't bother warning him against such behavior. The use of drugs and illegal stimulants was so prevalent in the dreg that there was no escaping it if one was so inclined.

He made his way to one of the lockers outside the combat chamber and placed the half-dozen knives and the small military pistol he usually concealed in various sheaths and a holster under his robe inside it before using his wrist implant to pay for it and lock it. Then he entered the combat chamber, locking it behind him.

As he stripped out of his robe and applied the skin-coats before hooking himself into the combat rig, he had to acknowledge that he was also addicted, only his addiction was to the combat stimulants that filtered into his blood in response to excess stress and anger. He could use meditation to soothe his mind and body while the stimulants dissipated, but he always chose the arena instead, punishing his body—and often the bodies of others—to chase a satisfying victory with as much determination as some males chased the illusive climax offered by artificial means in the stimulant lounges.

He lost track of time as the virtual system threw a variety of enemies at him, with a randomized level of intensity and difficulty. His focus remained entirely on the battles, allowing him freedom from the problems that plagued him beyond the confines of this VR combat room. He'd set the rig to cause the same degree of pain as he would feel in a real battle, even though he wouldn't sustain permanent damage. This setting ensured he remained careful not to make foolish or avoidable errors during battle.

His combat ability had only improved since he'd arrived on this planet. Even before coming here, he'd been an elite operative for most of his adult life, and his training and modifications were extensive. He maintained proficiency with every Iriduan weapon in active use by the empire, not to mention a vast array of alien weapons, and had even grown interested in ancient melee weapons in the past year after coming across a collection of smuggled artifacts from a long-dead culture on Iridu.

Before Ninhursag had trapped him and some of his squad mates with her scent, his skill level had put him on the fast track through the ranks and Command had once had him pegged for a leadership role. It hadn't been the affliction itself that had screwed him out of that role, but rather his own resistance to some of the less justifiable missions they'd been sent on.

Insubordination had been his setback on multiple occasions as he'd refused to perform tasks that he felt were dishonorable and unnecessary. He'd been written up and even detained more than once because of his disobedience. Still, his team had been his family, despite how often he'd failed them by defying his orders.

Their ghosts now haunted him, chasing him through his nightmares and hovering in the corners of the labs or the alleys of the dreg, demanding he finally cure the affliction that had led him and his fellow squad mates to commit so many atrocities at the will of a manipulative female.

Certain mind healers lived within the dreg who might have been able to help him banish those imaginary spirits back to the Grand Spinner's web, but he didn't feel that he deserved that kind of assistance, and he never wanted to confess to the crimes he'd committed to any other male. Instead, he used his focus on the cure and his daily trips to the combat arena to dispel the ghosts to the darkest shadows of his memory, at least temporarily.

After multiple victories that felt far less satisfying than a single victory against a real opponent but had certainly challenged him, he unhooked himself from the rig and peeled off the skin-coats. Though he knew the attendants would clean the rig itself before another combatant used it, he still cleaned off all the surfaces in practiced and efficient movements, simply from long habit, before dressing once again in his robe.

When he unlocked the door and left the VR chamber, he entered the lobby to find a small crowd had formed and the counter now had a line in front of it. After retrieving his weapons from the locker and quickly rearming himself, he responded to several greetings as his gaze scanned the lobby, always on alert for threats. Even for Iriduan males, the dreg could sometimes prove a hazardous place, though most of the predators that made their home in this criminal underground weren't foolish enough to choose the regular patrons of the combat arena as targets. Usually, it was the males who had escaped the leisure-class life who fell prey to the worst of the monsters in this dreg.

That reality was another thorn in Shulgi's side since he couldn't interfere in the black-market trade of slaves and body parts without jeopardizing his whole purpose here. As much as he wanted to hunt down and kill the leaders of the gangs that committed such atrocities against their own people, he had to remain focused on what he'd come to this merciless pit to do.

He only intervened when the males targeted by the gangs had come to this world for his cure. Then, his retribution was brutal, but he had to remain anonymous in those instances, leading to a rumor around the dreg of a shadow killer exacting vengeance and leaving behind an indisputable message to others.

Because he always remained alert, he spotted the young Iriduan male who entered the lobby before the other male saw him, so he was ready when Alad approached him, his blue eyes wide with worry that made Shulgi's already exhausted muscles tighten.

He recognized the male as one of Namerian's newest lackeys. One that the professor apparently trusted enough to bring him in on the secret project. Shulgi had objected to any additions to the team he'd originally selected, but Namerian had convinced him that he needed an assistant, and that the young male could be trusted.

"We... uh... have a bit of a problem, sir," Alad said in a low voice as soon as he was close enough to Shulgi to speak in a volume unlikely to be overheard in the swelling conversation now filling the lobby.

"Of *course* we do," Shulgi ground out, his now gnawing hunger giving bite to his tone that had the younger male flinching. "I don't suppose it is a problem any of the others can handle?"

Alad wrung his hands. "I brought the issue to Professor Namerian first, and he told me that this was something you would prefer to deal with."

In that case, the problem likely involved the probability of combat rather than some scientific endeavor. Shulgi wasn't ignorant of scientific matters, but he'd been selected for war-class rather than knowledge-class for a reason. He had little interest in the more cerebral pursuits of the professors.

"Tell me." His tone made it clear he had little patience at the moment.

Despite hours of training in the VR chamber, his body

already prepared for another fight, and glands that should have been tapped pumped fresh stimulants into his bloodstream.

The young male looked far too nervous to be a long-time resident of the dreg. Shulgi figured him to be just out of meta, which probably meant someone had helped him escape whatever fate the empire had in store for him. That someone had not done enough in Shulgi's opinion to protect Alad, but at least Namerian and the others had taken him under their wings and given him a place to stay and work.

Because of the skittishness of the youth, Shulgi tried to moderate his tone and demeanor, since both clearly intimidated Alad. "Tell me what the problem is, and I'll take care of it."

The other male's gaze flicked from side to side as he took in their surroundings, scanning the occupants of the lobby in way that told Shulgi he wasn't completely naïve. "Perhaps we could step outside," he whispered.

Shulgi gestured to the double doors and Alad rushed from the lobby with Shulgi stalking behind him, his wings flicking in irritation and tension. The youth had stowed his wings beneath his robe.

Shulgi sighed at that evidence that the young male wasn't prepared enough for this place. In the dreg, one's wings should always remain hydrated and ready for flight. The ability to outfly your opponent could mean the difference between life and death, and the more fragile and lean males often had an advantage in the air against stronger opponents.

Shulgi's harsh tone froze the younger male when he made to duck down an alley. "Stop here. You must not have been in the dreg long if you think an alley in the entertainment district is a good place for passing on information."

Still wringing his hands, Alad spun around to face Shulgi. "I... I had only just arrived when I joined the team. My sire smuggled me off Iridu when he heard that I was destined for leisure-class, and he set me up with a job at Ma'Nah. He was one of the first to receive the cure from Professor Namerian and he returned to Iridu to free me and some of the others of the harem from the same fate he'd escaped."

Shulgi put a hand on the youth's shoulder. "You should stick closer to the factory when you're alone, Alad. This district isn't safe during the best of times."

Alad nodded, swallowing. "I know, sir. But this news... Professor Namerian felt that it was urgent, and you weren't answering your com."

Shulgi cursed, lifting his hand from Alad's shoulder to tap his wrist, reactivating the communications implant beneath the skin. He'd deactivated his communicator during his time in the rig because it interfered with the combat experience. The fact that he'd failed to reactivate it as soon as he finished unhooking from the rig was an oversight that could have led to harm for this young Iriduan.

"What news is so urgent that Namerian risks one of our newest employees to pass it on?"

"H-he and the others of the team were busy, and I was the first one avai—"

Shulgi held up a staying hand. "Just tell me the news. You don't need to defend my creche-kin to me." After all, the failure was Shulgi's own. Namerian had to work with what he had, and he could have sent the message to Shulgi's com if he'd had it activated.

"The supply shipment the professor has been waiting for was sent to the wrong dock." Alad's words tumbled out in a rush, no doubt because he sensed Shulgi's growing ire and mistakenly believed it was directed at him.

"Which dock?" Shulgi growled, his spine prickling, causing his wings to extend erratically.

"Base-level," Alad said quickly. "The under-tier docking station."

"Blighted silk!" Shulgi hissed, running a hand through his hair as he turned to regard the sulfurous steam that rose out of ground vents from lower tiers. "What ship captain would be so foolish as to dock in the under-tier?"

"I believe it was an okihan cargo hauler, sir," Alad said, his robe shifting as his stowed wings began to fill with fluid.

He clearly felt agitated enough by Shulgi's reaction that his flight instinct was kicking in.

Shulgi snorted, shaking his head in aggravation. "Okihans. So, we've fallen to this. Relying upon *pirates* to bring our supplies."

"Sir, why is it so bad that the cargo was delivered to a different dock? Our tier's dock is usually crowded, leaving ships on hover-time. Doesn't that increase costs for us?"

"The under-tier docks are Sha Zaska's territory." Shulgi withdrew a tie from the inner pocket of his robe and caught up his hair with one hand, then twisted it into a knot to secure it at the base of his skull. "Do you know what a thida naf is, Alad?"

The youth shook his head, his eyes fixed on Shulgi's bound hair. It was rare for a male to tie up their hair, and even Shulgi wouldn't deny that it was due mostly to sheer vanity that they liked to leave it loose and flowing, even when they weren't trying to attract mates.

"No, sir."

Shulgi regarded the younger male, unsurprised that he hadn't learned much about some of the worst denizens of Za'K-luth yet. "Let's hope you never have to find out." He caught the younger male by the arm and drew him along in his wake. "I'll return you to Ma'Nah, then go speak with the dockmaster in the under-tier. If I'm lucky, I won't have to deal with Sha Zaska or his minions."

He escorted Alad back to the relative safety of the factory, where the sentries atop the building could watch over the young male. Stopping at the gatehouse, he traded his mask for a set of combat armor, opening the vents in the back of the suit for his wings to slide free. He didn't need a complete environmental seal and had no intention of being grounded in a place like the under-tier.

Once armored up, helmet included, with his knives sheathed in hidden compartments on his armor and his pistol openly worn on his hip, he made his way to the shipping elevator—the only other egress from the dreg besides the main gate. Like that gate, it was heavily guarded, and Ma'Nah paid high fees to have regular access to it.

The sentries let him through without comment, but when he told them his destination, they raised eyebrows in surprise above sealed heavy filtration masks. The mask Shulgi usually wore was unnecessary—or at least he'd believed that until Namerian told him of a re-afflicted patient—but he still used it to maintain the necessary illusion that he was an unmated male vulnerable to affliction. It also helped to conceal his expressions, though he had trained to remain stoic at any rate so he wouldn't give himself away even with the eyes, as these guards did.

As the elevator took him downwards towards the most depraved and bleakest tier in all of column 212, he reflected upon his words to Alad about Sha Zaska and his minions. He also reflected upon the fact that he wasn't usually lucky.

TWO

The helmet of his armor protected Shulgi from more than just attacks aimed at his head. The smell of the under-tier would be overwhelming without it. A miasma formed by far too many differing alien pheromones, garbage, sulfur from the volcanic vents, and a hint of rotten flesh no doubt left in the under-vents by Sha Zaska's prodigious and foul appetites lay so thick over the docks that it should have been visible.

He'd had little reason to come to this tier in the past and had only made one other very brief visit after first arriving in Za'Kluth, but he knew enough about Sha Zaska not to take this trip lightly. The thida naf ruled these crowded docks through fear—and with good reason. Hundreds of slaves disappeared from these docks every annum, never to be seen again, and it was said that Sha Zaska ate every last one of them himself.

Shulgi would love to kill a monster like the foul thida naf gang boss, but no one ever met Sha Zaska in person—at least, no one who had ever returned from that meeting. Instead, the creature worked through his minions and communicated primarily through intermediaries, usually his slaves.

Shulgi's wings flared and twitched as he stalked over the vents that dotted the docks, past dozens of full bays echoing with a cacophony of noise as dockworkers loaded and unloaded a variety of goods in crates constructed of every possible material. The ships that docked here carried mostly smuggled goods concealed from the notice of the city bosses occupying the highest tiers, a vast majority of those goods illegal in much of the settled galaxy.

The gang boss that owned these docks, not to mention a small fleet of ships of his own, dwelled beneath Shulgi's feet in the under-vents—an extensive system of artificially and naturally formed tunnels. Thida nafs could grow to hundreds of feet in length, with many tentacle arms to capture unwary prey. No one knew for certain what their bodies looked like, since they lived underground even on their home world, but Shulgi could guess that even Nemon's true form wouldn't match the hideousness of a thida naf.

Whatever he might look like, Sha Zaska controlled his docks effectively from below, and many people had been snatched through the vents, disappearing so quickly and silently that those around them hadn't even seen Sha Zaska's tentacles grab them. Some even suspected the monster used camouflage, but Shulgi hadn't heard that the thida nafs had that ability. They didn't really need it. Only a fool stumbled into an underground lair in search of one of them.

The ostensible business office of the docks contained a single, bored dockmaster sitting behind a small, reinforced window. The dock AI system did all the actual work in routing the traffic and billing, so the dockmaster clearly existed for show. The lack of guards didn't ease Shulgi's sense of danger, since he could see the pedestals of gun turrets lining the top of the boxy office building. He didn't doubt more remained concealed behind the ceiling tiles within Sha Zaska's business offices. The nuxanon dockmaster chittered at Shulgi in its language, and Shulgi's implanted translator allowed him to understand the creature's intent, though he would hardly call the sounds it made words.

Once it learned of the cargo that had been left on the docks for Ma'Nah, it made a series of sounds that indicated amusement, rubbing two of its six hands together in front of it with obvious greed, no expression evident on its chitinous, insectoid face. Instead of immediately turning over the cargo and debiting his account for the docking fees, the creature summoned one of Sha Zaska's minions and insisted he wait inside the lobby of the office.

Shulgi stood inside the lobby and waiting room of Zaska's Docking and Shipping with wings half spread and vibrating with tension. His hand rested on the holstered pistol as he faced the inner doors to the gang boss's offices.

Discordant and terrible sounds played from an overhead speaker that Shulgi suspected were supposed to form music. The chipped and battered waiting chairs sat empty, despite the docking bays being at full capacity from what he'd seen. Obviously, few of the regulars bothered to visit this office.

It didn't take long for the inner doors to swing open and Zaska's minions to enter the lobby. Though he kept his stance firm, he was taken aback by those who stepped out of a much more luxurious back office into the lobby filled with grime, cracked tile flooring, yellowed walls with peeling paint, and seats covered in questionable stains.

The two Ultimen guards didn't surprise him, though they lacked the ubiquitous network of energy beads and even the braids so typical of their species' more civilized citizens. Their long fur hung in thick hanks with nary an energy bead in sight. Their size and relative power were more than enough to intimidate though, and the pistols holstered on their hips sent an unmistakable message as well. Shulgi knew better than to underestimate them simply because they weren't wearing the Ultimen version of armor.

The towering, hairy beast men wore groin cloths to conceal their genitalia, and besides that small concession to modesty that not all their species bothered to make, they wore nothing else. Despite that covering, he could tell they were clearly both male, though the females of the species weren't much smaller or weaker than their counterparts.

Shulgi could take them both out, if necessary, but it wouldn't be a fight he'd win easily. He would prefer to deal peacefully and quickly with Zaska's servants.

Especially since the third minion—the one standing between the two guards—seemed so harmless—small and delicate.

For any other unmated Iriduan male, she would also pose a potential threat far more serious than the Ultimen guards. The female was undoubtedly human, even though her skin had been dyed an unnatural violet color with green pigments painted over it in a pattern of coiling tentacles, marking her as one of Zaska's "dyed flowers." What little fabric she wore over that marked and dyed skin covered her body only in the front and back with a tasseled silken rope as a belt and glittering sandals on her small feet.

She kept her head bowed and her gaze lowered to the floor in front of his feet. She clasped her hands low in front of her. The thin, silver slave collar around her neck blinked with lights indicating its armed status.

Shulgi ground his teeth in frustration at his inability to do anything to help this slave, any more than he could aid the hundreds of others that disappeared from these docks. He couldn't imagine what horrors this fragile female had endured at the many repulsive arms of Zaska—and perhaps within the many repellent beds of his minions.

Zaska's dyed flowers were renowned for their beauty and grace and their absolute obedience to his will. They were also known for being untouchable unless Zaska ordered them to service someone other than him. As far as the gang boss was concerned, those female slaves he chose not to eat he kept to serve his—and only his—other foul appetites, unless he wanted to reward a particular client or power broker in exchange for something useful to him.

"Honored Iriduan," the flower said in a high-pitched, whispery voice that he had to step a bit closer to hear, "my master welcomes you to our docks. It would seem that your cargo was mistakenly delivered here, and we understand that you are no doubt frustrated by that inconvenience. Please, allow my master to waive your docking fees as a gesture of his goodwill."

She never looked up once while talking, her narrow shoulders high even as her head remained bowed. Tiny bumps pebbled the surface of her exposed flesh that he'd been told were common for humans when they were chilled or afraid.

He felt more intrigued by the female herself than surprised by her offer to waive fees. He'd expected Zaska's minions to extort as much as they could from him before he had to resort to threats to finalize their price to retrieve his cargo.

"What's the catch?" he demanded, then softened his tone when she noticeably flinched. "Your master isn't known for his generosity."

He had to remember that she was not the target of his ire, nor could he allow his disgust and repulsion for her master to reflect upon her.

The flower glanced up briefly and Shulgi saw her eyes clearly for the first time. They were an unusual shade that seemed caught between green and brown, as if uncertain what color they'd rather be. The dark green sweep of dye beneath her eyes and over her nose enhanced that color within them, but the golden-brown shade provided a halo around the inner green color. She quickly lowered them before he could study them for long.

The fact that he wanted to study them at first surprised him, then it deeply disturbed him that one look into her eyes impacted him in such a way. He lifted a hand reflexively to touch his helmet, knowing full well that it wouldn't allow any of her scent to reach him. It was simply a lifelong habit to double-check when in the presence of a female—especially when something about her seemed too enchanting.

"My master hopes that his generosity will inspire you and your company to consider docking here regularly. Ma'Nah is known throughout Za'Kluth to be a profitable endeavor. Zaska Docking and Shipping would like more of your business. We are willing to work out a deal that proves beneficial to both parties."

"Ma'Nah shipments are generally delivered to our tier," Shulgi said, curious now about the unexpected offer, though he didn't like the idea of doing business with a creature like Sha Zaska. "It lowers the transportation fees within the column."

She glanced up again, a small, hesitant smile touching her small but shapely lips just briefly before she quickly lowered her gaze. "We have heard that hover-time fees are increasing on your tier, honored Iriduan. We are willing to work out a deal where we provide both docking and shipping at a price that will offset the difference in column transportation fees and still give your company a discount."

"I don't like your master," Shulgi growled, suddenly far too tempted to accept the offer solely because it might mean he could see this female again. "I don't like slavers or slave owners. Why would I agree to conduct business with such a creature?"

He didn't like that temptation at all. Iriduan males were not immune to visual stimulation, but only a female's scent could enrapture an unmated male. He remained aware that he'd been cured of that imprinting affliction, but not of the natural desire to mate. The deactivated genes only dealt with the compulsions involved with imprinting, not with sexual and reproductive functions. In fact, shutting those genes down unlocked reproductive functions without a male having to imprint. Because of this, it was best that he kept his distance from any female who made him want things he could never have. His mission was too important to jeopardize it with distractions.

Especially with a dyed flower of Zaska's. The gang boss specifically used them for their allure, and Shulgi would not take part in using a slave, especially one whose sole purpose was to manipulate through seduction.

The slave looked up sharply when he said he didn't like slavers, and he saw surprise in her widened eyes and raised brows, a soft gasp leaving her slightly parted lips. She quickly lowered her head, dropping her gaze even further until it hovered around her own sandal-clad, green-painted toes.

"Forgive me, honored Iriduan. My master was unaware of your... *distaste* for the practice of slavery. Many of the slavers do extensive business with Iriduans in the dreg."

Shulgi crossed his arms over his chest, the movement causing one of the Ultimen guards to growl low. That growl fell silent when the flower turned her head towards the guard, a movement so slight that Shulgi wouldn't have noticed it if he hadn't been watching her so closely, hoping for another good look at her eyes.

"Ma'Nah does not deal in slaves. You cannot judge all my people based on the repulsive actions of a few."

Her lips quirked in a skeptical expression, though she kept her head bowed so he only spotted the edges of that expression from where he stood a head and shoulders taller than her petite frame.

"Perhaps more than a few," he ground out, irritated by the reputation his people had earned in the wider galaxy, especially now that he knew for a fact how accurate it could be.

"Please, honored Iriduan," the flower said in a soft, pleading voice, "consider my master's offer." She stepped closer to him, lifting her head to look up at his blank helmet.

She placed a hand on his forearm, and even though impenetrable armor stood between her skin and his, he could swear he felt her touch. "The potential rewards of our partnership will far outweigh the drawbacks."

THREE

Molly's legs trembled, threatening to fail her as she watched the Iriduan leave the waiting room and make his way through the crowded dock area. She noticed how everyone gave him a wide berth, making certain to be out of his path when he passed them. He barely turned his head to scan his surroundings, but she suspected he didn't need to in that armor. His wings twitched, outspread at his sides as if he prepared to take flight at a moment's notice, which told her he remained aware of the danger on all sides of him.

She'd gotten the feeling from him that he would fight before he'd take flight, and she had no doubt he'd win most, if not all, of those fights.

"Shit," she whispered beneath her breath.

"You think he'll speak to his superiors about a deal?" Jenice asked, her voice suddenly rasping in Molly's ear from the communicator tucked inside it.

"I'm coming back there, Jen." Molly sucked in a deep breath, letting it out slowly. "We'll speak in a moment."

She glanced at her bodyguards, Mogorl and Grundon, and

THE IRIDUAN'S MATE   29

they nodded in unison, stepping aside for her to pass into the office, before closing in behind her.

She rushed through the luxurious outer office without seeing it, then through another door to the inner sanctum where soothing music played, and a pleasing floral and citrus incense burned to chase away the stench from the docks. She didn't linger there, either, though her bodyguards settled onto the seating crescent in front of a screen array to play video games.

She continued through a hidden door into a more utilitarian chamber outfitted with screens displaying feed from secret cameras that scanned the entire docks and even some of the other tiers.

Jenice spun around on her chair to face the door as Molly walked in, still covered in goosebumps from the encounter.

"Well?" Her cheeks bunched as she smiled toothily. "Do you think we'll get Ma'Nah's business? I had Rokoi throw in a free transport of the cargo to the dreg to kiss up a bit more."

Molly slowly shook her head, unhooking the slave collar to toss it onto one of the security desks before collapsing gratefully into an overstuffed office chair patched in multiple places. "I'm having second thoughts about doing business with Iriduans."

She didn't want Jenice to know how much the encounter had unnerved her. Something about that particular Iriduan had all her senses on alert, and she'd learned to trust her senses. He posed a threat to her, and she wasn't certain what type of threat that might be, but she feared it wasn't a physical one.

She could handle physical danger. She didn't think she could survive an emotional threat.

Jenice nodded quickly, her short curls bouncing around her heart-shaped face. "I understand your concerns, *but* they have a shit ton of money up in that dreg, not to mention goods we can't get anywhere else on this rock. Hell, if we make the right connections, we'll have a line to some of the rarest goods in the galaxy, right from Iridu itself! Ma'Nah is our way in. If that company legitimizes Zaska's Docking and Shipping, the other Iriduans will see us as a viable option to their overcrowded docks."

"You heard him say he won't deal with slavers." Molly still felt surprised by that revelation.

Everything she knew about Iriduans told her they were the bastards of the universe and that there wasn't a single atrocity they weren't more than happy to commit.

Jenice held up a finger. "No, he said he doesn't *like* slavers and slave owners, not that he won't deal with them. He left the waiting room without a definitive answer, so he could still take the offer to his superiors."

Molly sighed, smoothing her hand over her bound hair to touch the bun high on her head, prickling with ornamental pins and jewels. "He was... not what I expected."

She'd planned on meeting some arrogant masked bastard in fancy robes surrounded by a full escort of armed guards. Instead, a single Iriduan in full armor and far larger in size than she'd anticipated had shown up, stalking through the deadliest dock tier in the column as if he owned the place and feared nothing.

Given their reputation, most Iriduans probably didn't fear much. That armor he wore was some of the best in the galaxy. The pistol on his hip had been imperial military issue, which meant it probably fired multiple kinds of ammo, not to mention ammo with multiple devastating effects.

She also got the impression that he felt more than comfortable with combat since he moved in the armor like it was as familiar to him as robes were to most of the uptight Iriduans.

"Mm," Jenice said noncommittally. "It's a pity he wore a helmet. I've seen pictures of Iriduan males, and they're ridiculously good-looking, even with all those bizarre skin colors." Molly chuckled at Jen's ironic tone as she pointed to Molly's dyed skin.

She shrugged with far more nonchalance than she felt. "Sure, they're handsome, if you like that pretty boy type, but we need to focus on what matters here. The Iriduans aren't stupid, Jenice. We've played this game well with the lowlifes and scumbags who live and work down here but branching out to the upper tiers could end up screwing us, big time. Especially with a species like the Iriduans."

Jenice waved away her words. "Relax, Mol. Sha Zaska terrifies everyone, and his reputation has spread throughout the column. Hell, I'm pretty sure it's spread throughout all Za'Kluth. No one is gonna mess with his minions or servants."

Molly leaned forward, propping her elbows on her knees as she tapped her fingertips together. "Yeah, it's just too bad that we can't produce the boss himself if anyone gets too nosy and starts investigating."

"Well, no one with any intelligence will delve below the vents to see if he's real or not. As long as people keep disappearing off the docks and so many slaves go missing, no one— not even an Iriduan—is gonna want to risk messing with Sha Zaska."

"Speaking of which," Molly leaned back in her chair with a heavy sigh, "how many slaves were you able to smuggle off world in that last shipment?"

"We got seven in the crates bound for Pelin Jumpstation docks. Our contact there will see they get onto ships bound for Akrellia."

Molly tapped her knee with nervous fingers as she pondered the situation. "Just seven, huh?"

"We need more ships and more shipments, Mol," Jenice said, her tone all business now. "We can't launch half-empty cargo haulers without bringing attention from the city bosses. That's why we need companies like Ma'Nah to fill our holds with enough cargo that we can run more slaves out of here without arousing suspicion." She pointed to the decrepit waiting room of the dock office visible on one screen. "We could also use the credits. Our ships all need an overhaul, and the dock's forcefields are due for maintenance. You know how much that shit costs."

Molly stared at the screens, not really seeing the images depicted on them.

"You know," Jenice said thoughtfully, tapping Molly on the forearm to get her attention, "that Iriduan didn't exactly slap your hand away when you touched him."

Molly shot a quelling look towards Jenice. "We're not at the seduction stage yet, Jen. I don't want to push it with the Iriduans. They're... *weird* when it comes to sex and mating." Though she had no personal experience with the males of that species, she had heard odd and conflicting rumors about their sexuality and mating habits.

Jenice grinned. "It wouldn't be the worst assignment to seduce one of them."

Molly's stomach fluttered as she recalled the deep, impatient, sometimes even growly voice of the Iriduan. Normally, she only pretended to be frightened and submissive, but his species truly did unnerve her, and his size and commanding voice had made her act much easier—and much closer to her real feelings. It had been an impulsive and, in retrospect, dangerous decision to touch him, and she still wasn't certain what had possessed her to do so. A "dyed flower" shouldn't be so aggressive and obvious in their seduction attempts. They were supposed to seem elusive and delicate. Something to be pursued. That elusiveness and reserve had saved them on more than one occasion from having to engage with repellent creatures.

She also knew enough about the Iriduans to understand that attempts to seduce them rarely worked. They apparently imprinted on a single female in their lifetime, so casual sex wasn't normal for them. Conversely, she'd heard other rumors that unmated Iriduan males *could* have sex with females they hadn't imprinted on, but she had no idea how true that was, as the males from the dreg didn't visit brothels openly. Rare as those rumors were, they sometimes implied that things could get ugly and violent in those encounters with unmated males, some tales even claiming they behaved in an abnormal fashion in brothels, as if they were high on drugs.

Sometimes she and the other "flowers" used their bodies to close deals, though they always tried to avoid taking the seduction all the way if they could. Molly had been in positions where she'd had to follow through with one or another of the unpleasant creatures she'd seduced in her role as one of Zaska's flowers, but it was a rare enough occurrence that she could live with it.

She wasn't in a brothel anymore, so at least she had more control over who touched her body.

"Hey!"

Molly jumped when Jenice suddenly waved a hand in her face.

"You okay, sweetie?"

She nodded quickly. "I'm fine." She sucked in a hard breath. "I think I'll avoid the seduction route with the Iriduans though. I don't think that's a winning strategy. We'll court their business in a more professional manner."

Jenice grinned. "You mean bribe the captains of the cargo haulers to deliver more of their stuff to our docks?"

Molly nodded with an answering grin as she stood up to

leave the office and Jenice to her voyeuristic work. "Damned right," she said on her way out the door.

The okihan pirate captain who had delivered Ma'Nah's smuggled cargo had owed Zaska a favor, and Molly had cashed it in when Jenice suggested they find a way to court the wealthy Iriduan business, even though she had her misgivings about the plan. She still wasn't sure how she felt about their decision.

When she'd invented Sha Zaska, it had been an act of desperation. A work of propaganda to keep nosy and intrepid explorers out of the under-vents where she and other escaped slaves had hidden and scrabbled to survive on what scraps fell through the vents from the base-level tier.

The other slaves had helped her create the effects and sounds in the under-vents to begin the spread of fear, and over time their whispered rumors on the docks spread it further. That was when Molly realized they could use the myth of Sha Zaska to their advantage, and with the help of some of the savvier slaves, like Jenice—who'd been a successful business-woman before her abduction—started helping slaves to escape the docks and smuggle them into crates on outbound ships. Then they'd tell tales to whoever would listen that the thida naf living below the vents had pulled them down through the vents and eaten them.

Fake slave collars, fake gang marks, even fake tentacles, along with very real guards—most of whom genuinely thought they were serving Sha Zaska—helped the former slaves move back above the vents to take over the docks.

Now, their operation had grown far beyond Molly's wildest dreams, but it was still too small to help every human slave she encountered, much less the many other species that lived in slavery on this hellish world. Former slaves like Mogorl and Grundon, who now served *her* loyally, rather than the mythical boss they knew didn't exist.

Molly hated having to walk by the suffering victims of this criminal world, unable to free them all. She tried to tell herself it was enough that she managed to free some to return home to their own worlds, or find a haven where slavery wasn't tolerated.

Her own memories of the brothel haunted her nightmares. The patrons hadn't been the worst part about the place, and most had treated her well enough that she even found herself taking comfort in the physical intimacy, since she'd been deprived of any kind of kindness or comfort from the owners of the brothel.

She barely remembered her life prior to being sold to the brothel. She'd been very young when aliens had abducted her. She'd never even seen the ones that took her from Earth. She only recalled waking up in a slave market as a small child. From there, she'd been purchased by a colonial construction company and used for various labors in tight spaces where even their mechs couldn't fit. Once she'd grown too big to fit into those spaces, the company "recruiter" sold her to a brothel. She had no idea what her age had been then, but she doubted it was older than twelve.

As for what her family had been like on Earth, she couldn't say. When she'd finally had the freedom to return to that world if she wanted to, she hadn't bothered. She figured she had a greater purpose here, helping others to find their way back home.

FOUR

Shulgi paced in front of Namerian's desk, his wings twitching with his tension. "Zaska charged us nothing and sent our cargo to the dreg with no fees. I still don't trust the creature."

Namerian leaned back in his chair, dropping the stylus he'd been using to make biological sketches on his tablet. "Forming a contract with Zaska might not be a bad idea. The city bosses rarely sweep the under-tier docks, and the cargo we've been bringing in through this tier's docks have raised difficult questions, costing us a fortune in bribery payments."

Shulgi clenched his fists, pausing in his pacing to stare at the wall behind Namerian's desk, though he didn't really see the slowly cycling images of Iriduan landscapes within the elegant frame. "I was afraid you would say that."

Namerian scoffed, clasping his hands together on the desktop. "There isn't much that frightens you, Shulgi. Why do I feel like there is more to this hesitation than simple distaste for the gang boss?"

Shulgi opened his mouth to mention the dyed flower, but

quickly closed it again. He was unwilling to expose the fact that he'd felt vulnerable to her allure, even with his helmet seal firmly in place. This wasn't a scent thing. It also wasn't an admiration that had deepened to a strong attraction, like he'd felt for Paisley.

He couldn't explain it, and that meant he couldn't guard against it effectively. Other than to never see her again and hope he forgot about her as quickly as he'd felt an attraction to her. At the same time, he wouldn't send anyone else to deal directly with Zaska's minions or even walk the under-tier docks. The professors were not warriors, and Ma'Nah's guards remained, for the most part, ignorant of the details of their work, as well as the nature of their cargo. They could not be relied upon for intricate business dealings with canny gang bosses.

"As I said, I don't trust Sha Zaska. Only a fool would."

Namerian nodded slowly. "Your caution is understandable, but the dockmasters on our tier routinely skim from cargo, spy for the city bosses, and attempt shakedowns and extortions daily, and you can't deny that the cargo haulers we're sometimes forced to use don't always deal honestly with us. Sha Zaska, for all his vile habits and faults, isn't likely to be a worse option than what we already must contend with."

Namerian leaned forward in his seat, his violet eyes intent on Shulgi. "Besides, Zaska must be angling for a greater slice of Iriduan business. I'm guessing it was no mistake our cargo was delivered to his docks. Ma'Nah's custom would legitimize Zaska's company for the rest of the dreg."

Shulgi shrugged. "I'd already figured out that our haulers dumped our cargo there on purpose, no doubt threatened or bribed to do so. That doesn't inspire any more trust in me for doing future business with Zaska."

Namerian's wings slowly sliced the air behind his seat as his expression shifted from intent to thoughtful. "Zaska is clever enough to keep his word and minimize his extortion attempts with his associates and clients. If necessary, we can outmaneuver him, but for the moment, I believe we can benefit from his ships and his docks. I say you contact his minions and draw up a contract. If he doesn't keep to the terms, we pull our business from his company."

Ultimately, it was Shulgi's decision as the leader of the front company of Ma'Nah as well as their secret team, but he valued Namerian's advice even more than he valued the input of any of the other members of their team. He also knew Namerian was right and had already come to that conclusion himself by the time he'd arrived back at the dreg. He had just wanted a second opinion—and perhaps he'd hoped that Namerian would talk him out of doing a deal that might put him back in contact with the dyed flower who had not even given him her name. Assuming she had one. Many slaves weren't permitted to own anything—even something as intangible as their own name.

He left Namerian's office after a lengthy discussion of the details for a potential contract. Certain cargo had to be handled differently from the usual supplies required by the company's legitimate and public production. No doubt Sha Zaska would be eager to gain the shipping runs for Ma'Nah's off world exports as well, as the company ramped up the export end of their business after installing contacts on Iridu and even far-flung Iriduan colonies in preparation for phase two.

Shulgi finally settled into his small cell of a room that evening with a meal he'd picked up from one of the food stalls that dotted the factory sector to service employees. Unlike the others of his team, he eschewed the apartments at the top of the factory building in favor of a defensible room with a trapdoor exit into the basement. He didn't like being surrounded by windows vulnerable to sniper attacks, and the view of the dreg wasn't all that pleasant at any rate, try as the hologram artists might to make the false sky look beautiful.

He often isolated himself from the others, even those he'd taken into closest confidence, like his creche-kin. He doubted he would ever trust himself to form close relationships with anyone at this point. After all, he'd murdered members of his own elite military squad who were as close to family as he'd ever gotten, and he would never forget the look of their blood staining his hands. Nor would he forget the look in Retas's eyes as he'd turned, the blood welling at his throat from Shulgi's own dagger.

Instead of anger, or hurt at being so betrayed, he'd had pity in his expression as he'd met Shulgi's eyes one last time before his body slumped to the floor. He'd known from the moment Shulgi grabbed him from behind and sliced the blade across his flesh that Shulgi had been compromised in a way that would make him a slave forever.

And he'd pitied his murderer because he'd understood that Shulgi had no choice.

Only Shulgi still believed he'd had a choice. He could have found a way to end his own life instead of taking the lives of others. It was difficult to work against the survival instinct that imprinting only enhanced, but imprinted males *could* manage to commit suicide rather than fully submitting to their compulsion to serve their mates. It was a rare occurrence though, and the longer one was imprinted, and the more exposure he had to his mate's scent, the more enraptured he became and the harder it was to go against her will.

As much as he despised Ninhursag's memory now, he well

remembered how obsessed he'd felt with her when he'd been under her spell, before receiving the cure.

That was another reason the idea of working with Sha Zaska worried him. The petite and delicate flower of a slave that Zaska dangled like a lure in front of potential clients seemed far too tempting. He no longer had unmated impotency to protect him from rash actions. If she offered herself to him for more favorable terms on the contract, only the fact that she was a slave and not acting on her own desires would deter him from accepting something he could not afford to accept.

Ninhursag had taken his virginity with a cold callousness that made him ill to think about it. She'd used her harem solely for her own pleasure, with no regard for theirs. The fact that he'd felt powerless to deny her anything she'd wanted from him made him unwilling to take advantage of someone in that same way, especially a slave of a monster like Sha Zaska.

On the other hand, the flower appealed to him in a way a woman hadn't since Ninhursag. Not even his affection for Paisley had made him feel such strong desire. If the dyed flower managed to convince him that she was willing and desirous of his touch, he might not be able to retain his honor and reject her.

In truth, he wanted to free her from her enslavement and protect her from the monster that kept her in chains but knew that would invite far too many complications he couldn't afford at the moment. The cure had to be his priority. Nothing else could take precedence, and he couldn't allow irrational desires to spur him into actions that would jeopardize everything he'd built in this dreg to work towards pushing the cure out to all Iriduan males in the galaxy.

He could only hope that Sha Zaska would choose a different mouthpiece once he earned Ma'Nah's business and no longer needed to dangle a prize in front of Shulgi's face. Even though he still wanted to see her again. A part of him hoped he'd been misled by faulty memory. Perhaps she wasn't as appealing as he recalled. She was only human, after all, though her skin was dyed in colors that would appeal to an Iriduan.

She had human eyes, and a human face, and—no doubt— the grating human nature that irritated so many of his kind. Impetuous, impulsive, overly passionate in all things, and markedly impatient.

Unfortunately, Shulgi had learned enough about the human spirit to also acknowledge many traits that were admirable—and perhaps far too infrequent in his own people. Paisley's empathy, determination, kindness, loyalty, and capacity for love had impressed him to the point that even imprinted on Ninhursag as he had been at the time he'd been trapped on a derelict ship with Paisley, he'd been able to form an attachment to her.

This "flower" might have none of those traits—or all of them. He couldn't afford to find out. As he ate his meal in isolation, with no company other than the sound of an action play on his holoscreen providing background noise, he braced himself mentally for another potential meeting with Sha Zaska's minions. He would rest and recuperate first. The day had been long and exhausting, even for one such as him. This meal was the first he'd eaten in so long he could barely recall the taste of the last one.

The stew and the noodles tasted as unmemorable as the last, but the flash-fried flowers on his plate, grown from imports from Iridu, left a lasting impression, and not just one of nostalgia for a home world he likely wouldn't see again. As he crunched down on the first one, he thought of the Zaska's dyed flower, and he worried that Sha Zaska would eventually grow tired of her and perhaps decide to consume her as casually as Shulgi now ate the petals of the kizu blossom.

He reminded himself for the hundredth time that she was not his problem, but that reminder didn't silence his conscience as the breaded, grassy and light floral flavor of the fried blossom turned bitter on his tongue.

FIVE

The sound of water dripping somewhere nearby warred with the soft, pleading croaks coming from the bulging throat of the sagdui whose upper set of arms had been tied to a pipe above his head. His amphibious skin glistened from a mucus coat and the toxins that welled from the pores on his bared back.

The heat in the under-vent tunnels could be almost unbearable in some places, and for some species, it was. The sagdui preferred cooler climates, but Zaska's thokost enforcer, Thudar, hadn't brought the message runner here to suffer from long exposure to the heat.

They all knew he wouldn't live long enough for his amphibious skin to dry out and his body to whither.

"Please," the sagdui whimpered to Molly, his nictating membranes sliding over his huge, black eyes. "I swear I don't work for Uthagol! It was all a misunderstanding! Please!" He turned his head, his thick neck straining around the bulge of his distended throat as he desperately searched the tunnels on either side of his temporary prison. His terrified stare returned to Molly. "Tell Sha Zaska that Thudar is wron—"

Thudar's fist slamming into the sagdui's soft belly cut off his plea. The sound of flesh striking flesh made Molly flinch inwardly, but she remained still, breathing in deep to steady herself, even though her gut churned with bile and her heart raced in her chest.

"My master finds Thudar's evidence compelling, I'giar," she said in the soft, breathy voice she only used when playing her role as Zaska's mouthpiece. "You have been spying upon our operations for Uthagol and her minions. Sha Zaska will not accept this betrayal without consequence."

Thudar punched the sagdui a second time to silence him when he opened his fleshy lips to speak. A pained grunt was the only thing that escaped them as his lower set of arms strained against the bindings that kept them tied behind his back.

The thokost glanced in her direction, the shadow of his antlers shifting on the rock wall behind him when he moved. She felt his questioning look but didn't meet his amber eyes. He was a brute enforcer—one who believed in the existence of Sha Zaska, though he'd never seen the gang boss. It didn't matter. Zaska had his unquestioning loyalty, and he obeyed Molly as long as he thought she served the gang boss's will.

She kept her gaze on I'giar's dangling body as she gestured towards him with one hand, her stomach rebelling so she had to swallow hard to keep the bile down. She wanted to close her eyes when Thudar started beating the sagdui, the thokost's own toxic skin undamaged by the drops of toxin that spattered onto him from each impact with the sagdui's rubbery flesh. He demanded answers from the runner in a hollow toned voice, but they didn't actually need them. Thudar had already collected all the information they needed to trace the sagdui's actions in the past three months since he'd been approached to spy for Uthagol.

The skeletally thin, spidery alfgoi bitch had her suspicions about where her escaped slaves had run to, and now had a personal vendetta against Sha Zaska, believing he'd had something to do with the explosion at one of her brothels several years ago. She was technically correct, though her ire wasn't aimed at the right person, but Uthagol couldn't even comprehend the idea that the slaves themselves had managed to escape and build a successful criminal organization in the lowest bowels of the column.

Thudar took efforts to keep the sagdui conscious to suffer as much as possible, but eventually, he sagged in his bonds, and it was clear that he wouldn't regain consciousness. Then the thokost simply snapped his neck, leaving his corpse to dangle, flesh battered and swollen, bones shattered beneath layers of fat.

Mogorl and Grundon shifted their weight behind her as Thudar turned to Molly, his disturbingly humanoid face expressionless as I'giar's blood and toxin spattered his rough, textured skin. The Ultimen never felt easy in the presence of those who weren't aware of the truth, always prepared for Zaska's minions to turn on Molly. She wished she could take some of the other minions into her confidence, but the less people who knew the truth, the less likely it would end up leaked to someone like this sagdui.

"Leave the corpse for Master Sha Zaska," she said, stripping all emotion from her voice while keeping it as soft and submissive as possible.

She'd learned at a very young age how to mask her distress, no matter what horrors she'd been exposed to. The mask of stoicism had saved her life on more than one occasion.

The thokost cast a quick, nervous glance at the dark shadows that clustered in the tunnel exits. He then bowed his heavy antlers in her direction. "Please inform Sha Zaska that I will never allow another of my servants to be compromised again."

Molly had no intention of making an example out of Thudar for failing to stop Uthagol from compromising one of his team. He'd more than demonstrated his loyalty by detecting I'giar's betrayal and bringing it to her attention.

Sometimes, she hated being the primary mouthpiece of the mythical gang boss.

"I will, honored thokost."

She made certain her bow was lower than his. She was—after all—just a slave, and Thudar was a free and willing minion of the gang boss. What that said about him was more than obvious to her, as was the sagging corpse, but she understood the need to do terrible things to survive. None of Sha Zaska's minions had chosen their life out of an abundance of better alternatives.

Ultimately, the sagdui's death was her doing. Thudar was simply a weapon she'd used to silence a threat.

Thudar left, understanding the dismissal. Once Mogorl informed her that he was gone, Grundon cut down the sagdui.

"You don't have to stay to watch this," Mogorl said, noting her expression as she struggled to keep her bile down, blinking back tears as the corpse slumped brokenly to the stone ground spattered with I'giar's blood and fluids.

Molly shook her head, swallowing hard before daring to open her mouth to speak. "I do," she whispered. "I swore I would never turn my back on the consequences of my own actions, no matter how terrible." She looked up at the Ultiman's face, seeing the kindness and empathy there that he had to hide as much as she did her own emotions. "Leave some of his limbs to rot in the tunnels, near the runner's station. Throw the rest of his body in the lava well. Send his head to Uthagol."

Mogorl nodded and turned to the corpse, leaving her to

stand on shaking legs, her fists clenched against the desire to flee from the scene. Together, he and Grundon tore off two arms and a leg from the body, then ripped off the head.

Despite her determination to endure the grisly sight, Molly had to turn away when the first arm came free, trailing bloody ropes of tissue and muscle. She collapsed to her knees, then bent over and vomited everything in her stomach to spatter the ground in front of her trembling body. She covered her ears with both hands to shut out the horrifying sounds of the two Ultimen finishing their dirty work as hot tears burned her eyes.

She flinched when Mogorl gently touched her back, then bit back a sob as she pushed herself back to her feet. Swiping a hand over her lips, she turned towards him, her gaze skating over the small pile of dismembered body parts and the streak of blood from where Grundon had dragged the body out of the tunnel to take it to a lava well.

"Grundon will finish the work, Mol," Mogorl growled gently. "Let's return to the inner sanctum so you can rest."

Molly wanted to show a strong front, but she couldn't manage it at the moment. She'd seen so much in her life, endured so much, that she felt like she should be immune to such horrors by now. Yet this situation proved to her that she hadn't yet hardened herself enough to the realities of her existence.

She wondered what life on Earth would have been like for her. She'd heard many stories about it from the slaves she'd helped to escape and knew that parts of that world could be as brutal and bloody as this one. She had no idea what the situation had been like for her and her family when she'd been abducted, but she had a feeling her life would have turned out vastly different if she hadn't been taken.

She followed meekly in Mogorl's footsteps as they left the under-vents, not because it was an act she had long ago perfected, but because she truly felt broken and lost and needed someone else to rely on and protect her in that moment.

Jenice joined her in the inner sanctum after Mogorl left her to wash up in privacy. She caught Molly staring blankly into the bathroom mirror, wondering if her eyes looked a little more dead now.

Wondering if they were as lifeless as the sagdui's corpse.

"Thudar's an ass-kisser who wouldn't dream of questioning Zaska's mouthpiece," Jenice said with empathy in her tone as she approached Molly. "You could have left him to do the job himself. He wouldn't have protested you not being there."

Molly slowly shook her head, watching her movement in the mirror as the delicate bells on the chained netting that swung from her head ornaments tinkled. "I have to face what I am, Jen. This monster—Sha Zaska—he is me. And I am him."

Jen rushed to Molly's side, gripping her upper arm to jerk her away from the mirror, forcing Molly to face her. "Don't you dare take all the responsibility for Zaska on yourself!" She glared as she lowered her head to meet Molly's tear-soaked eyes. "We are *not* monsters! We do what we must in order to help the innocent escape this hellhole. Zaska is a terrible necessity, but he *is* a necessity."

She touched Molly's damp cheek. "And I won't let you regret what we've created here simply because a lowlife pond scum like I'giar met his well-deserved end at the hands of our minion. We've done the same to others, and will have to do so again, but we've never killed anyone who didn't earn it." She clutched both Molly's arms when she tried to turn away. "He worked for Uthagol," she hissed angrily. "Everyone knows what a monster she is. He *deserved* his death, Molly."

Molly finally pulled away and stumbled out of the bathroom and into the sitting room. She looked up sadly as she sank down onto one of the loungers. "What do *I* deserve?"

"A fucking medal!" Jenice snapped as she joined Molly on the lounger. "Stop all this moping. You chose to go down there and endure that scene for some misguided and masochistic reason. Now you have to suck it up and focus on what matters."

Molly sighed and leaned back on the seat, staring up at the star-studded ceiling, the hologram that played over it slowly moving the constellations around the room. "How long are we going to do this, Jen? We will never free every slave." She snorted. "We freed seven—*seven*, in the last shipment! That's such a pitiful number considering all the terrible things we do in Sha Zaska's name."

Jenice touched her arm. "Seven people who are now heading to a safe and possibly happy life don't find that number pitiful."

Molly smiled weakly, turning her head to look at Jenice. She winced and lifted her head off the seat to pluck out an ornamental pin that got stuck in the material and pulled on her bound hair. "I hate these things," she said, chucking it onto a nearby low table. "Why did I think we had to invent such elaborate costumes for Zaska's mouthpieces."

Jen grinned as she glanced at the fallen pin, a cheap imitation of gold and precious gems. Then her smile faded. "If I recall, you decided on these costumes and the dyed skin and markings to make it less likely we would be recognized as Uthagol's former brothel slaves."

Molly sighed heavily, sagging into the upholstery. "Right. I should have thought of a less labor-intensive costume." She lifted an arm to stare at the swirls of green tentacles covering her purple dyed skin. "I'll probably need to re-dye soon. My markings are fading."

"Glad to see you're finally focusing on the right priorities." Jen patted her arm as Molly lowered it back to her side. "Now, speaking of focusing, I actually came in here with good news that I think will cheer you up. Ma'Nah has contacted us, and they want to do business with us—if we can agree to terms they like."

Molly's heart thudded faster again, only this time, the fluttering feeling in her stomach wasn't from horror. "When will we be working out those terms?"

"Today." Jenice clapped her hands together. "In fact, you only have a few hours to get cleaned up before you'll meet with their rep in the office." She rose to her feet and strode to the wall, touching it so a panel slid aside to reveal a closet filled with green outfits.

"I really despise green," Molly said as Jenice plucked out a dress to examine it before shaking her head to put it back and select another.

Jenice grinned as she glanced at Molly, holding a silk robe that looked like the ones the Iriduans themselves often wore. It was elegant and demure in comparison to most of the outfits Molly wore as a dyed flower. "And here I thought green was your favorite color."

Molly stood up, smoothing the fabric of her current dress. "It was, until I decided to use it to represent Sha Zaska's gang." She approached Jenice, who handed the robe to her, then dug through the dresses for other potential options. "So, the Iriduan rep wants to meet in person?"

"He doesn't want to transmit details, even over encrypted lines."

Molly accepted the second dress—a far more revealing one—automatically, her gaze on Jenice's face. "That sounds like we won't be dealing with aboveboard cargo, Jen."

Jen smirked as she pulled out a final dress for Molly to consider—a flowing, billowy number with a romantic, fairy tale appearance. "My guess is that Ma'Nah isn't entirely operating on the legal side of things, even for Za'Kluth. They're probably trying to slip under the city bosses' radar."

Molly huffed as she took the final dress. "I don't think the word 'legal' even applies in this place, but I have to agree with you. It doesn't sound like Ma'Nah wants much attention brought to their business." She sighed as she regarded the three dresses in her hands. "We can help them smuggle stuff in and out without much notice from the city bosses. I just hope this deal will be worth it for us."

Jenice dug around the shelves below the dresses for a pair of shoes to match the different styles. "Look at it this way," she straightened, holding strappy sandals dangling from one hand and glittery slippers in another, "at least you get to see the Iriduan guy again."

Molly raised her eyebrows. "You mean the one in combat armor? Do they usually send soldiers to business meetings?" She shook her head. "That hasn't been my experience with them in the past. An escort of guards, sure, but I'd expect some pompous, berobed asshat to be leading the talks."

Jenice's eyes glittered as she turned to face Molly. "Apparently, that guy is someone important in the company, and he's the one making the decisions, so...."

She put both pairs of shoes in one hand and plucked the sexy dress out of Molly's loose grip. "*Maybe* you should wear this one."

Molly rolled her eyes. "We already got their interest. I don't need to seduce the guy."

"We might get better terms," Jenice said in a singsong voice. She wiggled her shapely hips as she followed Molly towards the bathroom. "Just flutter those long eyelashes of yours and show him a little skin and maybe a little kissy, kissy," she made smooching sounds as Molly laughed despite herself and tossed the romantic fluttery dress at Jen.

"Stop it, you loon!" She lifted the green, embroidered robe. "I need him to respect me, and humans are already at a disadvantage on that front with those Iriduan bigots."

Jenice snorted as she tossed the other two dresses on the bed. "As long as he respects Sha Zaska, it doesn't matter what he thinks of you personally. You're just a mouthpiece, as far as he's concerned. We'll be communicating through the terminal to fine tune the contract, and you'll be pretending its Zaska himself talking to you. What you *need* to do is keep the Iriduan distracted so he doesn't overanalyze our terms or get too hard-nosed and inflexible with theirs."

She stepped closer to Molly, holding out the strappy sandals. "Who cares if he respects you, Mol, as long as we get what we want? Keep your eyes on the bigger picture. This Iriduan is just one more mark we can use to our benefit."

SIX

After helping her select an outfit for the meeting, Jenice left Molly to get dressed, returning to her security room to watch the monitors. They had an AI that tracked and analyzed all the feeds for noteworthy activities and would alert them if it spotted anything that fit a set of parameters they'd entered, but Jenice found comfort in personally watching everything that happened on those cameras.

Molly knew they all coped with their lives in different ways. Jenice had her voyeurism, hiding in a small security room to watch others living their lives to the fullest. Mogorl and Grundon had video games to help them forget that they'd been taken from their home world, Ultim, before they could harvest their own eel-stones that would mark them as adults when worn in their long fur—those same "energy" stones that other species coveted for their shielding power.

Molly's way of coping with the things she was forced to see and do was to study. When she was a slave, any kind of unsanctioned learning had been forbidden. She knew enough about human children to understand that many went to schools where they learned many subjects before becoming adults. As soon as she'd gained access to the spotty Galactanet available on Igoth she'd begun taking official courses under a false name. At first, she could only take the free courses offered to all Cosmic Syndicate species that barely touched the surface of so many subjects the Syndicate citizens might need to know.

Now, she actually paid for some advanced courses in whatever subjects interested her, though she didn't bother working towards any specific academic goal. It was enough just to focus on something other than the under-tier, the docks, Sha Zaska, and the horrors of her current career. The types of scholastic assignments varied, some ridiculously easy and some impossibly difficult without assistance, but they all took her away from Igoth for a while, at least mentally.

Physically, she remained present in this world. The taste of bile clung sour to her tongue, the stench of blood and sweat and alien pheromones and rotting flesh forever clogged her sinuses, and the sounds of suffering, and scheming, and screaming rang in her ears even when she slept.

Despite her determination to help as many slaves as she could, sometimes, she dared to dream of a future beyond Za'Kluth. In her Galactanet searches, she'd found some content that purportedly came from Earth, content that was intrinsically human and spoke to her in a way no other media did. Her favorite was the collected fairytales that had been compiled by an Iriduan scholar intrigued at how humans had mythologized the presence of Iriduan colonial descendants.

In some of those fairytales, the heroine would find love and live happily ever after. Molly daydreamed of such a magical future, even when dark shadows, grasping hands, heaving bodies, and hanging corpses filled her sleeping dreams.

As Molly finished applying makeup that made the dyed marks on her face more vibrant and touched up her lips to make them a darker purple than her violet skin, she pondered her own face in the mirror. Malnourishment as a child meant that she probably wasn't as tall as she might have grown on Earth, and perhaps even now her body was too slim, though she made sure to eat regularly to maintain what curves she had, knowing that they gave her leverage with those aliens attracted to the human form. Her face, as Uthagol had reminded her on many occasions, was plain, though the markings added an exotic flair to the round shape with narrow cheekbones, a small chin and jawline, a lower lip that was fuller than her thin upper lip, and a slightly crooked nose that had been broken by an irate supervisor when she was a child and never fixed.

Her eyes were a striking feature, she'd been told, staring out of a rather ordinary human face with an indeterminate and arresting color that shifted with her mood and the surrounding lighting. Long lashes framed them, and she wouldn't confess to anyone but Jenice that those had been artificially enhanced to play up her best feature.

She wasn't a great beauty, but those who visited Uthagol's brothel hadn't seemed to care. They'd gone there looking for a human—most to serve some fetish—and they weren't particular about the details of her appearance. Now, she used those same fetishes for humans against many of the aliens who came to this tier to deal with Sha Zaska.

To her surprise—and at one time, her horror—it was the aliens that looked the least human that were most likely to have the human fetish. She'd outgrown her fear of such creatures and learned well how to manipulate and direct them to keep herself as safe as possible.

The alien she was preparing to meet belonged to a whole different category altogether. Many aliens, regardless of appearance, had an Iriduan fetish, not to mention a burning and lasting hatred of the species. Iriduans were known to be both beautiful and cruel. Their empire was a dominant one in the Cosmic Syndicate, though she'd heard tales that its power had waned drastically in the past dozen or so Standard years.

She'd seen full images of the faces of both Iriduan emperors on the Galactanet and had done some recent research on the species after her meeting with the Ma'Nah representative. She'd be lying to herself if she denied that they were exactly as described—gorgeous—although almost unnaturally so, their features too symmetrical, too perfectly formed to be markedly distinct from each other. As if a talented artist had used only a single model to draw all their images and only slightly tweaked each picture to differentiate them.

They differed most significantly in their coloring, and those differences could have a dramatic effect on their appearance. Just as Molly's unnatural coloring and markings dramatically altered her own appearance. Interestingly, the colors of their iridescent skin weren't what denoted their class or social position. It was more like the combination of colors that told whether they were considered valuable enough to engineer the most aesthetic color schemes for them if they weren't naturally gifted with it.

Details about their mating habits and reproduction remained confusing and conflicting at best. Molly only knew that their females were extremely well protected, and some accounts claimed they were actually locked away for a variety of speculated reasons. Not one of the sources she'd been able to find on the Galactanet had been able to describe an Iriduan child. The Iriduans protected their offspring so completely that they were never seen by other species, not even those trusted enough to visit Iridu.

She idly wondered if any Iriduan children had been abducted and sold into slavery like she had been. If so, she suspected they would have ended up in brothels like Uthagol's, given their physical beauty.

Molly waited in the inner sanctum for the representative. Jenice had passed on the information that his name was Shulgi. Apparently, he had an additional name—the Iriduan version of a family name—but he hadn't offered it. Since Molly couldn't even remember her own family name, she wasn't about to demand more information about his. People on Za'Kluth often dropped any identifying details like family names anyway. Not many came to this world without having a past that chased them off far more hospitable ones.

When Shulgi arrived, twenty minutes early, the dock-master—now obsequious to him because he might become a client—ushered him into the public office.

Molly studied the video feed of the public office from within the inner sanctum, watching the Iriduan male pace the confines rather than take a seat in one of the luxurious chairs. She got the impression of a caged predator, constantly checking the boundaries of its confines, seeking a way out.

The fact that he'd worn a more formal robe this time instead of armor told her he was aware that Sha Zaska wouldn't allow anyone on the docks to harm his newest potential client.

She'd seen Iriduan males before, though intelligent people avoided the dreg unless they were forced to do business around there. Sometimes, the Iriduans strayed from their own part of the tier to wander among the other species they clearly felt were beneath them. Their arrogance was always evident in their demeanors, even if their expressions were mostly hidden behind masks.

She'd read conflicting reports about the masks too, though most sites had agreed that their use tied into Iriduan mating habits. She suspected that the Iriduans themselves flooded the Galactanet with a hundred different versions of the truth and perhaps even more than a hundred different lies to keep the stories about them and their culture confused.

This Iriduan had green coloring. Not just his iridescent skin, which was a light spring green shade, while the smooth, sleek strands of hair that fell to the middle of his back between bottle glass green wings was the shade of a dark grass. His eyes glittered like flawless emeralds, larger than human eyes, though they were currently narrowed above his breather mask as he surveyed the empty office.

Molly's favorite color had always been green, for as long as she could remember. That was why she'd chosen it to be Sha Zaska's color. Still, it wasn't her admiration for the many shades of his appearance that stole her breath. He was as large in his cream-colored silk embroidered robe as he'd been in full body armor, and he still carried himself with the coiled tension of someone prepared to fight at any moment.

This was no willowy Iriduan male accustomed to a life of leisure. She knew their species had warriors—some of the best in the galaxy—but it was rare to see those guards and soldiers not wearing armor, so she'd just assumed that the armor itself lent them the added bulk that set them so apart from their berobed counterparts.

Shulgi looked more than capable of winning a fight even without armor.

His size unnerved her, but Mogorl and Grundon would be with her, and they had already risen from their seats on the lounger to stand at her side, waiting for her to give the signal to step out into the outer office, where she would have to face down one of the most intimidating clients she'd ever dealt with. She feared he would somehow see through her ruse when none of the others had. Not even the okihan pirates who leered at her with lolling tongues could see the truth, despite how canny and clever they were.

She nodded her head to Mogorl, who opened the outer door as Molly turned her gaze away from the screen and took a deep breath. When she let it out, she tried to release all her tension and nerves with it. She bowed her head slightly, taking on the posture of a meek dyed flower, ready and willing to serve in whatever capacity her master desired.

Her heart thudded so hard in her chest that she feared the Iriduan would somehow hear it pounding away as she followed Mogorl into the outer office.

A quick glance up showed her that he remained standing on the other side of the desk, though he'd stopped pacing. His wings continued to flick and shift behind him, as if he didn't like to remain still. At least not in uncertain surroundings.

"Welcome, honored Iriduan," Molly said in her breathy voice, grateful that the affected tone allowed her to conceal the quivering in her words. She gestured demurely towards the seat at the other side of the desk. "Please, be comfortable in my master's abode. He will speak with me through the console, and I will relay his words to you."

Shulgi's eyes narrowed further, furrows forming between the straight slashes of his grassy green brows. "Why doesn't he speak for himself?" He gestured to the console on the top of the desk as Grundon shifted at Molly's side, agitated by the disrespectful tone the Iriduan took.

Molly breathed shallowly through her nose, inhaling a delicious odor that was unlike anything else she'd ever smelled in the under-tier. She knew that scent came from the Iriduan, but she couldn't describe it based on anything she'd ever smelled before. It was fresh and exotic, with an undertone of something rich, like an irresistible desert. She wished she could bottle it up and wear it around her neck to keep away the stench of the under-tier all the time. Stench that even infiltrated this office and the inner sanctum beyond.

She struggled to focus on his words, rather than his imposing presence. "My master does not speak a language that most would understand, honored Iriduan." She kept her voice as soft as possible, being certain to strip any hint of emotion out of it. "I have been trained to interpret it for others, and I serve as his mouthpiece."

Shulgi's wings folded at his back, then spread outwards briefly, before folding again. "Thida naf communicate via sonic pulses. There are mechanized ways to interpret those signals." He gestured to the console. "I suspect that is what interprets those pulses, not you."

For a moment, Molly forgot to breathe. She blinked rapidly, her gaze still lowered so she didn't have to meet the Iriduan's beautiful eyes. Her mind went blank, and she started to panic. She hadn't expected him to do research on the thida naf, and she'd deliberately chosen that particular alien species because there was so little known about them. Most of the other clients of Sha Zaska's had simply accepted her explanation at face value. If they had their doubts, they hadn't bothered to voice them aloud in her presence. The rare few that did voice similar complaints as Shulgi's had been easy enough to convince to work through her.

Suddenly, words flashed on the console screen that faced her, out of the view of the Iriduan.

"Pull it together, Mol," they said, and she knew it was Jenice speaking them from the security room in a way that was translated into their coded language. "This is an easy one. It isn't the first time someone has questioned you. Give your standard response."

Of course. Molly breathed out, then bowed her head lower. "Honored Iriduan, I do not question my master's will. I exist only to serve him."

Shulgi's sudden growl raised the hair on the back of her

neck as she looked up quickly. Both Mogorl and Grundon tensed, following the sound with their own warning growls. Shulgi's posture subtly shifted, and Molly could tell tension was escalating in a way that could be counterproductive, if not outright dangerous.

"Your master is a vile monster," Shulgi bit out, his angry glare fixed on the door to the inner sanctum. "I despise such creatures." His emerald eyes shifted back to her, his glare softening.

She didn't like the look in his eyes when they met hers. Well, she *did* like it. More than she should. It worried her though because she recognized it. It was the same way she looked at every slave she passed, plotting how she could help free them.

The last thing she needed now was a savior, and she realized with a flash of insight born from familiarity with the sentiment that was exactly what Shulgi wanted to be when it came to her. As much as that thought warmed her, unexpectedly lightening her mood, she couldn't afford to entertain it.

She had to take a different tack with him. The more downtrodden and beaten she appeared to be, the more likely he'd make a move to rescue her. Her posture shifted as subtly as his had, though she wasn't moving into a fighting stance.

"Please, honored Iriduan," she said in a firmer tone that caused both Ultimen to glance at her in surprise. "My master takes excellent care of all his servants. He treats us far better than the rest of the galaxy would." She lifted her head to meet his intent gaze, her voice growing breathless again, only this time it was genuine. "I am happy here," she whispered in a low voice.

His glare returned though he didn't comment on her claim. She didn't think she'd succeeded in convincing him, but when she gestured to the chair again, he took a seat this time. His wings spread to his sides, framing him to adjust to the furnishing, their wingspan impressive, even when not fully extended.

"We should get down to business," she said in a more authoritative tone, realizing that she had to drop the submissive act completely for him, because it only created complications.

He leaned forward, his gaze shifting from her face down to the console, then lifting again to fix on her face. His strong hands rested on his knees, motionless. She noted the thin scars along the back of them with some surprise. Iriduan technology was more than capable of fully healing scarred flesh, and their purported vanity meant they rarely had any mark on their skin that they didn't want there.

It was becoming crystal clear to her that this Iriduan wasn't at all like the stereotype of their species. That could end up being a hindrance in their business dealings. She'd expected a representative to be as shady and willing to operate outside of any kind of law as any of her other clients. She feared that Shulgi would have limits that Sha Zaska's operations might push.

"I've agreed with my... associates to make a deal with your boss." Shulgi's gaze swept the office before returning to her. "I am certain it is clear I have reservations about working with Zaska in any capacity."

Molly slowly nodded. "I understand your concerns. However, Zaska's Shipping and Docking will benefit Ma'Nah so that you can continue your mission in the most effective way possible."

Shulgi stiffened, his fists clenching on his knees. "My mission?" His voice sounded strained coming from the distorting speaker of his mask.

An alarm bell went off in Molly's head at the sudden tension and antagonism radiating from the Iriduan. "I speak of Ma'Nah's mission of spreading affordable, quality nutrition to every corner of the settled galaxy. That is your company's mission statement, is it not?"

She lowered her gaze to the console, ignoring the flashing text on there from Jenice that would only tell her she was screwing this up. She didn't need that reminder.

"Forgive me if I have said something offensive, honored Iri—"

"Shulgi," he said, cutting her off. "Call me Shulgi, if you are to be the mouthpiece of your... of Sha Zaska."

To her relief, his tone sounded more relaxed and a quick glance at him showed that the tension had eased in his posture. Now, he leaned back in his chair, his hands open and palms resting on his thighs. Only his wings still shifted at his sides as if not all his aggression had disappeared.

Molly slowly let out her breath, lifting her fingers to swipe over the screen of the console to bring up the contract Jenice and the others who were more familiar with the business side of things wrote up in advance. She tapped a button that opened a console on Shulgi's side of the desk. "Please forgive me if I misspeak in any way... Shulgi."

She shot a quick glance at his face, then looked away when he met her eyes. Saying his name seemed too familiar. At the same time, she felt an urge to become even more familiar with him, even regretting that she didn't need to seduce him or even flirt with him any longer.

For the first time ever, she wanted to flirt with a mark. She actually wanted to do a little more than flirt with him.

SEVEN

Shulgi perused the terms of the contract with little real interest, though he paid careful attention to the details. He could tell by the bullet points that there wouldn't need to be much haggling on his end. From what he could see, Zaska really wanted Ma'Nah's business. Most particularly, the company's growing shipping concerns.

"Are you certain Zaska can provide this level of service," he asked skeptically, glancing up at the very distracting dyed flower.

It was only the fact that he suspected distraction was her primary purpose that kept it from working on him. Though, he wasn't completely immune to her.

She had taken a seat behind the desk, and no longer bowed her head like a beaten slave. Though he approved of the fact that she hadn't been completely broken by her master and could still show spirit, he still wished he could find a way to free her, without jeopardizing everything.

Her lips tilted in a reassuring smile that didn't meet her fascinating eyes. He had to stop himself from staring into them to try to determine their true shade. Instead, he shifted his attention back to the console in front of him.

"Please don't let the apparent condition of the docks concern you, Shulgi. They are far more serviceable than they look. Their decrepit outward appearance serves an important role."

Shulgi huffed, leaning back in his chair to regard her frankly. She met his eyes with little sign of her previous meekness. The abrupt shift in her demeanor made him deeply suspicious, but he also understood it. She had a role to play for Zaska, and she'd likely been well trained for it. Realizing her previous timid act didn't yield the results her master no doubt desired, she'd been forced to change her tactic.

He could respect her skill at manipulation, even if he also found it distasteful. He didn't blame the slave, but the master. He couldn't imagine what nightmares this woman had been put through to learn her craft so well.

The apparent deterioration of Sha Zaska's docks was another manipulation, a smokescreen to distract the city bosses from this tier. Clean, well-run, visibly repaired and technologically advanced docking bays and forcefields would draw their attention—and inspire more frequent visits from their tax assessors.

He understood subterfuge well. He could assess the true condition of the docks with an examination of the bays Ma'Nah would be using.

"What about your haulers? You're offering the dedicated use of two ships in this contract, with the possibility of additional ships as we expand our shipping routes, but I see very few details about their capacity, make, model, space-worthiness, or who will crew them."

Again, his words earned a slight smile, and Shulgi wished

she could give him a genuine expression. One that he believed was her own and not an act for her master's benefit.

"It was my intent to take you on a tour of our docks and show you one of the ships from our fleet that will haul your cargo." She gestured to the console in front of him with an elegant sweep of a small and dainty hand. "I understand you wish to verify our ability to perform our end of the contract before agreeing to it, but I wanted you to be aware of the terms when you toured our facilities." She slowly rose to her feet. "Shall we go now? Or would you like to read over any of the other points in the document?"

He'd skimmed the document already. There wasn't much to it. Business dealings in Za'Kluth didn't involve the layers upon layers of legal bindings and bureaucratic nonsense that would be found in inner system contracts. This one laid out the essential terms, financial obligations of both sides, and how either side could break the agreement.

If someone tried to break the terms of the contract, enforcement of those terms depended on how big an army either side could raise and mobilize before the city bosses took notice and brought their bootheels down to crush both sides.

Ma'Nah had no intention of riling up Sha Zaska, nor would the under-tier boss want to mess with the dreg. Upon consideration, Shulgi found it ironic that contract disputes in Za'Kluth were rare, and that business, foul as it might be, often ended up being far more civilly conducted in this criminal city than in some of the most civilized cities in the Syndicate.

He stood, his gaze shifting from her captivating eyes to trail down her form. This time, she'd covered more of her skin in a green dress with a billowing skirt, no doubt because her master felt he already had Shulgi and Ma'Nah on the hook. In that case, he was grateful she wasn't forced to display her body for his benefit, though he couldn't help wishing she would like to do so of her own free will.

Not that he would dare to remove his mask for her. Even if that single re-affliction was an aberration he didn't have to fear happening to himself, he didn't want anyone who might understand why Iriduan males wore masks to notice he didn't use one around a human female. Especially since humans were known to be so strongly fragrant—perhaps because they were also close to completely nose-blind and could barely detect a pheromone even if they were drenched in it.

He assessed the Ultimen guards as they shifted to allow the dyed flower to pass around the desk onto his side. The hairy species were well known for being intelligent and technologically advanced, but they were also known in the galaxy for being physically strong and more than capable of fighting, if necessary, though they usually sought peaceful ways to deal with conflicts. The combination of high intelligence and physical strength as well as a strong sense of diplomacy had made them one of the most dominant species in the Cosmic Syndicate.

Many members of the species served in guardsmen capacity in Syndicate-controlled space, but it was rare to find them on the Rim, since they didn't usually resort to criminal and violent activities by choice. The story behind these two was probably an interesting one, but the important thing was that they weren't likely to make a move against him unless he posed a genuine threat to their charge.

She certainly seemed comfortable around her guards as she walked gracefully to the door that led into the lobby. "Please, come with me and I will show you the bays we've set aside for Ma'Nah's use."

Shulgi tucked his wings behind him as he moved to stand next to her, shooting a warning glance at the Ultimen who came up beside him. They both towered over him, just as he towered over the petite female. This didn't intimidate him, but he also wasn't reckless.

The dyed flower glanced over at him, then frowned as her gaze shifted upwards to meet the eyes of one of the Ultimen.

Shulgi found it curious that the guard shifted away from him, almost as if he'd been given a command to give Shulgi more space as he stood beside the woman.

Perhaps they were so obedient to Sha Zaska that they viewed every glance from his mouthpiece as a verbal command. It was an interesting dynamic, but Shulgi found the woman herself far more interesting as he followed her through the lobby, then out onto the docks.

"What is your name?" he asked impulsively as soon as they stepped outside Zaska's building. He was tired of calling her a dyed flower in his head.

She shot a glance at him, the purple shade of her cheeks darkening. "My name?" Her gaze scanned the docks rapidly, as if she sought an escape from something. Then she sighed and shrugged. "My name is Molly."

Despite her almost defeated tone, she seemed surprised by her own words, her eyes widening as a hand lifted to her mouth. It looked like she wanted to push the name back behind her lips but realized it was too late.

"I won't tell your master you've given me your name, Molly," Shulgi said in a low, soothing voice, irritated that the speaker on his mask made it difficult to whisper.

If only he could talk to her without that barrier between them.

She met his eyes, and a smile spread on her lips that finally reached her own. It looked more genuine than any of the other expressions he'd seen on her winsome face. "You are truly a good person, aren't you?" she murmured, just loud enough for him to hear her over the dull roar of noise as they strolled towards the docking bays. "Why would you ever want to live in a place like this?"

Shulgi's pleasure at seeing a true smile from her dimmed as he considered her words. He knew he wasn't a good person. He was a murderer.

"I have my reasons." His tone had sharpened unintentionally, and he wanted to curse at himself when her smile disappeared and she stiffened, the mask of politeness sliding back over her features.

"Forgive me, Shulgi," she said in the breathy tone that he now knew was completely affected to fit her demure and submissive persona, "I should not have asked such a question."

Irritated at himself for being so inept in speaking to a female, he shook his head, reaching out a hand to stop her before they walked into the closest bay where Ma'Nah's ships would dock. "I'm sorry, Molly. I'm not... accustomed to speaking to... women. Forgive my boorish tone. I took no offense from your question."

Another brief flash of a genuine smile crossed her face, rewarding his honesty, no matter how humiliating it had been to admit to his failing. She glanced down at his hand, which had fallen upon her shoulder to pause her steps. When he shifted to pull away from her, she caught his fingers with hers.

Her pupils dilated, the shade of her eyes turning more green than amber or brown, a golden halo surrounding the irises. Her lips slightly parted as her breathing grew shallow and the dye on her cheeks darkened with a flush.

He felt paralyzed by the feeling of her fingers closing around his. When she lifted his hand to her soft lips and kissed one of the scars on the back of it, he didn't pull it away. Instead, he entwined his fingers with hers and tugged her closer to him.

Her small, warm body bumped against his chest, and her

head tilted back to look up into his eyes. He felt the weight of the mask covering his mouth and nose and a vague part of him realized it was the only thing keeping him from lowering his head to kiss her.

Panic at how captivated he felt by her made him push her away from him, though even then, he did it gently, feeling unable to cause her the slightest bit of harm.

"Forgive me, Molly," he said quickly at the hurt expression that crossed her face. "I did not come here to accost you in such a way. I am here only for business."

"What if I want you to 'accost me' in such a way," she whispered in a voice husky with desire as a slow smile spread on her lips, her eyes still slightly dilated and shaded forest green and soft gold.

He wished he could tell if her demeanor and expression were genuine—or a result of long, unwilling training.

The recollection that she was a slave was enough to cool his desire, which was a good thing, because his erection would soon become obvious if it grew much stiffer, and he cursed his decision to wear a formal robe rather than combat armor.

He might get away with an obvious bulge at his groin in the under-tier, since it didn't look like there were any Iriduans on this dock, but if it lasted all the way back to the dreg, his condition would attract unwanted questions.

Turning his attention to the docking bay, he tried to focus on the details of that space and what they would mean for his business, and the underlying purpose of it. He had to remind himself of the whole reason for him being in Za'Kluth, because Molly was proving far too distracting and appealing.

One of the Zaska's cargo ships sat in the bay, and Molly, perhaps sensing his deliberate shift of focus, gestured to it, though he didn't miss the small sigh that came from her. It made him think that her desire had not all been an act. He knew that Iriduan males were fetishized in some parts of the galaxy, especially on the Rim. He'd even been part of a team that broke up a slave ring while serving in the Iriduan military, where unmated males were forcibly imprinted and then ordered by their new queens to serve in a brothel.

It was possible that Molly had a fetish for his people. It was also possible that she was simply attracted to him because he didn't look that significantly different from a human male, and her exposure to those was likely limited.

Or she was simply talented at acting, and that final concern was the one that kept him from feeling any hope that this sudden and unwelcome interest in her would amount to anything.

EIGHT

Molly wished she could read the Iriduan's expression. His eyes gave little away, though his body language had implied that he might desire her. She couldn't deny that she felt aroused by him.

He smelled incredible, and she covertly sucked in deep breaths while standing close to him, when normally she made sure to breathe very shallowly on the docks. The stench of this tier was part of the illusion of a run-down and disreputable trash heap, unworthy of attention from the upper tiers and their tax assessors. Though, to be fair, it had been that way when she and her fellow escaped slaves had taken it over, using the myth of Sha Zaska.

Now, she could be proud of what they'd accomplished, as they'd taken great efforts to improve the docks, the bays, the force fields, the warehouses, and especially, the ships. Some of which had not been obtained in the most legal and aboveboard manner but were now completely the property of Zaska's Shipping and Docking. Perhaps their previous owners were dead. Perhaps some had met their end in the lava pits in the under-vents. Perhaps those deaths would haunt her nightmares for the rest of her life, but the cargo haulers that had once carried slaves to the market now helped them escape their enslavement. She tried to focus on that whenever she saw those ships.

"I did not expect Zaska to have a c'uk lar'cli ku cargo hauler," Shulgi said in a neutral tone as he scanned the sea-green hull of *Jonah's Whale*. He cocked his head, shooting a glance her way that she wished she could interpret. "This model is only a dozen Standard years old. It's unusual that a cli ku owner would sell it so early in its lifecycle."

She couldn't help but be impressed by his command of the difficult and bizarre cli ku language. She'd never been able to pronounce the full name the species used to refer to themselves without sounding like she was choking on something. He made it sound just like the insectoid members of the cli ku species did.

He also clearly knew enough about them to understand that they didn't often part with their newer technology, though they were still decades behind other space-faring species in their ship designs. They guarded their tech jealously, and after obtaining Jonah's Whale, she understood why. Her engineers—who believed they served Zaska—had expressed their admiration for the engine design, claiming that given a few more decades of development, it could end up surpassing some of the more advanced species' ship drives—and it was unique to the cli ku species.

"The owner owed Zaska a great debt and transferred the title to the ship over to him rather than struggle to come up with the credits to pay it."

Shulgi's eyes narrowed with obvious suspicion. "Ma'Nah cannot afford to draw too much attention to our shipping concerns. As impressive as this cargo hauler might be, we don't want questions to arise about its ownership."

Molly hastened to reassure him. "Jonah's Whale is legally registered to Zaska Shipping in all corners of Syndicate space. Our crew is primarily cli ku and they serve us loyally, and in return, Zaska pays them very well for their service." She added that last because she'd already seen he didn't like the idea of slavery. She felt certain he was on the edge of changing his mind about working with Zaska at any moment, because of his distaste for the practice.

She wished she could be completely honest with him and tell him that helping Zaska would actually mean helping hundreds of slaves find freedom but knew the folly of such a desire. She couldn't take anyone into her confidence who wasn't already part of her inner circle. The chance of the truth leaking out to someone like Uthagol was too great. Even those with good intentions might accidentally spill enough of the secret to get Molly and her fellow escaped slaves into big trouble and cast doubt on Zaska's power in the under-tier.

For a brief moment, she felt a terrible, drowning sense of loneliness and an overwhelming desire for a partner—a true mate—who could help her bear the burden of her mission, and who could hold her close and comfort her when that burden grew too horrible to bear alone. She loved Jenice and the others but could not find the level of intimacy with them that she knew she could have with a life partner. That kind of thing only existed in some human fairy tales, where people lived happily ever after.

He hadn't responded to her assurance, leaving her stomach knotted with concern that perhaps she should have designated different ships for Ma'Nah's use, but Jonah's Whale and their other cli ku vessel, Moby Dick, were the best and newest cargo haulers in Zaska's fleet, and she'd wanted to impress the Iriduans.

She followed him around the bay as he studied the details

of the deceptively ramshackle state of it. The ship itself looked beautiful as it loomed above them, half of it within the force-field and half jutting out into the lava-streaked darkness of the inhospitable planet beyond.

"Would you like a tour of the hauler?" she asked hesitantly after Shulgi finished his long circuit around the expansive docking bay.

He cast a pensive glance at a pile of detritus lying in one corner by the dormant cargo handlers standing like metallic sentinels against one long wall. "From what I've seen, Zaska is a master at hiding his secrets in plain sight." He scanned the pitted and scarred hull of the ship. "I will take a quick look around the cargo bay of this ship, but I doubt I will be disappointed upon taking a closer look at it."

His gaze fixed on the painted letters of the ship's name, then shot to her. "That name is a human one, is it not?"

Molly shrugged, feeling lightheaded at the speculation she feared she spotted in his eyes. She again wished she could see the entirety of his expression, because at the moment, his body language told her as little as his masked face did. Even his wings lay motionless against his back.

"Sha Zaska collects ideas for ship names from all his servants, before choosing the ones that most appeal to him." She gestured with a shaking arm to the ship. "In the case of these cli ku ships, he liked the idea of them being named after fictional sea beasts from Earth."

Her answer appeared to satisfy him as he slowly nodded. "I am unfamiliar with the stories behind those names, but the lettering is distinctly human."

She tried to smile flirtatiously, though worry still gripped her stomach and sent cold fingers along her spine. "Perhaps I can tell them to you sometime." When his gaze sharpened, fixing intently on her face, she impulsively continued, "over dinner maybe?" She tilted her head, lifting a hand to sweep over her bound hair in a demurely seductive motion, though the trembling of her fingers was certainly not practiced. "We could discuss the details of the contract further in a bit more... privacy." Her voice grew husky with desire she didn't have to fake as she thought of getting him alone in the inner sanctum, and then seducing him with the intent to enjoy herself for once by losing herself with a male who genuinely aroused her. "Zaska has an excellent chef." That much, at least, was true, though she supposed tastes were relative. The ramsuta male was in hiding on Za'Kluth now but had once cooked for kings.

"Careful, Mol," Grundon murmured from right behind her, covering the words with a low growl as Shulgi shifted his intense green gaze from Molly's face to her Ultimen protector, his brows drawing together over narrowing eyes.

She understood Grundon's warning, and it was a perfectly reasonable and sensible one. One didn't mess with the Iriduans lightly, and conflicting tales and rumors or not, she didn't doubt they took mating very seriously. There were plenty of other males in Za'Kluth who would gladly allow her a few hours of blissful physical intimacy without any complications, but none of them had ever appealed to her like this one did.

Shulgi stepped closer to her, his heady scent enveloping her and pushing back the reek of the docks. He eyed Grundon, who also stepped a bit closer to her, growling softly in protest when she flicked her fingers behind her back to tell him to move away.

As he took several reluctant steps backwards, giving her and Shulgi space, she tilted her head, looking up into Shulgi's gorgeous green eyes.

"Do *you* want to have dinner with me, Molly," Shulgi said softly, though the speaker on his mask somewhat ruined the effect. She didn't miss the stress he put on the word "you." His next words explained it. "Or is it your master ordering you to spend more time with me to close the deal?"

She had to be careful about how she handled this. It was now clear to her that the desire she suspected he might feel for her was tempered by his concern that hers was all an act for Zaska. If she made it clear that she genuinely wanted him and it had nothing to do with the contract, he might get suspicious of why Zaska—the slave-eating monster—allowed his mouth-piece so much freedom to pursue her own desires. Especially since she and the other "dyed flowers" used the rumor that Zaska kept them for his own pleasure to minimize the chances that they'd have to follow through on a full seduction of a client.

She placed a cautious hand on his, recalling how he'd pushed her away the last time she'd been so bold as to touch him, and then impulsively kiss his hand. "It is rare that I enjoy my duties, Shulgi, but in this case, I find that there is nothing I'd like more than to spend time with you."

Shulgi stared down at her hand on his arm for a long, tense moment, before closing his other hand over hers. When he looked back up to meet her eyes, she felt a moment of elation, because she saw that his resistance had wavered.

"I should not spend any more time with you."

"We need only discuss business, if that is your wish," she said hastily, though she made no move to withdraw her hand, and he made no move to release it.

She heard the huff of his short laugh amplified by the mask's speaker. "My wish?" He slowly shook his head. "My wish does not matter. Only my duty."

Molly sighed, feeling the strength of his muscular arm beneath her palm and the heat of his hand over hers. "I understand that sentiment completely."

She caught his wrist as he lowered his hand from hers,

moving his arm away at the same time. "Duty doesn't mean we have to forgo all pleasure!"

She stepped closer to him, until she was near enough that she could feel the brush of his embroidered robe against the inferior silk of her dress. "Especially if that pleasure makes our duty more bearable," she whispered, running her hand up his wrist to slip inside the fabric of his wide sleeve.

His skin felt warm and smooth beneath her palm, firm over hard ropes of muscle that told her he didn't live a life of leisure or excess. Vain as they were, the Iriduans didn't seem to view male musculature with the same admiration as human males did. They didn't have their own version of Mr. Olympia. From what information she'd been able to find about their culture, they were pragmatic about muscle mass, seeing it as the sign of a certain class of male, with the leisure and privileged class trending towards leaner, slender builds.

His strength made her wonder what type of work Shulgi did, because it seemed odd that he ran a food manufacturing company rather than working in security. Then his quick indrawn breath chased any idle observations from her mind as she slipped her hand further up his arm to brush her fingers over a bulging bicep.

He stepped away from her while he caught her elbow and pulled her hand away from him. "You will make returning to my dreg difficult," he said in a strained voice.

She caught sight of the unmistakable bulge at his groin and noticed that the fabric of the robe shifted not only in the front, but also at the back, reminding her that the Iriduans had two appendages attached to their spine whose purpose was specu-lated on in multiple Galactanet forums.

She could guess that a lot of that speculation was accurate, given that he was definitely aroused.

Normally, a successful seduction left Molly feeling hollow

and filled with trepidation, knowing that she would have a difficult time avoiding the expected conclusion of her efforts. She did what she had to, in order to further their mission, even when she couldn't wiggle her way out of following through, but in this case, she felt only a sense of elation. His arousal proved that he desired her the way she desired him.

"I have to go," he said abruptly. "Send the contract and any further details to my com and I'll go over them with my team."

He turned on one foot with a precise military style movement, then strode away without a backward glance, leaving Molly gaping in shock as disappointment and even a hint of despair filled her.

NINE

The memory of Molly's touch warmed Shulgi's skin as he rushed back to the dreg while attempting to keep to a pace that didn't look like he was fleeing the under-tier docks like a coward. Even though a part of him did feel cowardly for not taking what they both obviously wanted.

He avoided the cargo elevator directly to the dreg, choosing instead to take one of the public column elevators, though they were packed full regardless of what time it was. The crush of sentient life, all of them potentially dangerous, helped to distract him from an arousal that would be all too obvious to the Iriduan security guards and would raise many questions he wasn't prepared to answer.

The dreg was intended for unmated males. Occasionally, unwillingly mated males could go there to die of deprivation in some comfort, but the presence of mated Iriduans was generally heavily discouraged since their loyalties were always in question. Shulgi understood the caution well. It was almost always a mated male who betrayed the unmated males at the request of his queen. Ma'Nah generally snuck their patients in as deprived males on the brink of death, which sadly, most of them were.

If the Iriduan guards of the dreg were to see that he was aroused, they would either think he was using stimulants outside of an approved facility—in which case, he wouldn't be allowed back into the dreg until he proved he was unmated, and that could be an uncomfortable experience—or they would assume he was mated and served the whims of some female—in which case, they'd kill him.

It would be his preference to let all the Iriduan males in the dreg know that there was a cure for imprinting, but not all the males—especially the criminals in the dreg—had the best interests of the Iriduan people in mind. They wouldn't all welcome that news with relief and happiness. He also wished he could set up his clinic somewhere that would be more easily accessible for afflicted males, but any clinic run by legal citizens of the empire was a risk, because the empire itself didn't necessarily wish to free its citizens completely of the affliction—not when it was so useful to their power and control over the population. They would only free those who were in power, allowing only the elites to breathe free and easy and never fear being fully under the influence of another.

Establishing a clinic in Syndicate space not overseen by the empire ran the risk of exposing the existence of the cure to the enemies of the Iriduans, who would be highly motivated to destroy it, since the Iriduan species would grow stronger without that affliction hanging over them.

Thus, he was forced to a place like Za'Kluth, living within a dreg that was hostile towards mated males unless they were in the state of deprivation that made it clear they hadn't been in contact with their female for a while.

Up until now, that hadn't been a problem, but Molly had an effect on him that he'd never experienced before while not imprinted. Even his arousal around Ninhursag had come with a tinge of resentment, though his mind had been almost completely enslaved by her in the end, taking an enormous effort for him to betray her the way he had.

The crowd of non-Iriduan bodies packed the elevator and he was grateful for the filtering properties of his breather mask since it made him unable to smell the stench of their many differing and often clashing pheromones. He wasn't the only one who chose to cover his face to avoid that suffocating smell, but fortunately, there were no Iriduans about until he neared his own tier, as most of the citizens of the dreg avoided the lower tiers, choosing to instead conduct their business up the column, rather than downwards.

Most of the passengers on the elevator stood as still as possible, all of them aware that such a small space was no place for unanticipated aggression caused by limbs or bodies bumping in ways that inspired ire. Again, he noted that the criminal citizens of Za'Kluth were often better behaved and more polite than those found in Syndicate space. Perhaps because there was nothing to stop a fight from devolving into a full-on slaughter until it started to affect the bottom line of the city bosses and they sent in their own armies.

Still, the prospect of danger kept him focused on his surroundings, allowing him to push aside his arousal until the evidence of it was no longer obvious. The fact that he wanted more than anything to remain on the elevator and select the under-tier to return to Molly when the other occupants cleared off it made it difficult for him to continue to his tier.

He couldn't afford to let his mind linger over the memory of her touching his bare skin, because he'd end up right back in the unfortunate condition that forced him to take the long way back to the dreg. Instead, he pushed aside his desire for her and concentrated on the terms of their contract—and the mystery of Sha Zaska.

The gang boss had a fearsome, terrible, and monstrous reputation, even for Za'Kluth. There was no atrocity he wasn't accused of committing, and there had been plenty of evidence to show that those accusations weren't idle rumors. Shulgi had no doubt that the cli ku ships had been acquired in a less than acceptable manner, though he also believed Molly when she said they were now legally registered to Sha Zaska and wouldn't cause any issues for Ma'Nah. After all, one thing Sha Zaska hadn't been accused of was being stupid. He wouldn't make the offer of their use if he couldn't guarantee it would benefit both him and Ma'Nah.

Despite the horror that Zaska caused in even hardened criminals, Molly seemed less frightened by him than Shulgi would expect. Once she'd dropped the excessively servile demeanor, he began to suspect that perhaps she was even comfortable in her role as Zaska's mouthpiece. Given the monstrous things Zaska no doubt did to the slaves he didn't eat, that seemed odd to Shulgi. It was possible that Molly had simply acclimated to a life of misery, as some people managed to do, accepting their existence and making the most of it.

He didn't believe that, though. She didn't seem like the type to be content just existing at the very fringe of misery. She still had enough will to seek her own pleasure if her words could be believed. He wondered whether Zaska would approve of Molly's plan to seduce Shulgi, and that made him wonder just how possessive Zaska was of his dyed flowers. Shulgi knew that the gang boss did occasionally reward clients with them, so the vile creature could not be as jealous of them as some males might be, but that didn't mean he would share them idly, nor did it mean he'd ever allow them to act upon their own desires.

Molly could have been taking a risk by asking him to join

her for a meal with the intent to seduce him. Or she could have been following through on what was Zaska's plan all along, as Shulgi hadn't yet agreed to the terms of the contract. Perhaps she would have asked him to seal the deal halfway through their intimate encounter, or maybe when he was on the verge of climaxing. He had no idea how these kinds of arrangements worked, but he knew that he didn't want to do such a thing simply because her boss wanted his business.

The fact that he couldn't stop thinking about her words, and her touch, made him question his own honor. No matter whether she wanted him or not, she wasn't free to make her own choices. He would be wrong to take advantage of her.

At the same time, he believed that she meant it when she'd said she wanted to spend more time with him, and that she wanted to take pleasure in that time. She'd sounded so sincere, her gaze direct, not a single hint of her previous servile demeanor in her posture or tone.

Perhaps he was only trying to convince himself that it would be okay, just this one time, to turn his back on the values he'd tried to so hard to uphold since being cured of the affliction. The values he'd once believed were the very core of Iriduan society, until the harsh and terrible reality had been brutally exposed to him.

It would be wrong for him to ever give in to her seduction attempts, and he reminded himself how wrong as he passed through the extensive security checks to get back into the dreg, allowing his self-disgust to keep his arousal from returning at such an inconvenient time.

Though he knew Namerian and the others would expect an update about his meeting with Zaska's mouthpiece and the contract that had been proposed, he made his way towards the combat arena after clearing security, instead of heading back to the warehouse sector.

In the entertainment sector, he paused when he reached a stimulant lounge, the façade blank and utilitarian—far different from the garish displays found on such buildings in other parts of Za'Kluth. The Iriduans of the dreg didn't particularly appreciate the presence of the lounge and what it represented, but they also felt it was a necessity for some of their residents. It kept many unmated males calm, since aggression was often tied to sexual behavior, a fact which made the stimulants themselves dangerous in uncontrolled environments.

Because of their distaste for the presence of such a facility, it lacked any advertising on the front of the structure. Anyone who wanted to use the offered services knew exactly where they were going and what they would find inside.

Shulgi stood in front of the plain, sliding metal door, shifting his attention from it to the combat arena still a distance away. Then back to the lounge.

The door slid open, and an unfamiliar male walked out of the lounge, nodding briefly to Shulgi as he passed, dark circles under his eyes and his hair disarrayed. His robe was unkempt, and his wings shriveled from dehydration. Yet his body language seemed far more relaxed than many of the other males in the dreg.

Before the door slid shut again, Shulgi stepped over the threshold, causing it to open fully as he cast a glance over his shoulder at the retreating male. The stranger didn't look back, continuing his way through the entertainment district without showing interest in any of the other offerings.

The inside of the stimulant lounge resembled an upscale leisure-class spa. He'd only ever seen one of those while in the middle of a mission since war-class were rarely afforded such luxuries. In fact, austerity was a requirement of his class, and sexual stimulant use was strictly forbidden unless it had a mission-specific purpose. Extra aggression in the war-class was encouraged, and combat training was the only acceptable way to work it out if it grew too disruptive.

The males that worked within the spa were aided by mech-bots who no doubt did the heavy lifting, given the slender, almost sylph-like appearance of some of the spa workers. The sleek white mechs with black jointing were the most basic functional automatons used by the Iriduans. Inexpensive and therefore considered expendable if damaged, they could also be controlled remotely if their AI programming proved inadequate for a situation.

As he passed the mech guards standing just inside the door with only their heads moving around slowly as they scanned their surroundings, a slender male approached him with a broad smile.

"Welcome, my friend," the blue-skinned male said, then he gestured with one arm, his wide sleeved robe sliding down his forearm to reveal an arm as slim as any female's. "Have you come to partake in our services this fine evening?"

Shulgi had no idea why he'd entered this place. Then he acknowledged that was a lie and changed it to the truth in his mind. He'd gained control over the physical evidence of his arousal, but the skin of his arm still tingled with the memory of Molly's seductive touch. He'd wanted more. It would have been so easy to abandon his morals and his promises to himself and simply give in to the desire to enjoy all she would offer him.

Now, all he could hope for was an inferior experience with a hologram or perhaps a modified mechbot. He was aware there were other options, but the slender spa employees weren't the type to interest him. He also knew that, like Molly, they had a job to do. Though they were paid well to do it and could leave at any time if they wanted to, unlike her, it would still seem hollow to him.

"This is your first time," the spa worker said in a low voice.

His gaze took in Shulgi's appearance. "You're war-class—or used to be." He shook his head, his expression shifting to one of pity that raised Shulgi's hackles. "I'm assuming you didn't accidentally stray into this lounge instead of the combat arena?"

Shulgi glared at the spa worker's sudden smirk. Then he spun on one foot and headed back towards the entrance. The other male grabbed his arm and Shulgi easily shook off his hold.

"Wait!" the blue male said quickly, "I didn't mean to offend you, friend. You're welcome here!"

He rushed after Shulgi, jumping in front of him just before he passed through the sliding entrance door that opened at his approach. The spa worker's wings spread behind him as if to block Shulgi's view of his escape path.

"I can tell by your body language that you need to be here," the other male said in a cajoling tone. "Don't allow your discomfort to deny you pleasures you've never been allowed to experience before. You came to Za'Kluth to escape the empire. Don't bring its restrictions with you!"

The worker placed a hand on Shulgi's arm, right where Molly had touched him, reminding him of her fingers sliding over his bare skin beneath the sleeve, though thankfully, this male did not take such a liberty.

"We have many services here, my friend. As well as guaranteed anonymity." As Shulgi tensed, the other male lowered his hand back to his side, his wings flicking behind him. "I can tell you would prefer a hologram or perhaps one of the modified life-like mechs." He gestured to the guard mechs standing at the door. "I assure you they look far more convincing than what you see out here. You can make your selection once you enter the back rooms."

Shulgi ground his teeth together, frustrated by his own indecisiveness. What he wanted to do right now was return to the under-tier and find Molly so he could take her up on her offer. Instead, he must settle for something nowhere near as satisfying, and perhaps more embarrassing than he'd expected, since he already felt uncomfortable. Or he could go without and hope his unwanted erection didn't appear again at a random thought of the promise in Molly's voice and touch.

Making his decision, Shulgi turned away from the door, facing the intake counter at the other end of the lobby with a heavy sigh.

"Excellent," the blue male said as he left his post blocking the door and followed Shulgi's slow and reluctant steps to the counter. "Just sign in with our automated concierge, and we'll get you into a back room to make your selection. Then you'll get your stimulant injection and...." The slender male chuckled, shrugging. "I suppose you'll do whatever it is that pleases you at that point."

Shulgi studied the other male closely for the first time since the spa worker had approached him. "Do you like working here?" He wondered how anyone could enjoy such a profession.

He could tell by his expression that the blue male was about to give him some canned answer scripted for a question he probably received a lot. He held up a hand to silence the other male as his mouth opened to respond. "I'm only curious. It won't affect my patronage of this lounge. I just have many questions about your profession."

The blue male closed his mouth and eyed Shulgi thoughtfully. "Your build probably wouldn't do as well in an Iriduan lounge, to be blunt, my friend. Most of our clients are genuinely seeking female companionship and prefer spa workers who are close enough in appearance to pretend we are female. Although...."

His hesitation kept Shulgi from correcting his misunderstanding of Shulgi's reasons for inquiring. "Although?"

The blue male leaned in closer to Shulgi. "There are... *places* outside the dreg where you might find employment. You won't always need to be on stimulants, as some of their clients are only looking for the chance to dominate an Iriduan. It can be rough work, but you look like you've been through hard training and would be better conditioned to handle it. I've heard the pay is far more than anyone who works here at the spa receives."

Shulgi could only assume he was referring to the specialty brothels, the kind that people only learned about after they'd gained some trust from those who knew about them. He hadn't heard that there were Iriduans working in such places, but it didn't ultimately surprise him. Iriduans were a popular fetish, and a popular target of resentment and hatred.

"I'm more interested in your personal feelings about the job. I'm not really looking for one myself. I just wanted to know if you actually enjoyed what you do?"

This seemed to disappoint the blue male and made Shulgi wonder if he was a recruiter for one of those specialty brothels. Then the spa worker stroked his chin thoughtfully after a quick glance around to make sure they were still in relative privacy, though some other males had stepped through the entrance door and were being greeted by other workers. They all kept a distance away from each other, so only the murmur of low volume voices could be overheard but not the words spoken.

"Why are you so curious?" the blue male said after a long moment of consideration.

Shulgi shrugged, uncertain if he should continue his line of questioning or just finish what he'd come here to do. "I guess I just want to know if someone could take pleasure in something they have to do as a job."

The other male laughed loud enough that some of the other patrons glanced over. Shulgi felt their stares shift from the blue male to him, then back, and the spa worker apparently felt the looks too, returning them briefly before turning back to Shulgi.

"My ability to enjoy physical pleasure doesn't disappear the moment I accept payment for my services." The blue male grinned, slanting another glance towards one of the patrons that kept looking over at them as he went up to the counter to sign in.

"I came to Za'Kluth to escape my fate as a member of leisure-class," the blue male said in a low voice, sounding more serious now. "I learned during my mate training that I was more intrigued by the male bodies of my fellow trainees than the images and holograms and models of female bodies we were made to practice on. I know that would likely have changed in some respects if I had imprinted on a queen, but I also knew I didn't want it to." He pointed to himself. "I *like* who I am, and here in the dreg, I can be exactly how I want to be, never fearing being enslaved to a female's will, serving only her whims and not my own desires." Then he held his arms out to his sides. "This is my version of freedom, my friend. I can't believe I get paid to do this, but I'm not complaining."

His words sounded sincere, but he was in a far different position than Molly, though they performed similar work. This male had a choice in the matter. Shulgi should not let that influence his thoughts on Molly's offer and whether it would be right to accept it.

Still, he was looking for any excuse to convince himself it would be okay, because the thought of a hologram or life-like mech didn't seem nearly as intriguing as feeling her hand stroking over his naked skin. Besides, he wasn't entirely certain what the stimulants would do to him since he had no problem growing aroused already, and the workers would find it odd for him to reject the injection.

He'd been receiving potentially dangerous injections since

his military training began, so he wasn't overly concerned about that aspect. It was likely the sexual stimulant would make him more aggressively aroused to the point of engorgement, but if there was something to take that aggression and desire out on, he didn't think it would be a real problem.

He glanced around, noting some of the other spa workers now greeting the other signed in patrons to lead them to the back rooms. "Do all of these workers feel the same way you do about their jobs?"

The blue male sighed, watching the other patron that had shown interest in him be led away by another slender blue spa worker. Then he met Shulgi's eyes again, and Shulgi determined to give him a good tip, simply for satisfying his curiosity about a subject that had never even occurred to him before, much less concerned him.

"I can't speak for my co-workers," the worker answered with a tilt of his head. He regarded Shulgi thoughtfully. "I feel like you have a specific person in mind, don't you?"

When Shulgi failed to respond, the other male smiled crookedly in an expression that seemed genuine and not practiced as some of his other expressions appeared to be. "You want me to tell you it's okay to be with this other person, because they enjoy what they do." His smile faded as he slowly shook his head. "Without knowing who it is, I couldn't do that for you. However, I suppose the easiest way to find out is to simply ask."

"Aren't you trained to pretend you enjoy this?" Shulgi gestured to the surrounding lobby, then the back room.

The other male chuckled, his gaze scanning the lobby for other patrons. "Aren't you war-class types trained in reading body language? You should be able to tell the difference. Most people can, even when we're exceptionally good at acting. Some are fine with pretending; others want to know that we're genuinely into what we do." He shot a searching glance at Shulgi. "I can see you're one of the latter."

He leaned closer to Shulgi, placing one hand on Shulgi's arm in a familiar way that Shulgi didn't pull away from. "I suspect it is not someone in the dreg that has you so conflicted." His gaze trailed down Shulgi's body, pausing on his groin, which fortunately remained unaroused at the moment. "The use of stimulants outside a lounge or other monitored facility is genuinely dangerous," he said in a low voice. "If you kill an alien female, it will bring negative attention to the dreg." He met Shulgi's eyes again. "Be careful, and—if you need a supplier—I know someone who can hook you up."

Shulgi shook his head. "I don't... I have that covered already."

The worker nodded; his expression serious now, no longer searching the lobby for other clients as he fully focused on his conversation with Shulgi. "Listen, alien body language is not as clear as our own, but you can usually tell when they are into it, and most of them usually are with our species—especially compared to the kind of creatures they normally have to consort with. Just... don't *expose* yourself," he said, waving towards Shulgi's mask. "The last thing you want to do is imprint on an alien female!"

TEN

Molly sprawled on the crescent seating of the inner sanctum on her back, one hand flung above her head, her hair finally released from its bindings to flow down the side of the couch arm. With her other hand at her temple, she massaged it with her fingertips.

"I've lost my touch," she lamented.

Jenice rolled her eyes and patted Molly's outstretched arm. "Not from what you told me, you haven't. You said he was aroused. Obviously, he desired you."

Molly clenched her free hand into a fist as she circled her temple a little harder. "If he wanted me, why didn't he just take me, then?"

Jenice chuckled as she plopped down ungracefully on an elegantly upholstered seat designed for those who didn't have tails or wings, like the office's human occupants. It was situated across from the crescent couch that Molly had collapsed onto after re-entering the office.

"You know, Mol, he *does* have a problem with slavery.

You'll just have to convince him you really want to be with him, and it wouldn't be a job for you."

Molly slowly sat up, groaning as the intensity of her headache increased. Stress always brought on a miserable tension headache nowadays. She wondered if she was growing too soft being at the top of the food chain for once—well, relatively speaking.

She glanced at Jenice as she lowered her hand from her temple. "How do I do that, without making him suspicious of Sha Zaska's nonchalance about his 'dyed flowers' seeking their own desires?"

Jenice shrugged, her smirk unsympathetic. "He does sound like an overly suspicious pain in the ass, quite frankly, but that's all the more reason you need to find a good way to distract him. Maybe we can send him a message from Sha Zaska giving you permission to be with him."

Molly wished it were that easy. The problem she'd noticed with Shulgi was that he didn't care what Sha Zaska wanted. He appeared to concern himself with whether Molly herself wanted him. As unexpected and heartening as that was, it posed a difficult challenge, because she really did desire him, but didn't know how to make him believe that.

Either that, or he just wasn't that interested, and his arousal had only been a mild reaction to her touch. After all, he'd left so abruptly—his tone so formal and cold—that she'd almost suspected she might have imagined that arousal until she glanced at his groin again and noted that his robe remained tented even as he'd turned away from her.

"I need to go lay down until this headache goes away, Jen." She rose to her feet, wincing as the movement only shot more pain through her head.

Jenice also rose, putting a sympathetic hand on Molly's

shoulder. "You want Becca to take over for you on the meeting with Ygaot hysgodi?"

Molly sighed, debating whether she wanted to subject Becca to the tapiran smuggler, but Becca had been training to step in more frequently as Zaska's primary mouthpiece, because they all recognized that Molly couldn't always be available, and a personage like Zaska would need more than one main voice. In the past, Becca had done well with the role, but they'd been careful to limit her interactions with the more dangerous clients.

Fortunately, Ygaot hysgodi had already been brought on as a client and didn't have expectations from Zaska's flowers that would put Becca in an unpleasant situation. It was only a speaking meeting.

Finally, she nodded, then made her way to the bathroom to get a relaxer injection that she put against her neck over the knotted muscle there that was causing the tension in her head. The relaxer would put her out of it for a few hours, but she needed the rest anyway.

Jenice made the call to Becca, who claimed she'd be more than happy to take over for Molly, allowing Molly to change into a plain, oversized tunic that she used as a night shirt and then slump onto her bed with a heavy sigh. She lay back to stare up at the moving stars projected on the ceiling as Jenice closed the sliding wall panel to secure her room from the rest of the inner sanctum in a way that concealed its existence.

They all had rooms hidden behind the wall panels, heavily sound-proofed so even if they snored—or engaged in other noisy activities—no one else would hear them. It also allowed them privacy they so desperately needed, even from each other at times. They all bore a heavy burden with their secret, and they had to be acting at almost all times, so it was sometimes such a relief to just escape into their little bedroom alcoves and drop all their masks and just be themselves.

It was just too bad that Molly wasn't entirely sure who her real self was. She'd been enslaved for a long time but had never considered herself as one. In her mind, she was always just a free person in temporary bonds, always looking for a chance to escape. Sometimes, she studied her features carefully, trying to discern who she had been on Earth and what region she'd come from, based on the information provided by those who'd been taken from Earth when they were old enough to have learned more about that world.

She still had no real clue, other than her natural skin tone being a light tan color, and her hair being a dark blonde. Her natural eye color was something of an anomaly that Jenice called "hazel." She knew she wasn't beautiful by human standards, but the other women said she would qualify as "cute", or "like a pixie", or "adorable." She used the dye and makeup and elaborate hairstyles to add glamor to an ordinary set of features that told her next to nothing about herself.

Ultimately, she felt no real identification with Earth. That life was too far behind her, and too much forgotten, that she couldn't feel any real pull in that direction. Jenice and the other humans who'd elected to remain behind with her on Za'Kluth, even after gaining their freedom, had their own various reasons to avoid returning to Earth. Some of those reasons she didn't know, and didn't ask, knowing that the memories caused them pain.

Instead, she tried to focus on the identity she'd created for herself here, on this world, but realized that it felt as hollow as trying to be an "Earthling" like any other human. Despite a strong sense of self and independence, she'd never quite figured out where she belonged, and despite knowing every line and curve of her features, she still didn't know herself.

The question of where she really belonged plagued her as much as her uncertainty about the future did. When she'd initially dreamed up Sha Zaska, it had been a temporary thing to save their own asses. Once they all realized the potential of the fictional "boss," they'd jumped into creating the factual elements to lend credence to their tales. No one had really sat down and determined exactly how far they would take things, and by the time Molly really started contemplating where it would all eventually end up, Sha Zaska's legend had grown too big to simply abandon.

A part of her wanted to flee that growing burden, knowing that trouble loomed on the horizon with each day as the "boss" amassed more power. More power brought unwanted attention from other power players in the column—the kind who wouldn't normally bother with a place as low as the under-tier. The kind like Uthagol, and others of her ilk who resented the rise of a lowly resident of the under-tier while they struggled to hold onto their wealth in the higher tiers.

Every day, she awoke with a determination that in her next meeting with the others, they would discuss an exit plan. Despite that determination, every meeting ended up revolving around how to make Sha Zaska's influence even stronger so they could free more slaves and effect more changes in the under-tier.

Worse, as their power grew, she feared the ambitions of some of her close circle grew as well. Not Jenice, and certainly not Mogorl and Grundon, but she'd seen the first glimmerings of avarice in the others as the wealth they earned finally began to overtake the staggering expenses of their enterprise.

Even Becca seemed too eager to take on a bigger role in guiding their business. Molly hated that her trust had begun to waver in some of her closest friends and companions.

She also hated that she hadn't been able to find a partnership with anyone she trusted enough to share everything with them, including her concerns about the others that she didn't feel comfortable sharing even with Jenice. In fact, she didn't dare to have a romantic partnership at all, since her role sometimes required her to do things no ordinary mate would find acceptable. Some of the others of their circle paired up from time to time, but no one had made a serious romantic connection. Their business didn't encourage that kind of bond.

The sad truth was that Molly felt truly lonely, and the more secure their position became as Zaska's minions, the more time she had to dwell on that loneliness and that desire for a deeper connection than she had with even her closest companions and allies.

She really wanted a lover. Not for sexual pleasure so much as for emotional intimacy. She'd learned from a young age that sex could be had anywhere and sometimes even quite cheaply. Love, on the other hand, was usually far too costly, and the few times she'd even started to feel such an emotion, she'd learned the hard way how quickly it could disappear.

Initially, she'd looked at Shulgi as someone attractive enough that she wouldn't mind having sex with him, and indeed, it would even be a pleasure to stroke his body and inhale his heady scent. Then he'd made his disgust for slavery and his disdain for Zaska very clear. Molly felt like she'd found a kindred spirit—and a rare resident of Za'Kluth who still had values that were admirable, even if he was forced to work with those who didn't reflect them. He was canny too, rather than being some naïve idealist. She'd sensed his cynicism and his pragmatism, both being traits she could respect, having had to adopt them herself at a tender age.

In short, she'd felt a kinship with him that surpassed the fact that they belonged to two different species and were, in essence, complete strangers on either side of a business transaction that put them at a kind of odds with each other, as each wanted to get a leg up in the negotiations.

Of course, she could have been imagining that connection with him. After all, a connection couldn't be made with only one side being open to it. Shulgi wasn't exactly friendly, and his guard was up so high that she wondered if anyone had ever breached that barrier before. It might be too much to hope that she'd found a weakness in his wall at her level, one that she could exploit to touch the real Shulgi—the one literally hidden behind his mask.

It was those thoughts that chased her into sleep as her headache finally relented with the help of the relaxer.

AN ALARM from her wrist implant woke her many hours later with an urgent message from the dockmaster on duty. Apparently, a very agitated, armored Iriduan was currently pacing in the ramshackle lobby, demanding Molly's presence.

She sat up quickly in bed, opening a com to the dockmaster to tell him to stall the Iriduan, and get verification that it was, indeed, Shulgi. The dockmaster also said the male was acting very erratic and had barely managed to growl out his identity before stalking into the waiting room to pace in front of the door to the inner public office.

Molly jumped to her feet as the dockmaster urged her to hurry, because he didn't like the look in the Iriduan's eyes.

This news alarmed Molly enough that she summoned Mogorl and Grundon to man the security system for the lobby and inner office, her heart thudding as she wondered what could be upsetting Shulgi enough to make even the unflappable Yenbpi feel shaken enough to mention his concern.

Shulgi hadn't yet signed the contract, and in fact, had not

even messaged them back on what his team had to say about the terms. In fact, she doubted anyone had heard from him at all after he'd left. She knew Jenice would have awakened her with her own urgent message if Shulgi had contacted them.

Instead, he'd appeared here in person and apparently in an agitated state. She quickly dressed in her slinkiest dress, the one that barely concealed anything, not bothering to apply any makeup or bind up her hair, leaving it to flow down around her shoulders and fall halfway down her back to her waist.

Whatever had upset Shulgi, she hoped a little seduction could improve his mood and make him more amenable to signing the contract. Although, as she cast herself a last look in the mirrored panel on her wall before dismissing it to return to a flat surface that matched the rest of the room, she acknowledged that she had ulterior motives that had nothing to do with business.

Mogorl and Grundon waited outside her room when she left it. She smiled to them both, greeting them warmly, despite their serious demeanors. Mogorl held up an arm to block her path as she tried to walk past him.

"This one is dangerous, Mol," he said in a warning tone, shaking his head. "Let us deal with him."

Mol gently pushed at his arm, growing irritated when he failed to move it. "I can handle him, my friend. You know that."

"I don't." He still refused to let her pass, and her growing sense of urgency was bringing her headache back. "Iriduans are unpredictable. You can't guarantee your seduction attempts will succeed with them."

Molly laughed bitterly. "You can never guarantee *anything*, Mogie, but I know how to read people, and I know when I'm getting somewhere with a mark. Shulgi desires me, and it's just possible that he's here to act on that desire, so I don't want either of you interfering in that meeting." She narrowed her eyes on Mogorl, then turned a sharp look on Grundon. "Is that clear?"

"We won't let you risk your safety," Grundon said in his bass voice that felt like it vibrated the air in the room, crossing huge arms over a proportionately large, hairy chest.

Molly sighed, wishing sometimes that her most loyal friends and bodyguards would actually obey her wishes without question the way they pretended to when in the company of others who were not in on the secret of Zaska.

She tried a different tack, turning a pleading look on Mogorl. "I *want* this, Mogie!" she said with a low hiss. "I haven't felt this way about anyone in a very long time. Please, let me handle Shulgi without the two of you looming over us. Just man the suppressor turrets for me."

She slipped under Mogorl's arm, patting him on the triceps as she rushed towards the door to the public office. "He's not here to kill me. I'm sure of that. If he gets too out of hand and I give you the signal, use the turrets to take him down."

"We can't be sure they will affect him in that armor," Grundon growled, stalking after her, only pausing when she held up a hand and shook her head at him.

"Yenbpi said he's not wearing a helmet, only his mask. You can hit him in the head easily enough and we know the suppressor rounds will knock out an Iriduan. Just... *please* don't interfere unless I give you the signal!"

She paused at the door, her hand sweeping the panel beside it so it slid open, then she winked at both of her body-guards, who looked miserable at her command to let her meet the Iriduan alone. "And if it looks like things are going *well*, stop watching and switch the turrets back to my voice command alone." She grinned at their sheepish expressions, then stepped through the door.

Despite her certainty that she could handle Shulgi on her

own, she still felt her stomach twisting with nerves as she sat behind the desk in the public office, bringing up both her console and the public console with the contract ready to sign. Her heart thudded and her skin flushed with nervous perspiration as she considered what she was about to do.

If she weren't so certain that Shulgi would never hurt a slave, she would have allowed Mogorl and Grundon to stand at her sides and pose a visible threat if he tried to harm her. The problem with their presence was that it could be somewhat off-putting for clients she was attempting to seduce. The suppressor turrets were a compromise, existing beneath the ceiling panels both in the lobby and the public office. They usually didn't kill a target, but they sent a painful and undeniable message from "Zaska" that his minions and his mouth-pieces weren't to be messed with.

Finally working up the nerve to meet with Shulgi again, forming her expression into an impassive mask that hopefully gave none of her nervousness away, she told Yenbpi to let him into the inner office.

When the door to the lobby slid open, he stalked into the room without a backward glance, and she understood why Yenbpi had been unnerved. The Iriduan's agitation was palpable, his wings twitching and his hands clenching into fists, relaxing, then clenching again. His piercing green gaze went unerringly to her, barely scanning the room for threats in stark contrast to his more cautious demeanor from earlier.

He strode towards the desk as she slowly rose from her seat, gracefully waving her hand to the other seat in a practiced gesture. "Welcome, Shulgi. Please, have a...."

Her voice trailed off as he froze in mid-step, his eyes the only part of him moving as his gaze trailed down her barely concealed body. She gasped in surprise when his eyes lifted to meet hers again and they were nearly black, his pupils so

dilated that almost no green remained around the rims of his
irises.

"I need you," he said in with a guttural groan, lifting a hand
to touch a place on his breastplate that looked like the rest of
the sleek surface but apparently unsealed it, because the sides
of his torso armor opened, revealing that he wore a skintight
bodysuit beneath it.

"I'll sign your damned contract," he hissed as if he was
angry, then tore off the breastplate, even as more of his armor
parted on his body, allowing him to toss pieces of it to the floor
as he moved closer to the desk and the console.

Molly smiled seductively, and this time, there was nothing
practiced about the expression. Apparently, she hadn't lost her
touch at all. The fact that he was so agitated as he peeled off his
armor was a bit unnerving, and the fact that his eyes were black
now definitely surprised her, but she'd seen many strange signs
of arousal in different species, so it didn't bother her to see him
so visibly affected.

"I tried the holos," he muttered, and she wasn't sure if he
was talking to her or himself, "and the mechs. Nothing worked.
Nothing satisfied."

His gaze shifted to her from the console as he drew his
pistol, causing her to gasp even while the ceiling tiles slid open
in the corners of the room. He barely glanced at them as he set
the pistol on the desk, then proceeded to remove more of his
armor.

She relaxed when she realized he wasn't pulling a weapon
on her, but the turrets remained exposed as a warning to him.
At this point, she didn't think he cared. Between dragging off
his armor, he paused just long enough to touch the console
screen on his side of the desk to place his mark there, agreeing
to all the terms laid out in the document.

"I shouldn't have accepted the injection," he moaned,

pulling the last of his armor away from his lower body to expose the large ridge of his erection beneath his skintight undersuit.

Molly gasped in admiration at the sight of his body, which was very muscular and again made her wonder why he was a businessman instead of a soldier. Although all concerns about his profession abandoned her when he lifted a hand to his mask and jerked the seals open, the mask hissing as air escaped it.

He pulled it away from his face and tossed it onto the desktop beside his pistol even as he moved around the desk, stalking her with intent black eyes.

It wasn't just that he was the handsomest male she'd ever seen that made her breathless. The intensity of his gaze and movements made her wonder if she should flee, even while she wanted to leap into his arms in a very unpracticed fashion.

She was well trained and experienced. She shouldn't feel these butterflies filling her stomach, or the trembling of a body both eager and anxious for his touch. She shouldn't. But she did as she stood almost paralyzed like frightened prey as he rounded the desk and pulled her into his arms.

His scent surrounded her as she inhaled deeply. Then he lowered his head and his lips fell upon hers in a scorching kiss that made her whole body weak. She sagged in his embrace and his strong arms supported her, lifting her off her feet as he straightened, his mouth claiming hers with an undeniable hunger.

Molly generally avoided kissing anyone, especially a client. Sometimes, she couldn't escape it, but she rarely enjoyed the experience. It was far too intimate for the work she did, and up until now, sex had always felt like work.

This time, she hungered for his kiss and returned it with an excited whimper that drew a low moan from him as he deepened it, his tongue sliding along her lower lip. When her lips parted, his tongue delved between them. He tasted as delicious as he smelled, warm and savory with just a hint of spice, like a gourmet meal.

She wrapped her legs around his waist, feeling the two appendages that extended from his spine uncoiling beneath the stretchy material of his undersuit. A breeze from his wings flapping slowly behind him as he kissed her caused her hair to flutter around her face, at least until he buried his fingers in it, cradling her head between his hands.

She clutched his shoulders, feeling the muscle rippling beneath the slippery fabric of his undersuit. One of his hands released her head to stroke up her naked thigh, pushing aside the strip of a dress that provided the only covering to her body.

He moaned again when his palm slid over the warm skin at the crux of her thighs, his fingers slipping over the dampness from her slick.

She hoped Mogorl and Grundon had shut off their monitors by now. It wouldn't be the first time she'd been observed having sex. It was just that this time, she really wanted this, and she couldn't remember the last time her desire and arousal had been genuine. She had no idea how she'd behave while in the throes of genuine passion, but she already felt like she was acting way off script and losing control over her body, too excited and aroused for practiced movements or careful considerations.

Her hands shifted from his shoulders to slide into his thick, silky hair just as he turned to face the desk. He rested her bare buttocks on top of it and she barely noticed the cold of the sleek surface as he leaned his big body closer to her petite one. His hands explored her naked thighs, moving unerringly towards the heat of her wet core.

He only broke their kiss to jerk at the fastening on his suit which caused it to part all the way down the front to his groin. Molly purred in pleasure as she took in the naked green flesh he exposed, her gaze trailing down to his erection as it sprang free. She released her hold on his hair and slid both hands down his powerful chest to his shaft to encircle it, licking her lips, swollen from his hungry kisses.

He caught her mouth again with his, his tongue delving between her lips as she slowly stroked his shaft. At first, his hands were busy pulling the fabric of his suit away from his body, freeing him enough that she felt the long, segmented appendages attached to his spine wrapping around him to caress her thighs.

Rather than freaking her out, this turned her on even more, though she was surprised she could feel any more excited than she already did as the clawed appendages moved over her vulnerable flesh. His fingers were the first to make it to her core, sliding inside her with a wet sound that caused them both to moan.

As his fingers moved inside her and she stroked him, he broke their kiss long enough to whisper something against her lips.

His actual voice was so much sexier than what she'd heard filtered through his mask, and he spoke in his fluid native language, which made it even hotter. Since she'd been implanted with a translator, she understood his words, but didn't quite know their meaning.

"Spinner's curse, I'm lost," he murmured, before sucking her bottom lip into his mouth.

He tugged her lower body closer with one hand as the fingers of his other continued to move inside her, his thumb now shifting to focus on her clit.

Molly cried out with pleasure, his lips capturing the sound as he made her climax. Withdrawing his fingers, he caught her wrists and pulled her hands away from his shaft, shifting his hips so the tip of it probed her entrance while his hands fell upon her thighs to spread them wider.

"Tell me you want this, Molly," he implored, his lips brushing against hers with each word as they shared their breaths.

She clutched his shoulders, her fingers digging into his hard muscles, her nails bending at the force of her grip as she shifted her own hips until his tip penetrated her. "I want it, Shulgi," she cried aloud, "I need it. I want *you*!"

The fact that she meant that in more ways than one was in her tone. She wasn't certain if he picked up on it or not, but then he entered her fully, burying his length to the hilt with a low growl.

Then she stopped caring about anything but the feeling of him inside her, filling her, making her feel whole for the first time in her life.

ELEVEN

Shulgi knew the moment the stimulant injection kicked in that he'd made a serious mistake. Not being familiar with its use, he hadn't been prepared for the impact of the sudden flood of hormones that filled his blood and caused an erection so rampant it was painful.

The holos had done nothing for him, even when he'd created one that looked as close to Molly as he could. The life-like mechs were even worse, since all of them had been built to look like Iriduan females, and his only experience with one of them had been one of the worst in his life.

He wanted Molly, not a poor and inadequate substitute, and the pulsing power of the stimulant in his blood drove all common sense from his head. He knew the workers and guard mechs would keep him from leaving the lounge without finishing his business and exhausting the effects of the stimulant, so he'd escaped through the back employee exit after disabling the single guard mech stationed there to scan in employees.

Then he'd made his way through the dark alleys of the

entertainment center, avoiding any encounters with other Iriduans who would certainly question the fact that he was aroused. His robe did little to hide that fact, so he knew he'd have to wear armor to make his way back down to the under-tier.

The fact that he planned to do so wasn't even in question at that point. He had no choice, at least as far as his body was concerned. He took insane risks to get back to the factory and slip in through their secret passage to return to his single room and retrieve his armor. Even after successfully concealing the evidence of his state, he'd avoided as much interaction as he could. He couldn't fully hide the agitation the stimulant was causing in him, nor put an end to his recklessness until he'd sated his gnawing need.

Fortunately, he was able to keep calm as long as he was using the dreg's cargo elevator, so the guards didn't suspect him, but once he stepped off the elevator and onto the grated flooring of the under-tier docks, he made no effort to hide his eagerness.

The dockmaster on duty at first tried to give him the brush off, but then had taken a close look at Shulgi, his six eyes trailing down the sleek surface of Shulgi's armor, then back up to his wild eyes and mussed hair. Then they'd fixed on his wings, which were outspread in aggression, before finally ending up on the pistol at his hip and Shulgi's hand clenching into a fist just above it.

Then the dockmaster sent a message to Zaska's minions, letting them know he wanted Molly.

Despite how agitated he felt, he still wasn't expecting his reaction to seeing her in person. When she'd finally let him into her office and rose from her chair, he saw that only a thin strip of fabric covered her body, cinched at her waist with a narrow band, leaving her sides completely bare. He'd nearly lost control over himself right then and there. He'd reached an engorged state in that moment and realized that he would do anything at all to bury himself inside her. If she had asked him to kill for her, he was afraid he would have even done that.

It wouldn't be the first time, though he'd hoped the cure would have kept it from happening again.

Now, he could only think about her, and how much he needed her. The worst part was that his biology had betrayed him without him even being imprinted on her. It had to be the stimulant itself that had put him in such a vulnerable state, because his mask hadn't failed him. He wasn't afflicted by Molly.

He just desired her more than he'd ever desired anyone.

He didn't bother to read over the contract, aware that Zaska could have changed any number of terms. Instead, he marked it as he stripped off his armor, barely glancing at the console. When the turrets in the ceiling appeared as he'd drawn his pistol to set it aside, his wings barely flicked with concern.

He was too focused on her to give a damn what happened to him. He doubted Zaska would shoot him dead but figured the turrets would shock him or suppress his movements in some way if he did anything to threaten Zaska's mouthpiece.

He had no wish to hurt her, though his body wanted her so badly that he wasn't entirely certain he could manage to be gentle to her. He knew he'd treat her a lot better than she'd likely been treated in the past.

When he first inhaled her scent after removing his mask, he grew even stiffer, unsure how that was even possible. He would be in agony if he didn't sate himself with her body soon. Fortunately, she appeared more than willing to allow him to, and this time, he couldn't over-examine why. He had to take her at her word that she wanted him, because her lips felt so soft and tasted so sweet against his, her mouth was so hot, and her hands felt so good on his body, encircling his shaft, that there was no way he could stop.

Still, he'd begged her to tell him she wanted this, and he needed to believe the truth behind her breathy cry that she did want him.

When he entered her, her inner muscles clenching tight around his girth even as she rocked her hips forward to take him deeper, he couldn't stop himself from making an animalistic sound. She felt so good he had no comparable experience to compare to being inside her, his huge body firm against her petite, soft body, his head filled with her captivating scent, her taste on his tongue, and her sighs and moans in his ears as he began to thrust.

His cerci whipped against his sides, their tips stroking along her thighs, the sensory appendages sending delightful messages back to him about her body that only increased his pleasure.

He didn't doubt they were being recorded, watched by Zaska perhaps, or maybe just one of his minions. He couldn't give a single thread of concern for that, even knowing that his behavior would raise many dangerous questions about him and his state. If he'd left his mask on, he might have passed off any uncomfortable observations, blaming everything on the stimulant.

But removing the mask meant he'd exposed himself to a human woman, and he'd also been aroused by her. Anyone who understood his people's physiology would assume she'd afflicted him, making him a target of his own people. Or they would wonder how he wasn't afraid of being afflicted, putting his project and the cure at risk of discovery by those who would not mean well.

Still, he'd needed to kiss her. Something he'd wanted to do from the first moment he'd seen her, though he'd refused to acknowledge that need then.

Now, he was deep inside her, pressed against her, his lips against hers, and there wasn't anything else that seemed to matter to him.

He recognized that this was some new kind of affliction that made his need for her this great. Granted, it was likely driven further by the stimulant, but he hadn't been injected the last time he'd come here and then left so aroused that he'd had to take the long way back to the dreg.

He chased his orgasm, but not with so much selfishness that he didn't make certain she found hers. To his pleasure, she appeared to be as excited as he was, her sheath soaking wet. When one of his cerci rubbed over her sensitive nub, her inner muscles quickly convulsed in climax as her upper body arched in his arms. She broke their kiss to cry out, her lower body rocking against his thrusts to drive him deeper with each one.

He felt her legs trembling as she came and he smiled as he trailed his lips along the dyed skin of her neck, down to her collar. One of his cerci clawed aside the fabric that barely covered her small, firm breasts so that he could lower his lips to claim one, sucking the hard nipple that peaked it as she gasped and clutched his shoulders. Then she buried her fingers in his hair, tugging on it to pull his head closer against her body.

He chuckled against her skin, unfazed by the pulling on his scalp or the way she wrapped his long hair around her palm in her excitement. He moaned as she dragged her warm tongue along the edge of his ear, then nipped the pointed tip playfully.

He was having more fun and feeling more pleasure than he ever had in his life. His previous sexual experiences had been more abusive on the side of his partner, as Ninhursag had possessed a sadistic streak and resented the lowborn members of her harem, even while she used them for her own pleasure. She'd only really wanted one male, but even then, what she'd genuinely wanted was to recapture the power he'd possessed.

For the first time, Shulgi felt wanted by a female, and he wanted her in return, so badly that even while chasing his orgasm inside her, he felt like it wasn't enough. He needed more of her. He didn't want this to end, knowing it had to. Knowing the stimulant would wear off after he climaxed.

He lifted his head from her breast to bury it against the warm skin of her neck and inhale deep. "Let me take you away from here," he whispered against her ear, before nipping her lobe.

He couldn't keep her, he knew that. He certainly couldn't take her back to the dreg. His offer was one of desperation and need. He could save her, he was sure of it, and then set her free to return to her own world. The thought of never seeing her again, never feeling this again, made him panicky, but he pushed aside that idea.

Somehow, he'd figure out how to get her away from Zaska and make things work without jeopardizing his mission.

She'd stiffened at his words, not answering him. Instead, she turned her head to capture his lips, kissing him with fervor that scattered his thoughts. Her arms encircled his neck, pulling her tighter against him, her inner muscles clenching around his shaft.

He shuddered in the throes of his climax as he pounded into her, his hands gripping her hips to keep her from sliding on the desktop. When he finally broke the kiss and lifted his head to look down at her face, he noticed that her eyes glittered, now almost as green as his own, with only a slight halo of brown around them. It looked like she had unshed tears, but she turned her head to the side, breaking eye contact, even as her palm slid over his naked chest in a caressing manner.

"Thank you, Shulgi," she said in a soft voice, "for this. I enjoyed it." After a moment of rapid blinking, she met his eyes again, her expression solemn when she brushed his hair away from his face. "I can't go with you." She slowly shook her head, her fascinating eyes wide and damp. "I am happy here."

He knew she lied, and he suspected she was aware he could tell. He wondered if her words were for their watchers. Perhaps he'd chosen the wrong moment to offer to free her. He wouldn't give up that easily. Even though he couldn't keep her for himself, he could get her away from the monstrous Sha Zaska.

At the moment, he felt the chill of air against his naked skin and realized how vulnerable he'd made himself. The stimulant still hummed through his blood, but the worst of the lust had faded with his orgasm, allowing his erection to go down and it should dissipate. Now, exhaustion crept in, and he recognized it as an unnatural kind from using the stimulant. If he'd stayed in the lounge, he would have been able to sleep off the aftereffects in the private room he'd been given.

He didn't dare sleep in this place. Though he trusted that Molly herself meant him no harm, he couldn't guarantee what Zaska and his other minions might do to him. He'd signed the contract on behalf of Ma'Nah, which was within his power. Zaska probably wouldn't be stupid enough to jeopardize their business relationship by allowing him to come to harm in the under-tier, but he shouldn't take any chances.

He cradled her face between his hands, enjoying the feeling of her silky hair, admiring the shade of it that seemed far more natural to him than Ninhursag's overtly gold hair color had been.

"I should go," he said, tracing her lower lip with his thumb.

She nodded, licking her lip, and his thumb. "I'm sure I will see you again." Since her tone sounded hopeful, he also took hope.

"All the business Ma'Nah does with you will go through me," he promised, though he'd initially intended to pass off the duty of dealing with Zaska to another member of his team.

Now, he intended to take every opportunity to see Molly again. And when Zaska decided he'd had enough of allowing his "flower" to spend time with Shulgi, he would steal her away from the monstrous creature.

Or just hunt him down and kill him, so that she would be free for good. He liked the idea of that even better. He felt jealous and enraged at the realization that Molly was still forced to serve whatever twisted and perverse desires the thida naf might have, not to mention that Zaska could decide to simply eat her at any time and there was nothing she could do about it.

Though he didn't mention it to her as he withdrew from her embrace and righted his undersuit before donning his armor again, he had formed a plan, still vague for the moment.

He glanced over at her readjusting her own scrap of a dress. He spotted her using a cloth she'd taken from the desk to wipe between her legs with a practiced motion that made him both infuriated and deeply saddened for the life she'd been forced to live.

The life of use and abuse that he'd only taken advantage of, to his shame.

He would find Sha Zaska, and he would kill him. Then Molly could be free to make her own choices. Even though his mission kept him from becoming one of those choices, he assuaged his own sense of guilt by allowing himself to hope that she *would* choose him if she could.

TWELVE

Molly wanted to kiss Shulgi again as she watched him pick up his pistol from the desk and reattach it to his armor at his hip. She hadn't stopped wanting to kiss him since they'd broken from their last kiss.

She wasn't sure she would ever stop wanting to feel his lips on hers. Their time together had been far too brief, and though her body buzzed with her pleasure from their encounter, she also felt the return of the hollowness as he readied himself to leave the office.

He'd signed the contract. She'd gotten what she'd set out to get. In the process, she'd also enjoyed sex in a way she never had before, finding her own pleasure in the alien body of her partner. Yet, at the end of it all, he still had to leave, and she still had to stay and play her role.

When he'd offered to take her away from here, she'd been so tempted she'd trembled with her desire to say yes. Even though she knew better.

She knew how these things worked.

Still, she eagerly tilted her head back when he finished

dressing and arming himself, then lowered his head to claim her lips in a kiss that told her his hunger had no more abated than her own. After a long, breathless moment where they seemed almost as connected as they had been while he was inside her, he finally stepped back and reattached his mask around his head.

Though she could no longer see the lower half of his face, his eyes still seemed to burn as they met hers. They weren't black any longer, but the green shade of them glittered with the intensity of his desire. He was so beautiful, so perfect, that she knew he was too good to be true.

Reminding herself of that was the only way she could say goodbye to him without begging him to take her with him. He hesitated at the door, almost as if he hoped she'd ask him to stay, but then he finally bid her farewell, promising to contact her the following business cycle before stalking through the opening doors.

Molly slumped into the chair behind the desk as the doors slid closed after he'd passed through them. She flicked the console screen, bringing up video feed from the lobby so she could watch him leave the building, then used the other cameras' feeds to track him back to the cargo elevator that led to the dreg.

It was only after he stepped into the elevator with the armored Iriduan guards, and the door closed to shut off her view of him that she finally rose on shaking legs from her chair. The fabric of her dress was soaked from his seed that had spilled from her after she'd cleaned up the initial gush of it.

She wasn't worried about getting pregnant. She never had to worry about that, as she'd been sterilized as soon as she'd been purchased by the brothel. Dreams of having children of her own hadn't even had a chance to form before they'd been killed off permanently.

And the dream of escaping this life and finding a new, happier one had also died long ago. Shulgi wasn't the first of her clients to ask her to come away with him. He wasn't the first male she'd been with who'd made her feel a connection—and a painfully vulnerable hope. She'd once believed that another would save her from the hell of her enslavement.

Yet, he'd turned out to be just as she now knew most people were. Too good to be true. He hadn't really loved her. He'd just been caught up in the moment, promising to take her away with him, when he'd had no intention of following through. She'd found that out later when she'd approached him with a plan for how he could help her escape the brothel and then leave the planet on his ship. She'd daydreamed that they could be together forever.

He'd put her down as gently as he could, she supposed, though her heart had been broken when she'd realized that he'd been roleplaying with her like he was a caring lover, but he still saw her as nothing but a product.

That was the last time she'd ever allowed "hope" in, though she hadn't been completely immune to others who played the role of concerned lover, and her heart had been bent a few more times after him.

The problem with Shulgi was that she'd felt so strongly for him from the very first moment, and her feelings were only growing in that direction. With the others, her attachment had grown over multiple visits from them, as they'd been regulars of hers. She'd never been initially attracted to them.

"Is it safe now?" Jenice asked wryly, her voice echoing from the console's speakers.

Molly sighed heavily, then chuckled as she shook her head. "We got the contract."

"Honey, I figured that much. I assume he's gone?"

Molly nodded, touching her tingling lips as she recalled

their parting kiss. "He's gone. I'm going to take the fact that you weren't sure as proof that none of you were watching the show."

"It's been recorded for blackmail purposes, if necessary, but none of us brought up the feed to watch," Jenice promised.

Molly frowned as she swept her hand over the console, sending it and the partnering one on the other side of the desk back into the desktop. "Honestly, Jenice, don't you think that's a little...."

"Mol, you know we record it every time. Hey," her tone sounded concerned, "you want to talk about it, hon?"

"Later." Molly stepped towards the inner sanctum doors which slid open at her approach.

To her relief, neither Jenice nor the two Ultimen were around, giving her the privacy to retreat to the bathroom to clean herself up, then change.

During her shower, she touched her body where Shulgi had touched her, recalling with the return of her arousal the way his hands had skimmed over her skin, the way his mouth had kissed along her neck, then sucked her nipple, the way his feelers had trailed along her thighs. She shivered as she brought herself to another climax. Then she flattened her palms on the black obsidian tiles of the shower, tears leaking from her eyes to blend with the water droplets pouring down over her head as she bumped her forehead against the cool glass between her palms.

She could live with having no hope. She'd lived that way for so long. It was only when she started hoping for more that her life became unbearable, and each moment was a struggle.

Once she left the tube of the dryer and dressed in her lounging clothes—which Jenice called "jammies"—she made her way to the sitting area of the sanctum. She smiled hesitantly when she saw Jenice seated on the couch, her eyes lifting from a tablet in her lap that probably had a book on it.

"Hey there." She smiled encouragingly, but Molly saw the solemnity in her eyes.

Jenice didn't like what Molly and the other "flowers" had to do. She'd tried her hand at it a couple of times and had been so emotionally traumatized by it that Molly had insisted she never put herself through that again. They'd all decided that Jenice should be responsible for the business side of things instead.

Prior to their escape from the brothel, Jenice's short stint as a slave had been difficult. She'd never made it to the actual clients, because Uthagol and her minions were still trying to break Jenice's will in order to make her more obedient, using torture and deprivation. It was one reason they preferred to buy their slaves as young as possible, since those who were enslaved as adults tended to fight a lot more and a lot harder against their bonds.

Molly held up a staying hand as Jenice set aside her tablet and made to rise. "Relax, Jen. I'm fine." She grinned, her cheeks flushing as she thought about how much her body hummed from her encounter with Shulgi. "Better than fine, actually. He was...."

Jenice waggled her eyebrows. "Hot, right? I saw enough, girl! Those Galactanet forums weren't lying about how fine the Iriduan males are."

Molly gasped. "You saw how *much* exactly?"

Jenice grinned, waving a hand vaguely towards the monitors. "I didn't watch anything, but I had to check the feed before cataloguing it, didn't I? By the way, he has a really nice ass, even if he does have two strange thingies coming out of his back right above it."

"Jenice!" Molly shrieked, picking up a decorative pillow to chuck it at Jenice, who only laughed as she caught it.

She knew what her friend was doing. Jenice wanted to lighten the mood, and make light of the encounter, as she often tried to do when one of the "flowers" actually had to go all the way to close the deal. Most of them, Molly included, were so inured to the job that they weren't usually too bothered by it, but Jenice seemed to suffer vicariously, and always tried to make them feel better, when it was really more her own emotions that were deeply affected.

Not that it was always easy for Molly to put aside her feelings. She also appreciated the intent behind Jenice's teasing and attempts to make light of these things.

Their laughter died down as Jenice set the pillow next to her against the arm rest of the couch, then patted the other side. "Cop a squat, Mol. I want to hear the details." She swiped her other hand over the console on the arm of the couch to summon a bot carrying a tray of snacks and drinks.

Molly eyed the bot as it rolled in once the hidden panel leading to the kitchens slid open. She grinned when she spotted the offerings. "You've been flirting with the chef again, haven't you?"

Jenice shrugged. "What can I say? I think his horns are sexy." She waved towards the approaching tray. "Plus, I really wanted some pizza, and I would kill for some fresh, buttered popcorn!"

Molly chuckled as she inhaled deeply of the scent of food Jenice and the others assured her came right off an Earthling menu. How closely their ramsuta chef managed to make it probably had to do more with how much time Jenice spent in the kitchen teasing him mercilessly than it did with his familiarity with the cuisine.

"So," Jenice said, recalling Molly's attention to her as the pizza, popcorn, and "pop" as Jenice called some of the drinks, rolled up to the coffee table, "how are you doing?" Her expression sobered as she leaned forward and placed a hand on Molly's jammie-covered thigh. "He didn't hurt you, did he? I know the suppressors were set to your voice command, but it was difficult not to watch over you, just to make sure he wasn't...."

Molly patted her hand. "He was perfect, Jen. He treated me very well."

Jenice smiled and sagged back in her seat. "That's a relief! I swear, the problem with researching the Iriduans isn't the lack of information on the Galactanet. It's that there's too much of it. I can't tell what's real and what's bullshit, and the official sites hosted by the Iriduan Empire are so damned vague and even conflict with themselves on the information they provide."

She leaned forward to snatch up a handful of popcorn in one hand, picking up a pop in the other. "The only thing that everyone who *isn't* an Iriduan really seems to agree on is that they're real bastards. So," she took a sip of her pop, pulling a face because according to her, no matter how hard he tried, their chef couldn't get the recipe exactly right, "naturally, I was worried about how he might treat you."

Molly grinned as she plucked up a dish with two of the pizza slices on it. She'd tried them before and liked them, and Jenice and the others told her they were remarkably close to the real deal. "I ran into the same problem. Lots of rumors and urban legends and horror stories about their species. Many of them didn't make any sense at all."

She lifted a slice of pizza, about to take a bite, but then lowered it as she glanced at Jenice. "I did read some theories about why they always wear masks though. A few of them seemed... plausible. Yet, if the ones I suspect might be true really are, then I wonder why Shulgi was so willing to remove his mask for me."

Jenice swallowed the popcorn she'd been crunching on

while Molly spoke. "Are you talking about the deadly allergy theory? Or the air quality vulnerability theory? Or that pheromone theory?" She took a quick sip of her drink. "Or, ooh, the hideous face theory?" She frowned. "Obviously, from what I've seen, that last one is definitely not true. It didn't look like he had vampiric fangs either, so I'm guessing the blood-sucker theory is wrong."

Molly laughed aloud, shaking her head at Jenice's list of only some of the many different speculations on the Galactanet about the Iriduans' strange culture and habits. "Since Shulgi took his mask off for me, I wonder if the theory that the mask is for visual intimidation, anonymity, or for religious beliefs are the most accurate theories. Maybe it really is true that Iriduans only reveal their faces for those who are close to them."

She liked the idea that Shulgi felt close enough to her that he might want to reveal his face to her. Especially if such an act was truly meaningful for his people. Obviously, he couldn't have been concerned about air quality or allergens or pheromones.

Or the urge to bury fangs in her neck and drain her of blood. That last theory had seemed ridiculous even when she'd read it on a particularly lurid conspiracy site. Still, there had been some convincing stories told about such things, and despite the empire's official stance on slavery, way more than a few slaves disappeared from the Rim into the dubious "care" of Iriduans, never to be seen or heard from again. It didn't seem all that far-fetched that the species was doing something nefarious that required victims.

Jenice studied her face as she took another sip of her drink. "Mol, just... I don't want to be a wet blanket or anything. I can see that you're practically glowing. I don't think I've ever seen you so... satisfied, but I don't want you to get hurt, you know. I mean... emotionally."

Molly sighed, setting her plate down on the armchair of the couch without yet taking a bite of the pizza on it. "I appreciate your concern, Jen, but it isn't necessary. I learned long ago not to get my feelings involved in these types of transactions."

Jenice cursed, turning her head to glare at the wall as if she could see some monster through it. Molly guessed the one she saw was Uthagol. "I hate that you have to live this way, Mol. Especially since you've never known anything else!"

Molly shrugged one shoulder with more nonchalance than she felt. "The fact that I've never known anything else makes it easier, I think."

Jenice focused on her again, her eyes sad and misty. "Maybe. I don't know, but my heart breaks every time I think about what you've been through." She lowered her eyes, studying the bubbles fizzing in her drink glass. "And about the way we continue to use you and the others to achieve our goals. It's not fair! I should—"

Molly placed a hand on Jenice's arm. "Stop, Jen. What we do now, we do by choice. You have no idea how empowering that is for all of us. Me and the others are well trained for this work, and we have learned to appreciate our skills, no matter how hard won they are. I have no regrets, nor would I want to see someone thrust into this role when they suffer from it."

"I just don't know how you do it. I try to keep things light whenever one of you has to... *do* it, but it's so hard not to feel like I'm failing you. Like I should be the one taking the hit for the team, since a lot of times, it's my suggestions for how to expand our influence that force you all into these positions."

Molly released Jenice's arm and leaned back in her chair, plucking up her pizza slice again. She smiled at Jenice. "Sometimes, I'm really glad you give the advice you do, Jen." Her smile widened to a full-on grin. "Especially when it brings someone like Shulgi into my bed."

Jenice chuckled, and Molly could see her tension relaxing as she sagged again in her seat. "Well, as long as you really did enjoy yourself." She mirrored Molly's grin. "And technically, it was your desk, not your bed."

Molly tapped her chin, looking up thoughtfully. "Hm, you're right. I think I'll have to rectify that soon. My bed is looking kind of empty."

Jenice's laughter heartened Molly, and she joined in, but her mind was already thinking over how long she'd have to wait before she could see Shulgi again. He'd said that all Ma'Nah's dealings with Zaska would go through him, and Molly intended to be the only "mouthpiece" he spoke to.

She knew Jenice was right. She knew not to get emotionally attached, but she didn't see any reason not to enjoy the ride while it lasted.

THIRTEEN

Once Shulgi returned to the dreg, his first thought was to get to his room and clean off any trace of Molly's scent. It wasn't likely that the small bit that still clung to him would be enough to attract other males or cause an unintended imprinting, but if anyone did detect female pheromones on him, things could get ugly.

It was a pity, since he loved how Molly smelled and regretted having to wipe clean his entire body and the inside of his armor after cleaning any trace she'd left behind from running her fingers through his hair.

It was only once he'd completed cleaning himself that he dared to head to Namerian's office and give him the news about signing the contract.

He had to wait for his kin, as Namerian was in the lab. He paced around the office's confines, feeling exhausted but knowing he couldn't allow his condition to show and cause questions he had no intention of answering. The stimulant's full effects were finally wearing off, and his exhaustion had caused some of his combat stimulants to kick in, giving him a temporary boost to his flagging energy that would end up being costly later.

He'd have to sleep for a long time after this meeting, and he had little patience for extended questions. Thus, when Namerian finally entered the office looking distracted, Shulgi didn't greet him with his usual friendliness. This got Namerian's attention, and his violet-eyed gaze sharpened as he studied Shulgi.

"I take it things didn't go well with Zaska?" he asked cautiously.

Shulgi shook his head. "The terms were agreeable and favor both parties equally, so I signed the contract."

Namerian's eyes widened. "You signed without discussing the terms with the team first?"

Shulgi paced to the office window, activating the shade so it shut out the bleak sight of the factory district below and the silhouette of the ziggurat in the distance. "I did. There was no need to involve research scientists in the business negotiations." He shifted his attention back to Namerian. "You have more important matters to concern you."

Namerian studied his face in silence for a long, tense moment, before finally shrugging, his wings flicking with the only sign that his demeanor wasn't as nonchalant as he tried to project. "Very well. I suppose there's no harm in it. You are well aware of Ma'Nah's requirements, and the special requirements of our mission. If you feel that Zaska can be helpful, then I trust your judgement."

He wouldn't be so trusting if he knew about Molly's effect on Shulgi, and Shulgi was grateful Namerian and his fellow scientists were too distracted to insist on meeting Zaska's mouthpiece. "Have you come any closer to solving the issue of re-affliction?"

Namerian shook his head slowly, lifting a hand to run it

through his hair. "Not yet, though we've only encountered that one case so far. We're hoping it will be a rare occurrence. Otherwise...."

Otherwise, they'd sent males out into the galaxy with the mistaken belief that they could remove their masks safely around females.

"We can attempt the exposure protocol we've been discussing."

Namerian's upper lip curled at that suggestion. It wasn't one Shulgi liked either, but it had been used for the professors themselves, allowing them to be afflicted, then cured of the imprinting to better understand the cure itself.

"That means dealing with scent-peddlers again," Namerian said in a disgusted tone.

"We still have a collection of scent drench. That will last long enough to run trials on current volunteers."

Namerian moved to the window as if he could still stare out of it, and Shulgi knew it was a favorite position for him as he turned his back to the room to stare at the blind. "There is the other option," he said, without much hope in his tone.

"It won't come to that, Namerian." Shulgi was determined never to allow nanites to rewrite Iriduan genetic code at will.

Namerian couldn't understand how dangerous that was. He'd never met Ninhursag, or Enki. He'd never seen how much power they had wielded. Power that would be unstoppable if their memories were resurrected again.

Namerian sighed, turning to face him, his eyes dark purple now with his frustration. "Then might I suggest a more radical solution that can speed up the cure?"

Shulgi raised his eyebrows in question, crossing his arms over his chest. "You can make whatever suggestion you want. I'll listen to any of your ideas, Namerian. I brought you on for this mission because I trust you and know you have a better grasp of this aspect of the mission than I do."

"There is a... weapon currently in the hands of our enemies. One that is said to be capable of activating the imprinting response in any Iriduan male."

Shulgi slowly lowered his arms, his mouth falling open in shock as horror filled him. "Can such a thing possibly exist? How would it even work?"

Namerian shook his head. "I don't have the particulars of how it functions. I am concerned, however, that it might be a variant of the cure."

"You mean this weapon could be composed of nanites?"

Namerian nodded, his expression neutral. "This is possible, though rather than rewriting our genes, they simply activate the relevant ones." He stroked his chin thoughtfully. "It would be a far less complex process and program. If they attached to our receptors and replicated various chemical combinations until the victim is afflicted, it would be a simple enough program to create, without requiring the extensive artificial intelligence present in our cure."

"Who would be capable of creating such an abomination?"

Namerian's expression was grim. "The Akrellians are currently in possession of it, though I suspect they didn't create it. In fact, I fear it was our own people who did so."

"Why would the Iriduans do such a thing?"

Namerian's short laugh was grim and humorless. "For the same reason we can't afford to hand the cure over to the empire and let them disseminate it. The elites want to hold onto their power, and the affliction is a useful tool to control the masses. A weapon like this could put an end to any rebellion quickly."

Shulgi growled with anger and a feeling of impotence against the corruption of the empire and its leadership. If they were responsible for creating this abomination, then their arrogance and lust for power could be the downfall of their own species. "If the Akrellians have gained control of such a weapon, why haven't they used it yet?"

Namerian strode to his desk, running his fingertips along the smooth surface of it, bringing up multiple screens. "I suspect they have plans to but are holding off to see if the empire self-destructs on its own. The use of such a weapon would make them vulnerable to severe censure from the Syndicate, and perhaps even expulsion. Or dissection."

"Unless the Iriduans created it."

Namerian tapped a few symbols on one of the screens before looking up to meet Shulgi's eyes. "Even then, it would be the ones who unleashed it that would face the consequences. For now, I think the Akrellians are engaging only in small scale testing. We've picked up chatter that multiple imperial patrols have gone missing on the boundary."

Shulgi huffed, shaking his head. "Don't you mean *over* it?"

Namerian smirked. "I'm sure they crossed it at some point. Do not underestimate the ruthlessness of our enemies, however. Not to mention their desire to see us destroyed."

"I assume you have a reason for bringing up this weapon." Shulgi began pacing again, no longer feeling as tired as he had been.

Namerian swiped over a few more screens, then brought one up, flicking his fingers so it hovered above the desktop, visible now to Shulgi. He saw that it was a star map.

"I found a sample. If we can get ahold of it, I believe we can reverse-engineer it, and using the current tech of our cure, we can make it even more effective, giving us results rapid enough to potentially activate multiple gene clusters before the cure deactivates."

"So, you think using both this weapon and the cure in

tandem will make phase two possible?" Shulgi didn't like the idea of unleashing such a thing upon unsuspecting Iriduans, but at the same time, if it solved the problem of imprinting, wouldn't it be worth it?

He studied the star map, noting a familiar cluster as the image zoomed in. "I can put together a team to infiltrate—"

Namerian swiped his hand across the image, dismissing it. "That won't be necessary. I have some pawns in play in the facility where the weapon is being held. The issue will be getting it safely back to us. We've been fortunate that none of our smuggling of scent drench into the dreg was detected, but if security discovers this sample, our mission will be doomed, along with every last one of us."

Shulgi felt a rush of disappointment at missing the opportunity to head to an Akrellian research facility and execute a strike to retrieve the weapon, even as he wondered who Namerian had in place, and how the professor had made the contacts.

Namerian had never been a part of the rebellion officially, but his sympathies had always laid in that direction. Some members of the rebellion worked directly with the enemies of the empire, especially the Akrellians, who had made overtures to the rebels claiming they would support a coup if the rebels created a replacement Iriduan government that adhered to Akrellian values.

"Zaska's docks might be the best thing for us," Namerian said in a thoughtful tone. "We can have the sample sent there, and it's less likely to draw attention from city boss regulators than on our own tier docks."

Thinking of Zaska brought memories of Molly to the fore and Shulgi had to quickly turn his back to Namerian as his shaft stiffened, forming a noticeable bulge beneath the fabric of his robe. He regretted not wearing armor, but it would have been strange for him to do so within the factory.

To chase away his untimely arousal, he tried to focus on the monster that owned Molly. The one he fully intended to kill. Namerian's plan meant he might have to delay his own to obliterate Zaska, since the death of the boss would create chaos in the under-tier. They couldn't afford that with such an important shipment enroute.

"How long do you think it will take to acquire this sample?"

"A few Kluthian weeks." Namerian's tone sounded curious. No doubt he wondered why Shulgi had suddenly turned away.

Shulgi clenched his fists as he pondered leaving Molly in the clutches of that sick monster for even that much longer. "We can't get it into the docks any sooner?"

"I am pleased you want to begin phase two as soon as possible," Namerian said wryly, his voice growing louder as he approached Shulgi from behind, "but these things take time. If you really want to begin sooner, there is always the other option."

"That's not an option, Namerian." Shulgi sighed heavily, his wings flicking to wave Namerian away from him. He heard his kin step backwards to avoid their sweep. "I will deal with Zaska and his... minions personally. You let me know when the sample is expected to arrive, and I'll be certain none of Zaska's ilk grow too curious about it."

"Of course," Namerian said, his tone sounding neutral now, "though there are others on the team who could take over that duty. I know you have more important work to do as well."

Shulgi waved a dismissive hand, grateful his erection had subsided with the shift in the discussion so he could turn around to face Namerian again. "Minor business matters hardly keep me occupied. Ma'Nah runs smoothly now, and the dreg-masters are respectful enough of my abilities at this point to leave us alone."

"And what of your *other* activities?" Namerian's gaze sharpened on Shulgi's face, and Shulgi had a sudden fear that the other male had somehow figured out what he'd done with Molly.

"My other activities?" If the professor knew about Molly, he might decide Shulgi was too compromised to see her again and insist on someone else dealing with the under-tier dock situation.

The team would definitely agree with Namerian, even though Shulgi was ostensibly in charge. He couldn't complete this mission without the rest of them, and they all knew it. They also knew he wouldn't normally allow personal feelings to compromise their plans. They would expect him to concede and allow another to take his place in dealing with Zaska's "flower."

"The black-market smugglers," Namerian said in a low voice. "I have heard of the phantom killer who stalks the streets of the dreg, taking out the worst of its denizens. One who manages to stay unseen, even while assassinating some of the most dangerous criminals in the galaxy. There are few with that kind of skill set here in the dreg. Few trained for such work."

"You think it's me?" Shulgi regarded Namerian steadily, relieved that it was this suspicion in Namerian's mind, rather than the one about Molly.

"Personal vendettas are risky for our mission."

Shulgi snarled, his wings expanding behind him. Namerian responded by tucking his own close against his body, lowering his head, though his eyes never left Shulgi's.

"*If* such a phantom exists in the dreg, then perhaps he is only there to protect the weakest of the dreg's citizens from foul predators that would sell them into slavery or sell their body parts on the black market."

"I don't doubt the intent of this... phantom's actions." Namerian lifted a hand to rub the ports on the back of his neck. "But what we do here is more important, and it would be unwise to bring attention to us, for any reason." His expression shifted to an imploring one. "If we cure the affliction, then our people will finally be free, and life in the empire will change enough that innocent males won't have to flee to places like this."

Shulgi shook his head, folding his wings again as he turned towards the blind shrouded window. "That's a naïve and idealistic idea. I expected more pragmatism from you."

"*I'm* the idealist?" Namerian chuckled as he joined Shulgi in front of the obscured window. "There will always be predators, Shulgi. No matter what actions we take. My goal is to take the prey out of their hunting grounds, because I *know* I can't eliminate every hunter."

Shulgi remained silent, pondering Namerian's words. The combat stimulants that filled his blood whenever he went into battle or went on the hunt made him hunger for more of the same. Sometimes, the arena didn't completely sate his need for them. Hunting the evil that attacked their desperate clients did. But he knew Namerian was right. He could make a mistake at any time that ended up being critical. He was unnecessarily risking the mission. The most criminal elements of the dreg might someday track the killer's steps back to him, and Ma'Nah.

"I can disable your combat glands." Namerian placed a hand on Shulgi's arm to draw his attention. "That is the only way you will be free of your addiction."

Shulgi shook off Namerian's hand. "I'm not *addicted*.

Besides, I need the edge, at least until we complete our mission."

"And how many bodies will you leave in your wake before this mission is through, Shulgi?"

Shulgi shot a glare at his kin. "As many as I have to."

FOURTEEN

The week following her encounter with Shulgi was a busy one for Molly, though not busy enough to keep her mind occupied and away from dwelling on him.

And the fact that he didn't contact her at all during that time.

That wasn't to say that Ma'Nah's shipping office wasn't in contact. In fact, the very next day after Shulgi signed the contract, they received a request from Ma'Nah's shipment crew to commission Jonah's Whale for a large order.

Jenice oversaw the particulars, though their minions carried out the actions necessary on their end. Or Zaska's minions, as they saw themselves. Everything should go smoothly, as this was a standard shipment of food product to a colony bordering the CivilRim. Jonah's Whale had permission to travel through all the Jumpstations as well as any neutral territory within Syndicate space.

There was really no need for Sha Zaska to be personally involved in this end of the business, which meant there was no need for his mouthpiece. She realized there was no need for someone high up in Ma'Nah to be involved either.

Obviously, the company was smuggling some undisclosed products as well on Jonah's Whale, and that was fine with "Zaska" as long as they were well hidden. Jonah's crew was more than capable of dealing with nosy officials.

The good news was that they had a handful of escaped slaves in the pipeline and ready to smuggle off-world. The colony the Whale was traveling to required a Jumpstation transfer, and the slaves would be met there by a representative from an Akrellian organization dedicated to rescuing slaves, particularly human and Akrellian ones, though they would help all species—even Iriduans who'd been enslaved.

Ma'Nah's agents knew about some of the smuggling holds on the Whale, but not all of them, so there would be plenty of space for the slaves, and a full cargo hold wouldn't raise as many questions as one that was half empty.

Any success at smuggling slaves off Za'Kluth and onto the road to their freedom was a happy one, but Molly still felt dissatisfied. She was pleased that they had a way to get this group off-world, but she also wished she could see Shulgi again. She wondered if he'd forgotten all about her now that his part in the dealings was done.

Perhaps she really had been nothing but a product to him. Something to use while he had the opportunity, only to be forgotten and discarded after he'd sated himself.

She knew better than to expect anything else, yet it still hurt when he wouldn't even contact her at all. Not even to let her know whether he'd enjoyed himself.

She had nearly given up on ever hearing from him again when she received a message routed to her by Jenice.

It was from Shulgi's personal contact address, and it was very brief. Yet it still made her smile.

I was out of commission longer than I expected to be. Missed you. Can I see you again?

She didn't know what he meant by "out of commission" but suspected that it was an explanation for why he hadn't communicated with her since he'd left. She realized that it could just be an excuse, and she wasn't usually so naïve as to believe such an excuse. Yet she felt like Shulgi was too honorable to make lies like that up. If he wanted to use her for her body, she felt like he'd make that clear and not play with her emotions by pretending he cared about more than that.

She recalled Jenice's concern about her getting emotionally hurt, aware that was a distinct possibility in this case. Still, she replied to his message immediately, and directly, not routing it back through their central address for Jenice or anyone else to read.

Missed you too. Would love to see you again.

She bounced her foot as she sat on the couch, barely hearing the Ultiman video game going on in the background as Mogorl and Grundon engaged in a virtual battle. She'd been watching them when Jenice sent the message. Though really, she'd been staring at the holo screens without seeing them.

She thought she would have to wait a long time for a response, but he replied immediately, and since it was direct to her link, there was no delay.

His response appeared in a holographic display just above her wrist.

Tell me when. I need to see you soon.

She feared she might be misinterpreting his intent. She wasn't sure if he needed to see her personally, or as Zaska's mouthpiece. Why would he "need" her? Was it lust driving him to contact her? Or did he only need to discuss the contract, and the business Ma'Nah was now doing with Zaska's Shipping?

She wasn't in the mood for misunderstandings.

Mogorl glanced over at her as she whispered into her wrist com. Grundon crowed with victory as his avatar brutalized Mogorl's character because of his momentary distraction.

Is this for business or pleasure?

She waited nervously for his reply, her knee bouncing even more now until she noticed Mogorl staring at it with concern bringing his heavy brows together over soulful dark brown eyes.

She gave him a weak smile. "Just a business transaction. Don't let me distract you."

He studied her face for a long moment, and she knew he didn't believe her. Still, he nodded slowly, then returned his attention to the game, though she knew he remained alert to her mood.

She rose quickly to her feet and retreated to her room, knowing that would only raise both their suspicions. They were growing perhaps too overprotective of her. Fortunately, there wasn't anything romantic about their devotion to her that would make her feel guilty about hiding Shulgi's communications from them. She was more like a sibling to them.

Does Zaska monitor this contact?

Her heart thudded, aware that she was in a tight place with such questions. She had to be careful how she went about this. If she said no, it was completely private, Shulgi might wonder how a slave had so much freedom. If she said yes, Zaska did, he might not communicate fully with her.

"No," she whispered into her com. "But he has given me some freedom to work with clients as I see fit."

So I am only a client?

She slowly smiled, sensing he wouldn't have asked the question if he didn't really care about the answer.

As far as he's concerned. But not to me.

Several long minutes passed before his response scrolled over her wrist.

What am I to you, Molly?

She hesitated before answering that question, unsure what would be the best way to phrase what he meant to her, or why. Obviously, she couldn't be in love with him since she'd only just met him. Yet, she felt such a connection to him that she wondered if it wasn't something on the path to love. At the same time, she wouldn't want to assume too much on his side. She'd made that mistake before, and the pain of discovering she'd been wrong had almost been too much for her to bear.

You are something I don't dare to believe in.

She gasped as she saw her own words appear on her com, not realizing she'd said them aloud. Tears clustered in her eyes as she pondered how true they were. She didn't believe in love at first sight. Couldn't. She wasn't in a position to fall in love—least of all with someone like Shulgi. Someone who could never know her secret.

She sent the message anyway, her fingers shaking as she tapped her wrist. She took shallow breaths as she awaited a response, unsure what she wanted it to be.

It took a long time for him to reply, and each minute that ticked by without a response made her heart sink a little more. She was afraid she'd already went too far. Admitted too much. Made him more important in her mind than he intended to be. That was the biggest failing she'd always had, looking for someone to actually care about her so desperately that she ended up seeing it where it didn't exist.

You can believe in me, Molly.

When his reply came back, she released her breath in a gust, relieved that he hadn't completely denied any interest in her beyond her body. Still, the response was vague enough that she could take multiple meanings from it. He might be speaking of her being able to believe in his desire to rescue her from her slavery, rather than that he cared about her personally. She'd already seen that he disliked the practice, and Sha Zaska. She might be his project, rather than a potential love interest.

I will save you.

Her heart sank again at his follow-up message, realizing that her suspicions about his meaning were probably correct. She was a victim he wanted to save, not someone he wanted to love.

I don't need saving. Just love.

Again, her words left her lips without her conscious intent, but once they were out there, she didn't take them back, instead sending the message, even as she dreaded the response.

When he didn't reply for another long stretch where she waited, almost breathless, she felt again like she'd gone too far, pushed too hard.

Love for our kind is not like it is for humans.

His reply wasn't what she'd hoped, but it wasn't as bad as she'd feared, either. He didn't immediately shut her down and tell her she was a fool to even think he could ever love someone like her. Instead, he'd given her more questions than answers.

Before she could respond, he sent another message.

I want to explain, but some things should be said in person.

Molly's leg bounced as she sat straight on the edge of the bed, nervously debating what she should say next. She wanted to see him again, naturally, but she also now felt worried about his response, and what it might mean. Maybe he just wanted to sleep with her again. While she wanted that too, she wasn't sure that she could remain detached emotionally from him if she engaged in more physical intimacy. She might have already gone too far for emotional detachment.

I want to see you again, but I'm also worried.

She didn't like admitting to her vulnerability. Her mask of

professionalism was like armor for her. Allowing it to slip, even just a little, made her fear that she would lose herself to him, and that her heartache would be so much worse when he decided he'd finished with her, either growing tired of her, or discovering that she didn't need his rescue and moving on to someone who did.

We can meet away from the under-tier, away from Zaska's spying eyes. Perhaps we can find an excuse to get you away from him, even if only temporarily.

Clearly, he was aware Zaska saw everything that happened on the docks. She wondered if he knew their encounter had been recorded, then figured he did. She didn't leave the under-tier often, mostly to avoid the off chance that she might run into someone who recognized her, though the dye and markings obscured her features significantly from when she'd been in Uthagol's brothel. Still, there were tiers she could visit that Uthagol and her minions, as well as her usual clientele, wouldn't be caught dead on.

I might be able to meet you on second-tier. In the market-place. Sometimes I am permitted to shop there.

Her heart thudded in her chest as she waited for his response, realizing that if he agreed to meet her there, she would be away from the relative safety of under-tier and Zaska's shadow.

That place isn't safe for you alone. Is there any way I can come to escort you there without arousing Zaska's suspicions?

She shook her head as if he were in the room with her, a smile perking her lips.

I will have my guards escort me. There's an inn on second-tier where I sometimes meet clients who don't like coming to the under-tier.

Mogorl and Grundon would not be happy about this meeting away from the under-tier, but they would help her because they loved her, and also because they knew she would go on her own if they refused to escort her. She would not be controlled by anyone ever again.

Give me the details. I hope to see you again, as soon as possible.

Her heart soared again, though she urged it to settle and not get too excited. She'd been down this path before and had felt her heart bounce about excitedly as butterflies filled her stomach. She knew how hurt she could end up getting in these situations.

Yet she also knew it was already too late.

FIFTEEN

Second-tier was almost as much of a hole as under-tier. Shulgi didn't feel much safer in this place than he did on Zaska's turf. At the same time, the tier leaders for this level likely didn't belong to Zaska, which meant they wouldn't necessarily serve his bidding.

It bothered him that Molly would be forced to travel to this tier, though he suspected most of the casual criminals would be put off by the hulking forms of her two bodyguards. No one tangled with Ultimen on a lark. Even the more experienced criminals would seek a better opportunity than one where her guards flanked her, and they'd never find it, because once she was with Shulgi, they wouldn't be able to touch her.

He wanted to urge her to again consider allowing him to rescue her. It was likely she had a tracker implanted in her body from Zaska in addition to the slave collar that was ubiquitous around her neck, but he knew several medical techs capable of removing even the exploding kind. For someone like Namerian, it would be as simple as skimming the water, but he didn't dare tell his kin about Molly yet. His strong attraction to her and her connection to Zaska would be a definite concern for the professor.

The inn where she'd told him to meet her looked nicer than he'd anticipated, though still far below the quality and luxury of most of the resting houses within the dreg. Iriduans had a love of luxury that even the lowest citizens felt. Most of the furnishings within this inn were pragmatic and functional, with no eye towards beauty.

Still, it was cleaner than most of the establishments on second-tier, and he didn't feel like he would end up sticking to the bench when he sat while he waited for Molly's arrival. He also didn't feel like the available food would be poisoned or undercooked, though he wouldn't eat here. An Iriduan didn't remove his mask outside the dreg unless he was assured there weren't pheromones that could afflict him.

Time ticked by as he watched customers flow in and out of the inn. Many seemed to be only there for the food, some clearly there to rest, and still others were there for a short stay whose purpose was obvious, based on the people they had with them and their behavior.

It didn't surprise him that Molly was familiar with this place, but it really bothered him and made him more determined to get her away from Zaska. He only wished he had the ability to give her a home with him.

He looked down at his wrist com, bringing up one of her messages as he had done many times since she'd sent it to him.

I don't need saving. Just love.

If he were free to love her, he would make sure she never wanted for love again. He would treat her like the queen she was, and worship her the way any Iriduan male worshipped their mate. Not because he was afflicted, but because he genuinely wanted her.

Too many things kept him from even dreaming of such a

thing. Too many things that he could not afford to abandon. He also had a bloody past—a terrible past—that few mates could forgive. It was a past *he* could not forgive. He wasn't free to love, even though he was cured of his imprinting and Ninhursag was nothing but a despised memory.

He wished his position were different. Wished he could be with her the way she seemed to want. All he could do was help her as much as he could, and free her from her enslavement, the way he'd been freed from his.

The doors to the inn slid open, and the clients in both the lobby and the attached dining room and bar where Shulgi sat waiting in a shadowed corner turned to look at those who entered.

The towering Ultimen were unmistakable and easily recognizable, since they lacked the energy beads and braids typical of the rare Ultiman seen on this tier. The small figure between them wore a hooded cloak that concealed her features, but Shulgi straightened, his wings flicking around the back of the seat with his anticipation.

The green cloak had Zaska's coiled tentacle markings on it, and at least some of the clients appeared to recognize the threat, and the personage. They backed away from the trio as one of her guards scanned the lobby and dining room, his dark gaze falling upon Shulgi, who rose from his seat and waved them over.

The guard moved towards the dining room, but a slim, purple hand lifted to stop him, settling gently on his forearm in a way that made Shulgi grind his teeth. He felt a sudden surge of jealousy and possessiveness as he wondered about Molly's relationship to her two seemingly favorite bodyguards.

It was not like an Iriduan male to be jealous. At least, that was what they were taught to believe. Yet every imprinted male he'd ever known had resented the other males he'd been forced to share his mate with and felt jealousy daily. Their cerci had barbs for a reason. They despised the idea that their female had the seed of other males within her and used them to scrape it out before depositing their own—if she was willing to endure that, naturally, since they did nothing she didn't want. Most Iriduan females enjoyed the experience, taking an odd erotic pleasure in it, from what he'd heard.

He sincerely doubted a human female would appreciate it as much.

He wouldn't let it bother him. If anything, he should want her to find someone who could give her a home and love, and maybe even some kind of family. Except that the thought of her with anyone else made him angry. He felt like ripping Sha Zaska to shreds, not only because the thida naf was a monster in every sense of the word, but because he dared to put his foul tentacles on Molly.

Mine!

He felt a sudden desire to leap up and race to her to pull her away from her guards, then kill them both and flee this filthy world with her. It hit him so strongly that he moved towards them reflexively before he gained control over himself. Combat stimulants pumped through his blood, sharpening his senses as he scanned the crowd, quickly working out an escape scenario and potential threats that could interfere with it. He felt the rush of excitement at the prospect of a battle, and had to acknowledge that, yes, he was probably addicted.

However, he was feeling an even greater—and far more disturbing—addiction to this one petite human female. An addiction that could jeopardize everything he'd worked for.

Her cowled hood had turned towards him, and though a shadow concealed most of her features, he still saw her lips tilting upwards in a smile of greeting, flashing her even, white teeth. She waited for him to join her, seemingly unconcerned with the crowd of patrons that were now all wisely backing away from her and her guards, giving them space within the lobby.

A proprietor rushed out to greet Molly even as Shulgi drew close enough to overhear his familiar tone as he offered her "the usual suite."

More jealousy burned through him, sparking his rage. He turned a glare on the proprietor, a finrat, who noted his ire with a nervous squeak, backing away from Molly and her guards as he stared at Shulgi with wide, terrified eyes.

Shulgi's wings flared behind him, causing nervous mutterings from some of the other patrons. A handful of them slipped out of the inn through the front doors. Others watched from a safe distance, their curious gazes bouncing from him to the proprietor, to Zaska's people, no doubt anticipating some interesting action.

Molly's hand fell upon his forearm, and she nodded her head to the finrat. Her voice sounded gentle when she spoke to the creature, even as she shifted closer to Shulgi.

"If the suite is available, I would prefer it, Owngot." She subtly tightened her grip on his forearm, her message clear.

He was creating a scene that she probably didn't appreciate. Given the cloak and cowl, she likely didn't appreciate the focus of the staring crowd either. He was already screwing this up. He wouldn't be much use to her if he got into a fight with anyone who spoke to her.

The finrat's round ears remained pinned back against his skull but he clapped his little paws together, shifting his attention from Shulgi to Molly with a relieved exhalation. "Of course, mouthpiece! Naturally, Sha Zaska's servants are always welcome here, and we reserve the suite for your use!"

"Thank you, Owngot." Her tone was gracious, her accent

elegant as she spoke Ubaid Universal—one of many common Syndicate trade languages.

She had so much class and poise that he couldn't help but find it admirable. Even here in this filthy place—even as a slave of a foul master—she had the bearing of an empress, with the kindness of the humblest of souls.

It was one thing to see her in her element in the under-tier. It was another altogether to see her away from that place, vulnerable, even with her guards. Yet he already noted the way the crowd looked upon her with the same admiration he was feeling in their expressions. He also noted the gleam in the eyes of many of the crowd as they studied the cloaked figure with far more interest than he liked.

Some of that second group glanced at him, noting his expression and perhaps her hand upon his arm, holding him back with the merest touch, and they wisely left the area, either fleeing the inn altogether, or heading up to their own rooms.

To the proprietor's credit, the finrat had them seen to their suite very quickly and efficiently, barely glancing at Shulgi again. Also to the finrat's credit, he explained that the suite's air was filtered, and it had been disinfected. The fact that he glanced at Shulgi as he said this made it clear that the finrat, at least, had some suspicion about his purpose for wearing a mask.

Many suspected. Some knew for a fact. The empire tried to muddy the waters as much as possible. It didn't always work. Most people accepted what they were told by those they considered authorities on the subject, but some people had the sense to question everything and do their own research.

Shulgi didn't really concern himself whether the finrat knew for sure or not. Most of the resting houses had filtered air pumped into their rooms to limit the cross contamination of bacteria and viruses from countless different species. It had become a protocol, and he wasn't surprised that this inn, even on the lowly second tier, conformed to it.

At the door to the suite, Molly paused as her guards took up positions on either side of it, in the corridor. One of them met Shulgi's eyes, his expression dour. His upper lip pulled back in a slight snarl, revealing the huge teeth and sharp eyeteeth that the Ultimen still possessed, despite many thousands of years of advanced technology separating them from their primitive past.

Shulgi knew over thirty different ways to gain an advantage on that particular species, and if he had to take on these two, they wouldn't be the first Ultimen he'd killed. Still, even with combat stimulants rushing through his blood, he didn't relish a battle with them. They had a long reach and immense physical strength.

He also suspected Molly was fond of them, and though that thought filled him with a jealousy he had no right to feel, it meant he shouldn't hurt them unless he had no other choice.

Molly made a soft, distressed sound when she looked up at her guard and saw his snarl and its direction. Immediately, the Ultiman turned his face away from Shulgi, switching his glare to the wall on the other side of the corridor as he crossed his huge arms over an equally massive chest. His snarl remained.

A definite warning, and one Shulgi took to heart. They didn't know whether he would harm her or not, but they had to know by now that he'd already been with her intimately, and no doubt viewed him the same as all the other off-breeds who'd taken advantage of her.

He didn't blame the guards for disliking him. He turned his attention back to Molly, who hovered by the open door, her cowl shadowing all of her face now as she stood with head submissively bowed, waiting for him to move past her into the suite.

He gestured with one arm towards the door. "Please, enter first, my quee—Molly."

He was definitely losing his mind around this woman. Forgetting himself. He wondered again if he'd missed something. Perhaps he *had* been afflicted by her. Yet, this didn't feel the same as it had when he'd imprinted on Ninhursag.

She nodded slightly and swept into the room, her cloak billowing behind her. He followed on her heels after ensuring that the finrat had completely left the corridor, leaving it empty save for himself and the two guards who avoided looking at him directly.

"Hurt her and die painfully and slowly," one of them growled to his back as he stepped through the door.

He didn't doubt the guard was serious as he turned around to face them just before the door slid closed to cut off his view of them.

He felt Molly approach him from behind, his wings flicking reflexively. Her small hand trailed along the edge of one wing so lightly that he barely felt the touch.

"Your wings are so beautiful," she said softly as he turned to face her.

She smiled as she lifted her hands to remove her hood. Her blond hair was bound in a simple bun, with decorative ornaments dangling from golden clips that adorned it.

He frowned at the sight of them, touching one with the desire of removing it. He didn't want to see any ornaments in her hair that didn't come from him. In fact, he didn't want her hair to be bound like the hair of a mated queen, since he wasn't the one who'd mated her.

He again felt the surge of possessiveness as his fingers unclasped the clip and gently removed it from her hair. He wasn't doing it consciously, but he wanted those ornaments—

which he could tell now that he held one in his hand were cheap and fake—out of her hair.

Her gaze shifted from the clip he now held in his hand to his face. "Do you not like them? I wouldn't have worn them if I had known they would displease you."

He stared down at the clip with its dangling glass beads. It was far too light to be metal, and certainly wasn't the gold its color implied. "Do they please *you*, Molly?"

She was silent for a long moment, and he looked up to meet her steady gaze, noting that her beautiful eyes had turned more amber than green.

"Do you like wearing these?" He held up the clip.

"They are... pretty," she said, her tone uncertain. "They enhance my appearance."

He frowned and tossed the clip onto a short table beside a chair in the main entry space of the expansive suite. Then he framed her face with his hands, staring down at her features as if he needed to study them, when really, he'd already memorized them.

"You are beautiful without all of these cheap ornaments," he said, stroking one finger over her thin brows, then tracing the green lines of the markings dyed into her skin.

His own brows drew together as he did so, disliking the reminder of Zaska's ownership of her. The desire to slaughter that creature grew into an obsession as he looked into Molly's face, noting the sadness behind her eyes even as she smiled hesitantly. Once the shipment of the weapon sample was safely in their lab, he would hunt the thida naf in his own tunnels. He would find him, and he would leave nothing behind by the time he was done butchering him.

She lifted a hand to stroke a lock of his hair that was draped over his shoulder. "You are the beautiful one," she said with a sigh. "I am actually quite plain under all of this." She gestured with her free hand to her face.

Shulgi lowered his hands and stepped back, then lifted one to unhook his mask. For the first time since he'd crawled out of his cocoon after Meta, it mattered to him that his appearance pleased the eye. As long as it pleased *her* eyes.

"There is nothing plain about you, Molly," he said after removing his mask and tossing it onto the entry chair beside the table where her clip lay like the discarded trash it was.

She glanced at the mask, then turned to regard him with curiosity lifting her brow. "It doesn't seem like you need to cover your face. Is it part of your cultural expression to do so?"

She remained Zaska's minion, which meant that anything he told her could be relayed to her master. It was even possible that the room itself was bugged. He tapped his wrist com, activating a scanning program within his ocular implants, then swept the room with a glance, seeing nothing but the electronic signatures he'd expect for basic climate control functions.

He strode to the next room in the suite, noting the bed with a surge of his blood and the instant stiffening of his shaft as he thought of Molly splayed out on it, her body bare, and her arms held out in invitation towards him.

He struggled to focus his attention on the walls and furnishings, completing his scan without spotting anything of note before he turned back to Molly. She watched him with a curious expression and a slight smile.

"Electronic scanner?" she asked with a rueful tone. "It really lights up your eyes."

He smirked, returning to stand in front of her. "I'd rather not be recorded... this time."

Her smile widened into a grin as she lifted a hand to stroke it over his chest, her palm warm even through the fabric of his robe. "Why didn't you use it before?"

"I wasn't exactly thinking straight," he admitted, though he still felt chagrin at that. The sexual stimulant had made him reckless.

Molly nodded slowly, her smile fading as she glanced around. "This room had better be clean of bugs or cameras. Zaska pays well to keep it so."

His pleasure at having her touching him dimmed at the mention of that creature, but it didn't fully abate as her hand trailed lower, her gaze sweeping downwards to note the bulge of his erection.

He caught her wrist as she moved to rub her hand over that hard ridge. "You asked me a question, Molly, and I'd like to answer before I get distracted, because it's part of that explanation I wanted to give you."

Her eyes lifted to meet his. "Explanation?"

He wondered if she'd already forgotten what she'd said to him. Perhaps her message had simply been part of a script. Something to please him as part of a role she played for Zaska.

He also wondered if he would ever learn to trust a woman again after Ninhursag.

SIXTEEN

Molly noted the sharpening of Shulgi's gaze at her questioning tone and detected suspicion in his body language as he backed away from her, releasing her wrist. A slight frown touched his shapely lips.

She tried to recall exactly what they'd been talking about, though she'd been so distracted by Shulgi that she'd been hard-pressed to maintain her more professional demeanor. She'd wondered if she'd find him as fascinating this time as she had the other times she'd seen him, and now understood that he was even more so to her. Even just standing in his presence made her stomach flutter with anticipation. She had to concentrate to avoid touching him the way she desperately wanted to. His scent drew her closer to him and she had to fight the urge to press herself against him and inhale deeply until her head spun with it.

With his wings, and his pointed ears, and his inhuman coloring, she realized he looked like some fairytale prince from those tales that humans from Earth told. The fact that he was also handsome beyond what she'd seen from any human male also added to that ethereal, almost magical appearance.

But it wasn't his looks that drew her to him so strongly. She'd serviced males even more physically appealing than him who had only left her cold and unaffected. It was the core of honor and justice and strength that she sensed within him that made her feel so drawn to him. That core that spoke to her own desire to make the galaxy better and help those who couldn't help themselves. The core that found cruelty offensive and sought to put an end to it.

He'd been honest about that part of himself from the very first moment they'd met, even when he could have benefited from playing Zaska's game of corruption and criminal intent by flattering the "boss" to his mouthpiece as so many of Zaska's clients and business associates did.

Now, he looked disappointed in her, and she struggled to figure out what she'd done as he regarded her with his slight frown, his brows drawing together. She felt panicky as she sensed him withdrawing from her in more than just the physical sense.

"You mentioned 'love' in your message, Molly." He tapped his wrist com. "Or was that only part of the act?"

She gasped, surprised by the sharp pain his bitter tone caused in her heart. "It wasn't an act, Shulgi," she said, unable to keep her hurt from her voice. "I *do* want love." She blinked rapidly as she spun to turn her back on him, her cloak billowing out around her before settling its weight against her body again. "I just know that such a desire is futile, given my position."

"Blighted silk," he muttered in what sounded like a self-directed curse. Then she felt his hands fall upon her shoulders.

As she stiffened, he slid them down the front of her body, barely grazing her breasts before dropping to her waist to pull her back into his strong chest. He nuzzled her hair, inhaling deeply. "I'm sorry, Molly. It's difficult for me to trust women. I can explain some of that, but such secrets are not shared easily."

He was holding her, and though there was definitely a sexual element to that embrace, it also felt like more. Something more intimate and caring than what she was used to. One of his hands lifted to unclip another of her hair ornaments, and she didn't protest when he tossed the thing to the floor.

She and the others had to save money somewhere to carry out their true mission, and they'd chosen to do it in their costuming. She'd never liked the heavy weight of so many ornaments in her hair, but it had been part of the look of a dyed flower, the design of which they'd taken inspiration for from their brothel work. As he freed her hair from its confining bun, she sighed in relief, her scalp tingling when his fingers delved into the waves of it.

"I care about you, Shulgi," she whispered, acknowledging something she shouldn't.

She'd been hurt before after confessing to feelings a woman in her position was not supposed to have.

He kissed the top of her head, returning his hand to her waist to hold her close again. "I care about you too, Molly."

She turned in his arms to face him, looking up into his eyes. She didn't see a lie there, but she didn't dare to believe he could really mean it. Her heart pounded with hope and anxiety mixed, fearing that he would crush her fledgling emotions with the harsh reality of his true intention just to use her.

"Do you really?" She traced his lower lip with her finger, remembering how it had felt when he'd kissed her so passionately. "I've been told that before, only to find out it was a lie."

His eyes narrowed, his lips pulling into a scowl, making his beautiful features look fierce and dangerous. "Who played with your emotions? Give me a name and I will punish them for it."

Alarmed at the intensity in his tone, fearing he was deadly serious, she shook her head quickly. "It was a long time ago, and that part of my life is over." She cocked her head, regarding him thoughtfully as his expression slowly lightened, though his arms tightened around her, pulling her closer against his hard chest. "Shulgi, I know you're honorable—"

Her words were cut off by a startled gasp when he stiffened and stepped away from her. She stared at him in confusion, noting that he'd bowed his head and had half turned so he no longer faced her.

"I'm *not* honorable, Molly," he growled in a harsh tone. "I've done terrible, unforgivable things."

Her heart in her throat, she touched his arm, saddened that he only shifted further away from her. "Tell me. I have a feeling they would not be unforgivable to me. I've seen so much...."

She'd *done* so much. So much that still gave her horrid nightmares. So much blood that had been spilled that it made her sick. So much that, sometimes, even the reasons for her actions didn't seem like enough justification.

He lifted his head, but not to look at her. Instead, he stared at the wall of the entry room with a distant gaze. "I have already admitted more to you than I intended."

Her shoulders sagged and she lowered her hand from his arm, dropping it back to her side. "Of course," she said in a dull voice, "I am here only to serve, honored Irid—"

A startled yelp cut off her words as he suddenly grabbed her by her arms, lowering his head until his lips hovered above hers. "Don't *say* it!" His features were pulled into an angry scowl. "Don't talk to me as if I'm just like all the rest who have used you, Molly. You mean far more to me than that! Far more than I have any right to feel for you!"

Beneath the anger in his tone, she detected the torment.

She wasn't afraid that he would hurt her. She felt sad that he was hurting himself. Something inside him was tearing him up.

Lifting shaking fingers to stroke his cheek, she met his eyes, her own damp. "Tell me. I won't judge you."

He released her, lifting his head. "Everyone judges. Anyone who promises otherwise is lying."

Stepping away from her until they were at arm's length, he squared his shoulders, meeting her eyes with a hard gaze that she now understood was defensive. He was shielding himself, putting on a mask so he wouldn't be vulnerable to any more pain.

She understood that defensive behavior perfectly. "Very well," she bowed her head briefly, "I will be completely honest. Without knowing what you've done, I can't promise I won't judge your past actions." She met his eyes again. "But I *know* you aren't a bad person, Shulgi. I knew that from the moment I met you!"

"I murdered several of my own squad mates in cold blood," he said in a brittle, cold voice, his face an expressionless mask. "I participated in the torture of helpless prisoners, in kidnappings, and in more murder attempts." He lifted a hand to point to his chest. "I am a *monster*, Molly. Nothing will change that."

Her mouth gaped open, but she quickly gained control of her expression. She slowly shook her head. "I don't believe it was in cold blood," she whispered, unable to equate his confessions with the person she knew him to be. She felt his goodness in her blood and bones. She was certain of it. "I don't believe you had no reason for what you did."

"Does a reason matter, Molly?" he demanded in a tormented tone. "There are some actions that can't be forgiven, no matter the cause!"

She flinched at his brutal words. "If that is so," she said slowly, "then I, too, am a monster."

He shook his head sharply, closing the distance he'd put between them to pull her against him in a hard embrace. "No!" He lowered his lips to press against her hair, his hands sliding under her cloak to stroke her back, warm against the thin silk of her dress. "You have no choice in what you do. You are a slave, forced to obey a master who is a monster."

"And if I had a choice," she asked sadly, knowing now that she could never confess her truth to him, given how much he despised himself for what he'd done. Actions that were not much different from the ones she'd committed in pursuit of freeing slaves. "Would that make me a monster, if I'd done those things for a good reason?"

"A slave doesn't *have* a choice, Molly." His insistent tone shifted to something she couldn't interpret in the middle of that statement as he slowly released her, remaining close to her.

She stroked her palms over the high-quality silk of his robe, far more valuable and expensive than that of her own dress. His body was warm beneath the smooth fabric, his muscles large and firm. They flexed beneath her touch and even in her heartbreak over knowing she could never be fully honest with him, her mouth watered with her desire to taste him.

"Sometimes, you have to do terrible things for the greater good, Shulgi," she said, in a tone she hoped would convince herself as much as him.

He captured her wrists, sliding his hands down them to capture hers and entwine their fingers. "My people use that excuse all the time. They justify the most heinous of crimes because they insist they're trying to save our people. If we become monsters simply to save our species, do we deserve to be saved?"

She laid her cheek against his chest, listening to his heartbeat. "I don't believe you're a monster, Shulgi. And I do believe you're worth saving."

Releasing one of her hands, he lifted his to cradle the back of her head, holding her against his chest as his heartbeat thudded louder and faster in her ear. "Let me tell you a story. One I have not told anyone else in full. Then you tell me if you still think I'm not a monster."

SEVENTEEN

Molly tightened her arms around his strong waist, reveling in the feeling of his body pressed against her own. To her disappointment, he released her far too quickly, and without giving her one of his heady kisses as she'd hoped he would.

She looked up into his face, noting that his expression remained severe, his brows still together and lowered over eyes shadowed by a past he despised himself for. She sighed heavily, allowing him to step away from her without protest. He paced around the room, his agitation obvious. His wings flicked, fluttered, then folded repeatedly as if he struggled to settle himself.

He lifted a hand to run it through his hair, ruffling the silky, verdant length of it. "You said you wanted love, Molly, and I would give it to you if I could. Spinner!" He paused in his pacing to face her. "I *wish* it had been you! I think how much different my life would have been had I imprinted on you, sweet Molly."

She clenched her hands in front of her, twisting her fingers together. Her heart pounded in her chest as her stomach knotted with concern over what he would say next. She had a terrible feeling she already knew what it would be.

He already had a mate. A wife, a lover, something. They always did.

She could handle what he'd confessed to in his past, because she knew there was more to the story, and the fact that it was all tearing him up inside meant he had regrets no monster would suffer. What she couldn't handle was learning that another woman loved him and waited patiently for him to return while he'd used Molly's body for his own entertainment.

"What is her name?" she asked bleakly. "Is she... is she beautiful, like you?"

When he didn't immediately deny the conclusion she'd drawn, her heart sank until it felt like it pooled in a liquid mush in her toes. She struggled to remain standing since her knees felt too weak to support her.

"She was a goddess, Molly." He turned his back to her, his wings spreading wide, then folding tightly against his back. "A golden beauty beyond anything I'd ever seen before."

She felt grateful that he couldn't see her expression, but she still turned her head away from him, unwilling to look at his beautiful form without feeling deep regret that she'd allowed herself to grow so attached so quickly.

"She was also the greatest monster this galaxy has seen in my lifetime," Shulgi said in a harsh tone. Proof, if one ever needed it, that the outer appearance of someone is no way to judge them."

Molly gasped, looking up in surprise to meet his gaze as he turned back around to face her. "She... was?"

His expression hardened into something cold and angry. "Her demise wasn't my doing, but I like to think I had some hand in it."

"But... you loved her?"

He shook his head. "I was imprinted on her. That is the only version of romantic love Iriduan males understand. We are bound by our own biology, trapped into a sort of enslavement to the female whose scent causes us to imprint. We can't resist her after that, nor can we deny her anything she might want. We must obey. Over time, we don't even want to resist. All we want is to make our queen happy."

"That sounds horrible!" Molly's eyes welled as she thought about what it would be like to imprint on someone terrible. Someone like Sha Zaska would be if he existed.

Shulgi's gaze remained remote and cold. "It gets worse. We cannot be away from our queen for long without exposure to her pheromones. If we are deprived of them, we will slowly and painfully die. This aspect of our biology is used to control us—and to punish us."

Molly's brow furrowed even as her heart ached for Shulgi. "So, you said she had died, but," she gestured weakly to him, "you seem healthy."

"I am cured of the affliction. I won't imprint on another female."

"You mean you can't ever love me," she said sadly, nodding with understanding, though her heart hurt. "I can see how such a thing would be an issue. Now I understand what you meant in your message."

He stalked to her, catching her arms as she made to turn away. One hand lifted her chin so she had to look up into his face. The coldness of his expression had softened.

"I am not in a position to be what you need me to be, Molly. But I think I am more than capable of loving you."

His lips lowered to hers and he kissed her hungrily. Molly returned his kiss, her cheeks damp with tears she'd tried not to shed. If this was all they could have, then it was probably for the best.

She wasn't in a position to love him either.

He pulled away before she felt even close to sated, lifting his head to give her a rueful smile. "I promised you a story. I have told you only a fraction of it."

She brushed his hair away from his strong jawline with her fingertips. "I can't say I didn't enjoy the distraction." She smiled, knowing it didn't reach her eyes, but making the effort anyway. "Though I can see you need to tell me the rest."

"I don't expect you to be my confessional," he said as he released her and took a step back.

He inhaled deeply, his eyes closing for a long moment as he ran a hand through his hair. He slid his palm back to the nape of his neck, gathering his hair up to pull it over his shoulder. His wings practically vibrated with his distress.

Her tentative smile widened. "You'd be surprised how often I serve that purpose."

He opened his eyes and stared intently at her, a scowl forming on his face. "You deserve better than this life."

Molly shrugged one shoulder, a warning prickle crawling up her spine. She had to stop tempting him to save her from a life she couldn't leave. Not yet. "I actually enjoy talking to people—and listening. I want to hear the rest of *your* story especially, Shulgi. I enjoy talking to you the most."

His expression looked shuttered at her words, rather than reassured. "I will tell you the rest of my story, but I need you to promise me something first."

His tone sounded distant, and Molly worried that again, she'd said something to make him distrust her motives. "You can tell me anything!"

She stepped closer to him, but he backed away, holding a hand up to stop her. "I need to focus, and the closer you get, the harder it is for me to think."

Though his words flattered her, his tone worried her even

more. He was withdrawing from her in more ways than his physical position.

"What I tell you, you must never reveal to anyone. Especially not Sha Zaska or his minions."

"Agreed," she said immediately.

His eyes held suspicion, and she wished she could tell him the truth about her, about Zaska, about everything. Instead, she held a hand to her chest, meeting his gaze with her own, putting all her sincerity behind her next words.

"I will keep any secret you tell me to the end of my days and beyond, Shulgi," she said in the most solemn voice she'd ever used. "I vow this to you. I may be Zaska's slave, but I know how to keep my own secrets from him and all who serve him."

"I want to believe you," he murmured. "I know it's reckless to tell you these things, but even so, I've already told you too much." He started pacing again. "I suppose it won't make a lot of difference if I tell you the rest."

She wished she could comfort him by holding him in her arms while he told his story but could see that he needed to remain in motion given his agitation. Despite the reasons for that motion, his movements seemed to grow more fluid as he stalked back and forth, his wings finally settling as his shoulders squared.

"Tell me, Shulgi," she said in an encouraging tone, moving to the chair nearby to sink into it.

He nodded sharply at her, his pupils slightly dilated now. "I was part of a specialized combat unit in the imperial military. We were sent on a mission to break up a rebel cell and assassinate its leader. We'd successfully completed many such missions in the past. We worked well together, the members of our team so close that, sometimes, it was like we had a single mind."

He turned his back on her again, pausing his pacing to

stand completely still as his fists clenched. He was silent for so long, Molly wondered if he'd speak again or if she needed to encourage him.

When he finally did continue, it was only after he'd lowered his head, his voice coming out ragged and filled with grief. "We didn't have enough intel about what we faced. We went in expecting ragtag rebels and instead found a queen's harem of highly trained Iriduan soldiers. She sent them against us without a single concern for their safety, sacrificing some of them so she could add our team to her numbers."

"I'm so sorry, Shulgi," she said softly, her heart breaking for him. "The queen, was she...."

He began pacing again, glancing her way only briefly before focusing on the walls of the room as if he didn't want to meet her eyes. "She was no ordinary Iriduan female. I'm not even sure Command knew what she truly was. I like to believe they didn't. I don't want to think they sent us against someone like her with no knowledge of what we were facing."

"What was so special about her?" Molly tried to keep the spark of jealousy she felt out of her tone. He'd already said this woman had been a "goddess" and stunningly beautiful.

He slowly shook his head. "I cannot get into details about her true nature, but she had abilities we weren't prepared to counter at that time. Not only did she disable our infiltration team, but she somehow managed to remove our locked helmets without the explosives detonating."

Molly lifted a hand, the gesture causing him to pause and glance her way. "Wait a minute. What do you mean about the helmets?"

Shulgi's eyes looked haunted from this tale he told. "The helmets and masks of combat soldiers are biometrically locked during battle. If anyone tries to remove them other than the soldiers wearing them, or our medics or commanders, they will detonate, blowing the soldier's head off as well as causing extensive damage to anyone close to him."

Molly's mouth gaped as she shot to her feet. "The empire kills their own soldiers if someone tries to remove their helmets? That's *monstrous!*"

Shulgi shrugged. "They won't explode if someone fiddles with them, or even tries to pry them off manually. The only way they detonate is if the seals are broken and we end up exposed to unfiltered external air."

He regarded her outraged expression and it seemed to amuse him enough that the tight line of his lips softened into a slight smile. "Soldiers are expensive to train, and the empire values them as much as they value any life they control. We are not sacrificed on a whim—or without good reason." His smile disappeared. "The precautions are necessary. In fact, my own fall to the affliction only proved how necessary it is. If *she* hadn't possessed the powers that she did, I doubt she would have been able to afflict us and send us back to our ship to expose the remaining members of our team."

Here, his head bowed, his fists clenching again. "She ordered us to kill anyone on our ship who didn't imprint on her scent."

"I knew there was a reason," Molly said with sympathy.

In her Galactanet research on the Iriduans, Molly had read of the imprinting "theory", but it had seemed like one of the less believable theories posed, given how odd it was that a male would become completely subservient to the elusive and very rarely seen female Iriduans. In fact, the empire kept female Iriduans cloistered—many against their will, according to some 'net sources—which made it seem unlikely that females would have so much power in their society.

Shulgi shook his head. "Don't absolve me of what I've done, Molly. The imprinting was powerful, but I could have found some way to resist her influence long enough to warn my team-mates before we exposed them." His jaw ticked as his gaze went distant. "The fascination, the feeling of being enrap-tured... we didn't want to lose that. It was as heady as the combat stimulants in our blood. We were selfishly willing to do whatever it took to keep feeling that way."

Despite his evident agitation, Molly went to him. He didn't push her away, and this time, he didn't keep her from drawing close enough to wrap her arms around his waist. "You told me a slave doesn't have a choice, Shulgi. This 'imprinting' sounds like it enslaves Iriduan males." She propped her chin on his chest, looking up into his tormented gaze. "At the very least, it sounds like you weren't in your right mind after imprinting."

She hugged him tighter and after several long, breathless moments, his arms wrapped around her shoulders.

"You are too good to me." His hands stroked down her back.

The thickness of the material of her cloak kept her from feeling the warmth of his touch, and Molly lifted a hand to unhook it at her neck. It loosened, dropping from her shoulders to flap over his arms.

He impatiently tugged it off her as she looked up at his face, noting that his pupils had dilated further. As he pulled her tighter against him, she felt the firm ridge of his erection against her belly, and her core heated with excitement and anticipation.

She met his lips eagerly when he lowered his head to claim hers.

EIGHTEEN

Shulgi tasted amazing to Molly as his tongue delved into her mouth. Just as amazing as he smelled. Her hands slid from his waist up his chest to span the width of it. The twitching of his hard, bulging muscles beneath her palms thrilled her. She wanted him naked, suddenly viewing the beautiful robe he wore with a special kind of hatred that it kept the sight of his gorgeous body from her view.

Her fingers found the front seam of the robe just as Shulgi lifted one hand to the neck of it. She helped him jerk it open, sliding her hands beneath the fabric to stroke along his warm skin as he continued to shrug it off his shoulders and over his wings.

He broke their kiss to look down at her dress with a predatory gleam in his nearly black eyes.

"You're wearing pants," she accused in a teasing tone as her fingers trailed down his ripped abdominals and encountered the waistband of loose trousers.

"And you're still wearing your dress," he growled, his

fingers sliding beneath the straps on her shoulders, pulling them down so the top of the dress sagged open, revealing her pert breasts, dyed purple and marked with green coiled tentacles.

She laughed huskily, then moaned as he cupped one breast in his hand, his palm warm and callused against her sensitive skin as he trailed his thumb over her stiffened nipple. She leaned against him to pepper kisses over the wide span of his muscular chest, teasingly licking him between each brush of her lips.

As he toyed with her nipple, his other hand undid the catches on the back of her dress. "I didn't bring you here for this, Molly," he said in a voice that rasped with his desire.

She chuckled, slipping one of her hands beneath the waistband of his trousers. He groaned when her fingers stroked along the rigid length of his erection, then curled around its girth. "Maybe I brought *you* here for this, Shulgi."

"I've never wanted to be used more than I do now," he said in a strangled tone as she began to stroke his shaft, her other hand pulling the waistband of his trousers off his hips then pushing them down his thighs.

She kissed one of his pecs, then glanced up into his handsome face, noting the stark desire in his expression. "I really do care about you, Shulgi. I want to be with you." She paused in her strokes over his stiff flesh. "You make me feel good, just being in your company."

"Don't stop," he protested, the hand that wasn't on her breast lowering to grip her wrist and urge her to keep stroking him. "You definitely make me feel good too."

She smiled, then kissed a path down his chest and abdominals. His fingers dived into her hair as her hot breath sighed over his throbbing shaft. She licked the tip of it, tasting the salty flavor of his precum that welled from it. Then she closed her lips around it and sucked him deep, keeping her hand curled around his thick girth below her lips.

"Molly, you don't have to—Grand Spinner!" His tone turned guttural as his fingers tightened in her hair.

She lifted her mouth from his length just long enough to respond. "I want to do this," she insisted, then proved it by returning her mouth to him.

The wet sounds of her sucking his shaft were broken by his low, deep moans and the humming sound of his wings whirring behind him. The clawed appendages at the base of his spine had unfurled and the pointed tips dragged along the skin of her arm. They vibrated, the segmented, chitinous shafts slightly rattling with the shivering motion.

As she sucked, she used her free hand to push his trousers all the way down his powerful legs until they pooled over the expensive boots he wore. Then she traced the lines of his thigh muscles with curious fingers, reveling in the taste of his arousal and his hard flesh between her lips.

She was so turned on by this time that her panties were soaked by her slick. She didn't always wear them when meeting clients, but this time, she'd done so, uncertain exactly what would happen with Shulgi. She wasn't likely to be wearing them long. Her core ached for him to fill it, but she was also enjoying having him in her mouth. She loved the way it made him moan.

"Molly," he said in a rough voice, "you have to stop now. I don't want to climax yet."

He punctuated this plea with his fingers tightening further in her hair, gently but firmly pulling her away from him.

She gave him a last lick before relenting and rising to her feet to smile up at him seductively. He growled in response and bent to gather her into his arms, sweeping her off her feet to carry her into the other room.

He laid her gently on the bed, then tugged at the fabric of her dress impatiently until he'd pulled it over her arms, then dragged it down past her waist.

She stared up at him with all the desire she felt, hoping that the stronger emotions building inside her for him didn't also show so obviously in her hungry expression. When he met her eyes as he pulled the dress off her legs, she saw a reflection of her own hunger. Perhaps there was more there, but she didn't dare to hope too much.

He'd told her he couldn't be what she needed. Nor could she be the mate he needed. The one who could make him forget that evil bitch who'd forced him to imprint upon her and kill his teammates. She regretted that they couldn't be together, but she would make the most of whatever time she had with him. She wouldn't dwell on regret.

As he lowered his head to claim her nipple with his lips, she delved her hands into his thick hair, entranced by the silkiness of it as it slipped through her fingers. Then she traced the lengths of his ears as she moaned from the feeling of his lips tugging on her sensitive nipple. She felt each hungry pull like it was happening much lower. Her hips bucked upwards against his naked belly as his weight pressed her into the mattress.

One of his hands cupped and toyed with her other breast as he suckled her nipple. His free hand trailed down her trembling belly to the waist of her panties. He hooked the material on his fingers and pulled it down, exposing her mound.

She cried out with pleasure when his fingers trailed through her folds to brush against her clit. His lips smiled against her throbbing nipple and then he released it to kiss a path down her body. Molly sighed in pleasure as he settled between her legs, parting her knees further, his dark gaze fixed on her core.

She moaned as his head dipped and his tongue darted out

to lick along her seam, teasingly stroking over her clit. His fingers probed her soaking entrance, while his other hand pulled her panties down her thighs, then removed them completely. He tossed them aside as he licked her with long strokes over her tender nub. Her hips bucked when two of his fingers sank into her wet and eager slit.

With his tongue and his mouth, he brought her to a shivering climax that had her crying out in ecstasy. Then he rose to his feet, towering over the bed like a conquering warrior. He stood between her parted thighs, looked down at her with an intense gaze, his eyes now completely black. At his groin, his shaft jutted long and thick, the tip weeping with his precum. His clawed appendages writhed at his sides as his wings spread behind him.

"Take me, Shulgi," Molly said in a voice husky with her desire, running her hands up her naked body to cup her breasts. "I want you so badly. Don't make me wait any longer."

His eyes never leaving hers, he lowered his body until he had braced his hands on either side of hers, then crawled his way towards her head, settling his hips between her legs.

She moaned as his shaft probed her entrance, then slowly penetrated her, filling her deliciously. His verdant hair framed a face stark with desire as his dilated eyes took in her expression of pleasure. She gasped in surprise as the claws on the tips of his appendages settled against her hips, then dug in enough to dent her skin without piercing it.

She had a feeling they might, if he grew too excited, but she was so aroused she didn't care. He felt so good inside her that she cried out for more. When he responded by ramming home with a single hard thrust and a low growl, she clutched his powerful shoulders, holding on tightly for the exciting ride she knew was coming.

Shulgi thrust inside her with slow strokes at first, and one of his appendages left her hip to tease over her clit as he braced his weight above her. The vibration of the tip, the barbs that covered it lying flat for the moment, caused her to body to tighten in anticipation of another orgasm.

Trembling with need and arousal, she rocked her hips upwards into each of his thrusts, his thick length burying deep inside her before drawing out of her in a slow, teasing rhythm.

"You're so beautiful, Molly," he said in a guttural voice, his black eyes staring intently down at her face.

She framed his face with her hands, pushing his hair away from the hard planes of his cheekbones. "So are you." She moaned as he shifted his hips to drag his shaft upwards against her g-spot.

Then he lowered his head to her lips as if he wanted to capture any other sounds from her. He claimed them hungrily as his thrusts sped up. She lifted her legs around his waist to lock her ankles behind him as his rhythm grew more intense and powerful, shoving her upwards on the mattress with each hard thrust.

She felt consumed by him as he chased his climax, his vibrating appendage now trapped between them on her clit as he lay more of his weight over her. That vibration brought them both to the edge, and Molly's orgasm was followed shortly by a handful of rapid thrusts from Shulgi before he climaxed inside her. Her inner muscles convulsed around his shaft, milking all his seed from it as he pumped his hips a few more times before he lifted his head to look down into her eyes.

His own were returning to their beautiful green, his dilated pupils constricting back to a normal size again. He licked lips swollen from her kisses.

"Cursed silk," he muttered, and it sounded like he spoke more to himself than her. "I'm sorry, Molly. I was once again incautious." He slowly shook his head as he drew his shaft from her body, pushing himself further away from her with a flex of hard, rippling arm and chest muscles.

"Y-you regret this?" She tried to keep the hurt from her tone but suspected some of it still came through.

He quickly leaned over her again to kiss her deeply. "No," he whispered against her lips, "never."

He rolled off her and sat beside her on the bed, stroking one hand over her naked body as she propped herself up on her elbows to watch him, her heart thudding in concern over his withdrawal.

"I do regret not taking precautions." He glanced at the crux of her legs as she pushed herself up onto her palms, feeling the gush of his seed soak her inner thighs. "I wasn't thinking. I should not put you at risk like that."

Her eyes widened, surprised by his concern. "Are you talking about coming inside me?"

He scowled, turning his head to stare at the wall rather than continue to meet her eyes. "I should have worn protection. This was reckless, and I know better. I even brought some, but...."

She placed a hand on his hard shoulder, massaging the firm flesh there in reassurance. "I am sterile, Shulgi. You could finish inside me a hundred times without fear that you would impregnate me."

He bowed his head, staring down at his fists that clenched in his lap. The muscles in his thick forearms flexed and she marveled at how hard and strong his entire body was.

"Did Sha Zaska do that to you?" he growled in a low, deadly voice.

"I was sterilized well before I ended up in his service." She released his shoulder and turned away, her back facing him. "It's for the best. I... I don't think I will ever be in a position to raise children."

"That should not have been anyone's choice but your own," he said in an angry tone as his arms came around her shoulders, his hands smoothing down her arms.

He pulled her back against his chest, gently caressing her naked skin. "No one had the right to take that future from you."

She leaned back into his strength, lifting a hand to bury it in his hair as she turned her head to kiss his neck. "If we were in a different position, I think I would want to have your children. But I'm not even certain that would be possible given our differences."

He kissed her lips, one hand cupping her cheek. "It would have been possible. My people are more closely related to your own than you might think." He traced her brows, his solemn gaze studying her face. "I wish you were my queen. Then I would have an excuse to abandon everything to be with you. I would feel no guilt, or sense of duty to anyone but you."

She smiled sadly at him. "You said imprinting was like being enslaved. I wouldn't want that for you. I wouldn't want that for us."

"I would gladly choose to devote my life to you, Molly. You make me feel... whole."

Molly felt the same way, but she wasn't sure it would be wise to say it, though her heart soared to hear it from him. This felt different from the other time when she'd been played. She didn't doubt Shulgi's sincerity for a moment. They had a connection, and he felt it too.

But neither of them could act on that connection. Neither of them could commit to the other.

NINETEEN

Shulgi wanted to spend more time with Molly. He wanted to spend the entire day cycle with her, to make love to her again and fall asleep with her safely in his arms. The last thing he wanted to do was watch her leave him, with her bodyguards flanking her as she returned to the monster that dared to call himself her master.

After a long, parting kiss, he had to say goodbye to her. They both had to return to their duties, and he'd already risked too much by making this time for her. After the last time he'd been with her, he'd passed out cold after the stimulants had worn off and had not awakened for several day cycles. As soon as he'd managed to crawl out of his bed, starving and shaken by how weakened he'd felt, he'd been swamped with work. They had a lot to prep for with the upcoming arrival of the weapon sample.

They needed new equipment for the lab in order to store and process the weapon, and procuring that was Shulgi's primary responsibility. Beyond that, he had all his regular duties, including running the actual business of Ma'Nah and making a myriad of decisions to keep them solvent despite the massive expenses their true mission incurred. He really shouldn't have left the dreg to spend time with Molly.

He knew what he had to do, and though it killed him to let Molly go, he didn't chase after her. Instead, he made use of the bathroom facilities and cleaned up, washing away all of Molly's scent. He also decontaminated the room and his clothing to make certain not a trace of it lingered that would raise questions and doubts in the dreg.

He had to return to Namerian and would tell him that Zaska's minions were helping him to smuggle in some of the more difficult equipment to find. Making those arrangements shouldn't be difficult. Zaska's minions were already eager to ship anything and everything Ma'Nah required. Dealing with them meant he had a better excuse to be with Molly.

After he finally left the inn and was making his way through the crowded streets of second-tier, he received a message he'd been waiting for. He immediately opened it, reading it quickly on his wrist com before changing his direction. Before he could report back to Namerian, he had to make a stop on fourth-tier to meet an information peddler whose services were difficult to procure, but he'd been told they were well worth the effort.

Fourth-tier, like every level below fifth in the column, was overcrowded and filled with the press of alien bodies. Not many Iriduans bothered with this level, but he spotted a few in the crowd. Like him, they only made eye contact briefly, quickly nodded acknowledgement, then looked away. He doubted they were from the dreg.

Za'Kluth did business with every species in the Syndicate— and some too weak and poor to have membership in it. It wasn't impossible to encounter unaffiliated Iriduans, even imperial Iriduans, making their way through the crowds, rare though that was. The imperial Iriduans tended to avoid worlds like this, as their allegiance put them at risk from rebels and outcastes eager for vengeance.

Thus, the lack of prolonged eye-contact and the careful avoidance of each other.

Business fronts thronged the streets, so crowded and chaotic that it was a wonder anyone could make their way through the pop-up market stalls and vendors and temporary structures where countless different species peddled their wares in loud calls and vivid and garish advertisements.

He'd been given a location and his wrist com assisted him in homing in on it. That location was the only information that had been passed in the message sent to him by some old contacts who'd switched sides from imperial to rebel.

This information peddler didn't do business with the Iriduan empire—perhaps because they knew too much about that government to trust them. Shulgi couldn't blame them. The empire had a bad habit of betraying those who aided it, and "disappearing" those who threatened it.

In fact, it was risky to even follow the directions to this location, as one of his contacts might have switched back to the imperial side or was even serving as a double agent. Capturing Shulgi would be quite a boon for the second emperor, who all sources said was now completely in control of the government —the Oprimo being overwhelmed by his affliction to his empress. It wouldn't be long before the Secundo unseated the Oprimo and took his place—or selected some other male to take that place if he couldn't bear the idea of finding an empress of his own.

Few males who could choose wanted to imprint if they didn't have to.

Shulgi would choose Molly, if he'd had a choice, but he knew that he'd likely never have met her if he hadn't imprinted on Ninhursag. In fact, he likely never would have mated at all if he hadn't been entrapped. He might never have even had a sexual experience, never being one for using sexual stimulants. Though it wasn't the sex he had with Molly that made him so eager to spend time with her, he certainly enjoyed it. It also felt right to him, in a way that being with Ninhursag had not.

Molly truly felt like she was his when he had her beneath him. She seemed engaged and eager, her eyes only for him. She seemed connected to him rather than detached and cold.

He could see how good a life with her as his mate could be. He didn't think she would ever take advantage of her influence over him. The empathy in her eyes as he'd told the sordid truth about his past, and the way she'd insisted that he was a good person despite all the terrible things he'd done made him want to believe in himself as much as she seemed to. He wanted to be the male she thought him to be.

Proving himself worthy of her started with this meeting with the information peddler. He couldn't keep Molly as his queen, but he could free her from Zaska and destroy that monster and everything he'd built up in the under-tier.

The location turned out to be a small curiosities shop tucked deep within a shadowed alleyway between two eateries. Given the out-of-the-way location and the dangerous neighborhood, he wasn't surprised the shop had no customers, despite the intriguing items on display from all over the galaxy.

His wings flicked as he scanned his surroundings constantly, feeling tense from the moment he'd entered the alley. If he'd had the time after receiving the message, he would have returned to Ma'Nah for his armor and weapons. He could usually find a way to dispatch his enemies without them, but it was much easier and less potentially painful when he used them.

Unfortunately, this meeting was an appointment. One the

information peddler would not wait around for, so Shulgi had to make the time. Besides, Namerian would ask questions if he'd returned to Ma'Nah solely to grab weapons and armor. He didn't want Namerian to discover that he planned on destroying their newest ally and the corrupt businesses he controlled that would allow Ma'Nah to smuggle in their needed supplies.

If he did this right, he could take over Zaska's infrastructure after wiping him and his most loyal minions out, and Ma'Nah could install their own leader to run things. Most lower-level minions didn't really concern themselves with who was running things, as long as they continued to get paid.

For now, all he needed was someone who could gain access to information he'd been unable to obtain on his own. Zaska's movements were a complete mystery, though his minions had been well tracked by his enemies. No one could get close enough to the monster himself to truly pinpoint his location in the under-vents. Nor could anyone determine the true size of his organization and holdings as he used a variety of front companies to hide his dealings from city bosses and his rivals alike. His visible minions and businesses concealed far more below the surface, just like they concealed the monster himself.

The door to the curiosity shop slid open as he approached, revealing an interior packed with overflowing shelves, like a barter market in the slummiest sector of the dreg. Shulgi entered with caution, his body tense in preparation for an ambush, his gaze scanning the dimly lit interior of the shop, seeking potential threats as well as assessing his options if combat ensued.

A bored olem stood behind the counter, two of his three eyes focused on a screen that was below the top of the counter out of Shulgi's sight. His third eye glowed as Shulgi approached him. He straightened to his full height, which was nearly as tall as Shulgi's.

"Don't get your kind in here often," the olem growled out, his snout twitching as he sniffed. His pointed ears flicked towards Shulgi as his upper set of hands settled on the top of the counter.

"I have an appointment." Shulgi stopped in front of the counter, boldly meeting the three eyes of the olem male in a show of dominance.

The olem bared his sharp teeth in a grin, then lowered two of his three eyes again. "Of course, honored Iriduan. You are welcome to my shop. Our mutual acquaintance will meet you in the back room." He turned and gestured to a sealed door behind the counter. "Please, come this way."

Shulgi rounded the counter, his muscles tense and ears pricked as he neared the olem. The species weren't usually foolish enough to attack without being certain they could win the fight, and he knew that he didn't look like an easy target, despite wearing only a robe instead of full body armor.

"Your mate fill these shelves?" he asked in a carefully neutral tone as his gaze scanned the other side of the counter, noting a spiked club he could grab to kill the olem if the other male got any foolish ideas in his head.

The olem snorted at the question. "Sister. Haven't hunted a mate yet." The olem waved an upper hand towards Shulgi's mask. "See you don't have a queen yourself."

Shulgi chuckled, though he thought longingly of Molly. "I don't need a queen to travel off world."

"More likely she'd keep you downside, eh," the olem said, narrowing his lower pair of eyes. "Unless you're a parlor pet."

Shulgi cocked his head, regarding the olem with suspicion. "You seem well informed about Iriduans for a ground-sider.

You sure you don't have a mate? Surely your sister doesn't link with you."

The olem snuffled with open laughter. "I can see I've given offense, since you are quick to return it. It would seem we both know far more about each other's kind than either of us are comfortable with." He gestured again to the door, and it slid open as they both neared it.

"Please, wait within. Your contact will meet you there." He held up both lower hands, showing they were empty of any weapons or threats. "I mean you no ill will. I'm a professional, ground-sider though I be. Besides, I know how deadly the Iriduan soldiers can be. Even if they no longer serve their emperors." He grinned again, pointedly lowering his bottom pair of eyes in submission. The spines on his back flattened and his head hunched until it hung much lower than Shulgi's.

Shulgi acknowledged the gesture with a sharp nod then entered the interior of the backroom, quickly scanning it for alternative entrances and potential weapons. His wings flicked as he turned to regard the olem. The door slid shut between them, sealing him into a room with no other visible exits.

Still, it was a storage room, not a cell. A simple access panel for the door existed on this side of it, and Shulgi had broken through the like more than once in the past. He wasn't overly concerned yet. He was disappointed to see that the room stood empty save for more junk packed into crates, boxes, and barrels stacked against every wall of the small space.

He regarded the crates next to the door thoughtfully, patient enough to wait for the moment, though his senses prickled with unease that hadn't left him since he'd received the message of this meeting.

"I've heard the lamuchin statuettes are very popular with olemites," a lilting voice said from behind him.

Shulgi spun around, snatching up one of the small statuettes as he turned. He froze in mid-swing, the statuette just above his head, though not by his choice.

The female standing before him was slender, almost sylph-like. That wasn't what made her so startling—and terrifying.

She had a hand up in front of her, her palm turned towards him. He knew without asking that she froze him in place with her mind alone.

He also knew without asking that this female could disintegrate him with a thought.

"You're a Lusian?" he said with a grunt, still tensing to pull his arm out of her telekinetic grip. "A *female?*"

Her large black eyes slowly blinked as she lowered her hand, holding it out to him, palm upwards, three long fingers splayed open. Waves of silvery hair a shade lighter than her light gray skin covered a head that seemed smaller than Roz and his crew's had been, though it still retained the general and distinctive shape and features of a Lusian. Her lips were thin, her nose nearly flat with two small nostrils, her eyes as large and unnerving as any Lusian's were. Her slender body had slight curves in breast and hip. Noticeable but not overtly obvious, even in a skintight silver jumpsuit.

Without meaning to, he handed her the statuette, and her fingers curled around it. She lifted it to regard the carven image with the expressionless face of her kind, though one far more delicate and feminine than he'd ever seen before.

"I am an aberration." She glanced up at him. "You've met others." Her eyes narrowed slightly, and he realized she was probing his mind as he felt a slight internal tug on memories he'd buried deep.

He shook his head with a sharp jerk, forming the image of a wall inside his mind that caused her to frown in irritation. "I might have. I assume you've met a mate that made you this way."

"Your assumption is incorrect." She cocked her head. "Though it does explain something about the other aberrations. How curious."

"I came here to meet an information peddler. Should I assume that is you, or would that also be incorrect?"

He didn't bother to ask how she'd entered the room without passing through the door, now that he understood what species she was. He'd learned more than he'd ever wanted to know about them when he'd spent time on Roz's ship with his bizarre crew. Teleportation was easy for them.

"*That* assumption would be correct," she said with a small smile that seemed almost out of place on such an enigmatic visage. "Your case intrigues me. As does your connection with a rival cohort. A rogue operation, no less."

"I have no idea what you're talking about," Shulgi said through gritted teeth, bolstering his mental walls.

She lifted her free hand, gesturing in a smooth motion. He felt suddenly calm and relaxed, though he had enough sense to retain his mind shield. "There is no need for aggression. My kind engage in rivalries in a far different manner from your own. I suppose my own position puts me at odds with all other affiliated cohorts. I have more in common with your rogues than with the Progenitors' Council."

"I truly don't understand." He felt more sanguine and knew that was a direct result of her power over him, which conversely caused combat stimulants to release into his bloodstream.

She chuckled, showing even more animation in her features than Roz had. "The circumstances behind my transformation are different from the others you've known, but they have made me no less of an outcast of my species. Perhaps even more of one, as I am certain my existence would be extinguished were I to grow careless enough to allow any of my kind still affiliated to find me."

She lowered her empty hand, then set the statuette on the top of a crate standing next to her. "I have no interest in making enemies of your... allies. I am merely curious. Curiosity *is* my driving purpose, and the result is the product that I offer you—information that you can't find anywhere else."

Shulgi felt a spark of hope and anticipation. If anyone could find the illusive Sha Zaska, it would be a Lusian.

"Would you like to know my rates?" the female asked, her unblinking eyes fixed on him.

"I need this information," he said abruptly, "but I have limits to what I will pay for it." He did not wish to seem too eager so that she felt she had the upper hand in the bargaining. He kept the fact that he would pay anything to save Molly out of his head with effort.

"You ask for very privileged information. Information others have requested prior to you." The female glanced around the room as if searching for something. "There are those who would pay a small fortune to locate the one you seek."

"I haven't given you a name yet."

She smirked, meeting his eyes again. "As if I needed you to speak it aloud." She tapped her temple with one long finger. "I hear you shouting his name in rage repeatedly in your head. I know not only his name, but your reason for seeking his location." She studied him thoughtfully, tapping her pointed chin. "Your bloodlust is strong, but I sense something far stronger behind it."

"Just tell me what it will cost me to find the off-breed," he snarled, the false calm she'd sent to his mind dissipating. "What I will do to him when I find him is well deserved."

"Za'Kluth is a dangerous world," she said, her tone taking on a sharpness that he recognized as all business.

"For a Lusian?" he scoffed.

She grinned, revealing straight, white teeth, lacking the sharpened eyeteeth of Roz and his crew of males. "I am not invincible. Besides, I work through other sources less... *gifted* than myself. It would not be wise to risk revealing my presence to some of my kind."

"Name your price...." He raised his brows at her in question.

"My name is Luna." She lifted her chin, eyeing him with a hesitance in her expression that surprised him.

"Very well, Luna."

He knew from Roz that the Lusians did not generally have names. Only titles like Director, Associate, and Drone. He suspected there were more titles, but those were the only ones he'd been exposed to during his time on Roz's ship. Luna likely chose the name in defiance of her cohort, rather than being granted it by a mate, like Roz had received his.

She regarded him in silence for a long moment, though he still felt the prickling in his thoughts that told him she was trying to read them. He hoped the shields he'd raised were good enough to conceal the things he didn't want her learning. He made a conscious effort not to think of what those things were.

Finally, she seemed to give up, though he didn't let his guard down. She turned her penetrating gaze away from him, scanning the storage room as if it held objects of great interest to her. "My rates are high, and—as you must have been informed—I am selective about who I will work with." Her gaze shifted back towards him. "Iriduans generally do not make the list."

"And yet it was an Iriduan contact who set up this meeting." Shulgi crossed his arms over his chest, studying the delicate features of the shorter Lusian.

The fact that she was smaller than Roz and his crew made

THE IRIDUAN'S MATE 189

Shulgi curious about her status prior to her transformation. In fact, she had the petite stature of an Associate or even a Drone rather than a much taller and more imposing Director. Yet, neither of those classifications possessed the degree of power she seemed to have.

She smirked again. "I sometimes make exceptions for Iriduan rebels. Anything to bedevil the empire."

"You plan on making an exception for me?"

She met his eyes again, her gaze as uncomfortable as before. Lusian eyes were the hardest to meet, and for some, the most frightening to see. He had more fortitude than the average Iriduan, but he still found them unnerving.

"As I said, your case intrigues me. Until I met you here, I wasn't certain why you had so much interest in Sha Zaska." She cocked her head. "My rates *would* be as high as always." She smiled broadly, a startling expression on a Lusian. "Perhaps even higher. Your species is known for having access to plenty of wealth."

"You still haven't given me a number." He tried not to allow his impatience to show through, but he was eager to get this meeting over with.

He had to return to Namerian and give him an update on the status of the equipment he needed to procure. He felt torn between his duty and his desire to help Molly.

"My price has changed now that I've learned more about you," she said in a thoughtful tone. "I need something more important than credits to me."

Shulgi braced himself for news he suspected he wouldn't like. "And what would that be?"

She broke eye contact again, turning away from him. "I need protection. The protection of a cohort." She glanced over her slim shoulder at him, her silver hair framing her high cheekbone, her black eye gleaming above it. "You happen to know of one that might accept an aberration such as myself into their crew."

"Connecting you with others doesn't seem like a high price," he said suspiciously, unwilling to believe that a simple message to Roz would be all it took to get Sha Zaska's information.

She stared at the wall in front of her, hiding her expression from Shulgi. "It is not in our nature to mix cohorts. Convincing the other aberrations to accept one not of their kind will be a challenge."

"What of your own cohort? Did they expel you from their number because of...?"

She slowly shook her head. "That will be another hurdle. I cannot hide the truth from a director."

"I take it that truth will be a bad one?"

He wondered whether Roz would accept Luna into his cohort. He knew too little about the enigmatic Lusians to be certain, even though Roz himself had been remarkably friendly and helpful in comparison to the rest of their species. Yet always, Shulgi got the feeling that Roz worked towards his own ends and helped only when that assistance furthered those ends. Fortunately, he also suspected that Roz's ultimate goals were benevolent, given how much his aid had improved things for the people he'd helped.

She shrugged one shoulder. "It is. A terrible truth. One that would get me killed by most of my kind even if they could accept my... change." Her head tilted back, her hair falling to the middle of her back. "I had no choice," she said in a sad tone.

"I can contact the crew you're looking for," he said, "but I can't promise they'll accept you. I really need Zaska's location, so perhaps you can offer me an alternative price if things don't work out."

She glanced at him over her shoulder again. "Contact them.

Let them know that I murdered my cohort—and my director. If you can get them to hear me out, then I will have Zaska's location for you within a Standard week."

Shulgi's blood prickled with combat stimulants as he regarded the slender back of the Lusian. "And if they refuse to hear you out? If they decide to punish you for your crimes?"

"If that is their intent, then they won't find me," she said flatly. "I will contact you within two cycles. I expect you to have heard back from them by that time."

Before he could respond, she suddenly disappeared.

TWENTY

Molly smiled at the message on her wrist com, her mood instantly brightening when she saw who it was from.

I miss you already. I hope to see you again soon.

She looked up from the words flicking over the surface of her skin to study her face in the mirror.

The dyes that marked her as one of Zaska's "flowers" had been freshened and her violet skin looked vivid with the green markings coiling over it. Her makeup only enhanced the exotic appearance she made as Jenice helped her bind up her hair and decorate it with ornaments.

"Let me guess," Jenice said around the pins clamped between her lips, "another message from lover boy?"

Molly grinned. "That's such a strange way to refer to him. There's nothing 'boyish' about Shulgi."

Jenice stabbed some more pins into Molly's mass of hair before responding. "He certainly seems enamored with you," she mused, and Molly heard the warning in her tone.

Molly sighed heavily, pushing a stray curl off her cheek. "I think he actually does care about me."

"That's a dangerous situation, Mol." Jenice captured that curl and pinned it ruthlessly to the rest of Molly's updo.

"He would never hurt me."

Her friend met her eyes in the mirror. "You know that's not what I mean." She put in the last pin and patted Molly's hair gently to flatten any stray bumps. "Men who care can get in the way."

"Unless they join us, Jen."

Jenice raised her brows with a skeptical pursing of her lips. "You think he'll become one of us? Just like that? A boy scout like him?"

Molly slowly shook her head at Jenice. "I think he would do well in this business. He's not naïve, and he's also not afraid to get his hands dirty when he needs to. You underestimate him—and his experience."

She hadn't told anyone about the discussion she'd had with Shulgi about his bloody past. It wasn't her secret to share. Not even with her closest friends.

Jenice huffed, crossing her arms as she studied Molly's outfit with a critical eye. "I don't doubt he could put a hurt on some of Zaska's enemies. I just wonder if we can trust him to keep our secret—and not try to take over. He *is* an Iriduan after all. They're not known for playing well with others."

"That's a bigoted thing to say," Molly snapped, shooting to her feet to turn on Jenice. "I *know* you're better than that, Jen!"

Jenice sighed and ran both hands through her hair. "I'm sorry. You're right. I shouldn't have gotten ugly about this. I just... I'm afraid to trust anyone we don't already know we can count on, Mol. We've come so far, and our operation is expanding faster every day-cycle. We can't afford to take unnecessary risks at this stage." She regarded Molly with eyes darkened by empathy. "Especially the risk of letting someone new in on the secret."

Molly understood Jenice's concerns perfectly, though she still felt ire at her friend for the prejudiced statement about Shulgi's species. The Iriduan empire remained an immensely powerful player in the galaxy as one of the founding species of the Cosmic Syndicate, though their star had been waning rapidly in the Syndicate lately. Powerful entities gained a lot of enemies—and a lot of bad press.

The same thing was happening on a much smaller scale with Sha Zaska. The more powerful their gang grew, the more enemies they obtained that watched from the shadows, coveting the newfound wealth of an under-tier thug and resenting that such a creature could rise through the ranks of the column so quickly.

"I haven't told him anything that would make him suspect Zaska's true nature," Molly reassured.

"But you want to." Jenice sighed heavily, then gestured to Molly's dress. "That looks cheap and a little worn. We need to send a message to this mark. How about the brocade?"

"Of course, I want to tell him!" Molly stalked to the closet to punch in the request for the brocade gown on the panel that operated it. "I want to tell him everything. He cares about me. He makes me feel special—and loved."

"But does he actually love you? Enough to let you do what needs to be done?" Jenice watched her with a shadowed gaze. "What if this mark wants you in his bed tonight?" She jerked her chin at the brocade gown as the automatic hanger extended it from the closet. "What will your Shulgi think about other males getting between your legs on a regular basis?"

Molly swallowed through a lump in her throat, suddenly feeling reluctance to do her duty as Zaska's flower. A reluctance she hadn't felt since her first months at Uthagol's brothel, where she was brutally initiated into the business. She'd learned the hard way to cherish the gentleness of most of the clients, because it was heaven in comparison to Uthagol's people. She'd gotten over her squeamishness and disgust very quickly back then. The alternative was to die slowly and horribly.

Now, she felt that same initial repulsion for the idea of letting someone touch her body, unless that someone was Shulgi.

"Like you pointed out," she said instead of voicing her true thoughts, "he's an Iriduan. Their females keep harems of males. They're accustomed to sharing a woman in their culture."

Her friend straightened, an avid expression on her face. "So that's a true story then? I wasn't sure if that was just one of the many garbage theories floating around about them. It certainly sounded too good to be true." She shrugged one shoulder. "At least, from the woman's perspective."

Molly stripped off her dress carefully, trying not to dislodge any of her hair from its elaborate updo. She really wanted to rip the green gown into shreds, and then burn them, along with all the other garments in her closet that reminded her of the role she had to play. Instead of doing that, she tossed the gown onto the bed as soon as it was free of her arms, then unhooked the clasps on the heavy brocade emerald-green gown, which fortunately didn't have to go over her head.

Jenice snatched up the discarded gown, regarding it with distaste. "I think it's time to retire this one. We'll have to order some new clothing for you."

"What if...." Molly's breath failed her as she stood there with the brocade gown in her hands, ready to slip it on over her shoulders.

Jenice glanced up at her and noted Molly's expression. Her brows lifted, her lips parting to speak.

Molly rushed to finish her thought, not wanting Jenice to say anything that shut her down. "What if *I* retire? Then I won't be Zaska's mouthpiece anymore and I won't have to... I won't need to *perform* for the 'special' clients."

Jenice cocked her head, regarding Molly thoughtfully. "Is that what you really want? Or is it only because you hope to keep Shulgi around?" She sighed, her shoulders sagging as she bunched up the discarded gown. "Honey, I'm all for you retiring. You know how I feel about that! But if Shulgi can't respect you unless you give up your profession, he's not going to love you the way you deserve to be loved."

Molly lowered her gaze, staring at the smooth tile beneath her bare toes. "He's never said anything like that—that he doesn't respect me."

But she knew how many males felt about her and the other mouthpieces. They might not say it aloud, mostly because they didn't want to offend Sha Zaska, but they would be thinking it, and their thoughts would be obvious in their tone and body language.

"Mol, you're the best mouthpiece we have. You play the part perfectly. Briana is getting good at this, and the others are coming along well in their training, but right now, you are the one most of Zaska's clients prefer."

Molly had almost forgotten about that, so focused on her dread of having to follow through with tonight's mark, whom she'd been subtly seducing for weeks. He was a high-ranking official of the city bosses' administration and gaining his favor would cement Zaska's power in the lower tiers and expand their shipping operation as fees were "waived." This meeting was important, and Molly's savvy when it came to reading people and responding to their social cues in the proper way had allowed her to secure it.

Her skill didn't end at the bedroom door. She possessed a form of power that few of the males who interacted with her realized or appreciated, even as they fell under her spell. Not genetically gifted with great beauty, she'd enhanced what she had not only with makeup and dyes, but also with her grace and elegance, her soft voice and even softer gaze. She wielded her femininity like a weapon, or worked it like a well-crafted tool, to get what she wanted for their organization.

Though she hated to admit it aloud because it dashed her burgeoning dream of committing to a single male—one who actually cared about her, she *was* the best they had. She was one of the driving forces of Zaska's success.

Jenice seemed to note her expression and guess her thoughts. She took pity on Molly. "Why don't you think about things for a bit. Just get through dinner this evening with your usual charm and grace and use Zaska as an excuse to avoid anything too intimate with this mark."

"And our plan to gain blackmail footage?" They'd discussed the possibility of recording an encounter between her and the official if he didn't want to play along with their plans in any other way.

Jenice shrugged. "We'll consider an alternative if we have to." She approached Molly and put a hand on her shoulder. "I'm sorry, Mol. I shouldn't be so dismissive of how you feel about Shulgi—and this whole situation. You've done more than enough for us. You shouldn't have to do *that*."

Molly pulled the brocade over her shoulders and began clasping the frog closures down the front. "I will think of a way to put him off without fully discouraging him." She'd managed such a thing before, and she would manage it again.

Whether to share her bed or not had to be *her* choice now. Otherwise, she was still just a slave serving someone else.

TWENTY-ONE

The smuggler's market wasn't the safest place in the column, despite the excessive numbers of enforcement officers sent by the city bosses to patrol it. Shulgi kept an eye on their movements as he and young Alad made their way to the stall that provided a front for the procurer they had connected with in search of the equipment Namerian needed.

He wasn't the only one eyeing the enforcement patrols determined to collect the bosses' due from the market vendors. Every single stall had one or more thuggish guards who sized up the equally thuggish officers. Even the customers of the marketplace looked more than capable of holding their own in a fight. In this place, battles often broke out between rival factions, or between smugglers and city officials.

Shulgi hadn't wanted to bring Alad along on this expedition, knowing this marketplace well. He'd hoped that the minion of Zaska's he'd been in touch with could smuggle in the equipment in the under-tier, but it was rare enough that it would take several Standard months to receive it through those means. Instead, the helpful minion had connected him with a dealer in the smuggler's market on third-tier. Namerian had insisted that Alad accompany him, arguing that the youth needed to be hardened up in order to survive on this world. He'd claimed Shulgi was the best person to keep Alad safe while he learned about column 212 and all the dangers and iniquities of Za'Kluth.

Alad proved to be quicker on the uptake than Shulgi had feared. He remained close, and now kept his wings ready despite his obvious reluctance to have them brush other patrons in the press of the market crowds. Whatever training he'd been given hadn't prepared him for the chaos of the smuggler's market, so his blue eyes remained wide, his gaze darting nervously back and forth as it lighted upon aliens far larger and stronger than himself.

Yet he followed Shulgi's commands without question and jumped to obey him, and that was something Shulgi could appreciate, even if he found escorting civilians to be a tedious mission at the best of times.

This market was not in the best of times. A scuffle broke out after an ear-piercing shouting match between rival stall vendors. The press of bodies as some patrons moved away from the violence—and some moved eagerly towards it—pushed Shulgi and Alad backwards until the youth stumbled into a hulking thokost.

The antlered male stood a head taller than Shulgi, casting the young Alad in a long shadow as his lips pulled back in an enraged snarl that bared many sharp teeth. His rough, bark-like skin began to weep with toxin as he caught the front of Alad's robe in one meaty fist and jerked him off his feet.

Alad's wings fluttered wildly as he struggled in the thokost's toxic grip, apologizing profusely for any offense he'd given.

"Prissy little weakling," the thokost snarled, mossy green

eyes narrowed in a glare at Alad, "you dare to bump into *me*? Do you have a death wish?"

"Do *you*?" Shulgi asked in a hard voice as he caught the thokost's thick wrist, squeezing it until the thokost grunted in pain and slowly lowered Alad back to the ground.

The male dropped Alad onto his feet so suddenly the youth stumbled. Then he jerked his wrist out of Shulgi's grip and shoved Alad aside, causing the young Iriduan to go flying into the crowd that had begun to form around them with avid looks in their many different types of eyes.

"Now, *you* look far more capable of giving me a good fight," the thokost said, sizing Shulgi up. "It might take a little longer to kill you than the weakling."

Shulgi shifted his stance, his veins flowing with combat stimulants until time seemed to slow around him as his senses and reflexives and perception all sharpened. He heard subtle sounds now that had been barely detectible before as their new audience grew silent, watchful. No doubt curious to see if an armored Iriduan soldier could defeat a towering thokost male.

A quick glance told Shulgi that someone had taken Alad out of the mass of people now forming a circle around the small space they'd left for Shulgi and the thokost. He spotted a sky-blue hand waving from over the heads of some of the watchers, silvery wings flicking as the youth tried to take flight, but someone pulled him back down.

Shulgi snarled beneath his mask, aware that he had to make this fight quick. He needed to retrieve Alad before the youth came to harm. Namerian had entrusted him with the youth's safety. Perhaps that had been a foolish trust to put in Shulgi.

The thokost boastfully taunted Shulgi as he scanned the crowd, hoping to spot Alad again.

"Shut up, you overgrown shrub," Shulgi finally snapped, shifting his full attention to the thokost again.

"Your people are a dying breed," the thokost growled in rage as he clenched both clawed fists, vine-like muscles bulging on his arms. "Let me speed up their extinction by killing you!"

The thokost followed up these words by swinging his fist at Shulgi's head. Shulgi easily ducked the swing, though it had come at him fast. The thokost hit like a sledge and any punch that landed would have impact, even through his armor. More importantly, the creature wanted his bark-rough flesh to make contact with Shulgi's skin, which was only bare on his face. His toxin would do far faster damage to Shulgi than his brutal punches.

Shulgi didn't have the time or patience for this fight, though his blood pumped with eagerness for a prolonged and challenging battle. It was one he wouldn't be able to indulge this time. As the momentum of the thokost's punch drew his huge body forward, Shulgi slipped under his second swing, drawing a dagger from the sheath attached to his forearm.

Thokosts had only two weak points on their body that were easily accessible. Shulgi knew exactly where both of them were. He spun away from the thokost's other arm as it swung around to grab him, then stabbed the thokost below his ribcage in the narrow gap between the ropey muscles that protected one of his hearts. Two stabs in quick succession staggered the other male.

He roared in agony and stumbled away from Shulgi, both his hands covering the wounds that now wept with sap-like blood.

With the ease of long practice and the aid of the enhancing stimulants, Shulgi threw his dagger.

It struck the creature in the center breathing hole between his two green eyes, the force of Shulgi's throw rocking the thokost's antlered head backwards. Then the towering male slowly toppled like the twisted tree he somewhat resembled.

The crowd muttered with disappointment at the brevity of the fight, but Shulgi had no time to address them. He ran past the body of the thokost, bending as he reached the creature's head just long enough to retrieve his favorite dagger, which came free with a scraping sound. Then he charged the crowd that stood between him and the last place he'd spotted Alad.

The people watching wisely moved out of his way as he sheathed his dagger and drew his pistol. Even the city bosses' thugs kept their distance. He remained well aware of their threat and tracked them with other senses than his vision, but he focused on finding Alad.

He spotted the vivid blue coloring of Alad's robe further along the path towards the stall where they'd been heading and gave chase, shoving startled patrons aside. Angry protests died on their lips as they caught sight of who had pushed them. Realizing the impracticality of a ground pursuit, Shulgi leapt into the air, his wings expanding and then fluttering as he rose above the mass of bodies.

He dipped and darted around unmanned drones used to constantly record the market, skimming low enough over the crowd to keep his eye on Alad and the cloaked figure that pulled him along. The youth struggled to no avail against someone clearly far stronger than him. Shulgi couldn't make out what species he would face yet, but he had no doubt he could kill them. Especially now, with his blood pulsing with stimulants that filled him with euphoria and bloodlust.

He flew much faster than Alad's captor could run. Within only a few Standard minutes of him taking to the air, he passed overhead, and the cloaked figure glanced up with six eyes growing wide with obvious fear.

An alfgoi. A male, based on his smaller stature. Still much stronger than Alad, but he'd offer little challenge to Shulgi. Unless he managed to reach his mistress's web.

Shulgi had never had the misfortune to battle a female alfgoi in her own web before, and the creatures rarely left it, expecting their males to venture out and bring back "gifts" for them.

He dropped to the ground in front of the alfgoi, straightening as the creature squealed in fright, his hood falling away from a pale, humanoid face, six black eyes blinking as he desperately scanned his surroundings for an escape. Seeing the pistol in Shulgi's hand, he must have realized he couldn't run, so instead, he thrust Alad at Shulgi.

As the young Iriduan stumbled into Shulgi's line of fire, the alfgoi darted into a dark alley between ramshackle shops. Shulgi caught Alad and steadied him, then pulled him towards the alley as he checked for the kidnapper, already knowing the creature had undoubtedly gone to ground in some hole unknown to Shulgi.

It wasn't likely that he would find the creature, and he still had to get to the procurer before their contact grew too nervous to stick around with the equipment Namerian needed.

"I'm so sorry," Alad said in a breathless voice behind his mask. "I tried to fight the creature off, but he proved too strong."

Shulgi holstered his pistol and then clapped the youth on the shoulder. "I will take you to the combat arena to harden you up from now on. You're not prepared for this." He gestured to the market, noting the curious glances that some patrons shot his way. "It was *my* mistake to listen to Namerian and bring you here."

Clearly shaken, Alad audibly swallowed, the sound amplified by the speaker in his mask. "The creature—he said I would like my new role in the brothel." The youth's entire body trembled. "A *brothel!*" He shook his head, his long, mussed hair flying with the force of the motion. "I did not come this far from Iridu to serve another's sexual whims."

Shulgi grinned beneath his mask, pleased at the anger he heard in the youth's tone. "Good. I will see that you're trained so you can fight anyone who would try to force you to."

Though his blood still buzzed, Shulgi calmed his mind, keeping his attention on their surroundings as they left the area where the scummy alfgoi had escaped. He pondered returning to this place later to see if he could track the creature into whatever hole he'd used to disappear.

Then something caught his attention that chased all other thoughts from his mind.

A flash of a green cloak moving between two hulking Ultimen was enough to put Molly into his mind, and he sped up his steps, catching hold of Alad's arm to drag him along in his wake. As distracted as he was, he wouldn't let the youth out of his grasp again until they'd safely returned to Ma'Nah.

He followed the dainty cloaked figure, recognizing the billowing garment—and the two guards. It was definitely his Molly. No doubt she was once again serving as Zaska's mouthpiece. He couldn't fathom why else she would come to this marketplace.

The crowd swelled around him as he impatiently shoved aside protesting customers for the stalls that crowded the thoroughfare. He could no longer see Molly's hooded head, but still spotted the tall forms of her guards moving towards an intersection. They rounded a corner before Shulgi could pass through the crowd between him and them.

Alad protested Shulgi's rough handling, and Shulgi realized he'd been squeezing the youth's upper arm so hard that he'd come near to breaking it. He quickly released Alad, glancing around in frustration at their surroundings. There was nowhere safe he could leave the young Iriduan in this place. He was also already late to his meeting with the procurer.

This whole day cycle was turning into a disaster. Still, he wanted to see Molly again. He also felt like he had to know that she'd reached her intended destination safely in this dangerous place. She had her guards, but he wasn't sure even they would be enough to protect her from a crowd like this.

"Forgive me, Alad. I saw someone I know. I just need to head around that corner to see that they remain safe."

Still rubbing his arm with a pained squint to his eyes, the youth nodded his understanding. "I will remain close, sir. I won't be captured again!"

Shulgi gestured for Alad to fall in beside him and grit his teeth in frustration as he slowed his pace so the youth could keep up. Finally, he reached the corner where Molly and her guards had turned. The path they'd taken led into a nicer section of the third-tier. One where some of the city bosses' enforcers and officials made their homes.

Traffic through this area was much sparser, and Shulgi didn't like the looks he and Alad received as they passed buildings that grew progressively more expensive and lavish the further along the path they traveled. The path terminated at the gate of a mansion built in a boxy, old-world ramsuta style that left a lot to be desired aesthetically, but would no doubt contain luxuries far beyond the reach of the other residents of this tier. The gate protected the mansion but stood open at the moment. He quickly spotted the reason why.

The gatekeeper was in the middle of gesturing for Molly and her guards to pass him, just as a stocky ramsuta male walked down the stairs fronting the mansion.

The look on his face as he stared at Molly made Shulgi tense up, his fists clenching as he ducked behind one of the stone gateposts so the ramsuta didn't spot him.

Nor did he want Molly to spot him. He had no right to follow her. Not really. She wasn't his woman, even if he wished she could be. She had her guards with her, and the well-dressed city official clearly expected her arrival.

He glanced around the gatepost, taking another peek at the scene, unable to help himself.

Alad caught his arm before he could charge out into the open. "Sir, where are you going?"

The alarm in Alad's voice snapped Shulgi back to his senses and he ducked behind the gatepost again, his heart thundering and his blood burning with jealousy and anger—and intense frustration.

When he'd spotted that ramsuta with Molly's arm familiarly wrapped around one of his, he'd felt like he'd taken a blow harder than the thokost's would have been. When the ramsuta lowered his free hand to grip Molly's ass like he had the right, Shulgi wanted to kill him.

If Alad hadn't been there to stop him from making a fool of himself—not to mention jeopardizing everything—he would have.

TWENTY-TWO

Shulgi stood staring out the window of Namerian's office at the factory below and the spread of the dreg beyond. He failed to truly see the uninspiring view, an image of Molly in the clutch of the ramsuta official still burned in his vision.

"I'm pleased you were able to secure the equipment we required," Namerian said in a cool tone that didn't fool Shulgi. "Although Alad had an interesting tale to tell about your little... *adventure* on third-tier."

"No one will complain about one dead thokost," Shulgi said flatly, not bothering to turn around to face the other male.

He felt Namerian's approach but didn't glance at him when he joined Shulgi at the window.

Namerian didn't show the same courtesy, his gaze falling heavily upon Shulgi. Without meeting his eyes, Shulgi knew he would spot judgement in them.

"Let's not play games, Shulgi," Namerian said, his tone taking on a sharper edge. "The thokost barely offered a minor nuisance to you and poses no threat to us and our mission. That wasn't the part of the tale I found most *disturbing*."

Shulgi ground his teeth, his jaw twitching as he bit back the angry words he wanted to speak to defend himself from the condemnation he knew would come.

"Who is the woman?" Namerian said in a harsh tone, turning fully to face Shulgi, his arms crossing over his chest. "Have you been re-afflicted by her?" When Shulgi remained silent, pondering his words before he would speak them, Namerian spoke again. "Alad said you nearly charged onto the property of a city official. He claimed that the look in your eyes when you saw the woman with the official scared him."

Namerian grabbed Shulgi's upper arm, trying to turn him to force him to meet his eyes. He couldn't shift Shulgi, who shrugged off his grip.

"I am not afflicted," he finally said, his voice a harsh growl, anger prickling behind it.

"Then what insanity has gripped you!" Namerian hissed out. "Is it because of the stimulants that keep drawing you to the darkest alleys of the dreg to hunt and kill." He shook his head. "No, I don't believe it is. Even in your most incautious moments, you wouldn't hunt a city official. Especially not with Alad in your company."

He took a step back as Shulgi finally met his eyes with a glare of his own. He held up both hands in front of him. "You're letting your bloodlust consume you, Amanat!" His eyes widened and Shulgi saw fear in them. "We knew you were a murderer when we accepted this mission, but we understood your past, and believed the cure was the key to stopping good Iriduans from becoming monsters."

Shulgi returned his gaze to the window, noting his subtle reflection in the glass superimposed over the dirty dreg below.

"I fear you, my creche-kin," Namerian said in a harsh whisper. "I fear that you were always a monster, and your affliction only awakened you to your true nature."

"My true *nature*," Shulgi spat in a bitter snarl as he glanced again at Namerian, "was awakened the day I was dragged from my cocoon and pressed into war-class training."

Molly believed him to be a good person, but Namerian saw the truth of him. Now, Shulgi understood that truth fully and could no longer take comfort in Molly's reassurance about his nature. How many lives had he claimed before Ninhursag had entrapped him? How many enemies had he hunted and killed for daring to pose a threat to the empire?

Ninhursag hadn't awakened him. She'd merely taken a weapon already well-honed and stained with blood and turned it upon a different enemy. Now, that weapon had turned upon the worst of the criminals in the dreg, but it remained a blood-stained weapon, hungry for more death.

He would have killed the official without a second thought for touching Molly the way he did. For using her, the way he did. For reminding Shulgi that other males dared to take for granted what had been so precious to him. What was still so precious to him.

"She is mine," he growled, his fists clenching, muscles bulging with the movement. "It infuriates me that others use her like *chattel*." He slammed his fist against the window, the entire span of it flexing outwards, unbreakable but not unshakable. "It infuriates me that once again, duty compels me to ignore my own will!" He spun on Namerian, stalking towards the other male as he backed away, holding out both hands. "This cure was supposed to free us, so why do I still feel like a slave?"

"You gave up your freedom to help others achieve theirs!" Namerian said in a trembling voice, darting around his desk to put the expanse of it between them. "It is a noble—"

"Hang the Spinner with that 'noble' tangle, Namerian," Shulgi shouted, slamming his palms onto the desktop. "You *dare* to condemn me for caring about something beyond this mission? Beyond our rebellion against the empire?" He sank down into the chair in front of the desk with a heavy sigh, lifting a hand to run it through his hair. "You dare to condemn me for having feelings?" His voice remained steady but hung heavy with his melancholy. "For wanting love, when all I've ever known is bloodshed?"

Namerian still stood behind his own chair, keeping both it and the desk between them, his violet eyes wide, his lips and jaw tight.

Shulgi lowered his gaze to the desktop, noting his reflection more clearly now in the glossy surface. His brows lowered over his narrowed eyes, his cheekbones stood stark, his jaw squared, his hair ruffled. But it was the look in his eyes that disturbed him the most. The look of a male standing on the edge, looking down into an endless darkness that mirrored what dwelled inside him—and debating that leap that would free him from the bonds of a conscience, a sense of duty—or any hope of redemption.

"She pulls me back," he whispered, more to himself than Namerian. "She keeps me from surrendering completely to the lust for blood that boils forever inside me—the addiction that won't be cured by removing my combat glands." He lifted his head to meet Namerian's fearful gaze. "She is the only cure that will save me, Namerian. The only one that will truly free me."

Namerian sagged against the chair back, leaning forward on his forearms, regarding Shulgi with a cautious expression. "We are so close to phase two now, Shulgi! Just *control* yourself for a little longer! Help us complete this part of the mission. Then you can do whatever you like. Once we know the cure will work permanently, your role will be complete."

Shulgi shook his head. "No, it won't be. I was tasked not

just with disseminating the cure—but also guarding it against those who would misuse it."

Namerian straightened, his silver brows lowering. "You imply that *we* can't be trusted? *You?* The one who murders for a hobby?"

"My victims are the scum of the galaxy. If you manage to remove the limiter on the nanites, *everyone* in the galaxy would end up a victim."

Namerian lifted his chin, scowling. "Well then, I guess you're stuck with this mission. So why don't you see it completed, and then you can have your... woman." The way he said it made the word sound like a curse.

Shulgi wasn't surprised by the venom in Namerian's tone, and he'd sunk so deeply into depression that he didn't even prickle at it.

"Of course, if you change your mind, you could just give us the passcode to the nanites and be completely free of this burden."

He could do that. He could dump the responsibility for using the nanites ethically in the lap of his team and abandon this thankless mission altogether. Perhaps Roz and crew would hunt him down for betraying their trust. Perhaps Nemon would find him and strangle him slowly for betraying his.

But it would free him to save Molly and take her far from this terrible place. Then he might finally become the male she believed him to be, rather than the monster he was.

TWENTY-THREE

"Got something you want to share with the rest of the class?" Jenice asked Molly wryly from the other side of the dining table in their shared living space.

Molly blushed guiltily, covering her wrist com with a reflexive motion before recalling that she had nothing to be ashamed of, and Jenice and the others had no right to judge.

Still, she shook her head, leaning back in her chair as she met Jenice's eyes. "Nothing that would be of interest to anyone here."

Jenice raised her eyebrows, her lips tightening with skepticism. "If you say so."

"Mol is entitled to keep her own affairs to herself," Grundon said with a growl, sending a quelling glance towards Jenice before turning a smile on Molly.

"I don't know why you're getting so upset over this, Jenice," Briana piped up from her seat at Jenice's right hand. "It's like you're jealous or something." She gestured to Molly with a slender hand. "Let her have her fun with her lover. We already have Ma'Nah's contract. The company wouldn't dare to cancel it just because things don't work out well with her and lover boy."

Molly noted the tightening in the corners of Jenice's lips and hastened to intervene before any of the others at the table decided to make incendiary comments that would ruin what had been a nice, pleasant meal.

"Jenice has every right to be concerned," she said in a soft, placating tone. "It's not just my own position that is at stake, and I assure you, my friend," she turned her full attention to Jenice, "I am remaining cautious. I share nothing with Shulgi that would put us in danger."

"You do send a lot of messages back and forth," Mogorl said thoughtfully after swallowing a large mouthful of fish and eel stew as everyone else at the table fell into an awkward silence.

Molly blushed again, knowing the violet on her cheeks was now likely as dark as a bruise. "We speak of things that interest us both, not of business."

In truth, there wasn't anything she hadn't told Shulgi by this point that she could tell him. Though it had been several day cycles since she'd been able to see him, they did send a bunch of messages back and forth and had even chatted through holoscreen the last two evenings. A secret smile tilted her lips as she recalled last night's chat, and what it had ended up turning into. Shulgi was so incredibly desirable to her that she sometimes forgot herself. She was pleased that she made him do the same.

She had shared many details about her past, though nothing specific about those who'd harmed her, because she genuinely worried that Shulgi might try to do something about it. She didn't want him getting hurt by someone like Uthagol, whose web of influence spread far through the column. She didn't doubt he would prove capable in a fair fight, but Uthagol never fought fairly. She would have him taken out the moment she saw him as a threat, and he'd likely never see it coming.

Shulgi had been more reserved about the details of his past, and when she'd called him on it through a message that she worried might have reflected too much of her own insecurity, he'd confessed that he'd done too many things that shamed him, and he didn't want her to see him in that negative light.

Despite his concerns, she still believed in him and knew he was good at his core regardless of the things he'd been forced by his positions in life to do.

"I've seen that image you have of him in your room," Briana said with a grin, "I could think of many things to discuss with a man like that, and none of it would be about business."

Molly chuckled, noting the way Jenice's expression tightened as she shot a glance at Briana. "We do discuss entertainment often." As all eyes turned towards her, she smirked. "Like our favorite movies, and video games, and eateries." She picked up her eating utensil, which Jenice called a "spoon" since its design was like a utensil from Earth. "Do you know that the Iriduans in the dreg have a whole sector dedicated to entertainment venues?"

"Just one sector?" Mogorl grunted. "Sounds pretty austere to me. Not surprised though. They have always been so uptight and serious."

Molly dipped her spoon into her stew, inhaling deeply of the fragrant scent rising from it. Their chef really knew his business.

Her smile faded a little as she recalled her meeting with the ramsuta official several days ago. She'd managed to put off giving him any sexual favors, though he'd pawed at her until their meeting was concluded and she'd extracted herself successfully. Briana had offered to take her place from now on, claiming that she found the ramsuta males appealing anyway, but Molly suspected it was the official's wealth that truly appealed. She didn't blame Briana for enjoying the luxurious gifts that would be certain to come her way if she "serviced" the official in Zaska's name.

They'd lived in such terrible conditions for so long that any luxury seemed like a blessing. To be showered with gifts from a wealthy admirer was something even Molly had once longed for. Now, she'd grown too jaded—and too hungry for something deeper and more meaningful.

"Iriduans do have a lot of wealth, though," Briana mused aloud. "He must send you some pretty gifts."

He had. Molly had squirreled them away without showing them off to the others. Each one had been something that held meaning between the two of them.

He'd given her a dress made of Iriduan silk in a light gray that shimmered like silver, so she would have something to wear that wasn't green—that wasn't Zaska's. He'd also gifted her a hair ornament of such fine craftsmanship that she'd never seen its equal, certainly not in the cheap marketplaces of the lower tiers. Shulgi told her the ornament was his promise to protect her and always be there for her. She'd gained the impression it was a mating gift, though he'd never actually admitted such.

He'd sent her flowers imported directly from Earth, which had to be staggeringly expensive, but had the sweetest fragrance, and a perfume from Iridu that he told her enhanced her scent rather than covering it.

"They have been lovely," she confessed, though she intended to keep them concealed, not wanting the others to see just how much they meant to her.

How much he meant to her.

"You haven't shown them to us," Jenice said, her eyes narrowed. "I'm surprised. Usually, you display all the gifts our marks send to you for us all to admire."

Molly shrugged one shoulder, sparing only a quick glance at the others before looking down at her soup. "Shulgi isn't a mark. Not anymore."

Jenice made a huffing sound. Molly felt the curious looks of the others as they bounced between her and Jenice, but no one chose to speak again as they finished their meal in uncomfortable silence. When it was over, they all parted ways, Jenice sweeping past Molly without a word.

She understood why her friend was so concerned. Molly also understood that Jenice had good reason to be concerned. Molly was falling hard and fast, and women in love did very stupid things. She knew that from personal experience. None of them could afford for Molly to lose her head over a man. Especially not at this stage in their operations.

Despite her understanding of the risks, she still instantly agreed to meet Shulgi the following day cycle when he sent a message asking if she could get away from Zaska for a few hours.

She didn't have to answer to Zaska as Shulgi believed she did, but she still had people who did concern themselves with her whereabouts, and even Mogorl seemed reluctant to agree to her meeting Shulgi for a morning meal, much to her disappointment.

It seemed Jenice might be convincing him that perhaps this relationship wasn't a good idea. Fortunately, Grundon had more sway with him, and he had commented already on how happy Molly seemed to be lately—and how much she deserved to be happy. When he reiterated that to his closest friend,

Mogorl couldn't find a way to disagree that still honored the friendship they all shared.

She felt guilty about not checking with Jenice first before donning her voluminous cloak and heading out with her guards. She also felt guilty about the fact that she had no intention of meeting Shulgi on the under-tier, since she didn't want Jenice spying on them.

In fact, the strain her relationship with Shulgi was putting on her friendship with Jenice gave Molly a great deal of guilt. She couldn't help herself though. She couldn't stop seeing him.

He really did make her happy. Every message he sent made her smile, just knowing he was thinking of her. Every gift he sent her made her tear up, just knowing that he considered the kinds of things that might actually please her, rather than some generic gift meant to impress. Her every other thought was of him, and of how he made her feel, especially when he'd made love to her like there was something deep and true between them, rather than just because he wanted to get off using her body.

They both knew this relationship couldn't go anywhere, but neither of them was willing to let that stop them from carrying on with it.

Shulgi wanted to meet her on fifth tier, which was a high level for her, and one she rarely visited. Uthagol's brothel was only one tier higher, and her influence web spread its threads even as low as third-tier, so it wouldn't be wise to spend too much time where Uthagol or one of her minions might spot Molly, and possibly manage to recognize her, despite all her dyes and cosmetics.

On the other hand, Sha Zaska's increasing influence in the under-tier meant people were expecting to see his mouthpiece rise to higher tiers from time to time to conduct his business. It would be suspicious if his minions didn't move higher than third-tier as his wealth expanded.

Fifth-tier was also the home of the dreg, and despite that enclave being only midway to the top of the column, it held some of the greatest influence in all Za'Kluth. Uthagol's minions wouldn't be as thick on fifth-tier as the others. Iriduans really didn't like to share power, and the most powerful denizens of the dreg spread their own wealth and influence beyond its sheltering dome.

She would probably be safer on fifth-tier than fourth or sixth. At least, that was what she told herself. At this point, any risk was worth it to see him again. He'd warned her that they could not touch in an intimate way until they'd retired to a private place, lest one of the other Iriduans question his relationship to a female. While in public, they had to appear to be solely business associates.

She could handle that. She'd been in many such situations where her companion didn't want others to know their true interest in her. It hurt that she wouldn't be free to embrace him the moment she saw him as she ached to do, but she completely understood the dangers of that. For both of them.

Her heart lifted the moment they entered the morning eatery on fifth-tier when she spotted Shulgi standing near the bakery counter, regarding the many palatable offerings thoughtfully. Molly would eat any food that wasn't toxic to her—having learned the hard way the folly of being picky—but she had definite preferences, and this bakery offered several of them.

She knew Shulgi couldn't remove his mask in public, so he wouldn't eat where they could be spotted. In fact, she'd never actually seen him eat in front of her. Usually, when she had him at her mercy, they were far too busy to bother with niceties like food and drink.

As much as she'd like him in her bed again, she was willing

to take whatever time she could get with him. A feeling of impending doom had settled over her, making her feel like their time was rapidly ticking away and they needed to embrace every moment of it like it was their last.

He turned and spotted her as she and her guards entered the establishment—a Syndicate conglomerate owned eatery, with many different species' favorites on offer.

His wings flicked, but he made no move to rush towards her the way she wanted to run into his arms. Still, the intensity in his green eyes as they fixed on her shadowed face told her exactly how much he wished he could.

He held himself in strict control, and her many years of training kept her restrained as well, but she could feel the chemistry sparking between them as she swept closer to him, her cloak billowing around her.

She also felt the eyes of some of the patrons watching her curiously, either because of the green cloak, or because of the towering Ultimen guards who scanned the eatery with slight scowls.

Despite the feeling of being watched, Molly couldn't help but notice how clean, orderly, and safe the eatery seemed in comparison to the lower tiers. At mid-level, there was better enforcement for the common citizens—those who lacked the wealth or influence to pay security to watch over them. Residents of this tier paid dues to fund a community security force that provided blanket protection, keeping crime confined to the underground areas of the tier so that citizens could feel some sense of living in a civil society.

The heavy dues of the upper tiers were one reason so many residents crowded the lower, far more criminal ones.

Most of the patrons of the eatery looked respectable and rather ordinary, the kind of "regular" folks that Molly had been told about but had rarely ever seen in person. She spent most of her time either with criminals, or the elites—many of whom were also criminals—or the slaves she helped escape this place —none of whom she could see in this establishment, though she'd spotted a handful on this tier.

She already felt out of place on this tier, and this eatery made her feel almost shabby. She worried that the filth of the under-tier clung to her like a second skin. One she could never shed. It made her realize that Shulgi's life was much different from hers. Far removed from the only kind of living she could remember.

Still, that pull between them couldn't be ignored, though they greeted each other coolly and politely while the person behind the counter looked on a with a curious crinkling of his snout.

Shulgi gestured at the offerings behind the counter. "Would you like anything to eat before we conduct our business?"

His tone sounded so cool, so distant that she might have begun to doubt his feelings for her if his eyes weren't telling her a far different story about his emotions.

She glanced at the pastries, her mouth watering as her gaze passed over them. "Perhaps another time," she said in her most elegant and practiced tone.

She might not belong here, among the middle classes, but she would act like she belonged many tiers above them, because that was what she'd been trained to do, and she excelled at it.

"In that case, I have secured a private dining area for us to discuss our mutual business arrangements in further detail," he said, though she suspected he was aware she'd denied her interest in the pastries.

Her mouth watered more for him anyway.

She nodded regally. "Of course. That is why I am here, honored Iriduan. Please, escort me to this chamber."

In her daydreams, this meeting had begun so differently. In her daydreams, they rushed into each other's arms, like something out of a romance movie, kissing passionately.

She was experienced enough to understand that life rarely ever happened like her daydreams.

TWENTY-FOUR

Shulgi performed his scan of the private dining room as soon as they entered, the door sliding shut behind them, leaving Molly's two guards posted on the other side of it. He detected traces of electronic monitoring, but they had been deactivated recently, just as he'd requested.

He knew meeting her again, particularly on the fifth tier, was a huge risk. One he might end up regretting, but seeing her now, finally, made it difficult for him to worry about future regrets. The more they communicated with each other, the more he realized how much they had in common, despite so many differences between them.

Unsurprisingly, Molly felt passionate about freedom and abhorred the injustices of slavery. Her own situation was the likely cause of her deep anger at the practice, but he felt that she might be just as passionate were she free. She also despised the abuses of the lower classes in the city by the wealthy elite, including the city bosses who took increasingly higher shares of their income just for the privilege of living in the hellish lower tiers.

It wasn't just their fundamental beliefs that Shulgi and Molly shared. She also enjoyed many of the same forms of entertainment that he did, loved trying new foods and restaurants like he did, and also appreciated luxury but did not require it for her happiness.

Once assured they were alone and unmonitored, he turned his attention to Molly, who had removed her cloak and set it on one of the bench chairs surrounding the main table in the private dining room.

She looked so beautiful that it stole his breath. The gray silk gown he'd given her skimmed her subtle curves, highlighting her petite and graceful form. The hair ornament he'd sent to her glittered as she turned her head to meet his eyes, the gemstone beaded chains swinging with the movement. She wore only his and he pretended it made her his queen, even knowing that he couldn't make her so in any official capacity.

Even if he could spirit her away from this world and keep her for himself, he could never let their mating be known in Syndicate space without being hunted by the empire for illegally mating. Not that he'd had much of a problem avoiding imperial enforcers thus far.

She'd tucked one of the flowers he'd sent her into her hair right beside the golden ornament, and the subtle pink sheen of the delicate and fragrant petals gleamed against her blonde locks.

She watched him study her with a hint of uncertainty in her eyes, and he closed the distance between them and took her into his arms. Her slim arms encircled his waist as she laid her cheek against his chest.

"I can hear your heartbeat," she murmured, planting a kiss on the silk that covered his pectoral.

He shivered with pleasure at the feeling of her lips touching him through the barrier of fabric. His cerci unfurled at his back, pulling his robe tight so the ridge of his erection was easily noticeable.

"I only wanted to see you, Molly," he said, lifting a hand to trace the petals of the rose in her hair. "As much as I desire you, I didn't bring you here for sex."

Her chuckle sounded husky with her own desire, recalling their previous holo chat, when she had laid upon her own bed, gloriously naked, with her legs parted as she pleasured herself for him. She'd been sweetly seductive even then, exuding grace and class even as her back arched in climax, her hair spreading across her pillow and her fascinating eyes closing in bliss. She'd called his name as she'd come, which had brought his own orgasm, his hand fisted around his girth, stroking in time to her fingers moving inside her.

He'd wished then, more than anything, that he could have been in her bed with her at that moment. Now, it was enough that he could feel her in his arms again, even if he couldn't taste her the way he wanted to. It wasn't safe here to do so.

He could clean her scent off his robe before leaving this room, but if he made love to her here, he wouldn't be able to completely purge her much stronger aroused scent as well as his own from his skin without potentially drawing notice from other Iriduans.

"I wouldn't mind if you'd brought me here for sex as well," she said, her hand sliding from his waist to cup the hard ridge at his groin.

He moaned, shuddering as his hips bucked reflexively, pushing his erection harder against her palm. She sucked in a shivering breath, tilting her head to look up at him, her eyes sparkling with her arousal. She licked her shapely lips, leaving them glistening like an invitation it took everything in him to resist.

With much regret, he caught her wrist, tugging her hand

away from his groin. "We should think of other things, my queen, or I won't be able to leave this room for a long time after you without raising suspicions." He felt the edges of full engorgement creeping in on him and knew if he let his arousal go that far, he would end up in pain if he didn't make love to her.

Her lips spread in a soft smile as she lifted her captured hand to trail her fingertip along the upper edge of his mask. "Your queen?"

He reluctantly released her, stepping away from her before he lost control of his own will. "I shouldn't call you that. I have no right to claim you as such."

Yet he wanted to. As much as if he had been truly imprinted on her. Only this time, it felt like his choice, not his biology betraying him. Namerian had ventured to discuss this phenomenon of Shulgi falling in love with a female he hadn't imprinted upon, though Shulgi was still irritated with him since their discussion in his office. He hadn't been thrilled to listen to Namerian pepper him with further warnings about the dangers of continuing to expose himself to Molly. The professor speculated that he would still slip into the singularly devoted role of a mated male because it remained a part of his biology. Once he'd determined a female to be his queen, after she caught his interest—regardless of how she did it—he would feel emotionally bound to her, just as if he'd imprinted on her. The difference was that he would not die without her, but Shulgi suspected he might want to if he didn't put an end to this soon.

The best way to do that was to free her and send her home to Earth, where he would never have the chance to see her again now that it was under Akrellian guardianship.

She lowered her eyes, her smile fading. "I am no one's queen, I suppose. I'm just a whore."

He caught her in his arms again, pulling her tight against his body as his hands smoothed up her back, feeling the warmth of her skin beneath the sleek material of her dress. "Molly, you are not that! Not to me. Never to me! I love you, and there is nothing I want more in my life than you."

She sucked in a startled gasp, her hands pressing against his chest. He didn't want to release her, but he allowed her to push him far enough that she could look up into his eyes. "Do you mean that?" Her tone expressed doubt, but also a tinge of something else he told himself was hope.

He cupped her face between his hands. "I do. I would gladly claim you as my queen, and announce it to the entire galaxy, if I could."

Her lips parted as if she would speak, then her gaze fell. "I wish I was free to accept that claim, Shulgi, because I would—in a heartbeat." When she lifted her eyes again, they shimmered with unshed tears. "You make me happier than I've ever been. Whenever I get a message from you, it brightens my day. When I hear your voice, it lifts my heart. And when I see you...."

She ran her hand up his chest to settle over his heart. "When I see you, I feel like I've finally found where I belong." She rested her head against his chest, laying her cheek beside her warm palm. "I can't remember the last time I felt at home, but that's how I feel when I'm in your arms."

He embraced her gently, his arms folding her close to him. Though her body felt incredible against his, his mind seethed with frustration and despair at the thought of what he must do.

He had taken on the burden of the cure without hope of ever having anything else in his life that mattered to him. He'd believed that such a thing as love was forever beyond him, despite encouragement from Paisley to find a mate. Though he'd grown to admire and respect Paisley to the point that he'd even fancied he could fall in love with her, he hadn't truly believed that he would find someone who made him feel the way Halian had felt about her. Someone who could make him forget the horrors of being imprinted on Ninhursag, being manipulated by her, having her use him like a mechbot to do her bidding.

Molly had blindsided him with her grace and elegance, her soft voice concealing a strong will. She had suffered so much in her life and yet managed to remain unbroken by it. She held onto her true self, even as she was forced by Zaska to wear a mask for everyone else. He couldn't help but admire her and respect her.

He couldn't help but fall in love with her.

"Tell me we will be together someday, Shulgi," she whispered, her fingertip tracing the embroidery on his robe. "Tell me we will live happily ever after."

"I can never lie to you, my queen." But how he wanted to when it came to this!

She sighed, her breath warm as it swept over the silk covering his chest. "I know it is folly to dream. I thought, once before, that I would finally escape this life. He promised me many things, but all that mattered was that he'd sworn he'd love me forever. Then I discovered that he didn't love me at all."

"I am *not* him," Shulgi growled, wishing he could find this male who had hurt her.

He also realized he was no better since he couldn't give her his love freely either. Though he would at least have the decency to give her freedom before he left her life forever.

She stroked her palm down his chest, then slipped both hands around his waist to hug him. "No, you are so much better than him! You *are* a good person, Shulgi. You don't break my heart without reason. I understand that."

"I will find a way to set you free, Molly!"

She pulled away from him, stepping out of his arms so quickly that he didn't process she was doing so until she'd put a step between them. Then another. Though her eyes were lowered, he saw the dampness of tears on her dyed cheeks.

"I don't want to be free." She lifted her gaze, her eyes green with a golden halo. "I have nowhere to go. No home to return to."

"We can find your family," he insisted, shifting towards her, only to freeze when she shied away from him, holding up one staying hand. "I know people who are good at finding things."

She slowly shook her head. "I was taken as a young child, Shulgi. I don't even remember my family. I doubt they would recognize me or understand what I have become."

"Do not judge yourself so harshly!" He noted how her hand trembled as she lowered it, taking another step away from him. "You have become stronger, wiser, and more beautiful, both inside and out."

"I don't want to be free," she repeated, reaching behind her to grab up her cloak. "I'm sorry, Shulgi. I know you want to rescue me, but I don't need a hero."

He wanted to beg her to stop as she swung her cloak back around her shoulders. "Molly...."

She shook her head, the beads on her hair ornament sparkling as they swung. Then she lifted her chin, her spine straightening as she met his eyes, her own cool and distant. "I am better off where I am, and I should have recognized that from the start. I should not have allowed this to go on for so long."

"Don't," he pleaded, recognizing the walls she was forming around her heart. He'd been behind their shadow for too long himself.

She gestured to herself, then him. "This only hurts both of us."

Her long lashes fluttered as she blinked rapidly, tilting her head down as two tears slipped free. She swiped them away impatiently before lifting her gaze again. "It is also far too risky. I have been too distracted from my purpose, and from my duty to Sha Zaska. I cannot allow that to happen again."

Shulgi clenched his fists, his teeth grinding and jaw ticking. "You would choose that foul creature over freedom?"

She leveled a look at him that struck him to the core, as remote and resolute as an ancient empress leading her troops into battle. "I am more than just a slave, Shulgi. I am Zaska's mouthpiece. You have no idea how much power and consequence that gives me. I will not abandon all that to return to a world that no longer calls to me, and a family made of strangers who could never truly understand me."

She swept past him regally, her hands lifting to settle her cowl over her head, concealing the gleaming gems and gold of the mating gift he'd given her. She didn't turn to look back at him as the door slid open upon her approach.

He watched her guards fall into step beside her as smoothly as a military formation. He couldn't think of the words to say that would stop her from disappearing out of his life. He couldn't make the one promise that might have kept her in his arms. The one promise he would give anything to make to her.

Anything but what remained of his honor. He couldn't ever become the "good" man she wanted him to be if he abandoned the promise he'd made to others. The promise that now held him bound as surely as an imprinting would have. Namerian had been right. Their mission needed him. The other Iriduan males afflicted by this curse needed him.

He had been selfish to even allow things to go this far. He'd taken unnecessary risks that could have destroyed all that he'd already accomplished.

His wrist com notified him of an urgent message sometime

later as he sat in a dining chair, still staring blindly at the door where his queen had swept out of his life forever, because he hadn't proven his devotion to her.

He glanced at his wrist without much interest, expecting it to be yet another request from Namerian, who was careful now in how he addressed Shulgi, still apparently unnerved by their disagreement.

Then he stiffened as he spotted the identity of the sender. The message itself was brief and enigmatic, but like before, it contained a location, and a time. That time was very soon, the information peddler clearly unwilling to give him a chance to set up an ambush before the meeting. He jumped to his feet, then strode towards the door, not bothering to send a reply.

She would know when he arrived.

TWENTY-FIVE

Molly found Jenice waiting for her when she returned to their inner sanctum. The other woman paced back and forth in the main living quarters, clearly agitated. As soon as Molly, Mogorl, and Grundon walked in, all of them silent, Jenice started in on Molly.

"Why would you do something so reckless?" she shouted, flinging her hands up in the air as her feet carried her across the tile in another round of pacing.

Molly sighed heavily, barely holding herself together after an interminable journey back to the under-tier. Mogorl and Grundon had enough perception to respect her desire not to have a discussion at this moment, but Jenice was too angry to care what Molly was feeling.

"Precautions were taken," Mogorl said in a growling tone, defending Molly when she hesitated to answer, still afraid her voice would shake with unshed tears.

"Precautions!" Jenice cried aloud, spinning to face them in mid step. "The best precaution would be to avoid the upper tiers altogether!" She dismissed Mogorl with her glare, shifting it to focus on Molly, who still hid her swollen eyes beneath the shadow of her cowl. "Neither of your guards know Uthagol like we do, Mol. They can't understand the risk you truly took by going to that tier!"

Grundon flinched at the condemnation in Jenice's tone, and the way she referred to him as a "guard" rather than by name. After all, they were all like family, and Grundon and Jenice were usually as close as siblings.

"Don't take your anger out on Grundon and Mogorl," Molly said in a low voice, drawing in a deep breath to steady it, already hearing the quiver of tears on the verge of breaking through her control. "Direct it where it belongs. I am the one who insisted on going to the fifth tier. Mog and Grun acted as good friends do and made certain I was protected while I was there."

Jenice crossed her arms over her chest, shaking her head as she glanced from Grundon to Mogorl, then pinned her hard glare back on Molly. "Believe me, I know whose idea it was to go meet with Shulgi. I also know that these two never give you enough pushback when you make foolish decisions."

"You are not her slave-master," Mogorl snapped, "nor ours. Do not speak to us as if you imagine yourself in control of us."

Molly placed her hand on Mogorl's furry arm, softly smoothing his fluffed hair. "Please, Mogorl, Grundon, let's not fight amongst ourselves." She lifted her other hand to tug her cowl off, looking up into Mogorl's eyes, knowing her own shimmered with unshed tears. "Thank you, my friends," she shifted her gaze to meet Grundon's concerned eyes, "for standing by me when I needed it most."

With a grunt, Mogorl patted her hand on his arm, then strode to his own sleeping chamber, barely sparing a glance at Jenice, who still glared mutinously at the three of them.

Grundon gently embraced Molly, hugging her against his

massive, hairy chest. She breathed deeply of his comforting, familiar scent, returning his embrace.

"You deserve happiness, Mol," he rumbled, his deep voice vibrating against her cheek, "don't let anyone tell you different."

Her tears dampened his furry hide and she pulled away, swiping at them as she turned her back on Jenice. Grundon patted her shoulder, then strode away with heavy steps, leaving her alone with Jenice.

"I'm sorry," Jenice said from behind Molly, after a long moment of silence fell between them. Her hand fell upon Molly's shoulder. "Mol, you know I love you! I never wanted to see you hurt like this. In fact, this is one reason *why* I didn't want you to get your heart set on him."

"It's over, Jenice," Molly said in a dull voice, swiping more tears from her cheeks. "We both know this can't work. Shulgi has his own concerns that he can't abandon, any more than I can abandon mine. I was a fool to think he might join our organization and become a part of our mission. I realized that when I saw how different the fifth tier is from the under-tier. Why would anyone leave such a nice place to live down here in the slums, surrounded by criminals instead of wealth?"

Jenice sucked in a deep breath. "Did he dare to tell you you're too lowborn for him? Because if he did—"

Molly shook her head, turning around to face Jenice, feeling the swing of the gemstones on her hair ornament. "No, I don't think he would ever say such a thing. I... I think he loves me. I think he would be with me if he could, but I could tell that even if I was free to be with him, he isn't in the same position. There won't be a happily ever after for us."

Jenice's expression crumpled with sympathy and sadness as she hugged Molly. "Oh sweetie, I'm so sorry! I know life has never been fair to you, and it breaks my heart that you can't have the fairytale ending you've always dreamed of."

Molly couldn't hold on any longer. She broke into harsh, ugly sobs, clinging to Jenice like she would be swept away by all the tears that soaked her face. Her makeup washed away in colorful rivulets from her chin to drip onto the tile, but she still didn't feel clean. She didn't think she'd ever feel truly clean.

Nor would she ever be enough for a mate to choose her first and foremost, to put her before every obstacle that might stand in the way of them being together. She couldn't even blame Shulgi for not doing that, since she'd allowed her own concerns to keep her from putting him first.

Though, she realized that if he had asked her to leave this city behind today, she would have gone with him, without a second thought, despite all that she would be leaving behind. Her heart would ache for the friends she'd end up abandoning, but she knew they would recover from her absence. They would no doubt even blame her disappearance on Sha Zaska to add more fear to his legend. In time, she could have contacted them, maybe even someday saw them again.

Shulgi hadn't asked her to go with him to some new place, where they would both be free to show their love for each other. Instead, he'd told her he wanted her more than anything, but that he couldn't give her the promise of her fairytale ending.

Perhaps the hardest part for her to accept was that he'd never once told her what kept him here in Za'Kluth. It couldn't just be the business of Ma'Nah. Surely, there were others who could run the company. She knew there was something deeper there, but Shulgi didn't trust her enough to tell her what that something was.

Any more than she'd trusted him enough to tell him the truth about Sha Zaska. She could hardly blame him for putting these obstacles between them when she was doing the exact same thing.

The truth was that they weren't meant to be. She'd come to that conclusion while in his arms, knowing that there would never be another place she would want to be more. Even if she found love again, in some imagined future where her life didn't revolve around a terrible secret too dangerous to share, she would never feel the kind of desperate need that she felt for Shulgi. He truly had felt like her home, until she realized that she would never be able to stay there.

"It's okay, hon. Cry it out. I've got you." Jenice's voice had taken on a soothing tone now as she guided Molly to the sofa, settling them both down on it.

Molly felt her removing the hair ornament and the flower. She wanted to protest, feeling panicky at the thought of misplacing that ornament that had come to hold a value for her far beyond the expensive cost of it.

Jenice made a soft whistling sound as she set the ornament on the low table in front of the sofa, no doubt admiring the expensive jewelry. Then she returned her attention to Molly. "Listen, sweetie, Briana is ready to take over the primary mouthpiece role, okay. You can join me in the back, running the businesses from the shadows. It's honestly a lot of fun, though you don't get to do all those glamourous meetings and parties."

She smiled hesitantly, gently wiping away the tears that rolled down Molly's cheeks. "You know, once this organization gets enough wealth together, we can go legitimate. Maybe 'dispose' of Zaska altogether. Maybe we can move the whole operation save for the docks to another column, where we won't have to worry about bumping into Uthagol." She pushed the strands of hair that had broken free from Molly's updo away from her face. "I swear to you, Mol. Just hang in there a little longer, and we'll find a new home, one where you can be free to find love."

"I already found love," Molly said with a sniffle, turning her head away from Jenice. "I don't want to make that mistake again."

Jenice huffed impatiently. "Sweetie, Kuro was a scummy Urasol bastard who pretended to be someone he wasn't, and Shulgi," she softened her tone as Molly flinched, "might be a wonderful person, but he isn't putting you first. You *deserve* to be first in your man's life, Molly!" She cocked her head as she studied Molly for a long moment. "Are you *sure* you aren't interested in either Mogorl or Grundon?"

Molly chuckled weakly, shaking her head at Jenice's teasing. "Are *you?*"

Jenice grinned, shrugging her shoulders. "Maybe I was in the beginning, but they've become too much like brothers to me now." Her smile faded. "I have some apologies to make to my big, hairy bros."

Molly nodded her agreement, wishing for all the world that she could find love with someone like either Mogorl or Grundon—or both, though such couplings were rare with the Ultimen. They knew her secrets and were an active part of them, and always had her back and put her before themselves. They would be the perfect mates, if there was any chemistry that sparked between them and her.

"I think you really hurt their feelings, Jen."

Jenice sighed heavily, leaning back against the sofa. "I know. I have a mouth that is slow to receive messages from my brain. You know I say crap I don't really mean. I let my emotions take over and start snapping at everyone." Jen chewed her lower lip, a worried expression on her face. "Molly, sometimes I *do* things when my emotions take over that I regret, and I can't always take it back!"

Molly patted Jen's leg, lifting her other hand to swipe a final time at the tears that had slowed from a river to a trickle. "It's okay. We've all learned your quirks by now. We forgive you." She rose to her feet, feeling a hundred years older than she was, her body aching with her misery.

Jenice caught her arm. "Molly, I just... I fucked up, big time! I don't want you to hate me."

Molly smiled down at Jenice, though she knew the expression didn't reach eyes that felt like they were swelling shut from all the tears she'd shed. "I could never hate you." She bent down to hug Jenice. "You're the best friend I have in the whole galaxy."

Jenice looked like she wanted to say more as Molly straightened again, but then she bit her lower lip, dropping her gaze to her hands twisting in her lap.

"Good night, Jen," Molly said wearily. "Don't fret about Mog and Grun. They'll forgive you for your harsh tone. They love you as much as I do."

"Good night, Mol," Jenice said, worry still in her tone as Molly made her way to her sleeping chamber. "Hopefully, everything will look better in the morning."

TWENTY-SIX

Shulgi knew this part of the fifth tier, but only by mention. He'd never had a need to enter this sector, where Syndicate clinics routinely treated those citizens of Za'Kluth who couldn't afford the more expensive private medical care to be found all over the column, with varying degrees of effectiveness.

The dreg had its own extensive health sector, though the quality of service varied there, as well.

The crowd of many different fifth-tier species passed by him in a blur, though he always remained aware of potential dangers, even with the community security on this tier policing this section with more thoroughness than they did some of the others. The clinics paid a premium in fees to the community coffers for such a boost in security.

Some of the clinics had been set up by legitimate charitable organizations that operated within Syndicate space and spread their charity to the CivilRim as a misguided and pointless effort to improve the lives of the outcasts of polite society. Wealthy philanthropists and generous Syndicate citizens from every different member species threw money at these organizations, yet far too little of it made its way to these beleaguered clinics in remote areas of the CivilRim like Za'Kluth.

Still, many basic services could be found for almost any species in column 212. The non-affiliated clinics in the sector weren't so altruistic, but also offered a far wider range of services. Everything from bionic limbs to illegal implants and modifications to black-market transplants were on offer in such places. He actually felt relief to discover it was one of the shadier clinics that he'd been sent to, upon Luna's instructions. A legitimate clinic kept footage of patients entering and leaving, and possibly passed those records back to their headquarters in Syndicate space.

The bulky tapiran standing guard just inside the clinic's doors didn't bother to greet him. He merely eyed him with suspicion, taking in his appearance, then gestured towards a private treatment room with a grunt.

Shulgi scanned the clinic's lobby briefly, making note of all the other patients waiting listlessly in various seats designed for their biology, and the front desk, bustling with patients paying for their services. No one stood out as a particular threat, and few of the occupants of the lobby even glanced up from their varied forms of entertainment to meet his eyes. Those who did took in his appearance, and then quickly looked away.

He entered the indicated room, feeling the hum of the sound deadener kicking in as soon as the door sealed shut. He didn't bother to sit in any of the seats or on the table in the center of the room, eyeing the machines that surrounded it with only a vague curiosity.

This was an implant room, and he doubted they were using it to embed wrist coms under people's skin. No doubt the bulk of the work done here would qualify as illegal in Syndicate space.

"You've received word back." Luna's voice suddenly

speaking caused him to spin on one foot, drawing his pistol from the full sleeve of his robe.

He sighed and shook his head as he slowly lowered the pistol. "Are you testing me to see if I can kill you before you manage to freeze me with your mind?"

Luna chuckled, and again he found it strange to see so much animation in the expression of a Lusian. The genuine smile, almost a full grin, seemed unnatural on her. Yet at the same time, seemed like something she was comfortable with.

"I froze your weapon before I spoke," she said in a casual tone. "It would not have fired."

"What game are you playing, Luna?" He holstered his pistol, irritated that she'd managed to catch him off guard yet again, despite him expecting this very type of interaction.

Her smile faded and she lowered her unnerving eyes. "I apologize. I'm not trying to toy with you. It is rare that I speak with others anymore. I have lost my manners, perhaps."

"I've never known Lusians who had manners," Shulgi muttered.

This time, her smile was more hesitant. "Me neither."

He cocked his head, regarding her thoughtfully, keeping his mental wall built, careful not to think too much about secrets he needed to remain that way. "What's your story, anyway?"

She shrugged, glancing at the machines to the side of her instead of meeting his eyes again. "I have already told your friend. He has agreed to allow me onto his ship, though he has not yet said whether he will grant me a place with his crew."

Shulgi grunted, crossing his arms over his chest. "Friend? I wasn't aware Lusians had those."

"In general, we do not." This time, she did meet his eyes. "However, even an ignorant Iriduan like you should have noticed that the director you met is atypical of our species."

Properly chastened, he bowed his head in apology. "I didn't

come here to offend you, Luna. I seem to be saying all the wrong things to women today."

She tilted her head slightly, her dark eyes narrowing. He resisted the gentle probe at his mind.

She smirked. "To have such a handsome male even regard me as a female is flattering enough that I will overlook any offense you've given."

He had no idea why he felt startled that she expressed an awareness of sexual desirability. Roz and his crew were devoted to their mate in a way that made it clear they desired her on all levels, though Shulgi had not been fortunate enough to personally meet the human woman who had managed to transform their austere lives so completely.

"If only my heart was free, Luna." He couldn't keep the melancholy out of his tone.

He figured there was little point in trying to hide it from someone who could read his mind. After all, the only thing he could think of now was Molly, and the way she'd left him.

She blinked, then lowered her gaze. "If she has left you, then what need do you have to eliminate Sha Zaska?"

He clenched his fists. "That creature is a monster that does not deserve to live. I can never have Molly for my queen, but I can remove that burden from her life."

"And then what happens to your Molly?" Luna asked, and he wondered if he was imagining the tinge of compassion in her tone.

He shook his head. "She will be free. That's all that matters. Then, whatever happens to her, it will be her choice."

"Life is never that simple," Luna said in a neutral tone. "I suspect her choice would be to remain with you, but you have made a choice of your own that keeps that from happening."

"She was the one who left." Shulgi spun on one foot and began to pace in the small room. It only took two of his long steps to cross the span of the floor before he had to turn, making his pacing short.

"What did you offer her to stay?"

He shot a glare at Luna. "I offered her freedom from the monster who enslaves her!"

She watched him pace again. "You still don't see, Shulgi Amanat. I fear that you will not appreciate the truth when you discover it. I fear it will harm you more than even I can predict."

He paused, studying her face, looking for information from her expression. "You said Roz agreed to bring you on his ship, which sounds like he's willing to hear you out. You promised information in return."

"I would keep what I've learned to myself," Luna replied with a slow shake of her head, "but giving it to you is one condition the director insisted upon when I told him I balked at it."

"You think I will die at Sha Zaska's hands." Shulgi huffed. "Or arms. Whatever his appendages might be called. Roz knows I'm more than capable of defending myself."

Luna sighed, lifting her hand to touch a transmitter on her silver suit. "Yes, Roz knows many things that lesser beings like ourselves are never privy to, but *I* know that sometimes, the battle you go in search of isn't the one you find."

With that, she touched her transmitter, and less than a second later, Shulgi's wrist com beeped with a message from her marked simply "location."

"I have done what I can for you, Shulgi," Luna said. "I have been forbidden from giving you any additional information but what you have there. I do not question this director. I can't afford to at this point."

He froze in surprise when she laid a hand upon his shoulder, her long fingers curling over it. "Please, take care of yourself, Shulgi. Not just your body, but also your heart."

Shulgi stared at the blank space left behind when Luna blinked out of the room in a flash of light so fast it barely registered on his retinas.

He left the clinic in a thoughtful mood, though anticipation for the upcoming battle pumped through his blood. The message Luna had sent him offered coordinates, and a quick search showed that they led to a portion of the under-vents that likely contained the core of Sha Zaska's body—the part of him that Shulgi would need to destroy. The information also pointed him to an access point into the under-vents used by Zaska's own people. Shulgi planned to infiltrate the under-vents through that access.

When he returned to Ma'Nah, he found Alad awaiting him, his blue eyes wide as he practically bounced on his feet. When Alad spotted Shulgi, he skimmed above the ground, his wings blurring as they lifted him off his feet in his rush to intercept Shulgi.

"Professor Namerian says you must meet with him in his lab, immediately," Alad said in a breathless voice, dropping back to his feet in front of Shulgi.

"I have other things I need to take care of, Alad. He can send whatever he needs to tell me in a message."

All Shulgi wanted to do was to prepare for the upcoming battle with Sha Zaska. He had many preparations to make. He also had some contacts to tap in order to take on Zaska and his minions on their own turf.

The most important thing he needed to do was make certain Molly didn't get harmed in the ensuing chaos. That was paramount. He would make no move against Zaska until he could be certain Molly wouldn't end up harmed or killed.

Alad grabbed his arm, tugging on him without much effect. Still, the boldness of this act got Shulgi's full attention. Alad was usually far too timid for such behavior.

"Please, sir! The professor was very insistent that you see him immediately. He has sent out security to search for you!"

This couldn't be good. Namerian wouldn't waste manpower to find Shulgi just to pass on a simple message. Thanking Alad and bidding him to return to whatever duties he'd been doing, Shulgi made his way quickly to the secret lab.

When he arrived, the entire team waited for him, Namerian standing in the center of the group. They all turned to look at him as he walked in the room, but his gaze shifted from Namerian to the video playing on the holo screen beside the professor.

"Sha Zaska demands we double our payments to him for use of his docks and ships, or he makes this footage public to the dreg," Namerian said dully.

Feeling a sense of crushing betrayal, Shulgi watched the image of himself buried deep inside Molly, his mask-less face pressed against her neck as he fucked her without regard for protecting himself from imprinting upon her.

Now he understood why Molly had turned so cold and remote before walking out on him today. He wondered how he could have been so wrong about her.

Then he wondered what the point of being cured of the affliction was, if he could still make such a stupid mistake as to trust the woman he'd fallen for.

TWENTY-SEVEN

Deep within the humid under-vents, an Urasol guard paced near the primary access point to Sha Zaska's inner coil. Ceiling mounted turrets hung from the rock over his head, and scanners traced their light across the walls.

The bulky Urasol thug wore a full suit of armor and carried a Blauken rifle capable of taking off the head of the average Urasol with a single explosive shot. Collateral damage was generally high, but the species didn't often concern themselves with subtlety.

The creature lifted his head, his snout wrinkling as his nostrils flared, detecting something near the entrance access panel. Readying his rifle, he strode on heavy footsteps closer to the panel, his head cocked. Both turrets trained on the access panel in response to the shift of his eyes behind his helmet.

The only thing he found was a strange orb that had fallen through one of the vents in the access panel. He knelt to get a closer look at it, then spotted the light that suddenly flickered inside it, followed by a high-pitched whining sound.

"Hybernia's claws!" He jumped backwards, but not in time

to avoid the crackling explosion that sent him staggering, ropes of energy surging over his armor.

The damage from the EMP grenade spread to the turrets and scanners, and the Urasol fell to the ground, struggling against the weight of his own armor now that the mechanical assist from its AI had been deactivated.

With a loud growl, he yanked off his helmet, flinging it aside, then rolled onto his hands and knees. He looked up towards the access panel, but the end of the barrel of a rifle less than a handspan from his head caught his full attention.

His second curse cut off short as the back of his skull exploded, splattering the walls behind him with blood and brain matter.

Shulgi kicked the heavy body of the thug over onto its back, scanning it quickly for anything useful, but finding nothing that would aid him in his infiltration. He stepped around it, passing under the deactivated turrets, not bothering to clean up the evidence of his passage. It wouldn't be long before whoever oversaw Zaska's security noticed that their cameras were down in this section of the tunnels.

The sooner Shulgi reached his destination, the less likely Zaska's minions would discover him, though his blood burned for a good fight. That wasn't his mission now. He couldn't waste time battling low level thugs so that Sha Zaska had a chance to escape. He had to dispatch them quickly.

The stealth mode of his armor would keep him from being easily detectable by any cameras, even those with thermal imaging as it also concealed his body temperature. Still, Zaska had more patrols within his outer tunnels, not to mention the labyrinthine design of them meant to confuse and disorient any potential intruders.

The under-vents were massive, the basalt pocked in every direction by tunnels. Some had been worked by hand or machine to smooth their walls, but most were left in their natural rough state. As Shulgi proceeded through them, he encountered multiple lava wells spreading their heat through the damp tunnels so that steam filled the air.

Had he not been wearing a sealed helmet, the misty clouds would be suffocating.

He dispatched the next patrol of Zaska's minions with quick, silenced shots from his multi-function rifle, the heads of the cli ku triad rocking backwards as the rounds pierced them, one by one, so fast that they had no time to react. A brief scan of the tunnel they'd exited showed no sign of further patrols or turrets, and Shulgi continued his search, following the path laid out for him by Luna's message.

He had no idea how she'd gotten this information, nor did he think she would have told him had he asked. Still, he trusted it to lead him true. Roz would have stopped her from giving it to him if it would mislead him.

He hoped.

Shulgi detected multiple clutches of minions throughout the twisting maze of tunnels, but he didn't bother with them as their patrols seemed to keep them within certain areas of operation that wouldn't intercept his path. Unless they were alerted to his presence. Thus far, he'd managed to avoid the cameras scanning the tunnels, either by remaining in stealth mode as he passed beneath them or skirting around their view span.

He wasn't far from the inner coil where Zaska's primary body should be when something managed to ambush him.

He wasn't the only one using light-bending and temperature controlling technology to avoid detection. As he passed through a tunnel filled with steam thanks to a nearby lava well, a weight fell upon him from above.

The shriek of a scala filled the air as it slashed at the seals of his armor with two arms while knocking aside his rifle with the other two. Talon like rear claws wrapped around his shoulders as the creature's weight bore him down to his knees. Bony appendages from his shoulders slashed rapidly at Shulgi's helmet.

The force of the attack and the unexpectedness of it caused Shulgi to drop his weapon and use both hands to pull the scala off his back. He tossed the heavy beast against one wall, and its stony skin shifted to match the rock it struck briefly before turning back to a pasty grayish white. The bony, eight-limbed beast had no visible eyes, but the lower third of its face split nearly in half to reveal a mouth filled with multiple rows of teeth and a long, whiplike tongue with hard, serrated edges.

Each of its four arms terminated in three lethal claws, capable of slashing through lesser quality armor than Shulgi's. They'd still managed to score the surface of Shulgi's armor, which damaged the stealth coating that would allow him to sneak effectively past any further obstacles.

At the moment, he had bigger problems. The wing like appendages that the creature used to assist it in digging through tunnels or gripping walls to scurry up and down them were now darting towards his head, jagged claws on the tips aiming for the most vulnerable part of his helmet that covered his eyes and provided the screen for his heads-up display.

A quick sideways glance showed him that his weapon had fallen close to the edge of the lava well. The strap of the rifle burned where it touched the molten rock. He ducked beneath a slashing wingtip, rolling to the side towards his weapon.

The creature leapt after him, realizing what his intent was. It hit him in the chest with the full weight of its body, sending Shulgi staggering backwards as he fought to fend off all four of its arms and its two shoulder appendages.

His blood surged with combat stimulants, speeding his strength, agility, and speed as they wrestled. A satisfying snap sounded from the scala, followed by an agonized shriek, when Shulgi broke one of the four arms.

He managed to snap a second one after another brief flurry of strikes and counterblows, but the creature's frantic movements pushed them both closer to the edge of the lava well. Shulgi's foot bumped his rifle, sending it into the pool of molten rock.

With an irritated grunt as it melted into a useless fiery mess, he managed to free one hand long enough to draw a dagger.

The scala swung at his head with an upper arm, the broken one below it sagging uselessly. The blow rocked Shulgi's head back, but he retaliated quickly by slashing the tendons attached to the creature's shoulder, disabling that arm as well.

Brackish green blood welled from the cut as Shulgi turned his attention to the other side of the creature. He stabbed his dagger through the upper shoulder as a wingtip finally managed to crack his helmet.

The creature's last fully functioning arm kept his belly covered, cautious now that he no longer had the upper hand on Shulgi. Shulgi dodged another wingtip strike to his cracked visor, feinting another slash at the scala's arm. This distraction allowed him to draw his second dagger and punch it through the chest of the scala.

The creature shrieked a piercing cry of pain and used one taloned foot to kick him away, sending Shulgi stumbling into the lava well.

He heard the creature's triumphant cry as the molten rock engulfed him. His HUD filled with red alerts, alarms in his helmet drowning out its screams of victory. He flailed against the thick lava, catching hold of a portion of solid basalt at the edge of the well.

With effort, he pulled his body out of the molten liquid, flames licking from the lava pouring off his damaged armor. If his wings hadn't been tucked beneath his armor, they would be gone by now. He was grateful he'd decided he wouldn't need them in the tight tunnels.

The scala's victory cry cut off with a startled shriek as Shulgi charged him. His molten body struck the scala, setting its flesh aflame. It flailed, wingtips stabbing desperately as Shulgi clung to it, both arms around its waist as he pulled it tighter against him, flames engulfing it. His chest pressed the dagger that he'd left in its torso even deeper, driving it home.

As soon as the creature slumped dead, Shulgi cast it aside. He worked quickly to strip the damaged, melting armor off his body, tossing the pieces aside with frustration.

Without his armor or primary weapon, his battle against Sha Zaska would be much more difficult.

He wouldn't allow that to stop him.

Wearing only his undersuit, he retrieved his undamaged dagger, then continued through the tunnels, moving quicker now. Since he no longer had stealth on his side, he had to use speed to keep the element of surprise.

As he moved through the final tunnels to Zaska's inner coil, he noted the lack of minions guarding it. In fact, it seemed that the place even lacked cameras and scanners once he passed a certain point. It was as if Zaska didn't want to be monitored or have his inner sanctum patrolled, even by his own people.

Shulgi could understand why. It was usually your allies that ended up bringing you down in the end. He knew that better than anyone.

Though this development worked in his favor, he didn't allow himself to grow incautious as he approached Sha Zaska's lair. The hair on the back of his neck stood on end as he drew closer to the monstrous beast. Something definitely wasn't right, and he wondered if he should have trusted Luna.

Surely, a boss as powerful as Zaska was—with a reach as

long as he was rumored to have—should have sensed Shulgi's approach, yet not a single foul limb had unfurled from the deep shadows of the tunnels to snatch Shulgi up and squeeze him to death.

Shulgi had braced himself to face off against a monster he pictured to be built like Nemon, only on a much larger scale. Instead, he reached a locked door that blended so well with the rock around it that only his wrist com told him it was the location he sought.

With the hacking device he'd gotten from Namerian, the lock took less than a Standard minute to disengage. He hid against the wall beside the door as it slid open.

He'd expected a tentacle to unfurl, or perhaps a mass of them to shoot out of the opening and writhe around in search of whoever had unlocked the stone door. Instead, nothing exited through that portal and after a long minute of waiting in breathless silence, he cautiously glanced around the door frame.

To his surprise, the room beyond wasn't that large. Certainly not nearly large enough to fit the body of a monster that fed on hundreds of slaves each annum. Instead, he spotted a bank of monitors circling the walls of the round room. An elevator bisected the center of the room, the door closed and presumably locked. Sitting in front of the monitors that flickered with different vantage points in the surrounding tunnels, a single human snored softly, head leaning to the side. In front of the human male, a bottle of liquor sat on the desk that fronted the monitors.

Shulgi approached with silent steps, noting the muscular build of the human. He was rock solid but looked more like a laborer than a warrior. Once Shulgi moved close enough to get a better look at the male, he noted a slave brand on the man's neck.

The sight of it raised his brows. It was strange to see the

slave of a major warehouse company from third-tier being put in charge of security in Zaska's supposed lair.

Things weren't adding up, and Shulgi now felt more confused than ever about Sha Zaska—and about the information Luna had given him. Perhaps he'd been correct to mistrust her. He still didn't know why Roz would join in whatever game she was playing.

The only way to get answers he needed was to force them out of this human, who, despite the brand on his neck, did not appear to be a slave any longer.

TWENTY-EIGHT

Molly felt like a part of her had died inside, and she might just be a zombie, going about her day without any awareness of it. She couldn't stomach eating anything, and the words of her friends and allies seemed to buzz around her ears without her comprehending them. Her eyes itched and burned, dry at the moment, but likely to drip again with her seemingly endless tears when she once again retreated to the quiet space of her room.

She hadn't wanted to leave it at all, preferring to remain hidden away until she felt like she could breathe easily again, because right now, she felt close to hyperventilating every time she thought of the look in Shulgi's eyes when she'd walked out on him.

It was for the best, she kept repeating to herself, but those words also buzzed around her without meaning. What was the best? Did she even know anymore? Could she continue on in this role she'd never wanted in the first place, forever lonely and heartbroken, without snapping from the strain of it? Would she have to turn to drowning her sorrows and trauma in an ocean of alcohol, like poor Jem, who had grown so agoraphobic now that they let him stay down in the lower security room, so he didn't have to deal with people or new spaces?

She had no answers to those questions, but she knew in her heart that she'd made the wrong decision. She just couldn't tell what the right decision would have been.

She should have tried harder to work things out with Shulgi. She should have told him the truth and trusted that he wouldn't betray her and her allies. She should have believed in him, since she'd told him herself that she thought he was a good person at his core. If that were true—if she'd been completely genuine in that belief—she should have put her faith in him completely.

She did believe he was a good person, but his past told her that even good people could be swayed to do bad things. Sometimes, those things ended up harming the people closest to them. Her secret had not felt like hers alone, or she would have shared it without reservation, but if the people she loved ended up getting hurt because she'd trusted Shulgi with that secret, she never would have been able to forgive herself.

"Molly," Jenice said, laying a gentle hand on her shoulder.

Molly jumped with a startled yelp, blinking as she regained awareness of her surroundings. She glanced around, noting Briana and Jenice staring at her with concern in their eyes. "Sorry, what did you say again?"

Briana huffed, a small smile tilting her lips. "You've been out of it all day, Mol. Maybe you should take today off." She patted her generous bosom with the palm of one hand. "I don't mind taking over for you. This should be an easy day for Zaska's mouthpiece, and it will be good practice to step into your role."

Jenice nodded, shooting a speaking glance at Briana before turning her attention back to Molly. "We were talking about who we could bring in to take Briana's place as second, since you'll be joining me in the back."

"I still think Jusa would be a good choice," Briana said in a tone that suggested she'd already mentioned this before and had already been rejected.

Jenice sighed, slowly shaking her head. "Jusa is lovely, but she's been through too much trauma. I don't want her to take on this role, even though she says she'd be willing."

"We've all been through trauma!" Briana held her arms out at her sides. "Jusa has training. She's absolutely gorgeous, even to humans, and she has natural grace and charm. She's exactly the kind of female Sha Zaska would choose for a dyed flower."

Molly understood Jenice's caution. Someone broken by their experiences had a higher likelihood of inadvertently giving away Sha Zaska's secret. They couldn't afford to make the wrong decision when it came to bringing in new flowers.

There had been only a about a dozen dyed flowers since they'd come up with the concept, and only Molly had lasted this long in the role. It could be taxing even for those with an unbroken will. For those close to the edge, it could end up pushing them over. At the very least, it would mean they'd retire and leave Za'Kluth far sooner than a more healed flower would, forcing the inner circle to make this decision all over again, and take yet another risk with their secret.

Briana was similar to Molly in that she'd gained a strong degree of pragmatism during her enslavement. She'd learned how to play the game and make the most of her miserable situation. She also had little interest in returning to Earth, claiming she'd been nothing special there—just another face in the crowd—but now she felt like she was doing something truly important, and building a legend for herself in the process.

Jusa wasn't human. She was a hybrid nostria-onera, similar in build to a human female, though her breasts only swelled during her mating season and that happened only once in a Za'Kluth year. She also had six tentacles arrayed in two rows down her back, the lowest pair falling past her knees, writhing beneath a long fall of straight, filmy white hair. Her eyes glimmered like faceted diamonds in a delicate, almost foxlike tan furred face with a short snout and ultra-thin whiskers.

The hybrid had no attachment to a home world that would draw her away, but she had suffered dearly while enslaved to a wealthy merchant on seventh-tier. She'd been "created" for the pleasure of himself and his wife cluster, and they'd used her poorly in her short and tragic life.

"Jusa *wants* to do this!" Briana said earnestly. "Besides, since we bought her openly instead of secretly aiding her escape, there wouldn't be any awkward questions about why she's down here serving Zaska. It's what those bastards who sold her would expect Zaska to do with her!"

Jenice shook her head, but Molly spoke aloud before she could deny the request again. "I suppose Jusa has nowhere else to go," she said sadly, thinking about her own situation. "Perhaps it isn't such a bad idea after all. She knows enough about the truth that we wouldn't be telling her anything much more dangerous than we already have."

"Plus," Briana said with a sly grin, "I think Mogie has the hots for her. He'd be sad if you sent her away, Jen. Aren't you already on his bad side? Do you really want to make him angrier at you?"

Molly raised her eyebrows at the devastated expression on Jenice's face. "You know, I haven't seen either of them today," she said aloud, realizing that they'd failed to greet her when she'd crawled painfully out of bed that morning, and she hadn't seen them since.

In her sadness, she'd failed to notice their absence until now. Even when she didn't have somewhere to go where she needed their escort, they usually made a point to stop in and chat with her every day.

Jenice ran a hand through her hair, wincing as her fingers encountered tangles. "I sent them to Column 210 for that task we've been talking about. They should be back by tomorrow with a bunch of credit tokens in hand."

Molly's lips tightened in anger. "You didn't even discuss this with me first."

"They aren't in any danger, Mol." Jenice looked repentant, but her tone sounded firm. "You can take other bodyguards today, if you need to go anywhere."

Guards who wouldn't help Molly sneak away to see Shulgi was what Jenice meant. Guards who were loyal to the inner circle first, rather than to Molly personally. They would see Jenice's orders as better for the gang as a whole than Molly's selfish desire to see her lover again.

"If anything happens to Mog and Grun—"

Jenice lifted a hand to cut her off. "C'mon, Molly! I love them both too. You know I'd never put them in danger without reason! The dealer they're going to see is totally legit. They'll be fine!"

Molly looked away from Jenice's expression, which appeared torn between pleading and frustrated. She met Briana's eyes, and the other woman shrugged, clearly unsure what to say to reduce the growing tension between Molly and Jenice.

Jenice opened her mouth to say more when an alarm pealed, filling the inner sanctum with a klaxon of sound and a flashing of bright red lights.

"Sonofabitch!" Jenice leapt up from the sofa as Briana vaulted over it, landing lithely on her feet.

They all turned towards the door leading to the office as

they heard the whooshing sound of the blast-proof shutter sliding down on the other side of it.

"What's going on?" Briana said even as she rushed to the hidden panel that hid their cache of weapons.

Jenice and Molly joined her, each grabbing a pistol.

Jenice tapped her wrist com, then spoke into it. They all read the reply that scrolled over the skin of her wrist.

"Iriduans invading?" Molly felt as stricken as if she'd taken a physical blow. "Why? No! It can't be Shulgi. He would never do this to me!"

Jenice managed to get more information from the guards beyond their sealed sanctum, her voice shaking as she spoke into her com.

"We're losing ground fast!" she said as the text scrolled. "They brought a whole damned army! It mostly looks like hired mercs, but the dock guards are saying they see Ma'Nah's symbol on some of the armor."

"Shulgi wouldn't *do* this!" Molly insisted even as Jenice rushed towards the door leading to the inner security office. "He loves me! He would never put me at risk!"

"They're taking over," Jenice hissed as she spun around to face Molly, even while pressing her palm to the security door access panel, "we can't hold them off for long, Molly! Not without activating 'Hail Mary'."

Molly's heart thudded with dread as she thought about what would happen if Shulgi was out there when that happened. "No! We- we must be sure about why they're here before we purge the docks! A lot of innocent people will die if we use our last resort!"

"Don't act like you give a fuck about our people, Molly," Jenice sneered. "All you care about is whether Shulgi is out there."

Molly jerked back, stung by Jenice's tone and vicious

words. "What the hell has gotten into you, Jenice!"

Jenice's expression suddenly crumpled as she sobbed. "I'm so sorry, Molly! This is all my fault! I just wanted to keep him away, and I thought his people would stop him from seeing you if they thought he compromised their position with Zaska."

A deep and horrible foreboding filled Molly, just as the security door slid open.

Jem flew out of the room, slamming bodily into Jenice, followed by Shulgi, moving so fast he was a blur. Within the blink of an eye, he had a hold of the pistol Jenice had dropped, not to mention a fistful of her hair.

He jerked her head back, pressing the pistol to her temple as he dragged her up onto her feet. "Lower your weapons," he growled, his eyes cold as they shifted from Briana to Molly.

She and Briana both did as he ordered. Molly blinked back tears as she looked away from Shulgi's remote, chilling gaze. She spotted Jem lying unconscious on the floor, blood seeping from multiple cuts on his body.

"What did you do to him?" she demanded, shock and devastation in her voice, turning her gaze back to Shulgi. "Why would you do this? I thought you—"

"Do not pretend any emotion for me at this point, Molly," he said with a snarl, jerking Jenice's head further back until her body arched in his hold. "I know now that *you* are Sha Zaska— not a hapless slave. I understand everything now. The black-mail attempt wasn't from a monster dwelling below the vents, but from a greedy female who couldn't be content with the lucrative deal Ma'Nah had already made with you." His bitter chuckle held no mirth. "You played me well, little Molly. I almost fell for your innocent act. Ninhursag would have been in awe of your deviousness."

Despite the rage so evident in his expression as his lips pulled back from his teeth in a snarl, his brows lowered so much they cast a dark shadow over his cold eyes, and his jaw ticked, she still heard the hurt behind the deep bitterness in his voice.

Molly slowly shook her head. "Shulgi, please, I would never do anything to hurt you! You don't underst—"

Jenice gasped in pain as Shulgi pressed the pistol harder against her temple. "Do you think I won't kill a female, Molly?" His brutally cold eyes shifted to Briana. "Toss your weapon aside, or you will be the next to die."

Briana, trembling visibly, her face gone pale even with the dyes on her skin, threw her pistol onto the sofa, then held up both hands quickly to show she was unarmed.

Molly's fingers felt nerveless around the grip of her own pistol. Unlike Briana, she hadn't even tried to bring it up in a subtle way in the hopes of catching Shulgi off guard long enough to get a shot in on him before he could kill Jenice. Even if she thought she could get away with it—and she knew that was impossible—she couldn't bring herself to hurt him, at least not when she still hoped she could reason with him.

"Shulgi, I know you're upset that I hid the truth about Sha Zaska," she said slowly, her voice trembling as she set the pistol on the seat back of the sofa, then raised her own hands, "but please don't be hasty. I can explain everything."

"Where are the slaves?" Shulgi demanded, his voice hard and relentless. "Did you sell them off world instead of killing them? Claiming they died is an excellent way to escape paying excessive export fees, isn't it? Not to mention avoiding angry owners coming after you for the theft of their property."

"We freed them!" Molly said, realizing that Jem must not have made that known to Shulgi. No doubt he'd revealed as little as possible during his torture, likely unaware of the kind of person Shulgi was.

Molly wasn't even sure of the kind of person Shulgi was at

this point, though it hurt to acknowledge that she might have been wrong about him.

Still, some hint of the goodness she'd seen in him flickered behind his eyes at her words. "You *freed* them?"

Jenice's body relaxed a little and Molly suspected Shulgi's hard grip had loosened in his surprise at her words.

She nodded, clasping her hands in front of her in a pleading gesture. "Shulgi, we are *all* escaped slaves. We created Sha Zaska to be our 'master' to keep other predators away from us. Then we realized we could use his myth to help others escape this world and find their freedom—maybe even return to their home worlds."

Though his expression remained hard and remote, she saw his brows lift, just enough to spot the uncertainty that softened his eyes. "If this is true, why didn't you tell me this when I said I wanted to free *you*."

She despaired as the suspicion in his gaze returned, hardening it again. "I... I wasn't sure I could trust you to keep our secret. It wasn't only my own life at stake. Please, Shulgi, believe me when I say I wanted nothing more than to tell you the truth!"

His snarl only deepened, and Jenice yelped as his grip tightened. "The truth? You mean the one where you threatened to expose the footage of me fucking you to the entire dreg, knowing that such an act would destroy Ma'Nah and put me on the execution list of every Iriduan in the galaxy?"

Molly gasped, her mouth gaping open with her shock and horror. She shook her head so hard that her bound hair broke loose from its bun. "I would *never* do such a thing! Who told you this lie?"

"I *saw* the footage that was sent to my kin," he growled, his voice shaking with rage.

Molly shook her head again, not wanting to believe what he

was saying. "No, you *couldn't* have. There's no way someone could have gotten ahold of that footage. We keep it in a data vault that isn't connected to any other servers. We—"

"I did it," Jenice said dully. "I sent the footage to Ma'Nah, Molly."

Shulgi hissed, then thrust Jenice away from him like he couldn't stand being in contact with her, though he kept his pistol pointed at her head, his aim rock steady on her as she stumbled into Molly.

"God damn it, Jenice!" Briana shouted, turning her full focus on Jenice as if the lethally enraged male wasn't still pointing a pistol in their direction. "Are you fucking *kidding* me right now? Blackmail footage is supposed to be a last resort! Always! How could you do this? We had a great deal with Ma'Nah!"

Jenice covered her face with both hands, her body shaking. "I wanted him gone," she said between ugly sobs. "I feared that Molly would only end up hurt again, and this time, the heartbreak would destroy her! I didn't think he really cared about her. I thought he was just toying with her."

"So you pissed off the entire company enough for them to send an army of mercs our way just to get rid of one guy?" Briana's voice had risen to a shriek. "Haven't you ever heard of buying someone off? People do it all the time! Hell, we could have made Molly 'disappear' to keep the guy away! Why would you do something so stupid and reckless as this?"

Molly met Shulgi's eyes, still seeing no sign of softening in them as he shifted his gaze from Briana to her, to Jenice.

"She didn't just want him gone. She wanted to hurt him." Molly turned her focus to Jenice, betrayal gouging claws deep into her heart. "To destroy him."

Jenice lowered her hands, still sniffling, her eyes red and swollen as they fixed on Molly. "Kuro's lies nearly broke you,

Molly. I've seen these males toy with all of you with no regard for what it does to you emotionally. I was tired of watching you get hurt and being helpless to retaliate. This time, I wanted to make one of them feel as crushed as you would be when it ended."

Molly shook her head, her own eyes dripping with tears. "My heart is certainly hurt right now, Jen. My sense of betrayal is far stronger than the one Kuro left me with." She shook her head sharply, holding up a hand to stop Jenice from moving closer to her in supplication. "No, I don't think I'll ever be able to forgive you for this."

As much as it felt like they were being wrenched out of her, the words came out dully and without heat.

"Molly," Jenice wept, "I did it for your own good! I knew you wouldn't have the strength to stop seeing him until he'd finished playing with you and discarded you. I knew I had to do something drastic to keep him away from you."

"Yeah, you dumb bitch," Briana snapped, flinging a hand towards the outer door, "that 'something drastic' has led to an army knocking at our front door. Or should I say beating it down!"

Molly turned away from Jenice, who still stared at her with a wordless plea.

She met Shulgi's remote glare again. "Shulgi, please explain the misunderstanding to your people. We will pay any damages and turn over all copies of the footage, as well as a generous tribute, along with our sincerest apologies."

"It's too late for that, Molly," Shulgi said in the coldest tone she'd ever heard from him. "Ma'Nah has the manpower to take these docks, and we will, regardless of what resistance your minions put up. I went into the under-vents to eliminate Sha Zaska for that reason. If you want to end this without more bloodshed, tell your own minions to surrender now, and their lives will be spared. We will even guarantee the jobs of those who sign a contract with us."

"You can't take over our organization!" Jenice shouted, suddenly charging at Shulgi.

The sound of a pistol discharging caused Molly to scream in horror as Jenice collapsed to the floor in front of Shulgi.

She rushed towards Jenice, her heart pounding. Briana's shouts of alarm barely registered in her ears as Jenice's moans of pain blotted them out.

"Jen!" She hugged the other woman to her chest. "Don't you die on me!"

"She will have trouble walking until she's healed, but I have enough skill not to kill her unless I choose to," Shulgi said in an emotionless tone. "I recommend none of you force me to make that choice."

Molly looked up into his eyes, seeing no trace of the loving male she'd once believed him to be. "You came here to destroy Sha Zaska and take over, didn't you?" She huffed in mirthless laughter. "I was the fool being played all along. You seduced me because you saw me as a way to get closer to Sha Zaska. Close enough to strike him down."

Shulgi gestured to Briana with his empty hand. "Call off your minions and unlock that door. You've already lost this fight."

Then he returned his attention to Molly as Briana slowly made her way towards the door, speaking into her wrist com. "Believe what you will, mouthpiece. It doesn't change the fact that Sha Zaska is 'dead', and his reign of terror is over on these docks."

"And what new reign of terror takes his place?" Molly asked bitterly, her heart shattering until she felt certain that shards of it pierced her lungs, making it nearly impossible to draw another breath.

TWENTY-NINE

Shulgi didn't know what to believe now, the revelations that kept coming knocking him off guard. He wanted to hate Molly but knew he never could. Even if she truly had used him the way he'd suspected her of doing, he didn't think he could forget what she had meant to him.

Now, he watched her devastated expression as one of her companions opened the door to Namerian and a squad of armed security from Ma'Nah. Shulgi hadn't wanted Namerian to come along on this mission, seeing no need for his presence, but his creche-kin had insisted. Given the humiliation of the past day cycle and what Namerian and the rest of Shulgi's team had seen of his reckless indiscretion, Shulgi felt like he couldn't deny Namerian this.

They'd come not only to take revenge on Sha Zaska for daring to attempt to blackmail Ma'Nah, but also to destroy his operation completely and seize all the footage the creature possessed. It had been Shulgi's plan to take over Zaska's organization since meeting Molly and learning that the creature kept her as a slave.

Now that he knew the truth—that Molly and her companions were not only free, but had created Sha Zaska to give them power they never could have gained on their own—he didn't know what he felt about Ma'Nah's successful hostile takeover. If what Molly said about the missing slaves was true—if she and the others had truly been helping them escape Za'Kluth—then the takeover would be a mistake. There was no way Namerian and the others would risk Ma'Nah's operations and reputation by continuing Molly's underground work.

Still, it was too late to change things now. Ma'Nah held the advantage. Zaska's thuggish minions proved no match against the security force and mercenaries hired by Ma'Nah. The traps around the dock provided more of a challenge, and Shulgi now knew Molly and her people had set up some sort of last resort attack to wipe out an invading force. No doubt many of the minions would slip into the vents for whatever purge they had in place, but many innocent dockhands and ship workers would die.

He was glad she hadn't given the order to use such a desperate measure to wipe out the invading Iriduans—for her sake. Maybe she had manipulated him. Maybe he really was a fool to believe that she was sincere in her words and her use of the power she'd gained through Sha Zaska's myth. He wouldn't deny that his feelings for her blinded him.

Yet, even when he was imprinted on Ninhursag, despite his desire for the woman who'd ensnared him, he'd always known she was evil, had never felt any doubt about it. He didn't think Molly was evil. Ruthless, perhaps. Clever and cunning, no doubt. But evil?

He couldn't believe that.

That realization left him in a difficult place when Namerian's security detail surrounded the three women.

The voluptuous one whose name he didn't know screamed

obscenities in a human language at the guard who grabbed her to pull her towards the door. Another guard bent to grip the shirt of the human male that Shulgi had forced to bring him up into this inner sanctum. The man had been intoxicated and suffering from blood loss and had remained unconscious this entire time.

The Iriduan didn't bother to pick him up to carry him out, instead dragging his body as if he were already dead, when Shulgi knew he wasn't.

Yet.

Two more guards approached Molly, who still crouched beside her wounded friend.

Shulgi growled a warning when they drew too close. "I have these two under control," he said, his tone brooking no argument.

It angered him that they glanced over at Namerian instead of backing away. Namerian lifted a hand to gesture for them to move aside and give him space.

"It appears that one of these females is wounded," he said coolly, as if they weren't still finishing off a battle on the docks. "Allow me to tend to her." He lifted silver brows at Shulgi.

Shulgi nodded and lowered the pistol he'd taken from the one named Jenice. Namerian moved closer to Molly and Jenice, reaching into his robe for his medical scanner.

Shulgi's attention shifted to Molly, who looked up into his eyes, her own wet with tears that shimmered on her dyed skin.

"You used me," she whispered.

"I loved you, Molly," he insisted, still feeling stung himself that she'd kept such a monumental secret from him. It let him know that despite her words, she'd never really trusted him.

She parted her lips to say more, then shrieked in pain and surprise as Namerian grasped her by the hair and jerked her to her feet. He held an injector to her jugular.

Shulgi shouted in rage but froze in place as Namerian pressed the injector tighter against Molly's neck, backing away as his security force surrounded Shulgi.

"I didn't want it to be this way," Namerian said in a regretful tone. "I respect you, Shulgi. I've always looked up to you, ever since we hatched in creche. This is not how I would have our relationship end."

"If you hurt her, I will not rest until you are dead," Shulgi growled, his grip tightening around the pistol.

"Toss aside the weapon," Namerian ordered, pulling harder on Molly's hair.

Her eyes were wide and frightened as she stared at Shulgi, yet she kept her lips pressed shut, like she didn't want to beg him to save her.

Did she truly mistrust him that much?

Shulgi quickly dropped his weapon and kicked it aside. He could dispatch these fools with his bare hands, if need be, but not before Namerian could inject Molly with a poison Shulgi suspected would be instantly lethal to her. His creche-kin was no fool.

"She already offered to give up Zaska's data cache, Namerian," Shulgi said in a measured tone. "There's no need for this."

Namerian chuckled bitterly. "As if that is what truly matters! I want the override code, Shulgi. It is time for our people to rise to the top of the food chain again, and that will happen when the High Lords are resurrected. Nothing will stop the Iriduans then."

Shulgi shook his head slowly, disappointed in Namerian, but not as surprised as he should be. "You have a juvenile's dreams, Namerian. Perhaps you have been too sheltered in your labs. The high lords won't help our people. We mean no more to them than any other chattel. Did you not listen when I spoke of Ninhursag's evil?"

Namerian huffed as he backed further away from Shulgi, dragging Molly with him. "We won't raise any of the female ancients. In fact, we only need one of the high lords to help us wipe out the emperors and their council. We will be careful which one we resurrect, and *all* of our citizens will be modified by the time our new lord leads us to victory over all other species in the Syndicate."

"Namerian—brother—do not do this! You're not a killer. Don't let this misguided crusade turn you into one."

Namerian seemed to tremble, Molly gasping as the injector jerked against her jugular. Shulgi wasn't certain whether the professor was nervous or enraged. It was difficult to tell with most of his expression hidden behind his mask.

"How ironic coming from you, Shulgi. The resident murderer of the dreg."

Molly's eyes widened further as they met his. Her mouth dropped open as if she wanted to ask him what Namerian meant, but now wasn't the time for explanations. Especially the kind he didn't want to give.

"Once you start shedding blood, Namerian, it's difficult to stop. You can always justify it to yourself. You can always pretend that you're merely working towards a greater good with each kill." Shulgi slowly shook his head. "But you can't deny that you've become exactly what you hunt when you have to face yourself in the mirror. Trust me, Namerian, I *am* the one you should listen to when it comes to this."

"I *am* working for the greater good!" Namerian insisted, but the quiver in his voice told Shulgi the trembling of the injector was likely fear rather than anger. "Quit stalling, Shulgi. Give me the passcode and once I've tested it, this female is all yours." His wings flickered behind him as another sign of his nervousness. "You won't need to remain here on Za'Kluth any longer.

You can take her anywhere you want to, since your role in the mission will be over."

Shulgi studied Namerian without allowing his skepticism to show in his expression. They both knew one of them wouldn't be leaving this room alive. Whether Molly lived or died would determine which of them followed.

Jenice moaned as she struggled to crawl towards Molly and Namerian, leaving a smeared blood trail in her wake that showed she'd already moved several handspans while Namerian's focus was on Shulgi.

She was trying to get to Molly, but Shulgi knew there wasn't anything the woman could do that would help. She only risked her own life, because Namerian's security weren't all focused entirely on Shulgi and the threat he posed.

When Jenice slid a little further, her body made a slick sound on the tile that Namerian finally noticed. "Get that one out of here," he snapped, taking another step away from both Shulgi and the wounded woman.

"No," Molly said, struggling in Namerian's hold as one of the security guards roughly hauled Jenice up, causing her to cry out in pain. "Leave her alone!"

"Stop moving, woman!" Namerian shouted in her ear, his thumb trembling on the button of the injector. "I will kill you if you don't."

And then he would die seconds later, which Shulgi knew Namerian understood. Still, the professor was clearly nervous and that made his fingers twitchy.

"Molly," Shulgi said in the calmest tone he could manage, "they will heal her and get her back on her feet. Ma'Nah needs you and your companions to aid them in bringing the rest of Sha Zaska's minions under our control." He shifted his eyes from Molly's frightened face to Namerian's somewhat wild violet stare. "Professor Namerian is well aware of this, and he isn't foolish enough to destroy Zaska's most important assets, is he?"

"The women will be safe as long as they cooperate," Namerian snapped impatiently. "So be silent and quit fidgeting," he said to Molly. "If your lover gives me what I need, you can both leave this place!"

More security forces moved into the room as the guard who'd grabbed Jenice hauled her wriggling form into his arms while she screamed in protest. She begged Molly to forgive her as the guard carried her out of the chamber. Shulgi ignored the bulk of her screams, watching the fear and sadness play out over Molly's features. He remained aware of the dozen security guards filling the chamber now, all armed and well armored as they flanked him.

His blood might be filled with combat stimulants, and he might be a highly trained warrior, but even he could not defeat this many opponents without arms or armor of his own. Namerian had the upper hand, and he knew it.

With the last distraction out of the room, Namerian returned his full attention to Shulgi. "So, does this woman die, or do you give me a simple code that has only served to be a burden to you, Shulgi?"

Meeting Molly's eyes, Shulgi knew what he had to do. He had no choice in the matter.

THIRTY

The stranger holding Molly with such a punishing grip wasn't nearly as strong or imposing as Shulgi, but he proved much stronger than her. Though his slender body trembled against her back, the device pushing against her jugular made her more than certain that he was far more dangerous to her in this moment than anything else. In fact, his obvious fear only made him more unpredictable.

When Shulgi lifted his hand to tap on his wrist, the Iriduan holding her relaxed infinitesimally. Within seconds, she heard a beep from his wrist.

Namerian chuckled. "Nice try, Shulgi, but I won't be distracted enough to check that message. Send it to one of the others and they'll update me once they've run the code and verified it."

Shulgi's brows hung low over his eyes as he glared at Namerian, tapping again at his wrist. Molly's heart ached to see him forced to do this thing he clearly didn't want to do.

Forced to do it to save her life. He must feel something for her if he would go to this trouble. He'd told her he loved her.

But that had been in past tense. Did he still have feelings for her now, or was he only acquiescing to the demands of this Namerian because he didn't want any woman to die for his sake?

She suspected Shulgi wouldn't let a woman die if he could stop it, but she also wanted to believe that she meant too much to him for him to let her go like this. Maybe, just maybe, he was choosing her over anything else. It felt selfish to want him to do so, because from what the two Iriduans had been saying to each other, this passcode was important. Far more important than the life of a single prostitute in a criminal city on a backwater planet.

Yet it didn't take long for Namerian's associates to verify that Shulgi had given him the correct code, and Namerian's body tensed again, to Molly's surprise, even as the injector shifted away from her neck.

Shulgi watched that injector like a hawk, his eyes narrowed.

"I won't kill the woman," Namerian said as his guards all raised their weapons, aiming them towards Shulgi.

Shulgi barely glanced at them, his hard gaze returning to Molly and Namerian as Molly's thudding heart suddenly froze, her breath whooshing out of her.

"No," she managed after sucking in a gasp. "No!" she screamed as the guards opened fire.

Shulgi's body jerked as multiple rounds tore through his flesh, blood darkening the fitted suit he wore instead of armor. For a long, horrific moment that seemed forever burned in her memory, his eyes met hers and a slight smile kicked up the corners of his mouth. Then he toppled backwards, collapsing onto the unforgiving tile floor.

She screamed until her throat ached, then screamed some more, struggling against strong arms that kept her from running to Shulgi. She noticed nothing about her surroundings but his fallen body bleeding out on the tile.

How could this day have gone so terribly wrong? She'd had so much hope, so much love for him, and now, something had happened to him that was far worse than seeing him walk away from her.

"No!" she shouted, scratching uselessly at the impenetrable armor of the guard that yanked her off her feet and threw her over his shoulder.

She beat on his back, then tried to tear at his wings, but he battered her face with them, proving they were far stronger than their delicate appearance seemed to suggest. She realized the futility of fighting him.

As he carried her out of the room, she watched in despair as Namerian ordered his guards to dispose of Shulgi's body.

The Iriduans lined Molly, Jenice, and Briana up just outside their headquarters, all of them seated on the dirty ground near steaming vents. Jem and several of the other leading minions lay in a jumbled heap against the wall of the dockmaster's office. To her relief, they appeared to still be alive, since she saw some of them visibly breathing, and all of them wore restraints, which would have been pointless for corpses.

There were plenty of those scattered around the docks, and many of them were Iriduans that Zaska's minions had success-fully taken down before being overwhelmed by sheer numbers and superior technology. The battlefield of her docks was blood-soaked and gory, but no sight would ever disturb her as much as watching Shulgi die right in front of her.

She couldn't find it in her to care about anything else at this point but the grief eating her up from the inside. Devastation filled her at the terrible memory of his blood spattering as his body jerked backwards, his wings spreading behind him as if he could take off into the air to escape, his hair whipping around his body as the force of the rounds struck him.

The one called Namerian finally left their headquarters and joined the squad of mercenaries surrounding Molly and the others. He paused in front of her, ignoring Jenice and Briana's curses and insults leveled at him. Molly didn't bother to say what was on her mind about him. He'd just become her worst enemy, but at the moment, there wasn't anything she could do about that.

If he were wise, he would simply put a bullet in her brain right now, because she wouldn't rest until he was dead. Killing him, shooting him down like an animal in the street, had become her all-consuming purpose. For the moment, all she could do was glare at him with her hate in her eyes.

"I made a promise to my kin that I wouldn't kill you," he said in a cold voice that echoed from the speaker on his mask. "However, I can't have any of you running around, getting in our way now that we rule these docks." He gestured towards the crowd that had formed beyond the circle of Iriduan mercenaries a short distance away. "I don't want anyone's loyalty tested at this critical point in our operations, and it would be wasteful to destroy all of these useful laborers."

Most of them were dockhands, but many of Zaska's minions had surrendered after Briana's announcement to them that Sha Zaska was dead. They would take the offer of a job from the Iriduans, because in the long run, they didn't really care who paid their bills, as long as they still had food on the table.

Her eyes met those of Thudar, his antlered head towering above the crowd. His hard amber gaze held no emotion for her or the others. As far as he was concerned, they were only extensions of Zaska's will. He wouldn't risk his life to rescue mere slaves.

She thanked Jenice silently for sending Mogorl and Grundon to column 210. *They* would have tried to rescue her and the others, and they would have died for it, as so many of Sha Zaska's most loyal guards had. She didn't think she could handle losing them in addition to Shulgi.

She already couldn't handle losing Shulgi. It felt like a part of her had died, so when the Iriduan mercenaries raised their weapons to point them at her and Jenice and Briana, she sighed in relief. She would never get her vengeance on Namerian, but at least her suffering would end. She wouldn't have to see Shulgi's horrible death replayed over and over again every time she closed her eyes.

"You shouldn't have sent that footage to me," Namerian said with an obvious snarl in his tone, "because it didn't take long to identify you, woman."

Jenice stiffened at Molly's side, her hand sliding across the dock decking to grip Molly's, her palm clammy. "I'm so sorry, Molly," she whispered weakly.

Though the Iriduans had stopped the bleeding in Jenice's leg and splinted the shattered bone, they clearly hadn't given her any painkillers.

"There's a bounty on your head," Namerian continued, ignoring Jenice's words as he spoke to Molly. He bent down into a crouch to meet Molly's eyes. "*Yours*, not Sha Zaska's. I found that interesting. I contacted the hunters and discovered that a certain brothel owner with powerful connections wants her property returned."

Briana and Jenice gasped in horror, but Molly felt nothing. No fear, no outrage. Nothing. Watching Shulgi die seemed to have stripped every emotion from her but the desire to avenge him.

"I believe she'll be very grateful for the return of not only you, but perhaps a dozen more of Sha Zaska's minions to serve as her slaves." He regarded the other two women, then shifted his gaze to the pile of barely alive minions who apparently hadn't willingly surrendered but had been taken alive.

Molly was grateful most of the other women who served Sha Zaska in some way did not fight and seemed to have blended into the crowd of dockhands or taken refuge in a bolt hole. Uthagol wasn't kind to her slaves, and Molly, Briana, and Jenice would pay dearly for their actions against their former master. Some of the males would also be slaved out in Uthagol's brothels, though most would likely be resold.

Their lives would return to being a living hell, but Molly was already there after watching Shulgi die. She said nothing to Namerian, only staring up at him with her hatred on full display, her lips tight, her eyes narrowed until all she could see was him.

"Note the bright part of the pond," he said as he straightened from his crouch, still staring down at Molly as if he didn't notice how much she wanted to kill him, "I *am* keeping my word to Shulgi. You won't die by my hand."

THIRTY-ONE

Shulgi groaned as he rolled over onto his side from his back, his entire body filled with agony.

"You should take it easy," a familiar female voice said. "You're not completely healed."

He pushed himself up on what felt to be an operating table, groaning again as the movement of his muscles caused more shooting pain. He opened his eyes to glare at Luna, who stood beside the table, holding a portable Lusian healing device.

"I thought those things worked faster," he said with a pained grunt as she passed it over one of the wounds in his arm.

"You were almost dead when I retrieved you from the guards intent on disposing of you," she answered calmly. "In fact, several of your vital organs had been nearly destroyed. There was a lot of damage to repair, and even *we* aren't miracle workers." She lifted her dark gaze to meet his eyes, grinning broadly. "Though we like to pretend we are."

He ran a shaking hand through his hair, wincing as his fingers encountered tangles and bloodstained matting. "How did I even survive at all. Namerian's thugs pumped me full of rounds."

Luna chuckled, shaking her head. "Those nanites your Iriduan friend developed are something else. Quite impressive." She regarded him with a penetrating stare. "And that's coming from a species that considers ourselves the most technologically advanced. Perhaps we still have much to learn."

Shulgi huffed. "The nanites weren't created by any *friend* of mine," he muttered. "Besides, I thought the ones inside me had been destroyed after they cured me."

Luna shrugged one shoulder in a very un-Lusian-like gesture. "They were only dormant. They reactivated when your body was in mortal peril to mitigate the worst of the damage and keep you alive long enough for them to begin the healing process. I've managed to speed it up some, but you've been unconscious for several day cycles."

Shulgi stiffened at her words. "Day cycles? Where's Molly?" He struggled to stand, nudging aside the medical device Luna passed over his chest now. "I need to see her." He had to make sure Namerian kept his word that he wouldn't kill Molly.

At Luna's frown, his stomach dipped. "Luna, what happened to Molly?" he growled, his hands clenching into fists as he thought of what he would do to Namerian when he got ahold of him.

"Namerian knows," she said. "You must find him and make him tell you. I don't have that information and the entire column is on alert after Ma'Nah's takeover of the under-tier, so I've had trouble finding anyone on the inside of either the dreg or Zaska's old crew to give it to me. Thus far, I only know the women that were taken captive remain alive, because Ma'Nah reassured its off-world stakeholders that they didn't kill any innocents."

Shulgi pushed off the table to stand, swaying for a moment as his head spun. Luna's hand on his arm steadied him.

"I have to find Namerian," he said with a deep snarl. "I will make him suffer before I kill him, but before he breathes his last, he will tell me where Molly is."

"There's one other thing we need you to do, Shulgi," Luna said in a careful tone.

He glanced around the small, nondescript room they were in as she persistently passed the device over his wounds, barely seeing his surroundings as his mind focused on Molly. He feared what danger she might be in right now.

"I owe you my life already. You need only ask."

"You might have to kill innocents," Luna said slowly.

Shulgi met her eyes, feeling the soft touch of her mind probing at his.

"I know you don't like doing that, Shulgi Amanat."

"I will do whatever it takes to repay my debt to you, Luna, and to get Molly back."

She dipped her chin in a small nod. "In that case, we need you to destroy Ma'Nah and all its labs. I know you will want to evacuate the workers first, but you must be certain none of them take any of the nanite samples with them."

Shulgi closed his eyes, drawing in a deep breath that expanded his healing lungs painfully. "I understand. I'll do what it takes to stop the spread of the nanites."

"Namerian is back at Ma'Nah." Luna finally deactivated her device, then pushed a button on it that caused it to fold up and disappear in a flash of light. "You can kill two birds with one stone. Get Molly's location out of him, then blow up the factory."

He cocked his head curiously as he studied her face, noting that it seemed to have taken on a softer and rounder appearance since he'd last seen her. "That was a very human expression, Luna. I'm surprised to hear it coming from a Lusian."

She lifted her chin, her thin lips tilting in a slight smirk. "I'm full of surprises. Now, we should probably get you armored up. We can't afford any more delays."

His body still ached, but he wouldn't let pain stop him from finding Namerian, killing him, then rescuing Molly. Once he had her back in his arms, he would never let her go again. He'd been wrong to put any duty before the woman he loved. If he had just taken Molly from this place as soon as he'd realized what she meant to him, she wouldn't have been put in the danger she was now likely facing.

Luna provided him with a suit of armor and a rifle. Though they both were well made and of decent quality, neither were Iriduan made. Nor had the Lusians made them. Roz and crew had not yet arrived on Za'Kluth, though Luna assured him they were on their way, but they wanted to make another stop first. According to Luna, Roz felt Shulgi was capable enough of handling the mess he'd created himself.

Shulgi donned his armor and performed a check of his weapon, disappointed that it wasn't a multi-function rifle, as Iriduans were the only ones who'd been able to manufacture those properly. The rifle would serve its purpose. Especially when he called in assistance.

He bid Luna farewell and promised he would keep the cure from escaping this world in the hands of those eager to use it to resurrect the worst of the Iriduan species. As he strode out of the small dwelling tucked into the back alley between a grocer and a drug den, he activated his wrist com. Within seconds the person he contacted responded, opening an encrypted communication line.

"Are you still interested in the job?" Shulgi said as soon as the other person identified themselves.

"Is it finally time for mayhem?" the rebel Iriduan named Urbarra asked.

Shulgi's helmet hid his grim smile. "It's time for chaos. Bring Tiamat's kiss to the dreg, my old friend."

Urbarra chuckled. "I thought you'd never ask."

THIRTY-TWO

Molly and a half dozen others who'd served Zaska now dangled over a pit of reeking venom, the deceptively slender threads of Uthagol's web swaying as they struggled fruitlessly inside their silk cocoon prisons.

Uthagol had left their heads free so they could see and hear all that would happen to them, as well as hear the suffering screams of the others as they were tortured and raped, one by one. Uthagol had already told Molly that she would be the last, forced to watch the slow and agonizing suffering of all those who'd been loyal to her in Zaska's name, not to mention Briana and Jenice, who would be taken down before her so she could endure watching Uthagol's minions break them.

Instead of selling off any of the minions Namerian had handed over to Uthagol for some compensation Molly hadn't been privy to, Uthagol kept them all. Some, she killed for fun. Some, she fed to her own minions, or her spindly males with their gaunt faces and dark, eerie eyes. Some, she kept for her own harem, drugging them into an almost zombie-like state so they obeyed her every command.

The rest, like Molly and the other females, she planned to press back into service in her brothel. Only this time, she would not leave their minds free. Her intention was to punish them all, then lobotomize them so they never gave her trouble again.

Molly heard all Uthagol's plans for her, but she barely listened. She flinched and wept at the sounds of suffering from those who'd once served her, but her heart already felt numb. She almost welcomed the idea of being lobotomized into forgetting herself, forgetting her memories—forgetting Shulgi.

Not that she wanted to let the others come to harm because she'd given up on life. She still planned to escape, but in the last two day-cycles since the transfer of prisoners to Uthagol had been made, she hadn't been able to devise an escape plan. Uthagol left them enshrined in their cocoons, forcing them to eliminate their waste all over themselves as they hung over a lethal soup of her and her males' venom that would slowly and agonizingly kill them if their skin touched it. Even the fumes burned their eyes and lungs, and Uthagol would increase those fumes using heat beneath the vat whenever she wanted them to suffer more.

She didn't feed them, and they were all dehydrated by now as well. They'd been weakened, and that had been entirely deliberate. Uthagol wasn't taking any chances this time. Molly and the others had done significant damage to her operations when they'd escaped years ago.

Jenice moaned inside her cocoon, and Molly shot a worried glance her way, grateful to have a reason to look away from the horrors going on below them. Horrors she knew would be visited upon her and those she cared about most.

Jenice didn't look good. Her wound had not been fully treated by the Iriduans, who'd tossed them into a transport vehicle as soon as they finished taking full control of the docks. Some of the other former minions of Sha Zaska had aided the

Iriduan invaders in deactivating all the traps and security measures that hadn't been of much use in stopping their invasion. Zaska's former empire was now fully under Ma'Nah's control.

Jenice probably had an infection, based on her paleness, flushed cheeks, and sweat-drenched skin. Instead of struggling in her cocoon like she had at first, now she dangled limply, moaning and muttering. The only movement in her body was her constant shivering. Dehydration was hitting her the hardest after her blood loss.

"Hang in there, Jen," Molly said, worry now piercing her fog of numbness. "Don't give up fighting," she whispered just loud enough for the other woman to hear her.

"Tell Mog and Grun I'm sorry," Jenice said without opening eyelids that had fallen closed nearly a day cycle ago and hadn't lifted since, her words coming with effort through a throat that sounded dry as a bone.

"You'll get to tell them yourself," Molly insisted, wondering why she bothered to lie even as she felt like she couldn't bear to speak the truth aloud. "We're going to get out of here, Jen! I promise you!"

Jenice finally opened her eyes, what little moisture remaining in her body glistening over her irises. "This is my fault, Molly," she rasped, her words coming slowly and with difficulty. "I own that. I hope you can forgive me someday."

"Stop it, Jen," Molly said on a sob, shaking her head as Briana murmured behind her in a reassuring but hopeless sound. "Don't talk like that! You have to live long enough to grovel."

Jenice's chapped lips tilted in a weak smile as she wheezed out a chuckle. "I...I'm afraid I'm not gonna be able to get down on my knees anytime soon," she finally managed to get out. "But I would do anything to make it up to you, Molly."

She turned her head, grunting at the effort as she strained to glance back at Briana, who was dangling at their backs, between the two of them. "And to you, Bri." Her eyes lowered to the torture chamber below, her smile vanishing. Her lids closed, tears sliding down her cheeks. "To everyone."

She opened her eyes to meet Molly's again. "Let them know I groveled in spirit, Mol."

Molly shook her head fervently. "No! Jenice, don't you die on me, you hear me! I can't lose you too. I already lost...." Her eyes filled with tears. "Don't you die on me, damn you!"

"I love you guys," Jenice said in a weak murmur. "Don't ever forget that."

Then she closed her eyes again, her head lolling to the side as her breath rasped slowly in and out between her slightly parted lips.

Molly struggled in her bonds, wriggling as hard as she could, crying out to Jenice to open her eyes again.

"Mol," Briana said sadly from behind her when Molly finally ran out of energy, far too weakened by now to even cause her cocoon to swing on its slender thread. "I don't think she's gonna wake up again, hon."

Molly didn't want to acknowledge Briana was right, but she could see how bad of shape Jenice was in. The other woman barely breathed at this point, and the fumes from the venom hadn't helped any of their lungs. With Jenice's wound and advanced dehydration, she wasn't likely to recover unless she was saved at this very moment.

Given the fact that Uthagol's minions had stopped their gleeful torture of their current victim to watch Molly lose her shit, and were now mocking her and her dying friend, she sincerely doubted that anyone would make an effort to save Jenice.

Uthagol herself had said Jenice had never really been

worth the trouble of breaking her into the service of the brothel. She hadn't been concerned about seeing that Jenice's leg was properly set and healed. She hadn't cared at all. Why would she? Her slaves had always been expendable to her.

Jenice passed away several hours later, rasping out her last breath without another word to either Molly or Briana, or any of the others still dangling inside their cocoons, most of whom had sunk into their own despair and also didn't bother to speak or even interact with the other captives. They all knew their time was coming. It was almost a blessing to remain in the cocoon rather than face what would happen to them once they were cut down.

Molly heard Briana shedding precious water through her sobs as she mourned Jenice, but Molly's eyes remained dry. Not because she wasn't stricken with more grief, but because she couldn't make any more tears. She'd already cried so hard over Shulgi and now Jenice that she'd used up all her weeping.

Though Jenice had died blaming herself for their predicament, Molly felt like it was really all her own fault. After all, if she had only dealt with Shulgi on a business level, Namerian likely wouldn't have made a move on Sha Zaska's holdings. Shulgi himself wouldn't have bothered to delve in the undervents in search of Zaska. Life would have gone on with Zaska's power and influence continuing to grow. Maybe someday, they could have all retired and moved to a Syndicate zone planet— one with lots of tropical beaches and sunny days.

Molly couldn't even remember seeing a real sun. The last time she would have seen one would have been as a very small child on Earth.

Za'Kluth remained always on the dark side of a molten world.

She'd dreamed of what it would be like to walk beneath a warm but not scorching sun, her toes buried in soft sand, with the sound of the ocean licking the shore in the background as a gentle breeze carried the scent of flowers to chase away the brine.

She'd often wondered if that dream was also a memory because it seemed so real. Perhaps her last day on Earth had been spent visiting the beach. She'd probably splashed in the waves and searched for seashells along the shore.

Now, as she stared at Jenice's peaceful face, her eyes aching with the need to shed tears she couldn't make any longer, she felt her first bout of true homesickness for Earth since she was a child. She added mourning the family who had lost her—who had probably never discovered her true fate—to the mourning over Jenice, all of the others they'd lost, and Shulgi.

Always Shulgi, whose death haunted her the most, though she had known him for such a short time.

He really had been her home, for the far too few blissful hours she'd spent in his arms.

Uthagol's minions were cutting down another victim, the last one before they would come for Briana, then Molly, when one of her males rushed into the torture chamber, chittering wildly. The sounds were too far below her for Molly to make them out clearly, but then Uthagol herself strode into the chamber, several more of her males trailing behind her.

She towered over them, standing well over eight feet tall. Her limbs were as slender as a human skeleton, though chitin covered them. Her torso was also very narrow and sylphlike. She had an austere humanoid face, though six eyes clustered above her narrow nose and thin lips. Sharply defined high cheekbones and a gaunt jawline where the skin clung to her mandibles created shadows on her face that made it look far too similar to a human skull.

Though she walked on two legs—bipedal like so many Syndicate species were—she possessed eight total limbs, her two lowest set of arms significantly smaller than the other four, and solely used to pull and spin threads from a seam in her almost concave belly.

She was graceful and elegant, according to some who either didn't know how evil she could be—or simply didn't care. She was also one of the worst monsters on Za'Kluth, and that was a high bar to meet.

Molly still reflexively shuddered in fear when Uthagol's six eyes fixed on her, and the creature still seemed to tower over her, even when viewed from above.

"The dreg is on fire," Uthagol said shortly, cutting off her male's chittering with a sweep of one imperious hand. "I find that very... *interesting.* There has never been a riot of this level in the dreg since it was first established on Za'Kluth." She swept a second hand towards Molly and one of her males rushed to cut Molly down, using a barbed hook to haul her cocoon away from the vat of venom first.

"I wonder," Uthagol said in a thoughtful tone as her cold eyes studied Molly's face, "whether this sudden chaos has anything to do with Zaska." She spat the name out as if it tasted bitter to her.

As far as Molly knew, Uthagol still thought Zaska had existed. She believed him to be dead now, though, and Molly wondered if Namerian knew the truth and had decided to keep it from her, or if he'd never bothered to find out for himself if Shulgi had left a corpse behind in the under-vents.

Uthagol regarded Molly without a readable expression on her face as her male cut Molly from the cocoon. She chuckled when Molly collapsed onto her hands and knees at Uthagol's expensively shod feet.

"Is it possible that Sha Zaska still lives?" she demanded as Molly sat back on her haunches with a groan, her eyes lifting to meet Uthagol's defiantly.

Molly raised her chin. "Do you really think my master could be so easily defeated? He had multiple escape routes to choose from. The Iriduans found nothing in the under-vents because Sha Zaska escaped. But he will return for us. And he *will* punish you."

Uthagol struck her casually across the face, rocking her head to one side. Then she struck her again with one of her hands on the other side, much harder. Molly fell over onto her elbow and Uthagol kicked her in the stomach several times as she grunted in pain and tried to curl into the fetal position.

"Sha Zaska has been defeated," Uthagol snarled. "I don't care if he still lives. His minions belong to the Iriduans now, and his slaves are mine. He doesn't have the power to threaten *me!*"

Molly struggled for the breath to speak once Uthagol stopped kicking her. When she found it, she took a moment to spat blood that welled from the wound where she'd bitten her tongue. Her red-flecked spittle stained Uthagol's silken heel and Molly chuckled weakly.

"He's coming for us," she insisted, determined to make Uthagol live in fear, at least for some time before she finally realized no one would come for them. "He's so much more powerful than you know. He has minions everywhere. Powerful allies who owe him much, and he will bring them to help him destroy you, and the Iriduans of Ma'Nah. Even now, his retribution has begun. The dreg burns! You've said it your-self. Sha Zaska is already at work on his plan of vengeance!"

THIRTY-THREE

Shulgi strode through the burning streets of the dreg, immune to the chaos that roiled around him. Namerian wasn't the only one capable of raising an army. Shulgi had kept in contact with some of his old allies and had re-established contact with those who had turned against the Iriduan empire. Many of them had retreated to the CivilRim to avoid imperial enforcers and bounty hunters. Some had come to Za'Kluth lately, settling in.

Waiting for a moment like this.

Urbarra's pack wasn't large. No more than a dozen of his rebels lived in Za'Kluth's dreg—a minor cell mostly cut off from the primary rebel forces. Cells like his were chaos cells, their mission mostly focused on creating mayhem in key locations to draw attention from local forces and distract from the primary rebel strike teams.

Urbarra's pack was skilled and experienced at what they did, and they knew exactly where and how to strike tinder to kindling to set an entire city on fire. It didn't take long for riots to start, and those riots continued to rage without any additional fuel from Urbarra's team. A few rumors here, a few explosions in the odd warehouse there, a gang boss assassinated, and the next thing the residents of the dreg knew, the entire place turned into a war zone.

Shulgi used the chaos as a shield, making his way through the dreg from the cargo elevator, where he'd left two dead guards after they refused to take him to the dreg while it was locked down. The journey to the factory district left more bodies in his wake, his patience thin, his blood pumping with combat stimulants. Anyone who attacked him signed their own death scroll.

Ma'Nah's new mercenary army found themselves hard-pressed in the dreg, since so many of them were down in the under-tier using their martial presence to maintain order among the more rebellious of Sha Zaska's minions. The swell of the rioting mob had reached the factory sector, trampled the security team blocking that sector off to unauthorized citizens, and now poured through the deactivated gates.

Multiple factory forces amassed to beat back the mob, but Urbarra's pack moved among the crowd, slipping past the most distracted guards to set up explosive devices behind their lines. Shulgi shifted into place in the crowd, elbowing aside some of the more foolish and excitable rioters who dared to see him as a potential target. He was trying not to kill civilians, but they were making it difficult for him. He felt relief when the explosions rocked the factory district, some of them sending heavily armored security guards flying.

With Iriduan armor, those guards would be shaken but not killed, but the explosions caused the security forces to retreat to their own factories, concerned that the saboteurs had already made it into the sector and were using the mob as a distraction.

A valid concern.

Shulgi followed the crowd of Ma'Nah's security forces, sensing several members of Urbarra's pack slipping through the shadows around him. They carried more explosives with them, but Shulgi himself had the one that would do the most damage and level the building. He bore the device on his back, and it was a heavy weight upon his shoulders. One he would live with for what remained of his life—if he didn't die during this battle.

He met his first true resistance at Ma'Nah's gatehouse as a sniper on the parapet fired a warning shot, causing Shulgi to seek cover behind the wall. The gate itself stood frustratingly close, but Urbarra's distraction hadn't fully reached Ma'Nah yet.

Urbarra's people made it to the wall not long after Shulgi, the rippling of their stealth armor barely visible even to one who knew they were there and knew what to look for. He watched one of them scale the wall, heading towards the generator that powered the gate. It was his turn to distract the sniper and gate guards.

He peeked around his cover, spotted the sniper with his eye to his scope, and then ducked back behind the wall just before a round struck the edge of it. Stone chips rattled against his armor. He poked his rifle around the wall, firing a burst of rounds blindly, listening for the shouts of the other gate guards. Their booted feet sounded loud above him as they moved into position to fire down on his head. He shifted the rifle to point it upwards.

A burst of rounds took out one of the gate guards, who fell off the wall with nary a scream, striking the ground nearby with a thud. A cacophony of noise broke out in the courtyard of the factory as reinforcements arrived while Shulgi fired again at another guard trying to get a bead on him from their position on the wall.

The sniper kept him pinned, firing off a deadly shot every time any part of his body poked out of cover. Fortunately, he hadn't been struck yet, but if Urbarra's infiltrators didn't accomplish their job soon, he would soon be overrun by rein-forcements.

Their voices shouted as they ran along the parapet to where Shulgi had dispatched the first two gate guards. Then their shouts turned to screams as a minor explosion swelled into a conflagration when the generator's energy core ignited, filling the courtyard with a massive ball of flames.

The blast shook the concrete wall, causing it to crack and buckle in places as bodies flew off the parapet, landing several spans away from where Shulgi stood. Burning shrapnel crashed through the gate, leaving a gaping hole. The energy shield crackling over the gate flickered out.

The sounds of gunfire rattled in the ringing aftermath of the blast as Urbarra's infiltrators engaged the sniper, allowing Shulgi to break cover and slip through the hole in the gate.

He moved from cover to cover in the hellscape of a court-yard as fires continued to burn wherever flaming debris had struck. Some of Ma'Nah's guards and employees tried to put out the flames, but most of the civilians were now running towards the gates to escape.

Shulgi was pleased to see them evacuating of their own accord. He intended to activate the evacuation protocol if Namerian hadn't already done so before blowing the place, but he was working with a very limited window of time and couldn't risk any delays. The sooner the innocent civilians cleared the place, the better.

More of Urbarra's pack congregated beyond the gate now. Shulgi had asked them to scan the evacuees and detain any of them who appeared to be carrying anything that might contain a sample of the cure. There was still a risk that one sample might slip through in the chaos, but Urbarra's men were experts at operating in such conditions and weren't likely to let that happen.

Shulgi had no choice but to put that responsibility on others as he made his way through the courtyard. He had his own part to play in this mission.

He killed every guard he encountered but allowed the civilians to spill past him if they didn't attempt to play the hero. At the entry doors he discovered that his biometrics still worked, shaking his head at Namerian's oversight, but pleased he wouldn't have to go to extra effort to break into Ma'Nah.

More resistance met him inside the lobby, but he made quick work of the half dozen guards who tried to stand between him and his goal. He skipped the elevator platform to Namerian's office, spreading his wings to fly up to Namerian's floor. Guards spilled onto the balconies on each level, aiming their weapons to fire upon him, but a spray of rounds from Shulgi's rifle took most of them out. Several of them got a few hits in on him, and he was pleased that the armor he wore deflected the worst of the damage, though the impact staggered him enough that his wings had to work overtime to keep him in the air.

They didn't bother trying to shoot his wings. Given how fast they moved, they were a difficult target to hit, and every Iriduan knew that. Most Iriduan soldiers didn't even bother with such tactics, finding the body a much larger and more solid prospect. A good body hit usually brought down a flying Iriduan. Fancy shots to the wings belonged only in the action video plays and games not intended to simulate genuine combat.

Shulgi landed lightly on the top floor of the building, raising his rifle to destroy the broad glass window that looked out onto the lobby of the factory. Namerian really should have chosen bullet-proof material for the inner window as well as the outer one, but he'd preferred the look of true crystalline glass.

Not that Shulgi couldn't find another way to break into his

office, but this one was more dramatic, and gave Namerian less time to react.

The shattered pieces of the window rained down like a waterfall that made it difficult for the three guards protecting Namerian to target Shulgi effectively. Shulgi's heightened senses, speed, and training allowed him to drop them quickly, even through the obscuring broken glass. By the time the last of the glass shards drifted down between Shulgi and Namerian the final guard crumpled to the ground.

Not one of them had scored a hit on Shulgi.

Namerian held a pistol pointed at Shulgi, his hand trembling, his violet eyes wide and frightened above his mask. "Who are you? You can't possibly work for Zaska!"

Shulgi flicked his wings as he stepped over the threshold of broken glass, his boots crunching on the pieces scattered over the lush carpeting.

Namerian's eyes widened as they focused on the verdant length of his wings. "Shulgi!" His face paled until it turned a sickly gray. "I-I killed you!"

Then he fired his pistol desperately, forcing Shulgi to duck behind a solid stone block that served as a side table for one of the office's lounging chairs. "Give it up, Namerian. You can't defeat me with that little rock skipper."

"If you were bullet proof, you wouldn't be hiding right now!" Namerian's voice shook with fear, despite his confident words.

Even he didn't believe them.

"You'll never make it out of this office," Shulgi said, glancing down at his rifle to check the power and ammunition status.

The weapon wasn't the best one he'd ever used, but it had proved adequate thus far, and the ammo capacity was exceptional. Namerian's little pistol wouldn't last long in a firefight.

"Reinforcements will come." Namerian's voice trembled as much as his hand. "You can't kill them all, Shulgi."

Shulgi smiled grimly. "You sure about that? You willing to bet your life on it, Namerian?"

"Curse the blighted web!" Namerian's voice came from a different position, but Shulgi's heightened hearing had already detected his movement from the swishing of his shoes on the carpet. "What do you want from me, Shulgi? What can I do to convince you to spare my life?"

"Where is Molly?" Shulgi growled, shifting in his crouch as he poked his head around the block.

Namerian fired on him as soon as he spotted movement, but his aim was wild and Shulgi moved far too quickly for him. His change in position made it possible for Shulgi to sneak around the block, then dart behind one of the lounging chairs, working his way towards flanking Namerian.

"I didn't kill her!" The direction of Namerian's voice told Shulgi he still faced the side table.

"Where is she, curse you!"

Shulgi heard Namerian's gasp as he shifted, then targeted the lounging chair. Several rounds punched through the upholstery, sending stuffing flying. Shulgi had already moved on to the next block table by the time Namerian reacted to his change in position.

"I sold her!" Namerian's tone sounded pleading now, even as he backed towards the elevator that would take him to the lab. "I can tell you where you can find her, if you just leave here now."

Shulgi needed him to enter in his access code before he killed him anyway. Might as well have him do it now.

"Don't make me torture it out of you, Namerian. Because you know I will. You know exactly what I'm capable of. You said yourself I am a monster. I've never felt more like embracing that title than I do right now."

Namerian tried to be stealthy as he entered his code into the panel, but Shulgi heard the biometrics scanner as it passed over Namerian's retina. It was such a soft sound Namerian likely barely noticed it, but he'd never experienced combat stimulants before.

Shulgi burst out of cover, firing his rifle low. He wasn't a fan of aiming for legs. They were generally far more difficult to hit than the center mass of the body, but he couldn't afford for Namerian to die just yet.

Soon, though. Definitely soon.

Namerian yelped in pain as a round struck his thigh. The elevator seemed to taunt him as the secret door panel chose that very moment to slide open.

Shulgi fell upon him before he could aim his pistol, moving so fast that he had ahold of Namerian's robe before the other male's yelp of pain died out.

"Drop it!" Shulgi demanded, pushing the barrel of his rifle so hard against Namerian's chin that the scientist was forced to stare upwards to ease the pressure.

The pistol made a thud as it struck the carpet and Shulgi kicked it away with one foot without sparing a glance at it.

"Where. Is. *She*?" he growled in Namerian's face.

"Uthagol," Namerian whimpered, his trembling now so bad that his wings shivered, making a rasping sound. "I sold her to the brothel queen. She had a bounty on the female."

"And you call *me* the monster, Namerian," Shulgi snarled, recalling what he knew of Uthagol.

It wasn't as much as he'd like to know, given that the creature now had Molly in her clutches, but Uthagol wasn't a figure of mystery either. He could locate her headquarters with a little assistance now that he had her name.

"We were trying to do the right thing," Namerian insisted, the tremor in his voice breaking up his words. "The cure is the most important thing any Iriduan could ever do! She stood in the way—a distraction for you that could have ended up destroying Ma'Nah. You can't let a *woman* be the reason you end all of this. We can still salvage the mission!"

Shulgi glanced at the elevator, then returned his unforgiving gaze to Namerian. The other male's violet eyes widened when they met his.

"Shulgi," he hissed, clutching at Shulgi's hand fisted in his robe with both hands, struggling fruitlessly in his hard grip. "Don't do this, creche-kin! We-we can work this out!"

Shulgi wanted to make Namerian suffer for what he'd done. He wanted to hurt him for a very long time before he gave him the peace of death. Unfortunately, he lacked the time for such measures, so he pulled the trigger on his rifle, spattering Namerian's blood and brain matter over the elevator access panel and the wall it was set into.

He tossed Namerian's corpse aside and stepped into the elevator. It took only a short trip to reach the lab, and he stepped out firing when the door opened. Two of the scientists desperately trying to pack up samples went down in the first hail of bullets. Shulgi continued to fire, destroying equipment and work benches as screaming scientists dived behind them.

Alad huddled in one tight corner between two shelves as Shulgi cleared the rest of the lab, walking over broken crystalline and destroyed electronics, plastics, and tortured metal. His boots crunched on the debris as he approached the young Iriduan. Alad held a case of sample vials in one shaking hand, the other held a pistol that he didn't lift to aim at Shulgi.

The youth shuddered and shook, his eyes gleaming with an unnatural light. Shulgi sighed sadly, bringing his rifle to bear on Alad.

This was one kill he did not relish, but it appeared to already be too late for Alad.

The youth shoved him back with a mental push, sending Shulgi sliding across the tile floor. Alad cried out in triumph as he slowly rose to his feet, his eyes glowing brighter as he tossed the pistol aside and lifted his hand, palm towards Shulgi.

"I have *returned*," he said in a deep voice that sounded nothing like the timorous youth. "Lower your weapon and bow down to your lord. Bow to Enlil!"

Shulgi emptied the rest of his ammo into the youth, shredding his body so that the nanites would struggle to rebuild it before the blast went off that even they could not survive.

With a heavy sigh, he shrugged the bomb pack off his back and set it up on the work bench, arming it quickly.

Then he set off the evacuation announcement, though he hoped all the civilians had cleared out by this time. There wasn't much time left for them to do so.

There wasn't much time left for him to do so.

He contacted Urbarra to let him know to withdraw his men, then made his own way back to the factory floor, pleased to see that the building was nearly emptied, and those who yet remained were running for their lives.

Small explosions set by Urbarra's men had destroyed many of the pools, leaving the factory floor spattered and slippery with algae. Shulgi skirted the worst of the mess, striding towards the exit and meeting no resistance on his way out.

Once outside, he made his way to the destroyed gate, scanning the courtyard to make sure no civilians remained. Seeing the area was clear, he followed the last stragglers to the rally point, standing among the confused and traumatized civilians as Urbarra's men checked them all for vials.

His wrist com beeped an alarm and Shulgi sucked in a

breath, closing his eyes as the factory went up with a massive, booming explosion.

It wasn't until the screams died around him that he finally opened his eyes to regard the blazing wreckage with an odd feeling of numbness. His wrist com beeped again. This time with an incoming message.

He checked it, then grimly smiled behind his helmet. Roz was always way ahead of everyone else.

He spoke aloud into his com as he turned and walked away from the panicked crowd that Urbarra's men were effectively managing to calm down.

"How are you at acting?"

The person on the other end of the com replied quickly.

I don't know, but I'm always ready to try something new.

Shulgi grinned in anticipation as he requested assistance in locating Uthagol's headquarters—the center of her web—and then he explained the details of his plan.

THIRTY-FOUR

Uthagol seemed nervous. Molly hadn't thought there was anything that could truly disturb the female. Yet she paced uncharacteristically in front of Molly and Briana as they hung within new cocoons, this time in her "showroom."

"Ma'Nah was leveled by an explosion in the dreg," she said in a voice that contained no hint of the nerves that were evident in her tense body language.

Molly kept her surprise out of her expression even as Briana gasped aloud.

"Sha Zaska takes his revenge on all who dare to strike at him," Molly said, her mind racing as she sought to turn this shocking information to her advantage.

Briana glanced at her, and Molly met her eyes as Uthagol huffed in a sound of annoyance that did contain a hint of worry now.

Briana slightly nodded her head, a smile growing on her dyed face. "Our master will come for us—his most favored mouthpieces. He might spare you if you return us to him alive."

Uthagol hissed, turning on them with an enraged scowl. "I

do *not* fear Sha Zaska!" She eyed Briana and Molly with all six of her hideous orbs. "It is he who should fear *Uthagol*!" All four of her upper hands tapped her narrow chest.

Then she grabbed Molly's chin in one hard upper hand and snatched up Briana's in the other, squeezing them painfully as both women gasped.

"I could turn the two of you over to Sha Zaska's minions—if he dared to send them into my web—in little, bite-sized pieces."

"But you won't," Molly said with difficulty, her eyes never wavering as she met Uthagol's. "Because if you do, and you discover that you were wrong not to fear our master, he will visit a nightmare upon you that will have you begging for death."

Uthagol released them both with a hard jerk, sending their heads rocking to the sides. Again, Molly met Briana's eyes with a speaking glance.

"Our master destroyed Ma'Nah," Briana ventured, testing her cocoon with a slight wriggle. "He wiped out the Iriduan interlopers on their own turf. Do you really think he would dare to take on the dreg, but fear *your* web? You have not a tenth of the power of an Iriduan corporation."

Uthagol slapped Briana hard across the face and Molly winced at the sound, but Briana only laughed mockingly. She licked the blood from her split lip as if she relished it. "You know we speak the truth, queen of the web. Sha Zaska will come for you, and he will tear you limb from limb if you do not return his mouthpieces to him in one piece."

"He will make an example of your death," Molly said, picking up the narrative as Briana paused to take a breath. "Just as he made an example of Ma'Nah."

She wondered what had really happened to the company, since obviously Sha Zaska had nothing to do with its destruction. Had some of his minions escaped the Iriduan invasion of the under-tier and gotten some of their own revenge back?

She couldn't think of any of their minions who might have had the power or resources to undertake such a daring challenge. It was more likely that one of Ma'Nah's enemies—or even allies—had decided the company went too far in invading the under-tier and claiming Sha Zaska's assets. No doubt Ma'Nah's competitors didn't want the company gaining an advantage. They might have taken advantage of unrelated chaos in the dreg to strike at Ma'Nah, perhaps even planning to place the blame on Sha Zaska or his associates.

Or they *caused* the chaos in the dreg, which spoke to a much higher degree of organization than the typical gang boss.

Perhaps it was a more corporate move.

She prayed to whatever deity might exist somewhere in the darkest reaches of space that Mogorl and Grundon had nothing to do with the attacks in the dreg. She also prayed they wouldn't attempt to take on Uthagol and her minions here within her own web. They were strong and clever, but without Sha Zaska's resources, they didn't have a chance against Uthagol on her turf.

"Ha!" Uthagol laughed harshly, snapping Molly's attention fully back on her. "You both are so transparent. You really think I believe that Sha Zaska would come for two paltry humans, even if he did survive the Iriduan's invasion?" She grabbed a fistful of Molly's hair, jerking her head back as she towered over Molly, forcing her to look up into Uthagol's terrifying face. "You mean noth—"

The sound of some of her males rushing into the showroom, chittering wildly cut off her words as she released Molly and spun around to face them.

Her body twitched, her lowest set of arms moving reflexively as she chittered back at the males.

Then Molly heard gunfire nearby. Far closer than she would expect this deep within Uthagol's web—which consisted of multiple buildings inside a compound sealed off from the rest of her tier with an actual web.

"How did he get his minions inside my sanctum?" she shouted as she spun to face Molly and Briana. "Tell me how he did this!"

She grabbed Molly's hair again, shaking her head as Molly cut off her instinctive yelp of pain. Another of Uthagol's hands caught Molly by the throat, slowly strangling her as she shrieked in rage.

Then two shots rang out from behind Uthagol. The evil female gasped and turned to face an armored figure who was clearly an Iriduan, given the green wings extending from his back.

Molly also gasped, because her heart lifted at the sight of those beautiful wings, though she knew better than to hope for the impossible. There was no way this could be Shulgi. She'd seen him die with her own eyes.

She would never stop seeing it.

The Iriduan strode into the showroom to stand over the fallen corpses of Uthagol's males. "Sha Zaska has his ways," he said in a strong, deep voice that carried, amplified by the speaker in his helmet.

Molly cried out in shock, struggling inside her cocoon. This stranger sounded exactly like Shulgi though he didn't even glance in her direction. At least not that she could see through the helmet.

"Sha Zaska is dead," Uthagol snarled. "And *you* will be soon."

She gestured with one hand and automated turrets extended from the walls and ceiling to open fire on the figure in the center of the show room.

He dived to the side, ducking behind a stone pedestal that the rounds from the turret pitted as they struck. Molly screamed, tears running down her face as she watched the turrets tracking the rapidly moving figure. Though he managed to make it to new cover every time they destroyed his previous cover, she knew he would eventually run out of places to hide before he made it to Uthagol.

She rocked in her cocoon, wriggling back and forth as hard as she could as Uthagol watched her turrets chasing the Iriduan with cackling laughter rolling from her narrow chest.

"Sha Zaska will tear you to shreds and display your head for all to see," the Iriduan yelled before he rolled behind another pedestal.

Uthagol continued to laugh mockingly until one of the turrets suddenly snapped off its base, crashing to the floor in a shower of sparks. She gasped and turned to face that side of the room even as the other turrets continued to fire at the Iriduan.

"No!" She staggered several steps backwards until she stood right in front of Molly, just a short distance away. She remained unaware of Molly desperately struggling in her cocoon. "It *can't* be!"

Another turret snapped off its base, and the remaining three turrets tried to target the wall behind that broken one, but they seemed unable to lock onto whatever was causing the damage.

Uthagol had apparently spotted it though. "No! Sha Zaska, you cannot defeat me!"

Molly's focus remained entirely on the Iriduan, watching him use Uthagol's distraction to move closer to the dais where she stood with Molly and Briana. Uthagol suddenly realized that he was on the move and ordered her turrets to target him again.

On the other side of the room, another turret tore from its

base, this time flying across the room as if someone had tossed it aside with ease.

As focused as she was on the Iriduan that her foolish heart dared to hope was Shulgi, she couldn't help glancing over at the other wall to see what was destroying the turrets.

She screamed as she spotted the ripple of tentacles moving in a brief flash before they blended back into the wall. The camouflage of the creature was nearly flawless. It only became visible when it moved and only then because of a slight rippling and distortion of the wall.

But what she had seen in that brief flash had been terrifying. Based on the size and length of those tentacles, the creature tearing apart the turrets was exceptionally large, and extremely strong.

She wondered whimsically if they'd accidentally conjured up a real Sha Zaska. What else could the creature be?

Uthagol certainly feared that was who it was. She turned on Molly and Briana, her expression desperate as she debated what to do.

By now Molly had her cocoon swinging and Uthagol noticed her momentum. Her mouth twisted with an angry snarl just before Molly slammed bodily into her, sending her flying off the dais.

She hit the ground in a heap but quickly recovered to skitter across the floor on all eight limbs, heading towards an escape hatch. Molly shouted out her location, but the strange tentacle creature had already apparently spotted her. It became completely visible as it moved rapidly across the wall to intercept her path.

She moved faster but could not outrun the creature's reach. It snatched her up in a huge tentacle while two more lifted to rip the last two turrets off the ceiling.

"Don't kill her yet... Sha Zaska." The Iriduan rose to his

feet from behind his cover now that he was no longer under fire. "We still must make an example out of her."

"Molly," Briana whispered as they both stared in horror at the tentacle monster now wrapping more of its massive bulk around the screaming and struggling Uthagol, "did... uh... did we summon something?"

Molly slowly shook her head, her mouth gaping as her swinging cocoon finally slowed to a mere sway on its thread. "I don't even know if that's a thida naf," she whispered just loud enough for Briana to hear.

"What remains of your minions gather beyond these doors," the Iriduan said as he strode towards the creature and Uthagol, struggling wildly in its tentacles. "They will not be able to break through until nothing remains of you but the echo of your screams."

"What do you want, Sha Zaska?" Uthagol said with desperation in her voice. "I'll give you anything! Everything! My brothels, my other businesses. All of my slaves! Just let me go!"

The Iriduan glanced over at Molly and Briana, and Molly dared to hope, again, that it might be Shulgi behind the helmet. She knew it was folly to allow that hope to lift her heart. If she was wrong, this time, its fall could destroy her heart completely.

Still, who else could it be? What other Iriduan cared enough about her to come to her rescue?

Of course, the Iriduan could be anyone. Someone she'd never met.

Just like she'd never met "Sha Zaska," much to her relief because the creature was terrifying. All she could see of it from this angle was a mass of writhing tentacles, but she spotted a ripple of an amorphous mantle at the other end of those killer tentacles.

"Let us ask Sha Zaska's mouthpieces whether you should be spared," the Iriduan said, his voice sounding so much like

Shulgi's that it made Molly's heart pound as he approached their suspended cocoons.

He shouldered his rifle, then lifted both hands to remove his helmet as he stepped onto the dais. Briana whistled softly as Molly gasped, her heart soaring. Her eyes filled with tears, but they were joyous ones for once.

"Shulgi!" she cried, wriggling in her cocoon with the desire to wrap her arms around him. "You're alive!"

He tossed his helmet aside and it fell unheeded to the ground as he lifted his hands to cup her face. "I failed to rescue you before, Molly, but I wouldn't allow death to claim me until I found you again."

"I hope you didn't come here just to rescue me," she whispered as he lowered his head. "I love you, Shulgi. I'm so sorry I kept the secret of Sha Zaska from you. I should have told you sooner. I should have trusted you."

His kiss cut off any more words from her and Molly reveled in the feeling of his lips caressing hers.

"Uh, as sweet and heartwarming as this all is," Briana said, "this cocoon isn't as comfortable as it looks, so maybe we can postpone the reunion?"

Shulgi lifted his head, his expression sheepish even as his eyes gleamed when they took in Molly's bright smile and swollen lips. She licked her bottom lip as he took a step back, withdrawing a dagger that was sheathed within the forearm of his armor.

"I did not kill your mouthpieces," Uthagol said, still desperately struggling in the unforgiving hold of the tentacle creature. "Zaska! They yet live! They are all yours, along with everything else I own. Spare me, and I will become your most loyal servant!"

Shulgi ignored Uthagol's pleading as he cut first Molly down, then Briana. They both groaned as he gently laid their cocoons down on the dais, then went to work on cutting the strong silk of the cocoons so they could finally break free.

Molly cried out in pain as her limbs finally burst through the sides of the cocoon once Shulgi's knife slit through it. Needles stabbed into her hands and feet as the blood rushed back into them.

Briana expelled a heavy breath of relief, followed by another moan as Shulgi cut her cocoon loose and she managed to break through it.

"So," Shulgi rose to his feet, "what fate does Sha Zaska's mouthpieces wish for Uthagol?"

Molly struggled to rise to her feet and Shulgi quickly bent to help her up, wrapping an arm around her waist to support her when her feet proved too numb to take her weight.

"I wouldn't mind the help of a hot guy," Briana complained as she also struggled to rise from the dais.

Then she yelped as a tentacle from "Sha Zaska" snaked towards her, wrapped around her, and pulled her up until her feet barely touched the dais. The tentacle creature slowly set her down on her own two feet as Briana's face turned pale beneath the dyes, her eyes wide with fear, her mouth agape.

"Sha Zaska would never harm his mouthpieces," Shulgi said in a reassuring tone, then turned his attention to Uthagol. "As for those who dared to touch them...."

He glanced down at Molly with a questioning look in his beautiful green eyes.

"We should make an example out of anyone who offends Sha Zaska," she said, straightening in his embrace, her chin lifting as she met Uthagol's six terrified eyes. "Let her minions witness the terror that awaits anyone who dares to defy the might of Sha Zaska!"

Uthagol screamed as Shulgi glanced over at the tentacle creature. It responded by tightening its writhing tentacles around Uthagol. Then it moved towards the door with her still held in its unrelenting grip. The tentacle wrapped around Briana's waist retreated, and Briana sucked in a deep, shaky breath, like it was the first one she'd taken since the creature had grabbed her.

Molly watched "Sha Zaska" carry Uthagol to the door, beyond which waited her minions, her heart unmoved by the female's terrified screams. She shuddered when she spotted the full horror of the creature's amorphous mantle. It rose above the mass of tentacles once it reached the door, and a huge opening appeared in the mass of it, exposing rows of sharklike teeth.

It seemed that Sha Zaska had somehow come to life in all his horrific glory. Molly shifted her gaze from the monster to Shulgi. As he met her eyes, she smiled.

The universe had created Sha Zaska out of a myth and brought her beloved back from the dead. Perhaps someone out there really was listening to her prayers.

THIRTY-FIVE

Uthagol's death was gruesome. Shulgi had been unfazed by the goriness of it, though he'd insisted Molly and Briana turn away as the evil female's screams rose in intensity, just before Nemon pulled her apart in full view of all her minions.

Molly had protested his command at first, but he saw the paleness of her skin even with the dyes and ended up covering her eyes and pulling her into his embrace to muffle her hearing. Briana had turned away as well. She then fell to her knees, retching at the sound of Uthagol's limbs tearing.

Since both mouthpieces were unable to speak at the moment, Shulgi spoke for "Sha Zaska," letting all Uthagol's beaten minions know never to defy the powerful under-tier boss again. Then he announced that Zaska and his army would soon retake the under-tier, and he would pay well to any of Uthagol's minions who joined his side.

Nemon was having far too much fun playing the gang boss, Shulgi decided later as they stormed the under-tier. Nemon and Shulgi led a large group of Uthagol's defectors—mostly former slaves but also some of her minions who'd seen sense and had accepted "Sha Zaska's" generous offer of employment. Urbarra's people had decided to join in on the fun, though they blended into the background, moving like ghosts around Zaska's little army, seeking the best opportunities to put their skills to use.

The contingent of Iriduan mercenaries and Ma'Nah remnants who hadn't the sense to flee after the destruction of the company and a good portion of the dreg formed up in a belated attempt to meet the invasion pouring off the public lift. Nemon decimated a good portion of the front line before Shulgi and the rest were even able to fire upon them.

He was certainly grateful he was on Nemon's side instead of fighting against him. They made a good team, and the Iriduans and those minions of Zaska's who'd switched sides and knew they would pay for that traitorous choice didn't stand a chance. Many fled the battle, racing for the docks in the hopes of hijacking some of the ships to get off Za'Kluth.

Shulgi smiled grimly, knowing that Urbarra's men were already heading towards the bays to lock down the forcefield, which meant no one was leaving the under-tier unless they went into the vents.

Though he hadn't liked Molly's suggestion that she and Briana be allowed to head to the under-vents to rally those still loyal to Zaska who would have used the bolt holes in the vast maze of tunnels, she'd convinced him that her efforts would give them a distinct advantage. She knew the territory far better than he did, and certainly better than the Iriduans did. The under-vents had been the haven of the escaped slaves long before Sha Zaska was invented to keep the bounty hunters out of them.

His only concern as he and Nemon and their small army of Uthagol's defectors took back the docks was for Molly and Briana. They were both exhausted, weakened from their captivity, and dehydrated—though Urbarra's medic had given them both IVs and combat stimulants at their request. The last thing they should be doing was heading into battle.

Molly wouldn't hear of sitting on the sidelines, waiting for someone else to take her territory back for her. She was determined and far stronger than even Shulgi had realized. She endured when so many—regardless of their sex—would have given up and begged for mercy. His respect for her only grew even as his desire to protect her nearly overwhelmed him into making a mistake by forcefully keeping her from joining in on the battle.

He hated letting her out of his sight but sensed that he would be doing them both a disservice to deny her the right to fight for her people and her cause. Thus, his sole purpose was now to keep the bulk of Ma'Nah's invaders occupied and distracted on the docks while Molly and her people took back the under-vents.

They were to meet at Zaska's offices, and it felt like it took an age for Shulgi and his forces to make it there, though the battle was actually over very quickly. The dock defenders barely had the chance to ready their weapons before Nemon and Shulgi fell upon them. Uthagol's former slaves and minions proved effective in their offense, and most would end up being good long-term additions to "Zaska's" forces.

They encountered the heaviest resistance outside Zaska's offices, where Ma'Nah's forces had entrenched and set up a variety of deadly traps, including reactivating the purge system that Molly's people had in place as a last resort. That system was one thing Molly and Briana intended to disable before it could put an end to Shulgi's offense. Given the fact that they were all still alive, Shulgi had to believe that Molly had succeeded.

Their forces hammered the troops entrenched around

Zaska's offices, which were a fortress in their own way, having been reinforced when Molly and her people were in charge to hold off just such an invasion as this from the surface.

They clearly weren't expecting to be invaded from beneath the offices. As the snipers and their turrets kept Shulgi and his people pinned on the docks, chaos broke out from within the shipping offices. Shouts of alarm quickly shifted to screams of pain and terror. The snipers and turrets were forced to turn their attention to their own fortress, and that momentary distraction was enough for Urbarra's people to get through, followed by Nemon in full camouflage, visible only to those who knew where to look as he moved.

Shulgi remained on the docks, peppering the offices with a volley of rounds to shift the attention of the snipers and turrets back to him and the forces with him rather than have them pursue the infiltrators.

He managed to take down one of the snipers with a stray shot, but the others were pulled down by the mob of Zaska's loyal minions that poured onto the roof of the office building, cheering in victory, raising fists holding the heads of slain Iriduans by their hair.

The troops with Shulgi sounded their own cheers as they rose from behind their cover, recognizing that the battle was over, and Sha Zaska was the victor.

Then Shulgi's heart thudded harder than it had been even with all the combat stimulants flowing through his veins. Molly and Briana, their skin dyed violet and green, stepped out onto the roof, moving like two small and delicate flowers swaying in a warm breeze. They were both graceful and elegant, but Shulgi only had eyes for his petite Molly as she and Briana lifted Uthagol's head between them.

Then Molly lifted her other hand to reveal that she held an Iriduan head dangling from its hair in her raised fist.

No doubt that Iriduan was the leader of the invaders. The battle had truly been won.

The cheers that rose up around the docks were deafening as the two small females stood with their grisly trophies, clothed in dresses that were stained with blood, looking like the fierce and cunning warriors they were.

When Nemon joined them on the roof, whipping his tentacles around in an exaggerated fashion so that everyone below got a good look at them, the volume of the cheers rose even further, and it took a long time for it to die down.

The show was a good one, as far as such displays of power went, but it got even better when the noise of the crowd finally died down, allowing Zaska's "mouthpieces" to speak. Once Molly opened her mouth to shout her cries of victory in Sha Zaska's name, everyone on the docks fell silent, listening expectantly.

She was a natural, her voice ringing out with power and conviction despite her small stature. As she spoke of Zaska's victories and his vengeance, she and Briana tossed Uthagol's head off the roof. The crowd cheered again when it tumbled to the ground below with an ignominious splat, the cruel face of Uthagol splitting upon impact.

Once that cheering died down, Molly held up the head of the Iriduan, displaying it in a slow sweep to everyone watching as Briana took over the speech, reveling in Sha Zaska's victory over the Iriduans both here on the under-tier and in the dreg, claiming the leveling of Ma'Nah as Sha Zaska's doing.

Shulgi knew the truth wasn't what mattered. It was the stories people told about those truths that created legends, and Sha Zaska's had grown exponentially. In time, his people would likely face too much scrutiny from the city bosses, but even then, they could end up allied with the most powerful people in Za'Kluth if they played things right.

His smile of admiration for Molly fell when he realized that now that Sha Zaska had returned, she would want to remain here, to continue her mission of freeing slaves. That also meant she would continue to serve as Zaska's mouthpiece, because she was a natural at it.

He would give everything to remain at her side. He would fight for her until no breath or blood remained inside him. If it meant he would have to endure the thought of other males touching her, then he would endure even that.

For Molly, he would do anything.

Her cause was important to her. This legend she had built meant so much to her. It would be selfish for him to take her away from this place now.

Briana fell silent as Molly impaled the Iriduan's head on a pike handed to her by one of the minions. Then Molly handed the pike off to Nemon, who wrapped his tentacle around it, then slammed it into the roof's surface, which was concrete. The steel pike ended up buried in the rooftop—a reminder and example that would stand there until the flesh rotted away and the skull was retrieved to make another grisly trophy, no doubt.

The message was what mattered—the show of force and lack of mercy that would strike fear into the hearts of any who dared to defy Sha Zaska or stand in his way. It was impressive, their ceremony. Shulgi felt almost jealous of Nemon being so close to Molly—and being such a huge part of her victory speech.

There would be time for Shulgi to be beside Molly later. Time for him to finally tell her exactly how much she meant to him, and how much he wanted to be with her.

Then her eyes swept the crowd below until they found him. He lifted both hands to remove his helmet, tossing it to Urbarra, who stood nearby, fully encased in stealth armor. A broad smile crossed her face as she stepped closer to the edge of the roofline so all could see her clearly. Her gaze remained fixed on him for a long moment, as if she wanted to take in the sight of him.

He wanted everyone, including all the Iriduans in the crowd, to see that he wore no mask. To know that he belonged to a queen.

"My generous master, Sha Zaska, is greatly pleased with the loyalty of his minions." She tapped her chest, then gestured to Briana. "Especially his mouthpieces, who have always served him well."

A seductive and secret smile tilted her lips that made Shulgi burn with jealousy despite knowing for a fact that she'd never been touched by a single tentacle of any "Sha Zaska."

The crowd responded to her thinly veiled implication with cheers and whooping. They fell instantly silent as Nemon waved an imperious tentacle in the air.

"Because of our unflinching service to our beloved master," Molly continued, the volume of her voice carrying without her having to shout, "he has granted us our freedom."

More cheers met that announcement and Shulgi caught himself nodding in approval reflexively. This was a wise decision by Molly and Briana. They wouldn't be quite as constrained in their behavior if they were free minions of Zaska's instead of his slaves.

"My fellow dyed flower has decided to remain in the service of Sha Zaska," Molly continued, gesturing to Briana, who stepped up to the edge of the roof beside her.

Then Molly's eyes met his, her smile less certain. "But I have accepted my master's generous offer of retirement."

The breath left him as the rest of the crowd cheered again. Shulgi wasn't even sure now that they knew what they were cheering for. They just seemed caught up in the ceremonious feeling of the moment. But he knew why he felt like cheering. He had no doubt about his feelings on the matter.

Molly didn't want to remain here. She didn't want to continue being Sha Zaska's mouthpiece. Was it because she wanted to leave this world with him?

Without thinking, his wings flared, then buzzed as they lifted him off his feet. He flew quickly towards the roof, the entire crowd falling dead silent. He alighted on the edge of the roof beside Molly, his eyes only for her. Her hesitant smile grew broader as she met his gaze. He took her hands in his, then tugged her closer.

"Our master has given his blessing to his most loyal of minions and his most loyal of slaves," Briana said to the crowd in a well-projected voice as she gestured to Shulgi and Molly.

Nemon curled his tentacles around the two of them, pushing them into a closer embrace, much to the amusement of the crowd.

"Nice save," Molly murmured to Briana, her smile never wavering.

Then she lifted her arms to lock her hands around the nape of Shulgi's neck. He made no effort to resist her gentle tug, gladly lowering his head to claim her lips with all the hunger he felt for her openly on display.

This time, the roaring cheers of the crowd did deafen him, his sensitive ears ringing, but nothing else mattered save the feeling of Molly's lips under his, the heady taste of her as her tongue wrestled with his. The delicious scent of her nearly overwhelmed him, despite the odors of blood and sweat and grime that clung to her after her ordeal in the under-tunnels.

The crowd continued to cheer even after they broke the kiss. Molly stared up into his eyes as if no one else existed.

"I will follow you anywhere, Shulgi," she whispered, just

loud enough for him to hear her above the cacophony of noise from their audience.

He caressed her cheek, reveling at the softness of her skin and the delicate curve of her face. "I would stay right here with you, if that is your wish, Molly. As long as we're together, I don't care where we are."

"I love you, Shulgi," she said.

"I love you too, my Molly." He cupped her chin and lifted it so he could claim her lips again.

The crowd went wild, and Nemon's amorphous form rippled with pleased laughter as Briana looked on with a wide grin.

THIRTY-SIX

Molly felt the weight of her exhaustion like it was a physical creature sitting on her shoulders. She wanted to rest so badly that she kept losing sense of time as she daydreamed about a nice, soft bed.

And hard, strong arms holding her snuggled close to a firm, powerful body while she slept.

Shulgi loved her! Now, she had no doubt. He'd made his devotion to her clear with a very public display that she understood was irrefutable. With his face unmasked and his eyes only for her, anyone who knew about the Iriduans would understand she was his queen.

His visual declaration was as good a vow as any wedding promise. No more would he allow his own duties and concerns to stand between them. Molly had realized that she couldn't give any less of herself to him than he'd given to her. She couldn't sacrifice any less to be with him. She couldn't prioritize him below anything else in her life because he had made her his first priority.

It was a relief to finally find a cause that had an even

greater hold on her than the one she'd worked for these last years on Za'Kluth. Granted, she still wanted to find ways to help those who suffered under the yoke of slavery, and she knew that Shulgi would agree with her desire to assist them in some way. But now it was time to make a new life for herself. A new life for the both of them, and Molly didn't want that life to be in the filthy, crime infested, and deeply corrupt city of Za'Kluth.

She wanted them to find a home that felt clean and bright, perhaps a place where she could walk out along a beach and feel the sun warming her skin. She wanted to chase that vague memory or dream from childhood and see if sinking her toes into the sand would bring back any more memories.

But most of all, she wanted to stand within the protective circle of Shulgi's arms and look out upon a distant horizon far from the dark basalt columns of Za'Kluth and know that for that blissful moment, she had finally found peace.

She had yet to discuss the particulars of their future with Shulgi. In fact, she hadn't been able to discuss much with him at all. As a celebration broke out among Zaska's minions below them, Briana, Molly, Shulgi, and his friend Nemon—who everyone currently believed to be Sha Zaska—all retreated back into the office building.

Nemon remained with Shulgi in the public part of the building while Briana and Molly returned to their inner sanctum to discuss the future of the organization.

Some of their inner circle had escaped into the under-vents during the invasion, including Jusa, who would take Briana's place as the second mouthpiece for Zaska, since Briana would be stepping into Molly's role.

For now, the remaining members who knew that Sha Zaska didn't exist gave Briana and Molly some privacy, some of them joining the revelers outside the offices, some of them retreating back to the safety of the under-vents to decide their own futures.

Briana hugged Molly in a fierce embrace that Molly returned.

"I'm going to miss you," Briana said, tears in her voice. "It won't be the same around here without you."

Molly blinked back her own tears, some of them slipping free to roll down her cheeks. "It won't ever be the same, even if I stayed, Bri."

Briana sighed heavily, slowing releasing Molly. "I know. I don't even know what we're going to do without Jenice. It still hasn't fully sunken in that I'm never going to see her again."

Molly's heart ached whenever she thought of Jenice. She wondered how long it would take before she would stop feeling such painful grief at the thought of her friend. They had been through so much together, and though Jenice had betrayed her, Molly knew it was because she didn't want Molly to get hurt. She'd thought she could head off disaster by getting Shulgi out of the picture. She'd allowed her own love for Molly to blind her to the potential repercussions.

And she'd paid far more dearly for it than she should have.

Shulgi had been deeply upset to hear that Jenice died from complications because of the wound he'd given her, immediately taking the blame on himself because he'd never intended for her to die from his shot. Molly understood that and didn't blame him at all for Jenice's death. Their captors could have treated her wound easily so that it didn't get infected. They could have given her hydration. Instead, they'd left her to suffer and Uthagol's cruelty had done the rest.

Molly didn't want Shulgi to feel the guilt of Jenice's death, but they hadn't had a good chance to discuss things after Uthagol's defeat, because Molly and Briana wanted to take back the under-tier without wasting any time. They'd only allowed for a quick shower, a change of clothing, and a check over by a medic Shulgi had produced. The medic belonged to a group of more friends of Shulgi's she would probably never see again. They were the covert kind of friends, like the ones of hers that he wasn't likely to ever meet. Those kinds of people preferred to remain in the shadows, and Molly understood that well.

Once she had a chance to really sit down and talk with Shulgi, for once without fear of the secrets that lay between them being revealed, they could talk about all that remained between them. All the lies and heartache and hurt that they needed to put aside. Molly knew that the love they felt for each other was strong enough to overcome everything else.

"He better deserve you," Briana said after a long silence had fallen between them, both of them lost in their thoughts.

Molly smiled, managing it even through her grief. "He does. I could tell all along that he has a good heart. A worthy heart."

Briana chuckled, though her amusement didn't meet her eyes, which held a deep well of grief that Molly completely understood. "Not to mention a very nice outer wrapping for that worthy heart."

Molly's smile widened to a full grin as she shook her head at Briana. "You're terrible!"

Briana shrugged both shoulders, her hands out at her sides. "What can I say? I love males—especially the really attractive ones."

Molly's smile slowly faded as she regarded her friend. Their ordeal had brought them closer than ever, right before they had to say goodbye to each other.

"Are you sure this is what you want?" she asked, knowing she wouldn't have to explain further to Briana.

Briana nodded, her smile reassuring. "I've never been a 'settle down and have a family' kind of girl."

She lifted a hand to pat hair that had been spattered with blood during their brief battles in the under-vents with the little resistance the Iriduan invaders had put up in that labyrinth. Those fools hadn't stood a chance in Molly and Briana's territory.

"I like the game too much to leave it," Briana said with conviction, lowering her hand. "This lifestyle makes me feel powerful—and alive! Back on Earth, I was just another face in the crowd." Her smile twisted into a rueful wince. "Not even a very pretty one. I was just dragging along, day in and day out, in a job I hated, dating men who never seemed to understand me but always expected me to settle down with them, even though I said I didn't want anything serious. I just felt like I was out of place, even though I faded into the background."

She gestured with a sweeping hand to their inner sanctum. "Here, I am the mouthpiece of a gang boss—one of the true leaders of this gang. I have consequence, and power, and wealth." She tapped her chest, over her heart. "And a purpose! One that actually *means* something. One that changes lives and helps people!"

"I'm so glad you're happy here, Briana," Molly said with sincerity. "You're an excellent mouthpiece for Zaska."

Briana hugged Molly again, briefly this time. "You'll always be the best we ever had. You understood Zaska better than any of us. You gave birth to him."

Molly pulled a face, then laughed as she returned Briana's hug. "Ugh, that gives me a terrible mental image!"

Briana laughed aloud as they stepped back to grin at each other. "Yeah, I suppose having a bunch of tentacles coming out of your womb wouldn't be pretty." She shifted her gaze towards the door that led into the public offices of Zaska's Shipping.

"Although, having a tentacle or two going *inside* of you might not be so bad, come to think of it."

"Briana!" Molly's eyes were wide even as laughter filled her voice. "You are *incorrigible*! Besides, I think Nemon has a woman already."

Briana giggled, sounding young and innocent, belying the worldly experience she wore like a queen's mantle. "I know. But that doesn't stop me from being curious. Maybe I'll see if I can import a thida naf one of these days, so we have a real Sha Zaska to trot out whenever the occasion warrants."

"You know, I heard they really *are* dangerous," Molly warned, though Briana's tone hadn't sounded serious, and who knew what kind of logistics it would take to bring such a creature into Za'Kluth—then tame it to play a role without trying to take over for real.

Briana winked at her. "I like danger."

They both laughed aloud at her words as they stood in their blood-stained dresses on tile streaked by blood from corpses that the others had fortunately already removed from the inner sanctum.

Molly glanced at the damaged lounge chairs and sofa, her laughter dying. "I worry about Mogorl and Grundon," she said, realizing that it wasn't likely she would get the chance to say goodbye to them before she and Shulgi left Za'Kluth.

Briana's chuckle held less certainty and amusement. "Well, at least we were able to get their message. I guess the Iriduans couldn't decrypt it, or they just didn't care to."

"I can't believe they left Za'Kluth to save a slave without sending word to us first for assistance!" Molly shook her head. "I've never seen them act so impulsively before."

Of course, if Mogorl and Grundon hadn't hopped onto the transport cruiser just before it left column 210, they would have lost the poor human woman to whatever terrible fate awaited her, because the Iriduans had control of Zaska's resources at the time, so they wouldn't have been able to track the cruiser's course until it was out of Zaska's reach.

In the long run, their impulsiveness might have worked out for the best, though they had still been in pursuit of the woman and her captors when they'd managed to send a message that had arrived a day cycle ago. Mog and Grun were no doubt still unaware that Ma'Nah had turned on them. Molly wished she could speak to them again, one last time, and explain everything that had happened in their absence.

She dreaded what they would go through when they discovered that Jenice was gone. They had loved her like their sibling, just as they loved Molly and the others in their circle. They were a family, and that family was now all split up.

It was difficult and heartbreaking to deal with such drastic changes, but Molly still believed the future held so much more promise than the past, for all of them. Mog and Grun would find their lost slave and rescue her and see to it that she had a safe place to live without fear of being recaptured, before returning to Zaska and the crew. They would experience some heartache when they did return to Za'Kluth and learn all that had happened in their absence, but hopefully they would be satisfied with the good deed that they had accomplished.

And hopefully, someday, Molly would get a chance to communicate directly with them again, even if only to say their final farewells.

For now, she had preparations of her own to make. She also had a long discussion with Shulgi ahead of her.

THIRTY-SEVEN

Molly couldn't believe she was actually on a Lusian ship. So few people had ever been on one who weren't Lusian that Molly had never met a person in her life who could brag of having had such an experience.

Save for Shulgi himself, although he hadn't told her about his affiliation with a Lusian crew until they'd sat down to seriously discuss their future.

That talk had been a long and, at times, painful one. Shulgi revealed all his secrets to her, and all of his past. He explained the mission he'd been on Za'Kluth to perform. He'd also explained how he'd failed, and Molly could see the toll that feeling of failure took on him. Even though he insisted that he didn't regret his choices, and that he never would have sacrificed Molly to keep Namerian from getting the code, she now understood just how much that decision had cost him.

Her beloved turned out to be far more complicated than she'd imagined, and his life had been one of struggle and sacrifice. Much like her own. Shulgi wanted to do good things, but he'd had to resort to bad methods more than once to achieve his goals. She could certainly relate to that and told him about the things she'd not only witnessed in her role as mouthpiece, but had actually been a party to, in her role as one of the leaders of Zaska's organization.

Neither of them was coming into this relationship with clean hands. Both of them had done things that would haunt them for the rest of their lives. Both of them sought their own kind of redemption. They found forgiveness in each other and believed they would find that redemption in love.

As for their future, when Shulgi suggested they leave Za'Kluth for good, Molly hadn't hesitated to say yes, even though she had no idea where they could go. Shulgi had a suggestion, but he seemed reluctant to voice it. When he finally did, he confessed that he wasn't certain it was a good idea, given that it meant living the rest of their lives with the enemies of the Iriduans.

"You'll love Hierabodos V!" Ava insisted as she gave Molly the tour of the Lusian ship, one arm locked in Molly's in a companionable fashion.

Molly had instantly liked the other human woman who'd greeted them the moment she and Shulgi had been teleported to the ship, along with a drastically different looking Nemon. As bizarre as she found the change in Nemon's body from an amorphous mantle with tentacles to a handsome Iriduan male —at least from the waist up—she found it even stranger that Ava was the mate of not only one, but pretty much the entire crew of Lusians that ran this ship.

Ava's enthusiastic friendliness and engaging manner quickly put Molly at ease, though she was grateful that she didn't have to spend much time around Ava's mates, some of whom engaged Shulgi in conversation she wasn't privy to. She suspected that discussion was about the cure that Shulgi had been entrusted with and hoped he wouldn't be in any trouble from those who had given him that responsibility.

The Lusians themselves unnerved her, though Ava insisted they were wonderful. She *would* think that, after all.

"All my friends live on Hierabodos V," she continued as Molly searched for the right way to express her doubts and concerns without giving any offense."

Ava paused, shaking her head with a smile. "I mean, not *all* my friends! Some of my buddies are scattered throughout the galaxy. But some of my closest friends live on Hierabodos." She waved her hand vaguely towards the teleportation room. "And you've already met Nemon, who is one of the strangest inhabitants." She squeezed Molly's arm in her infectious enthusiasm. "I heard all about the battle and Roz even showed me some footage from it, but it's never the same as being there. It must have been very scary for you!"

Molly smiled ruefully. "I didn't have a lot of time to think about it. Things happened so quickly that we didn't get the chance to be scared until it was all over."

"You're so brave!" Ava said, staring at her with a wide-eyed and admiring expression. "I think you'll really like my friends on Hierabodos. They've been through some really crazy things too." Her gaze grew thoughtful as she studied Molly's dyed skin. "My bestie is an artist. I think she'll really dig your tattoos."

"They're actually just dyes." Molly held up one hand to study her skin critically. "They'll fade in a few months. It'll be strange to see my skin without them for the first time in years." She touched her face, tracing by memory the lines of Zaska's "markings," the artfully coiled tentacles writhing over her violet skin in a strong green shade. "I hope Shulgi still thinks I'm pretty when he sees me without all of this."

Ava impulsively hugged her. "You're absolutely beautiful,

Molly, and it's obvious Shulgi's crazy about you! He will always think you're beautiful. No matter what!"

Molly's smile widened into a genuinely pleased grin as she returned the hug with a fierce one of her own. Ava's bubbly and upbeat attitude seemed so out of place on this austere ship, yet Molly could completely understand why the Lusians loved having her around them. It was a pleasure to be in the company of someone who always searched for the bright side and looked for the goodness in others.

Ava was also a full-blown romantic who still believed in "happily ever afters." That belief had no doubt been reinforced by the fact that she'd found her own—albeit in an unconventional way that wasn't quite like the fairy tales Molly had been told.

Molly wanted to believe that she and Shulgi would get their happily ever after too, and she wished she had Ava's unwavering faith in such a possibility. She still had fears and doubts. She still worried that the darkness of her past would return to haunt her, or that Shulgi's past would come for him.

Then there was the fact that Hierabodos was in Akrellian territory, and the Akrellians weren't fond of Iriduans, though they apparently extended a welcome to Iriduans who defected from the Iriduan Empire and actively worked to thwart it. Shulgi wouldn't be the first Iriduan who'd sought refuge with them, but even the ever-positive Ava had to admit that there could be occasional rough spots while the Akrellian pioneers on Hierabodos got used to Shulgi's presence.

They really didn't have a lot of other options that would guarantee the same degree of safety. Despite being a dangerous world in its own right due to the untamed wilderness that covered most of the planet, its location deep within Akrellian space made it nearly impossible for the Iriduan empire to reach, and the exact star map to it was a well-guarded secret.

Shulgi's enemies wouldn't find him easily there, and the Akrellians were apparently already working with the Iriduan rebellion to overthrow the emperors, so they weren't completely against working with one more of their number. As for Shulgi, he would be killed on sight by imperialist Iriduans for mating illegally, so if he went anywhere else in the galaxy where he might encounter others who served the empire, he would have to conceal his mated status as much as his identity.

The Akrellians had communicated through Roz that they welcomed any efforts she or Shulgi could make towards finding and rescuing slaves from the CivilRim, as well as anywhere within Syndicate space. This gave them the chance to continue Molly's work, and they would even make it possible for her to coordinate with Briana and the others of Zaska's organization.

The offer was a good one, though they would be confined to Hierabodos V indefinitely until the Akrellian leadership decided they could be trusted to travel within Akrellian space. Ava seemed to think that wouldn't take long, but Molly knew her optimism might blind her to the cold reality of the political and social difficulties they'd be facing with Shulgi living among his former enemies.

But what had really sold Molly on the idea of moving to Hierabodos V was that it had beaches, and a sun that was not much different from the one that warmed Earth. In fact, apparently the world of Hierabodos wasn't much different from Earth in many ways, falling well within the same Goldilocks zone to its star and boasting a dense variety of ecologies that rivaled Earth's diversity.

Ava showed Molly to the cabin she would be sharing with Shulgi, promising with a wink that there wasn't any surveillance in the cabin and that the Lusians would respect their privacy.

"I know you'll want to spend most of your time with Shulgi," Ava said after that promise, her own cheeks red even though Molly was unfazed by the suggestion that she would make love with Shulgi.

That certainly was her plan the moment she had him alone, and she felt no shame for that. She also felt no shame about the life she'd led, nor how she'd leveraged her own sexuality for power. Fortunately, no one had made any judgmental remarks about her former profession, and she highly doubted a sweetheart like Ava or the enigmatic Lusians or Nemon would say anything negative about the life she'd lived. They all had showed her nothing but respect and admiration. She hoped Ava's friends were as welcoming and lacking in judgement.

"If you decide to leave your cabin," Ava continued with a broad grin, "I have a bunch of Earth stuff in mine if you want to check it out. I have comic books, movies, some video games, lots of romance novels... you know, all the good stuff! It sometimes helps when you're feeling homesick for Earth."

Molly sank down on the firm mattress in her surprisingly spacious cabin. "I was taken from Earth when I was so young that I don't remember much about it, but I will definitely stop by during our trip because I'd love to see some human-made things." She sighed. "It was so expensive to import true human artifacts to Za'Kluth. Most of the things we found in the markets were fakes, or poor copies of the originals."

Then she regarded Ava curiously, her head cocking to the side. "When would you be available for visiting, Ava? It seems like you have a lot," Molly raised her brows as she gestured to the surrounding cabin with the intent of indicating the entire ship, "on your plate, so to speak."

Ava's grin broke into tinkling laughter that made Molly want to laugh too, especially as she spotted the blush rising to the other woman's cheeks again.

"I *do* stay busy," Ava said in a sly tone, her smile still

playing around her lips, "but you can drop by my cabin anytime. Don't worry about catching me in the middle of something. My mates know when I'll have time for them or when I'll be otherwise occupied—even before I do."

This raised Molly's brows, causing Ava to giggle at her startled expression.

"Roz can see the future," Ava said casually. Then she shrugged her plump shoulders. "To a certain extent. Don't ask me how he does it or what his limitations are, because once he starts talking about paradoxes and alternate dimensions and parallel timelines and the flux, I get a headache. I'm not entirely sure the human mind is ready to comprehend a lot of these concepts involving time."

"He can really predict the future?" Molly blinked several times in surprise, then realized why the Lusians were considered by many to be the most powerful species in the Syndicate.

After all, they'd created the Jumpstations that made intergalactic travel so much faster and easier. Bending time and space didn't seem to be a problem for them, so telling the future was probably child's play for them too.

Ava slowly nodded. "Don't ask him for lottery numbers though, or you'll get a lecture on the dangerous futility of gambling." She flipped her blond hair over one shoulder as she leaned against the sliding door of the cabin. "He can get a bit pedantic, but I usually just tease him until he gets over it." She tapped her temple. "Since he can read my mind, I just imagine the last erotic scene I read in a romance novel, and he completely loses track of what he was saying when I project that image to him."

Molly laughed aloud at Ava's expression as she wriggled her well-groomed eyebrows. "You're wicked, Ava. Now I know why I instantly liked you the moment I met you!"

Ava pressed a hand to her chest. "Aw, thank you! I like you

too, Molly." She clapped her hands together. "I'm so excited to have another human woman on this ship for a while. I do miss visiting with all my girlfriends when Roz decides we need to travel all over the galaxy doing Lusian things." Her brows drew together in a slight frown as she stepped a little closer to Molly, glancing at the sliding door that currently closed the cabin off from the rest of the corridor.

"I'm kind of...," she bit her lip, "*jealous* for the first time in a long time, about the other woman we've just brought on the ship." She held up both hands. "Not that I think my mates would ever be unfaithful to me, but she's... she understands them like I never could. She's one of them! Only she's also like a human in a way. It's...." Ava slowly shook her head. "I'm sorry. I shouldn't be dumping my issues on you like this. You just got here and I'm sure you're completely wiped out. Plus, Shulgi's on his way, and I'm sure you both want to catch up."

Ava turned back towards the door as Molly jumped to her feet to catch Ava's shoulder. "Wait! Listen, Ava, I haven't met this woman yet, but I don't need to see her to know that you shouldn't be jealous. You're a wonderful person, and just talking to you has brightened my day—and we just met! I can't imagine any male who'd be fool enough to consider another woman over you."

Ava turned to give Molly another hug. "Thank you, Molly! You're so sweet!"

"If you want to talk about it, I'm more than happy to lend an ear," Molly offered readily.

She missed Jenice so badly, and already felt lost without Briana and the others—like Jusa—who had been there for her to talk with whenever she needed a compassionate ear. She welcomed having another female friend like Ava to talk to.

THIRTY-EIGHT

It wasn't long after Ava left that Shulgi entered their cabin through the sliding door, looking refreshed, even though his verdant eyes remained somewhat haunted by what he considered to be his failure.

Molly jumped up from the bed where she'd been lounging, her eyelids lolling closed after a very exhausting time. Now, she felt alert, and that had everything to do with Shulgi's welcome presence. At last, they were alone, in a private place where they could finally be together without fear of discovery or dark secrets forming obstacles between them.

Now, Molly felt strangely nervous, butterflies going wild in her belly as she went to her mate, her hungry gaze admiring the strong lines of his body and the fine chiseled features of his handsome face. He wore a robe now. One probably given to him by the Lusians as he'd essentially abandoned all his property in the dreg, where the chaos was only just dying down.

Though Molly found Shulgi very sexy in his armor, looking like the warrior he was, she preferred the way he looked in the traditional Iriduan robes. His wings folded against his back, gleaming among the silken embroidered dark green fabric of his robe. His hair hung sleek and shiny down his back, with thick locks framing his face. His skin practically glowed with vigor and health.

He studied her in silence as she closed the distance between them, a smile stretching on his handsome lips. "You're so beautiful, my mate," he said, holding out his hands to her.

She slipped her fingers into his, her own smile wide as happiness suffused her entire body. "You really make me feel like the most beautiful woman in the galaxy when you look at me like that, Shulgi."

He released one of her hands to caress her face, then cupped it as he lowered his head. With his lips hovering above hers, he said, "you *are* the most beautiful woman in the galaxy, Molly. For me, you are the only woman in the galaxy."

His lips falling upon hers cut off any response she might have made, though her head spun too much to think of what she could possibly say to that. She wrapped her arms around his neck as his kiss claimed her lips, both demanding and enticing her equally hungry response.

She slid one hand from the nape of his neck to the collar of his robe, her fingers toying with the catch at his throat. One quick flick of her finger unhooked that top catch and the seam of the robe parted as she drew her hand down the front of the silken material.

Shulgi moaned against her lips as her other hand trailed the first, pushing aside the silk that hid his powerful body from her view. She caressed his hard, firm muscles, reveling in the feeling of their power twitching and tensing beneath her gentle touch.

Once the robe's seam was fully parted and it hung loose on his shoulders, Molly's fingers trailed down his sculpted abdominals to the waistband of his trousers. He lifted his head from their kiss to stare down at her with eyes nearly black from his arousal.

"The things you do to me, my queen," he said in a guttural voice, his eyes closing as she parted the seam of his trousers and pushed the material aside.

His body shivered when she encircled his thick shaft, slowly caressing the length of it as she watched the pleasure play over his handsome features.

His eyes flew open when she sank to her knees in front of him, both her hands pushing at the waist of his trousers to shove them down his thighs.

"Molly," he said, then seemed to lose his voice as she parted her lips, exhaling a warm breath over the silky skin that covered his rock-hard shaft, tracing the veins crossing the firm flesh with a fingertip.

Then he groaned and slipped his hands into her hair as she followed the movement of her finger with her tongue.

"Oh, Spinner's mercy, my Molly!" he cried as she took him into her mouth, sucking him as deep as she could, wrapping her fingers around his girth below her lips as she slowly drew them back up his length, her saliva lubricating his skin so her hand slipped easily up and down his shaft.

Her head bobbed as she hungrily sucked him, loving the wordless sounds of pleasure he made, his fingers gently clenching in her hair. When his spinal appendages—he called them cerci—moved to stroke her head and trail across her hollowed cheeks, she used her free hand to stroke each one in turn. He'd explained that they were sensory organs sensitive to her touch, and they vibrated under her palm as she drew it along their segmented length to the barbed and clawed tip.

"Molly, please," he said, his voice rough with his arousal, "as much as I'm enjoying this, I don't want to climax yet, and your mouth is bringing me to that point very quickly."

She relented, dragging her lips one last time up his shaft to lick up the drops of precum welling from the head of it with relish, her eyes shifting to stare up at his face. His features were tense with lust and his struggle for self-control. His cerci coiled on either side of his lean hips, the barbs on the ends rippling from flat to extended and then flat again with his excitement.

One of his hands slid from her hair down to her chin as she lifted her head away from his thick erection. "I am just as eager to explore your body and taste you, Molly."

She heard the hunger in his voice and her inner muscles clenched in anticipation as she rose to her feet. Shulgi unhooked the clasps on the silvery gray dress he'd bought her, whispering in her ear how he would buy her a thousand more, each more beautiful than the last.

"I would rather have no clothes at all," she said with a wicked lilt in her voice, tracing his lower lip as he lifted his head to watch her while he drew her dress off her shoulders. "As long as I'm spending time with you."

His chuckle sounded strained and ragged as he pulled the fabric of her dress down past her petite breasts, his dilated gaze growing even blacker as it fixed on the hard nipples peaked from her excitement.

He pushed the dress all the way past her subtly rounded hips and Molly felt the silken swish of fabric brush past her legs to pool on the floor at her feet. Then his warm lips met hers, but only briefly before trailing over her jaw, then down to the column of her throat. She moaned in pleasure as Shulgi kissed his way to her collarbone, then lower.

She clutched his nape with one hand, tracing his ears and playing her fingers through his long, beautiful hair with the other as he caught one nipple in his hot mouth and suckled it. His hands trailed down her body until his fingers delved beneath the waistband of her panties. He shoved them down and cupped her buttocks in his large palms, gently squeezing them before pushing her panties further down her thighs.

The cooler air of the cabin brushed over her soaking core, but it wasn't long before the warmth of his fingers replaced that drafty feeling. His mouth sucked hungrily on her nipple while he drew the fingers of one hand through her folds, teasing over her swollen clit.

The hum of his pleased moan when he discovered how wet she was vibrated against her hypersensitive nipple, causing her to gasp and clutch at his strong shoulders.

Then she cried out in surprise when he lifted her up by her thighs and walked her backwards to the bed. He laid her out atop it, only then releasing her nipple. He teased the other one, licking it and then suckling it as his fingers played over her clit.

Molly's back arched on the soft blanket of the bed as she cried out softly, her voice panting and nearly breathless as Shulgi teased her clit until she approached her peak, her body tensing in anticipation of toppling over it.

Then he freed her other nipple, leaving it as swollen and tingling as the first as he kissed his way down her body. His hot tongue and warm lips teased over her naked skin as he tugged her panties off her legs and tossed them aside. He parted her knees, spreading her legs wide so he could position his large body between them as he moved lower.

Molly gasped as his lips reached her mound. Her hips writhed with her pleasure as he kissed his way to her clit. She shivered with delight as his tongue swept over that sensitive bud in a teasingly long stroke. Shulgi tongued her clit over and over as she panted and gasped and pleaded with him never to stop. He slid two fingers inside her soaking entrance, fingering her as her inner muscles clenched in preparation for her orgasm.

When the rising pleasure from his tongue and fingers sent

her over the edge, Molly cried out in ecstasy, her entire body tensing as her eyes closed. Her back arched, her knees reflexively trying to pull closed, but Shulgi's body blocked them as he continued to move his fingers inside her convulsing passage.

Clutching fistfuls of the blanket, she writhed in the throes of a powerful climax, feeling the hungry, dark eyes of her lover watching her. When she finally fell limp in the aftermath, Shulgi withdrew his fingers from her sensitive slit and positioned the head of his erection there.

They both moaned in unison as he slowly pushed his length inside her. This time she felt no surprise when his cerci moved into place to vibrate on her clit as he began to thrust, pushing his shaft deep before slowly withdrawing it until only the tip remained inside her.

Their slow, deliberate movements didn't last long. As much as they both wanted to draw out the pleasure of this lovemaking, the arousal proved too much. His cerci quickly brought Molly back to the peak of another orgasm, and as soon as she convulsed around his shaft, he lost control of himself and pounded into her, rocking her body on the bed until both of them were panting.

Her final internal convulsions milked his seed from him as he came with a loud grunt followed by a long moan. He pumped a few more times inside her as he spilled the last of his seed, then sagged over her, his strong arms bracing his weight above her so he didn't crush her to the bed.

In the glowing aftermath of her orgasm, Molly stroked her hands over his body, caressing his warm, smooth skin and enjoying the shift of powerful muscles beneath it as he slowly withdrew his length from her. He moved from between her legs to lay on the bed beside her, gathering her into his arms as he turned to face her.

As she continued to slide her hands all over his beautiful

body, reveling in the luxury of having him all to herself, with no obligations waiting for her attention and no one to tell her they couldn't be together like this forever, he returned her languid caresses, his eyes meeting hers.

"I will make you happy, Molly," he swore as if he was a knight making a solemn oath.

She traced his high cheekbone with the tip of her finger, a broad smile on her lips. "You already have, Shulgi."

"I mean forever." His gaze looked no less intense, even though his pupils had shrunk back to a more normal size with his orgasm.

"I like the sound of forever with you," she said softly, her finger moving to trace his lips. "You're my happily ever after, Shulgi. I've waited so long for you, but now I know the wait was worth it."

His lips tilted in a soft smile as he studied her face. When his hand lifted to touch it, he traced the markings of Zaska that still crossed her features. "I will do whatever it takes to make you happy, my mate." His brows furrowed. "But I hope it never involves allowing you to put yourself in such danger again."

She chuckled then kissed him. "I'd rather avoid danger, if possible. I was never married to the life of the leader of a criminal organization."

"Good." His smile faded into a more solemn expression. "Will you marry *me*? Ava mentioned something about a 'wedding' in the human tradition, and I would give you that, if you wanted it."

Molly kissed him again, her eyes misting with tears. "I will marry you, yes! But you don't need to give me anything else, Shulgi. You've already given me the best gift in the galaxy." She traced the straight line of his nose. "You."

THIRTY-NINE

Shulgi had many reservations about Hierabodos V, and the inhabitants he would meet there. Roz had already explained to him that he must never mention his role in the destruction of the Akrellian ship—the Star Dancer—to anyone, least of all, the Akrellian spiritual leader, Tirel, whom some claimed to be the avatar of the Dark Partner.

Shulgi figured if the Akrellian was truly in tune with some deific spirit, he would already know what happened to the Star Dancer and its crew. If he wasn't, Shulgi had no intention of informing him. That part of his life was buried now, and he didn't want to bring it back to the surface. That was one reason he'd strongly questioned Roz's very firm advice to relocate to Hierabodos V. The Akrellian leadership allowed this request for sanctuary because they believed Shulgi had become a fugitive of the Iriduan Empire due to working with the rebellion.

At least, that was what he'd been told. He found out differently after Roz teleported them to the surface of Hierabodos. A small crowd of unusual people met them at the teleportation pad. Fortunately, Nemon had already told him who to expect, and had shown him images of what they would all look like.

Nahash was one of the most startling, simply because he had once been an Iriduan soldier like Shulgi. He had become something so much more terrifying because of Iriduan experimentation. The one called Thrax hadn't actually been an Iriduan but had been modified with the genome of one, again because of Iriduan experimentation.

But those creatures seemed welcoming, and Molly greeted them as if they were no more unusual than any other aliens she'd ever met. She possessed so much poise and class that she made him think of her more as an empress than a queen. The fact that Ava had teleported to the surface with them and made introductions in her exuberant manner between Molly and Shulgi and their odd little family of "test subjects," no doubt also helped smooth the way.

Until Shulgi came face to face with a powerfully built Akrellian who regarded him with cold eyes and a chilling expression. A voluptuous human female with dark hair and light brown skin clung to his arm more like she was holding him back rather than being affectionate, though the way she looked up at him showed that she cared about him.

The greetings from the others fell silent, even Ava's bubbly voice dying from the weight of the tension that fell upon the group. Roz appeared beside Shulgi, his enigmatic gaze fixed on the Akrellian.

The scaled features of the male twisted into a hard scowl as his eyes shifted from Roz back to Shulgi. "By the Dancer's will, you've been allowed to settle on these lands, but I do not forgive so easily."

"You must be Tirel," Shulgi said with far more calm than he felt.

The Akrellian would be a challenge, even if his combat

glands were still functioning. He'd requested that Roz deactivate them so he could overcome the addiction to battle and bloodshed now that he wanted to create a peaceful life with Molly.

"You murdered my crew and destroyed my ship," Tirel growled, his claws flexing as the quills on his back and head stood erect.

So much for not telling about his past. It appeared that the Akrellian had somehow figured it out anyway.

His connection to the Dark Dancer is far stronger than I anticipated.

Shulgi glanced at Roz, whose expression still looked serene and unfazed, despite the words he'd spoken inside Shulgi's mind. Shulgi didn't know if he'd ever grow accustomed to having someone in his head. Roz invaded a person's mind far less gently than Luna.

Suddenly, Molly left the small group of females who had surrounded her and eagerly welcomed her into their fold, admiring her dyed skin. She made her way straight to the Akrellian and his lovely, dark eyed mate, her steps graceful, her bearing regal, even as she bowed her head in a submissive manner.

"Honored Akrellian and honored human," Molly said in a gentle, cajoling tone, "I beg that you find it within you to forgive my beloved for his past. He has suffered dearly for the crimes he once committed because he believed in the wrong cause." She glanced at Shulgi, all her love for him in her eyes before returning her pleading gaze to the Akrellian and his mate. "He is a good person who desires nothing more than to right the wrongs of his past and his people." She pressed her palms together in front of her, sinking into a low bow before them. "He will prove himself worthy of your forgiveness and generosity in time, if you will give him the chance."

"You have such lovely manners!" the Akrellian's woman said with a wide smile. She patted Tirel's stiff arm as her gaze shifted from Molly to Shulgi. "You are a very lucky Iriduan to have a woman like her as your mate."

Shulgi bowed his head respectfully, already sensing he had an ally in the Akrellian's mate. He could tell she had the heart of a romantic. "I'm the luckiest Iriduan in the galaxy." His voice rang with his sincerity.

"That's my line," Nahash growled in irritation from where he still coiled next to Nemon and Thrax, all of whom were watching the standoff between Shulgi and Tirel with more curiosity than concern.

Nahash's mate chuckled, which seemed to break the tension among that group, though Tirel still stared at him with anger in every line of his body.

"My queen speaks true," Shulgi returned his full attention to Tirel. "I deeply regret the actions I've taken in the past in service of an unworthy empire." His brows furrowed as he scowled. "And an even less worthy female."

"You speak of Ninhursag." The Akrellian proved he knew a great deal more about the situation than Shulgi had expected.

Then Shulgi recalled that Tirel had been a part of the showdown between Halian's fractures and Ninhursag and her minions. Shulgi himself had been kept isolated both from Tirel and from that battle. Not only had he still been recovering at the time, but Roz didn't want the others to question his loyalties, claiming it would be an unnecessary distraction.

"My Shulgi was bound to that woman when he committed the crimes against your people," Molly said, rising gracefully from her bow. "He had little choice in his actions, and yet he owns them completely and desires to make amends."

Shulgi stepped up to stand beside Molly, not wanting her

to have to speak for him. This brought him closer to the Akrellian, who tensed, his eyes narrowing.

"My mate speaks so eloquently, but I would not have her bear the burden of my apologies." He met the hard gaze of the Akrellian. "I cannot change the past, though I can promise you I would if I had that power."

"That would be unwise," Roz said mildly from behind Shulgi. "Changing the past would undo the present."

Tirel frowned, shooting his narrow-eyed glare at Roz before returning his attention to Shulgi. "A very large part of me wants to kill you for what you've done," he looked down into the eyes of his mate, his features softening, "but the wisdom of the Dancer prevails over my darker urges."

His mate smiled softly, leaning her cheek against his arm.

"I can't promise I will ever forgive you," Tirel growled in a hard tone as he returned his focus to Shulgi, "but you'll get the chance to prove you deserve forgiveness."

"I'll do what I must to earn it," Shulgi vowed, internally sagging in relief, since he recognized that he needed the Akrellian's cooperation to remain on this world, safe from the Iriduan empire.

Tirel stepped closer until they stood eye to eye. "Be the male your mate believes you to be, and we won't have a problem."

"You still desire bloodshed," Shulgi murmured in a volume so low that even Molly didn't seem to hear it.

Tirel's lips split in a sharp toothed grin. "I do."

Shulgi's grin was just as deadly if not as sharp. "Best to postpone that until the females are otherwise occupied."

His voice was still very low, but Molly watched him suspiciously, creeping closer to Shulgi as if she debated jumping between him and Tirel. Though at the moment, there wasn't enough space for her to fit.

"What did you just say?" Molly demanded, reaching to take Shulgi's hand.

"You'd better not be considering what I think you're considering, Tirel," the Akrellian's mate said in an exasperated voice.

"We better get to watch the battle," one of the other males said.

Shulgi suspected it was the one called Thrax that had spoken, because it was his mate—a curvy human female with a hair color that was vibrant and unnatural for a human—who made a shushing sound even as she wrapped her arm around her towering male's waist.

Despite what went on around them, Shulgi and Tirel didn't break eye contact for a long moment, neither wanting to be the one to look away first. There was no question about it. There would need to be bloodshed before he would ever have the chance to earn this male's forgiveness. The dark look in his eyes reminded Shulgi of his own joy of battle, and also reminded him of what little he knew about the Dark Partner that this Akrellian apparently hosted within him.

That entity was the spirit of battle and bloodlust.

Shulgi's smile widened. "This will be a good fight!"

MOLLY'S PROTESTS fell on deaf ears. Shulgi was determined to engage in combat with the Akrellian named Tirel, but they were given the opportunity to retreat to their pop-up housing placed on the shore of an unspoiled beach that bordered a gorgeous ocean. The ripple of waves glittered beneath a warm yellow sun as they approached.

She wished she could take a moment to enjoy the view and the experience of being outside on a world's surface, with an actual ground beneath her slipper-shod feet. Instead, she had to worry about Shulgi and the Akrellian coming to blows.

Something that the other males eagerly anticipated based on their conversation. The other women weren't at all happy about the turn of events. Least of all, Tirel's mate, Theresa.

"I'm so sorry," she said as she walked arm in arm with Molly to their new home—temporary as it was until they could build something more permanent. "I'll talk sense into Tirel. Don't worry. This fight won't go down if I can help it."

Molly understood how things worked when it came to repaying an insult or injury. On Za'Kluth, people killed each other over even minor displays of disrespect. Shulgi had done great harm to Tirel and his people, and it was clear that the Akrellian would have a hard time forgiving that. Still, she worried about Shulgi, especially since he'd given up his combat glands because he wanted to live a life of peace. It would be the first time he'd been able to do so since he'd entered his Meta.

He'd told her all about how the Iriduan lifecycle worked and how the empire chose an Iriduan's path for him once he left his cocoon to begin his adulthood. She still had a hard time imagining Shulgi as a "child," looking far more like a giant dragonfly skimming over the waters that bordered his creche than a plump two-legged toddler stumbling about on the ground.

"Shulgi had little choice in what he became. The empire decided the path of his life for him. Coming here was supposed to be a way for him to finally make his own choice about how he wants to live. And he chooses peace and serenity." She turned a pleading gaze on Theresa. "If you can convince your mate to drop this idea of a battle, I would be forever in your debt."

Theresa nodded her head firmly. "Have faith in me, my new friend, I know how to convince my Partner. There is a darkness in his heart, but it still beats in tune to my own. When he dances tonight, it won't be a dance of blood."

As they reached the temporary dwelling that the Akrellians had set up for Molly and Shulgi, Theresa hugged Molly close, reiterating her promise in Molly's ear before releasing her with a confident smile. She glanced over at Shulgi, who stood listening to Nahash speaking of some Iriduan topic that brought a slight smirk to Shulgi's lips and an unnervingly toothy grin to Nahash's scaled face.

The other "test subjects" and their mates had dispersed not long after bidding that she and Shulgi rest up. Ava and the other human women, including Theresa, promised to get together the following morning.

None of them mentioned that it would likely be after a bloody night for Shulgi and Tirel.

Molly wanted to trust in Theresa to talk her man out of this. Yet, Shulgi felt equally determined to see the fight through. He insisted that blood needed to be shed in fair combat to make up for the murders of Tirel's former crew. He refused to plead with Tirel to drop the idea of combat.

"You don't have your combat glands anymore!" she said heatedly as she paced in front of him in their new and sparsely furnished bedroom.

Her new friends had promised they would help Molly find or build the furnishings to make this pop-up a home until their permanent residence was built. The building of it was something both Molly and Shulgi anticipated, as it would be their first major project as a couple.

His expression tightened from stoic to stubborn. "I am capable of fighting without those glands," he ground out, a muscle ticking in his jaw. "I will hold my own, my queen. You needn't fear I will shame you or embarrass you."

She gasped in outrage, spinning in mid-pace to face him.

"How *dare* you suggest that's why I don't want you to go through with this!"

She rushed to him where he sat on the edge of their bed, then wrapped her arms around his neck, pulling his head against her chest. "I'm not afraid you will *lose*, Shulgi. I'm also not afraid of you being hurt. I can tell that our new friends and neighbors won't let the fight end in either of you getting too seriously injured that you can't be healed."

She stroked her fingers through his hair as he leaned his head against her breasts, his hands sliding around her waist.

"I don't want you to fight because I know that you feel like it defines you, Shulgi. You think this violence is simply a part of you. That it's in your blood. You think that it is second nature for you, and you can never escape it. That's why you aren't even trying in this case."

She pulled away from him to look down into his eyes, stroking his hair away from his brow with her fingertips. "We both came here to find peace from our lives of violence and bloodshed. You know as well as I do that starting out our lives here with a vicious battle won't bring us the peace we crave."

"Your wisdom shames me, my queen." He bowed his head, tugging her close to him again. "I will not fight tonight. If I must fall to my knees and submit as soon as the battle begins, then so be it. Let the burden of choosing violence be on someone else's head this time."

Molly held him close, smoothing her hands down his thick, silky hair. When his embrace turned more purposeful, she sighed in pleasure, pushing aside her worry.

They had a few hours yet before sunset, when Tirel and Shulgi had agreed to meet on the beach for their battle. She and her mate would make the most of that time. If they had to endure pain—and she would feel his pain as if it were her own because of her love for him—then they would preface it by pleasure.

His warm hands slid under the skirt of her dress and up her thighs until his fingers caught on the waistband of her panties. He tugged them down her legs slowly, lowering his head to plant hungry kisses on the subtle curve of her belly, just above her mound. She felt the heat of his mouth even through the thin silk of her dress.

Leaving her panties bunched around her calves, he lifted her skirt, exposing her bare mound to his hungry gaze. She gasped and clutched his head as he kissed her clit, then stroked his hot, wet tongue over the sensitive bud. His hands shifted from her waist to caress her buttocks as he feasted on her clit.

Molly's moans and soft cries seemed to urge him on and excite him more. He grabbed her thigh and lifted it, spreading her legs wider so his tongue could trail from her throbbing clit down her seam to her soaking entrance. He growled in pleasure when he encountered her slick, tasting her excitement.

She braced herself with both hands on his shoulders when he pulled her thigh to rest it over his shoulder, delving his tongue deeper inside her. In this position, she felt spread wide for him, unable to escape his hungry mouth. Not that she wanted to, the volume of her cries and moans increasing with each fervent flick of his tongue inside her.

He rubbed her clit with the fingers of one hand while the other held her thigh on his shoulder, pinning her in place and supporting her as her knees grew weak.

Molly's back arched, pushing her mound harder against his face as she climaxed with a loud cry. Her fingernails dug into his shoulders as her inner muscles convulsed around his tongue. His flickering wing brushed her calf as he seemed to revel in the taste of her orgasm.

When he finally allowed her to set her leg down, he

grabbed her by the hips to guide her down to his lap. Molly smiled seductively as she shifted into position. He'd freed his erection and the tip of it now probed her slippery entrance, but he let Molly set the pace. She tormented them both as she slowly impaled herself upon his thick length.

His cerci broke free of his robe, the clawed tips dragging along her thighs as she sank down on him until he was buried deep enough to bump her womb. The barbed ends vibrated as they trailed over her skin. She moaned with pleasure as one of them found her clit.

Molly framed Shulgi's face with both hands, pressing her lips to his as she rode his lap, his thick girth pumping deliciously inside her as his cerci stimulated her clit and teased her naked body. The one not vibrating over her clit slipped up the bodice of her dress to tear it away from her breast, freeing her stiff nipple. Shulgi wasted no time cupping her breast with one large hand, caressing it as his thumb flicked that tender bead.

He captured her moans and whimpers of pleasure as his lips and tongue claimed hers, his cerci and hands running all over her body to drive her to another orgasm. He came as soon as her inner muscles convulsed around his shaft.

She shuddered in the throes of her powerful orgasm, rocking her hips on his lap as his shaft jerked inside her, filling her with his seed. She mourned the fact that it would never take root but knew that what she and Shulgi had would endure, even though she could never give him children.

They would make their own kind of family together, here on this wild jewel of a world, surrounded by some of the strangest, and most welcoming people she'd ever met.

FORTY

Shulgi and Tirel sat on the dock that pierced the bow of the beach not far from Shulgi's new home. Both of them held fishing rods, the lines bobbing in the gentle waves as the sunset darkened into a mellow twilight.

"I don't see the point of this activity," Shulgi said as he felt a slight tug on his line. "Are there no more efficient methods to capture your food?"

Tirel chuckled, staring out into the falling darkness as glow lamps lit up around them on the dock. He'd already explained that the light would attract the fish they were seeking, although it also attracted some annoying insects.

"*My* food is harvested on Akrellia. However, I do enjoy fishing whenever I visit my friends here on Hierabodos." He glanced at Shulgi, a slight smirk on his scaled face. "It isn't about efficiency, or even about capturing your next meal. Fishing is supposed to be a bonding experience."

Shulgi reeled in his line, sighing as the hook on the end of it came up empty, the bait gone. "I think I prefer a fight to this."

Tirel barked a laugh at Shulgi's tone. "Believe me, I was

looking forward to it. However," he shot a glance towards the pop-up further up the shore, lights glowing within it as Theresa and Molly visited, discussing female things, "sometimes, we must put aside our own desires to please our women."

Shulgi slowly nodded. "I would do anything to please my queen." He regarded the hook on the end of his line hatefully as he drew the bait can closer, dreading the moment he'd have to dip his fingers into the foul stench contained within to bait his hook.

Tirel returned his attention to the ocean, watching his fishing line bob hypnotically. "I once pitied you Iriduan males for your mating habits. I wondered how anyone could feel so devoted to a female that their whole life revolved around her. And then I met my Partner. My beloved Theresa." He shot a toothy grin at Shulgi. "I knew in an instant that she belonged to me—and that I belonged to her. I think it was the first time I ever understood the Iriduan way of thinking."

"Most of my people view imprinting as a curse." Shulgi winced as he opened the bait and pinched off a chunk of the stinking dough. "For me, it was."

Tirel cast him another glance, his expression solemn. "A lot of good Akrellians died because of that curse."

Shulgi squished the bait around his hook, wrinkling his nose at the smell. "They did. I regret that."

"If we can't learn to forgive our enemies, then the war never ends." Tirel grinned at Shulgi's mound of bait clumped lopsided on his hook. "And then Iriduans never learn to fish."

Shulgi looked up from his work with a wry smile. "This is your punishment, isn't it?"

This earned another laugh from Tirel. "You Iriduans are always so fussy. Just wait until you have to clean the fish."

"Given my lack of success in catching one, I doubt I need fear the unpleasantness of that task anytime soon."

Tirel regarded him with a smile still playing around his lips. "Do Iriduans never go fishing? Don't your people love water?"

"*Juveniles* fish." Shulgi stood and flicked the rod, casting his line farther than where Tirel's bobbed. "But we don't use rods to do it." He sank back down onto the dock, spinning the reel a bit to readjust the position of his line. "Even our children are more efficient at catching their food than this."

A companionable silence fell between them for a several minutes before Shulgi spoke thoughtfully. "You should have seen the pond that surrounded our creche. The shimmer of colors as we darted and skimmed over the still water. When we're young, we feel so free, even though we never stray past the boundary markers. Our days are glorious, dipping and diving to grab a fish or amphibian we spot moving below us. Our nights are peaceful, the violence of the galaxy beyond those boundary markers so far removed from us that we aren't even aware of it."

"It sounds like the kind of life you'd never want to leave." Tirel regarded Shulgi with an empathetic expression.

Shulgi glanced towards the pop-up again, recalling the taste of Molly that he'd enjoyed not so long ago. "If I didn't leave my creche, I would never have met my queen. Had I known in advance what my life would be like when I broke free from my cocoon... I still would endure it all, knowing she would be there waiting for me to find her."

"I understand that feeling completely." Tirel's gaze shifted to the pop-up.

Another companionable silence fell over them as the twilight darkened into true night and the pale shadow of fish flickered beneath the dark blue waves, seeking the light from their glow lamps.

"What will you do about the cure now?" Tirel's question

caught Shulgi off guard and he shot a wary glance at the other male.

"It's no longer in my hands," he said, and he couldn't dredge up any feelings of guilt about that. He felt nothing but relief to be free of that burden.

Free to focus on Molly.

Tirel nodded slowly, his expression thoughtful as he gazed out at the water. "The cure, the bioweapon sample you had, these things are still my concern, but one I can delegate to others. I don't blame you for being happy to wash your hands of them."

"Heavy burdens seem so far away on this world." Shulgi scanned their surroundings, breathing in deeply of the fresh, brine-tinged air.

Tirel chuckled. "Now you see why I come here so often with my mate." He shrugged one scaly shoulder, his quills rustling. "Of course, I also come to see my friends. Though I suppose they are more like family to me now." He glanced at Shulgi, then returned his gaze to the fishing line. "Someday, perhaps I will view you as the same."

It was an admission that Tirel was willing to put the past behind them, and one Shulgi felt overwhelming gratitude for. He couldn't make up for all the things he'd done in his life, nor could he undo all the blood he'd shed. Perhaps that would be his greatest regret. Still, he had a chance to make amends by proving himself. He never would have imagined he'd be so concerned about earning the forgiveness and respect of one of his enemies.

But the days of being at war were over for him. To put the bloody past behind him, he needed this kind of future. The kind where old enemies became allies, and maybe, someday, friends.

He regarded his fishing rod with a grimace. "Is fishing a prerequisite for earning your regard?"

Tirel's bark of laughter drowned out even the sound of the rolling waves, especially when Shulgi's laugh joined it.

"I OWE YOU A GREAT DEAL!" Molly said to Theresa as they sat on the sofa in her living room, both of them glancing out the window towards the dock at the distant sound of laughter. "I'm sorry to admit, I didn't think you could convince your husband to drop the idea of combat."

Theresa's smile faded as she turned back to face Molly. "Tirel is an honorable Akrellian, despite the Dark Partner within him. He realized that Shulgi was not the evil person he'd thought. Tirel was a soldier himself. He understands that sometimes, you kill people because they stand in your way, even though you would rather avoid their deaths. Their blood still stains his soul, and he said that he sees that same regret in Shulgi."

"My Shulgi is haunted by past violence," Molly agreed, thinking of how their peaceful sleep was sometimes broken by Shulgi jerking awake, his eyes wild as they searched the room, his powerful body tense.

She would soothe him back to sleep, usually by making love to him, but sometimes all it took was letting him hold her close until his body relaxed back into slumber.

Theresa reached a hand to lay it upon Molly's. "I sense he isn't the only one, Molly." Her eyes practically glowed with compassion and empathy. "If you ever need someone to talk to, I'm here for you."

Molly blinked back grateful tears, turning her head to swipe them away discreetly before smiling broadly at Theresa.

"I lost a very dear friend and said farewell to many others when I left Za'Kluth. I truly appreciate the welcome I've received here, and the promise of new friendships. Thank you!"

"You are a remarkable woman, Molly." Theresa took a sip of her tea. "You are a survivor of things most cannot even imagine. Welcoming you to our little sanctuary here on Hierabodos is the least we can do to make your life easier. I know that everyone here is eager to help you both settle in and make a life for yourselves here."

Molly grinned as she leaned back in her seat, shooting another glance at the two males on the dock, visible from the wide picture window in the living room. "We are very eager to get started on making that life. Both of us are tired of the lives we led before this. We want to enjoy the peace and quiet." Her smile softened as her eyes grew misty. "We want to feel what it's like to be surrounded by family and friends as we live free. So far, despite one little hiccup," she shared a commiserating look with Theresa, "it has been amazing!"

EPILOGUE

Ava bit her lip as she surreptitiously studied the slender form of the Lusian standing near the food replicator.

Luna glanced over her shoulder and smiled at Ava, and Ava cursed the fact that she'd dropped her mental shields in her distraction, allowing the other female to read her thoughts. No doubt she'd even projected her concern because Luna turned away from the replicator and made her way to Ava's table.

"May I sit?" she asked, her voice taking on a more human rhythm with each passing day.

Ava nodded quickly, gesturing to the other side of the table. "Sure, have a seat! We really haven't had a chance to talk much since you joined our crew."

They'd only just left Hierabodos after a lovely visit with everyone that Luna had not taken part in. Like most of the crew, she'd remained on the ship, still retaining her Lusian distaste for prolonged exposure to groups of mentally unshielded people.

Luna regarded Ava with her large, ovoid eyes, framed by silvery white waves of hair that Ava envied. The other female was so ethereally beautiful and slender, with only very subtle curves to her body in comparison to Ava's curvy form. She was also elegant and enigmatic.

Just like Roz.

"Too much like him," Luna said with a wry smile. "We will not be at peace for much longer."

Ava gasped, a flush of embarrassment burning her cheeks. "Oh! I didn't mean to...." She waved both of her hands in front of her in negation. "I'm sorry! I wasn't suggesting... I didn't think—"

Luna dipped her head, her smile widening slightly. "I merged my mind with that of a human female. I understand your concerns and your doubts." She chuckled softly. "I have inherited many of my own insecurities through the process."

Ava shook her head, staring at Luna with fascination overtaking the small spark of jealousy that had begun to prick at her since they'd brought Luna on their ship. "I'm still amazed that you could do such a thing! It must have been very strange for you both!"

Luna's smiled faded into a tight line of her thin lips. "To do such a thing is forbidden. My species does not allow it for many reasons. Nor would most of them allow me to persist in this condition." Her gaze never wavered from Ava's. "The process also destroyed the human woman, leaving me with her memory and identity—and her anger at being so callously murdered."

Ava gasped, her hand lifting to cover her mouth. "Oh no! That's terrible! Roz didn't tell me that part."

A smile played again around Luna's lips. "The way he protects you—cares for you," she glanced around before returning her focus to Ava, "I've never seen anything like it among my people before." She waved a slim, three-fingered hand vaguely in the direction of the door that currently blended so seamlessly into the curved wall of the room that Ava couldn't see it.

"This entire crew is so bizarre and unique." Her smiled widened until it showed teeth that were more human than those Ava's mates had grown during the changes they underwent when they fell in love with her.

"Their devotion to you is unwavering, Ava." Luna's tone held awe. "They don't have eyes for any other female. My presence here won't change that, though as I said, I won't be able to remain with this crew long. We do not... *mesh*." She shrugged one lean shoulder. "It was my human optimism that thought this would work, even though I know my species far too well to entertain that naivety."

Ava grasped Luna's hand impulsively, then gasped and quickly released it when the other female flinched. She'd momentarily forgotten about their telepathic sensitivity increasing through touch.

"Luna, you can stay here as long as you need to!" Ava insisted, knowing that Roz wouldn't cast this poor, lost female to the stars without any aid.

Luna's smile widened even as she shook her head. "You see only the best in them, don't you? It's... remarkable. In your eyes, in your mind, the director is a hero. It is little wonder he loves you when you allow him to see himself like that. It is not surprising that they all do."

"Roz really does mean well," Ava insisted, knowing that her beloved mate had his flaws, like all people did, but he worked towards the good of the galaxy—so some of his less pleasant actions could be forgiven when looking at the bigger picture.

"I hope I find someone who can love me as unconditionally as you love them," Luna said with a fervent tone that sounded all human.

Ava's heart broke for the Lusian burdened with the mind

THE IRIDUAN'S MATE   363

and identity of a human woman, filled with the same desires as any woman Ava knew. Even Luna's body had changed to better reflect the mind that now shaped it.

Ava was struck with an exciting idea. So exciting that she clapped her hands together in anticipation as she announced it, though given Luna's suddenly wary expression, she'd read Ava's thoughts as soon as they occurred to her.

"We'll find you a mate!" Ava said, practically bouncing in her seat. "There's a whole galaxy out there filled with lonely males... or uh...." She gave Luna a questioning look.

Luna chuckled. "Preferably male, but I am more concerned with any potential partner's mind than their body."

Ava nodded, her own mind racing with ideas on how to find "the one" for Luna. She was certain Roz could help with that, doing his future-telling mojo to see the best possible destiny for Luna.

Even if he'd been blind to his own destiny with Ava until she'd made it very clear to him that he belonged with her and that he was *her* destiny too.

"Will you let me help you find a mate?" Ava asked belatedly, even though Luna wasn't exactly protesting the direction of her thoughts.

Luna slowly nodded, an uncertain expression on her face as if she wasn't sure this was a great idea. "I am willing to try. At least, the part of me that feels very human is willing. What remains of the drone," she shrugged, "is nothing but knowledge at this point."

HIERABODOS, one year later....

"Mama!" little Jenice cried out as she rushed towards Molly, one small hand pointing towards Nashi. "Nashi says he won't marry me because I'm just a little girl and little girls can't get married!"

Molly shook her head at her daughter, grinning widely as she glanced at Nahash's son, who little Jenice had developed a strong crush on since coming to Hierabodos last year. "Maybe he'll change his mind when you're both all grown, Jen." She hugged her daughter's fragile body close, patting her back. "But even if he doesn't, you will find the perfect person to give you your happily ever after!"

Jenice wriggled in her hold after returning her hug hesitantly. The six-year-old was still growing accustomed to parental affection. She'd been taken from her human parents, who had both been slaves in a breeding facility before she'd had a chance to bond with them. She couldn't remember her mother and had never even seen her father, but Molly and Shulgi had discovered that both had died, long before Sha Zaska's secret mission was able to break the humans free and relocate them.

When Mogorl and Grundon had brought the young child to the Akrellian facility where the freed slaves were processed and given options for relocation, the girl had come right to Molly, her frightened eyes wide as she'd tugged on the skirt of Molly's dress. She'd asked where the waste bucket was, her little body just skin and bones, already bearing the scars of a slave, lashing across her small back.

Molly had struggled not to weep as she'd shown the child the bathroom and explained how to use it. It wasn't long before the child refused to leave her side, following her everywhere as Molly told her about the wonderful future she could now look forward to and introduced her to everyone working at the facility. When she'd had to leave to return to Hierabodos, the girl had cried inconsolably, prompting Molly to contact Shulgi and tell him she'd be staying for a little longer.

When she told Shulgi she wanted to adopt the child as their own, he'd immediately agreed, joining her at the facility to meet their new daughter. She'd taken to him even faster than she had to Molly, fascinated by his wings and his "pretty" hair. He'd picked her up and flew her around the facility, much to her endless delight. They'd given her a name because she'd never been allowed to have one before—one that she vocally approved of—then went through the paperwork to make her their own and bring her home to Hierabodos V.

Little Jenice had been hesitant at first—about everything. Then she'd met the other children, and had been instantly intrigued, drawn out of her nervous shell. To Molly's relief, all the hybrid children had welcomed Jenice into their group, and she'd quickly latched on to Nashi, becoming his new shadow. Given how gentle he was with her and how he protected her when the others got too exuberant in their roughhousing, it wasn't surprising that she'd taken to hero worshipping him. Molly didn't assume anything bigger was growing between them, but Cass would often smile at the sight of her son playing with Jenice like she sensed that he cared more than he let on about the girl.

Even as their daughter grew more comfortable in her new home, Molly and Shulgi were already in the process of adopting two more children from the facility who had no home to return to, realizing that this was always the way they were meant to grow their family.

There were so many more in need that it made Molly's heart break every day that she received communications from Mog and Grun that showed the crowd of freed slaves seeking new homes. Far too many of them were no older than she had been when she was taken from Earth. Some of them had even been born into slavery, like little Jenice.

Molly and Shulgi worked through an often flawed and frustrating bureaucracy to decrease the incidents of slavery in the galaxy, especially in Syndicate space. Though a lot of legislation already existed to stop slavery, it wasn't evenly enforced, so organizations like the Akrellian facility and Sha Zaska's secret work on the Rim were vital to their efforts in putting an end to the horrific practice.

Their work would never end and that was a sad truth that Molly and Shulgi understood well. Yet, even though their efforts often seemed fruitless, they would never stop working to make the galaxy a better place. Nor would they give up their efforts to bring the same happiness they felt now that they'd found each other into the lives of others.

AUTHOR'S NOTE

I hope you all enjoyed reading Shulgi and Molly's story. If you did, I'd love it if you left a review to let other readers know about it! Reviews have such a huge impact on spreading the word! But regardless of whether you leave a review or not, I still want to thank you SO much for giving my book a chance. I know time is precious and the fact that you wanted to spend some of yours in one of my worlds really means a lot to me.

I am always amazed and honored by all the support and encouragement I receive from my fantastic readers! You all make this endeavor so worthwhile that it brings me back to the keyboard time and time again. I can't thank you enough for allowing me to live my lifelong dream of being an author!

I also really want to thank the amazing friends I've made in the romance writing community. You all know who you are, and you are all incredibly talented and inspiring. Thank you for being such a wonderful group!

This author's note will be much briefer than my usual end note, but I am eager to get this book published so that you all can read it, so I won't take long on this part, but I hope I can answer some of the questions that might be raised in this book.

Ava's story is definitely planned, but it isn't the next book in the series. That one is a surprise that I hope you all will love, and it will be very unexpected, I think. The characters in it you haven't met before... well, except for one, but I don't think you'll expect to see him again. ;)

Mogrol and Grundon will eventually have their own books. I have plans for both of them, and I'm eager to explain some of the culture and lore of the Ultimen more in their stories, as well as revisit these two characters that I fell in love with while writing this book!

Urbarra will appear in future books, probably, as the rebellion against the Iriduan Empire gains steam. I have some tentative ideas for a book for him, but nothing concrete yet. If you'd like to see more of this mystery rebel, let me know! I'd love to get further into the chaos cells and the rebellion, and Urbarra is a fascinating character to write. I would have added more about him in this book but I didn't want to go off on a tangent. ;)

Luna will eventually have her own story, but I plan on writing Ava's first. The idea for Luna came to me in a dream and I knew she belonged in this book. I'm often inspired by dreams. I don't generally share that, because I get some sideways looks when I do, lol. I have many ideas for Luna's story, and even though she is an "alien" heroine, I think she will still be very relatable to my readers, as she has a very human mind. I hope you'll agree when I get around to writing her story.

Briana is exactly where she wants to be in her own version of a happily ever after, so she won't be getting her own book, but she might appear in the books of other characters from time to time.

If there are any other stories you'd love to see in this series, please let me know! I have so many ideas for the Iriduan Test

Subjects universe that I am sometimes overwhelmed when trying to figure out what to write for the next book! Your suggestions help to narrow down the options for my next project!

I will be beginning a new project soon, as well as picking up where I left off on Kevos' story, so stay tuned to my social media (I know I'm really slow to post, sorry!) and be sure to follow my newsletter for exclusive sneak peeks and updates!

http://eepurl.com/gudYOT

Thank you all again for taking the time to read my book.

You can also follow me on my Facebook page:

https://www.facebook.com/The-Princesss-Dragon-343739932858

Or you can check out my blog:

https://susantrombleyblog.wordpress.com/

You can also drop me a line at my email addy:

susantrombley06@gmail.com

Bookbub: https://www.bookbub.com/authors/susan-trombley

Goodreads: https://www.goodreads.com/author/show/3407490.Susan_Trombley

Amazon author page: https://www.amazon.com/Susan-Trombley/e/B003A0FBYM

Book Links:
Iriduan Test Subjects series

The Iriduans are up to no good, determined to rule the galaxy by creating unstoppable warriors using monstrous creatures found on their colony worlds. Can the courageous heroines captured by the Iriduans to be breeders to these monsters end up taming them and turning the tables on the Iriduans themselves? This is an action-packed science fiction romance series where each book features a new couple, though there is an overarching storyline in addition to each individual happily-ever-after.

The Scorpion's Mate
  The Kraken's Mate
  The Serpent's Mate
  The Warrior's Mate
  The Hunter's Mate
  The Fractured Mate

Into the Dead Fall series

Ordinary human women are abducted by an enigmatic force that pulls them into a parallel universe. They end up on a world that is in the aftermath of a devastating apocalypse and is now just a vast, inter-dimensional junkyard. There they will encounter alien beings from many different dimensions and discover the kind of love they never imagined, forming a life for themselves out of the ashes of a lost civilization. This series is an exciting reverse-harem, post-apocalyptic alien romance that introduces beings from many different worlds and includes a mystery that spans the entire series, though each book ends on a happy note.

Into the Dead Fall
  Key to the Dead Fall
  Minotaur's Curse
  Chimera's Gift
  Veraza's Choice

Shadows in Sanctuary series

The humans of Dome City have been raised to view the horned and winged umbrose as demons, but when their separate worlds collide, these brave heroines must face the truth that nothing is ever what it seems. Can love alone bridge the divide between human and umbrose and put a stop to the tyranny of the adurians, who are the enemies of both? This futuristic science fiction romance series features a new take on the demon/angel paradigm on a world where humans have forgotten their origin, but still cling to their humanity. Each book features a new couple and can be read as a standalone with an HEA, though there is an overarching story throughout the series.

Lilith's Fall
   Balfor's Salvation
   Jessabelle's Beast

Fantasy series—Breath of the Divine

When a princess is cursed and transforms into a dragon, she falls in love with a dragon god and sparks a series of events that plunge the world of Altraya into grave danger. Myth and magic collide with the cold ambitions of mankind as those who seek power will do anything to get it. The dragon gods work to stop the coming danger, but it might be the love of a human woman that holds the key to the salvation of the world. This fantasy series features a different couple in each book and a satisfying ending to each story, but there is also an overarching story throughout the series.

The Princess Dragon
   The Child of the Dragon Gods
   Light of the Dragon

Standalones or Collaborations

The well-known story of Rapunzel gets a science-fiction twist in this fairytale retelling featuring an artificial intelligence and a plucky princess determined to prove herself to be much more than a pretty face. This is a futuristic science fiction romance that introduces a new universe where humans live on colony worlds after being forced to flee a deadly AI on Earth centuries prior to the story.

Rampion

Children of the Ajda

Guardian of the Dark Paths

·

Printed in Great Britain
by Amazon

65728485R00214